ALSO BY CATHRYN GRANT

THE WOMAN IN THE BAR

A PSYCHOLOGICAL SUSPENSE NOVEL

ALEXANDRA MALLORY
BOOK FIVE

CATHRYN GRANT

ISBN: 978-1-943142-36-1

This book is a work of fiction. References to real people, events, establishments, organizations, or locales are intended only to provide a sense of authenticity, and are used fictitiously. All other characters, and incidents and dialogue, are drawn from the author's imagination and are not to be construed as real.

Visit Cathryn online at CathrynGrant.com

Cover design by Lydia Mullins Copyright © 2017

CHAPTER 1

*S*an Francisco, California

* * *

Forty years ago it was quite remarkable to see a female bartender, despite the meme that a woman's place was in the kitchen. Nearly fifty years after a wave of suffragettes turned women into functioning citizens of the United States, women were still prohibited from entering bars in some cities. The reasons for barring them from public drinking were varied.

In one case, it was the belief that all women were potential b-girls.

A b-girl was a woman planted in a bar to entice men to drink more alcohol. Perhaps it's true. Of course it's true, planted or not. Perhaps this is why female bartenders take home more tips. The enticement is there, even when it's not deliberate. The more alcohol consumed, the bigger the tip. Unless, of course, the man is a mean drunk and the overindulging ends in violence.

It might be the kitchen thing that has some men believing

women belong behind the bar after all, serving them cocktails, listening to their tales of self pity and how they were screwed over, wiping up the spills, laughing at their jokes, gently massaging their egos.

Despite the shift toward female bartenders, much of the US workforce remains wildly imbalanced along gender lines. Executive suites are dominated by men, elementary schools are ruled by women. Billionaire investors are primarily men, social workers are women. Therapists are female and all but four percent of orthopedic surgeons are male. Eighty percent of film directors are white men and I won't even get started on young female actors paired with grandfatherly males. I'm still waiting for that movie where Ansel Elgort is Sigourney Weaver's *love interest*.

One career path, if you can call it that, which is very under-represented by women is the crime industry. Rarely do you hear of a female gang. The women serving time for white collar offenses are few, although Martha Stewart comes to mind, proving you can mix homemaking and business ambition after all.

Except for a few well-known exceptions, there aren't many women locked up for kidnapping or espionage. Most women who are in prison for murder have been convicted of killing the lovers and husbands who brutalized them. Is that murder? Self defense is more accurate, even hours or days or years after the fact. More than self defense, it's justice. Punishing a crime that had been overlooked, dismissed, minimized, trivialized. A crime that's mocked by the lower forms of human life as not a crime at all — lurking in some men's minds is the belief that women occasionally need a bit of physical *discipline*.

Many people consider this lack of female convicts a good thing — viewing it as a sign of female superiority, or female restraint on the necessary contributions that testosterone makes to the world. I really don't know.

I prefer not to think about killers who are identified and arrested and convicted and, worst of all, imprisoned. It may be a case of textbook arrogance on my part, an enormous blindspot that makes me vulnerable, but I don't believe I'm at risk for being caught in the act, or the aftermath, of murder. Nevertheless, I don't like to think about that outcome.

It's not that I'm super smart. That's the downfall of many criminals — they believe they're smarter than average. They believe cops aren't very bright. They think people in general aren't very bright. They think they're so clever and so many steps ahead of the game they'll never make a mistake. I don't see myself that way at all. But...I am calm, extraordinarily calm. And I think things through. I overthink. I look at problems from many angles. I carry on internal debates with myself. Calmness is underrated. So is the ability to consider life from a variety of perspectives.

It's also that female stereotype, that female meme — I'm good at cleaning. My siblings and I were raised with more chores than average for kids of our generation. We practically ran that household once we reached our teens. Everyone knows about the risks of DNA now, but how many killers clean with fanatical devotion to meticulous detail? Bleach. Q-tips. Toothbrushes. Duct tape. Tossing dish towels in the trash and removing vacuum cleaner bags.

Thirty years ago, The Chimera Bar in San Francisco opened for the first time. The proprietor was a woman who went on to launch another bar and three successful restaurants, but The Chimera remained her baby. It was the only place where she continued to show up several times a week rather than delegating to managers that were on-site whenever the doors were open. The constant presence of savvy managers at all her establishments was part of the reason for her success.

For the entire thirty years, every bartender at The Chimera has been female. Since the day it opened, it's been a popular place — for women and men. Over a decade and a half into the twenty-first century, hardly anyone notices that everyone behind the bar is female. A few still do, and it's surprising who they are, sometimes men in their twenties or thirties. Occasionally, women are troubled by it. An equal number are thrilled by the prevalence of females, and that's a small part of the draw to The Chimera. But most people couldn't care less. They aren't even consciously aware of the bias. And it's a bias as strong as any other. It's not clear how the owner gets away with hiring only females.

With customers who are unaware of the bias, but feeling the subterranean pulse of sex that drives the world, those women behind the bar rake in the tips. It's possible they're b-girls after all.

The Chimera also serves the best martini in San Francisco. It doesn't seem like a martini could be the best. After all, measure the vodka or gin, measure the vermouth, stab a few olives...how much better can they be?

CHAPTER 2

*T*he morning her plane from Sydney was due to land in San Francisco, Tess sent me a text message.

Tess: *I'm staying.*

Alex: *??*

Tess: *I'm staying in Australia.*

Alex: *For how long?*

Tess: *Not sure yet.*

Alex: *But what about...*

I accidentally hit send before I finished my thoughts about her cockatoo, her condo, and her job, which affected my job.

Tess: *Do you mind staying in my condo? For another few weeks until I decide my next steps? I'll owe you.*

Alex: *I can't.*

Tess: *Why not?*

My thoughts took off, a full sprint, my heart beating faster, even my breath responded as if my body were running to catch up with my brain. I'd murdered an elderly woman and her son less than five hundred feet from Tess's front door. And the woman to whom I'd exposed a glimpse of my function in the world was still living in that building. I trusted her more than I've trusted anyone, making it easy for her to guess I was a killer. It was necessary trust, not blind trust. Still, I needed to disappear from her world. I couldn't allow the detectives who were now investigating the murders to catch a glimpse of me.

I'd stood on Tess's balcony and watched the detectives and crime techs arrive. I'm sure they were perplexed by the murders of three family members within less than two weeks of each other. I could imagine the questions they were firing at Jeanne Clayton. I was mostly confident she wouldn't betray me. But there were several twisty things she had to explain, such as why she was locked up in her apartment for several years, and if she truly was locked up, how had she escaped?

If Jeanne mentioned me at all, I had no doubt the detectives would come knocking on every single door in Tess's building. It wouldn't take much for them to recall the overly curious woman who stopped to chat with them.

Several more texts arrived from Tess, filled with question marks. I ignored them.

I went into the kitchen and mixed a martini. I took it to the balcony that ran the length of the living room. I tugged the canvas cover off the lounge chair and sat down. It was breezy, but I hoped the chill of vodka and the wind would help me think quickly. I took a sip. The icy alcohol slipped over my tongue, down my throat, and settled into my veins.

It wasn't as if I had some sort of plan that had been disrupted. I had no plans and maybe that's why my mind had become a whirlpool, sucking me down. Working at Coastal-Creative generated a good income. Tess had paid for my membership at a very nice gym. I had an excellent sex life, a modestly growing savings account, and had been living in her luxurious condo for the past month. I had it all, some would say.

On top of that, I still had my studio apartment subsidized by the company for an entire year.

And that was the problem. They were taking care of me, I wasn't taking care of myself. I had no forward momentum. I'm determined to have money of my own and a sweet piece of property and a gorgeous, classy, comfortable home. A place where I can walk through a garden filled with pleasing aromas hearing the sounds of birds, a warm breeze caressing my skin. Space and privacy and the satisfaction of all my creature comforts.

I didn't want to have to attend idiotic meetings conducted by phone. Conference calls often included twenty or thirty people. Everyone talked over each other, constantly. Many of them pretended to listen while surfing social media, thus requiring the repetition of what had been said in order to give a simple *yes* or *no* answer to a question.

Of course, staying in her condo a while longer would be glorious. It had spectacular views of the San Francisco Bay and Russian Hill. There were bathrooms with every amenity, a luxurious bed, and a lovely kitchen. There was a talking bird — a beautiful white cockatoo with a yellow crown and intelligent black eyes. He said the most outrageous things, and although he'd unnerved me at first, I'd learned to enjoy his chatter. He made me laugh at least once a day with his mostly nonsensical, yet sometimes unnervingly astute comments.

If I stayed at Tess's, I could do a bit of a re-set on my life. I could use the time and space to figure out a better way of upping my income at a faster rate. The next rung on the corporate ladder was elusive. I'd been offered a position in sales, sort of, but it was probably a dead end. The man offering was not someone I wanted to spend another minute with, much less work for and hand over significant control of my life to. Waiting for Tess to deem me ready for a promotion might take a year, even longer. And now that she had no definite return date, if she planned to return at all, my current position also had the potential to collapse beneath my feet.

My mind circled back to the detectives investigating the murder next door. They already had my contact information, so it wasn't as if it mattered where I was living. They probably would not come and knock on Tess's door, demanding an interview. They'd call.

I was counting on Jeanne Clayton having my back. I'd released her from her prison, even if it meant murdering her mother and brother. After a lifetime in a psychological prison, her gratitude would keep her from turning on me. I was her hero of sorts. She was a smart woman, she'd figure out a way to explain her weird captivity and escape, and her dead family, without involving me.

Still, I needed to change my appearance, even if only a little bit. Just in case.

I took several sips of my drink and sucked an olive off the stick. I chewed it slowly. I pulled my phone out of my pocket and called a hair salon I'd visited once before.

I sent a text message to Tess: *I guess it will work to stay here for a while. Let me know your plans as soon as you can.* She replied with a smile emoji and a thumbs up.

I took another sip of my drink and closed my eyes, trying to picture the look I would adopt for the next phase of my life. In addition to making me unrecognizable to the detectives and to Jeanne, it might set me on a new course, leading away from CoastalCreative, and San Francisco. Changing your look can do that.

Shopping first. Haircut and color second.

CHAPTER 3

*J*en couldn't shake the feeling that everything in her life had been going perfectly since she'd met Alexandra Mallory, as if Alex carried some kind of magical power. She giggled. It was ridiculous. She could imagine Alex's aloof, almost sneering look if Jen said such a thing in her presence. But the thought wouldn't leave her.

She'd made a friend, her first in a long time. And having a friend made her feel like she had options. After Jake betrayed her, sabotaged her job, and evicted her from his house, she'd done the easiest thing a woman can do to support herself — selling sex. Even though Alex had sort of suggested Jen might find life easier if she charged more and reduced her list of clients, which was kind of disgusting, having Alex listen, and not judge her, made her see herself from a different perspective. And Alex's boyfriend had been so nice, standing up for her in front of that creep who threatened to expose what she did for a living.

Everything just seemed...better.

Instead of spending her days eating snacks and drinking soda and smoking weed, she'd started taking long walks. She was thinking about spending a bit of money on running shoes and a sports bra. Not that she wanted to copy Alex and become a jogging addict. She just felt as if she could do things to make her life even better, now that she no longer needed to spend all her energy focused on trying to stay alive and numb the pain.

Without even realizing how it had all happened, she was living in Alex's studio apartment with Isaiah. It was cramped beyond belief — three hundred square feet. A single room for living, cooking, eating. Isaiah sleeping on the floor one week, Jen the next. But they managed. And it was free! She actually giggled out loud every time she thought about it.

And then, her life continuing to change so fast it took her breath away. A classmate of Isaiah's had hooked her up with a woman who owned an upscale bar — The Chimera. It had been around for decades and was one of those places that was always crowded and always felt modern even though it was quite old. It was housed on the first floor of an adobe mission-style building from the 1930s. There were several offices above, one of which opened through French doors onto a small wrought iron balcony overflowing with red geraniums.

Of course she wasn't at all qualified to work as a bartender, but here she was. A bar back with responsibility for collecting dirty glasses, wiping counters, restocking alcohol and mixers, and watching the bartenders, hopefully taking a step closer every day to becoming one herself. Everyone said this job was an easier step up to bartender than it was from cocktail waitress, where you were relegated forever to a short skirt and smacks on the ass. Already they'd allowed her to pour tap beer when the place was packed, or one of the bartenders needed to use the restroom.

They even shared a percentage of their tips with her. It wasn't much, but her rent was zero. She giggled. She hoped

Alex wouldn't be in trouble if anyone at her company found out she'd invited other people to stay in the place they'd provided to the employees they wanted to lure to work in their San Francisco office. The apartment was only available for six more months, maybe a little more, but by then, Isaiah would be finished with culinary school and Jen was sure she would have moved into bartending with her own tips to share with the new bar back girl.

She worked five nights a week with a girl named Chelsea. Already, Chelsea was becoming a friend. She'd taught Jen how to make three different cocktails. Every night after the bar closed and they'd cleaned up, Chelsea made a drink. Jen watched and took notes on how to do it exactly right. Then, they sat in the dark bar, only a single light overhead, and sipped their drinks and talked.

Chelsea had long hair, almost to her waist. She straight-ened it with a flat iron, making it look like a sheet of metal with its streaks of mahogany, copper, and white-blonde. She didn't wear any make-up, but she didn't need it. Her skin was perfect and her lips had a charming natural dusty rose color. She was slim, her figure almost like a boy's, which made Jen wonder why Chelsea made such fantastic tips.

Maybe working in the sex trade had distorted her perspec-tive. That's what Isaiah had said that night — *your perspective is distorted*. That night had been the turning point for her. More than her own vow to stop the downward slide she was on, his insistence that there were *a lot of good men*, that most men were good, had jolted her. She'd let go of the despairing view that men only wanted sex and the opportunity to make sure women knew they were unworthy and unimportant, really not equal human beings at all.

It might have been Chelsea's voice that raked in the extra cash. She sounded like an angel. Her tone was clear, the sound of two crystal glasses chiming against each other.

Chelsea's voice made you turn your head to see who was speaking.

The people who came to The Chimera alone wanted to surf through social media, or they wanted to talk about themselves. So it wasn't as if Chelsea was constantly doing the talking, her voice luring them into a trance that left them scribbling large numbers on their credit card receipts, or leaving twenties for her to drop into the glass vase on a small shelf just behind the bar. Maybe it wasn't her voice at all, it was that cliché about bartenders — they need to be good listeners. Or, maybe she was just nice, and all the customers felt that, even if she didn't speak more than four words to them — *Hi, how are ya?*

The third day Jen was working there, Chelsea suggested the after-hours drinks. And the next day she'd bought Jen a pale blue notebook. It had ribbon markers attached to the spine and an elastic strap that held the covers closed, giving it a suggestion of privacy.

Chelsea had the same kind of notebook in red. She kept it behind the bar, stuck it in her purse, and often carried it with her when she went to the restroom. She wrote in it diligently whenever there was a lull in activity.

"What are you always writing?" Jen said.

Chelsea smiled. "I'm planning my life."

"What do you mean?"

"It's a bullet journal?"

Jen laughed. "Bullet journal? Like people you want to shoot? The same as a fuck list?"

Chelsea wiggled her fingers at Jen as if she were casting a spell. "It's a thing now. You write down all the stuff you want to do, your goals and plans." She flipped open her book, fanning the pages past her thumb, holding it far enough away that Jen couldn't see much. There were tiny drawings of cocktails and animals, flowers and trees, a surfboard. There were large numbers in elegant script with lists of things beside them, the numbers drawn with borders and filled with colored pencil. She had arrows and charts, all of them equally colorful.

"It looks like a coloring book," Jen said.

"Everything in my life is in this book." She closed it. "It helps me not put stuff off — like cleaning the apartment, or working out. I don't have to keep thinking about things over and over again because I'm afraid I'll forget them if I don't keep repeating them in my mind."

"Couldn't you just make a list in your phone? Or get an app?"

"This is more fun. And it makes all the things in your life seem more important. Your whole life is in one place. I have movies I want to see, TV shows I'm watching — what season it's on and what I think of them."

Jen nodded.

"You should do it."

"Maybe." She wasn't sure she had enough things in her life to fill an entire notebook.

CHAPTER 4

The shopping trip I'd planned for my new look required only one stop. Because parking was a hassle, I called an Uber. The driver took me to Haight-Ashbury. She told me she loved the area herself and was jealous that I got to spend a few hours soaking up the echoing whispers from the sixties along with the renovated twist on alternative lifestyles.

For two hours, I prowled through second-hand shops and rather expensive boutiques that offered funky, hippie style clothes. I bought a knee-length jumper and several loose-fitting dresses in pastel colors, vests, tops that were like long underwear shirts, peasant blouses, and tie-dyed skirts. I bought a pair of thick brown leather sandals and Doc Marten lace-up boots. The Doc Martens aren't classic hippie shoes, but I envisioned a twenty-first century hippie. A hybrid.

I ate lunch at a small, nicely decorated Thai noodle place and then took an Uber to the hair salon.

The stylist thought I was crazy when I told her what I wanted done to my hair. Just before I moved to San Francisco, I'd cut my hair to just off my shoulders, added loose waves, and had it colored a safe, corporate medium brown. In the four or five months I'd lived in the city, it had grown quickly to my shoulders and the wave had relaxed.

The stylist set to work, first giving me a minimal trim. Very minimal. I wanted to keep it as long as possible for my new look. She dipped the fat brush into the dye and stroked it across the roots of my hair. When she was finished, she stepped back and looked at me straight on. "Are you sure about this?"

"Absolutely."

"It's the weirdest thing I've ever done."

"I can imagine."

I flipped through a celebrity magazine while the dye set. When I was fully baked, she parted my hair in the center and blew it dry with a diffuser to keep the gentle waves.

The women in the chairs on either side of me stared as I studied myself in the mirror. My roots all along the parting in my hair were dark brown, almost black, the rest of my hair a soft, pale blonde. No one had the courage, or the lack of tact, to ask why I deliberately added trashy-looking roots to my hair, advertising a dye job in desperate need of attention.

I returned home to change the rest of my look and check the effect in a full-length mirror.

I put on makeup, heavier than usual, although that didn't really matter as far as hiding myself from Jeanne and the detectives. Still, new hair requires new make-up. I put on cream foundation for that smooth, rich, almost synthetic look. Most of the time I use tinted moisturizer, changing the shade slightly depending on whether I want to look healthy and sun-kissed or wan and aloof. For hippie persona, the only other makeup I used was light brown mascara.

When I was fully outfitted in a soft, pale blue cotton jumper with a white long-sleeved t-shirt underneath and my Doc Martens, I paraded in front of the full-length mirror in

Tess's master bedroom — a piece of glass large enough to reflect a group of five women. I practiced a sauntering walk, trying for a posture that was meek compared to my usual demeanor.

After an hour of this, I ate a small bite of a pot brownie I'd picked up during my shopping trip. I was ready to try my new look in public.

Jen was working at The Chimera, a perfect place for a test run.

The change was definitely over the top. The odds of not being discovered were in my favor, as long as I only left Tess's building after dark. I suppose my dramatic changes were telling. Deep inside, I didn't trust Jeanne. I don't trust anyone, really. Just myself. I know what I'm thinking. I know what I'll do. I'm predictable to myself ninety-five percent of the time. Possibly ninety-nine percent.

I fed Tess's cockatoo a plate of strawberries.

Thank you very much. The bird's sharp, almost human voice, was startling, even when I expected him to speak.

I put on my new floppy wide-brimmed hat with a huge flower made of ribbon, and went out. I pulled out of the parking garage, confident that the woman who had been living there, leaving for an early morning run every day, standing around smoking as she watched the curious behavior in the window of the Edwardian building next door, was gone for good. No one would recognize this twenty-first century hippie.

I parked two blocks from The Chimera and sauntered up the street to the door. I went inside and looked for a place to sit. It was packed. Thursday night, only six-thirty, most people still at work, and the place was filled.

Jen was behind the bar, picking up glasses and wiping the counter, passing out cocktail napkins to people who'd wadded theirs into wet balls. She didn't look up. She was frantically busy but completely at home after only a few days. I moved toward the bar and stood behind the row of people seated on the heavy oak chairs. Those chairs with their dark green leather cushions, secured by brass tacks, gave the bar a classy appearance.

I'd left the hat in the car and finger-combed my hair so it covered the sides of my face, a bit plastered down on top. Jen glanced at me. She squinted. The bartender asked her a question and she turned away. For several minutes I watched her and the bartender move around each other like performers in a well-choreographed dance — pouring alcohol, mixing drinks, Jen serving tap beer with an expert tilt of the glass and pull of the handle as if she'd been doing it for years.

A man on the last chair, closest to the entrance to the back hallway, put a few bills on the counter and slid off his chair. I darted in and shimmied onto the chair before anyone else could even look in that direction.

I sat there for several minutes, my fringed leather bag dangling from my shoulder. I felt very mellow from the pot. For a few minutes I stared blankly at the shelves of alcohol. I was pretty sure hippies didn't drink martinis, so I tried to figure out what I would order once the bartender looked in my direction. Without my usual aggressive exterior and demand for attention blazing out of my pores, I seemed to be fading into the scenery.

Beer was the obvious choice, but I don't really like it, and the calories per ounce of alcohol don't make it very appealing. I finally decided on a glass of red wine. Zinfandel seemed right. Wine is not what I like to order in a bar where they're pouring from a bottle that's been open for an entire day, maybe longer, but I wanted to keep the effect going.

Jen moved along the bar, wiping up spills and the sweat of melting ice cubes sliding off the outsides of glasses. She stopped a few feet away and looked directly at me. "Oh. Oh, hi. What?" She smiled. "What's that all about?"

"Just trying on another look."

"I'll tell Chelsea you're waiting. Unless you want beer or wine?"

"A glass of Zinfandel."

She went to the shelf of wine glasses and I returned to my marijuana trance.

CHAPTER 5

I nursed my glass of Zin for nearly an hour. I didn't want to go too crazy with the alcohol. It had been a while since I'd had pot, and I needed to be in a decent condition to drive back to Tess's.

Bottles glistened on the shelves behind the bar, refracted colors streaming up to the ceiling. The face of the bar and walls were rich, dark wood. The bar itself was black granite, slightly curved so people sitting at each end could see those who were drinking opposite from where they sat.

Keeping my eyes from meeting others', my soft clothes falling over my body like a blanket, and possibly my somewhat shitty-looking hair, changed my bar experience. Or maybe it was choosing a glass of wine rather than a martini. A woman drinking wine at a bar sends a completely different message from a woman with a sleek, cold, aggressive-looking glass of pure alcohol and that spear of olives that always reminds me of decapitated heads, red tongues protruding.

No one talked to me.

To my left was the hallway leading to the restrooms, a storage area, and stairs to the second floor. A woman was seated at my right, two men standing close behind her. The men leaned forward, elbows on the bar, so they could carry on a three-way conversation. She was drinking a Cosmo and the two guys had Long Island Ice Teas. Only a few bits and pieces of the conversation made their way into my ears — something about a reunion, but I couldn't make out whether it was for school or family or a former group of co-workers. My neck ached from straining to listen without shifting my body to let on that I was trying to overhear.

Past those three were two guys sitting alone. Normally, two straight guys will be checking out the women without a lot of subtlety. And they were, but they hadn't noticed me. It almost seemed as if they didn't see me at all. Their heads turned frequently as they surveyed the room, and their glances passed by me, but never hesitated, even for a moment.

Throughout my adult life, I've changed my appearance on a somewhat regular basis. Usually it's mostly hair color and glasses, and my approach to makeup. I change clothing styles from business to high fashion to trendy to punk, but my choices are always rather assertive, I suppose. For a woman trying to conceal who she is, I'd never made a very good effort at dressing to fade into the background.

This lack of attention shocked me, but not in a terrible way. It was interesting, and kind of fun. My new look might allow me to eavesdrop on more conversations where I wasn't welcome. It might allow me to walk through stores and take small items, although that sort of thing doesn't interest me. Shoplifting is low class, and so needy, and so unnecessarily risky, but if it did...

The three beside me picked up their drinks simultaneously. They finished them off and the woman waved a credit card at Jen. She walked over, took the card, and brought it to Chelsea. As soon as the card was returned, they were gone. Despite the crowd, no one moved in to fill the space

I'd finally reached the bottom of my wine glass. I ordered another Zin and a glass of water. I drank half the water. I turned slightly on the stool and looked across the room.

A moment later, the door opened and two men walked in, headed straight for the bar. They were average guys, one of them leaning toward good looking. The first one was tall, easily six feet. He had dark hair and two or three day's worth of very dark stubble, almost black. He wore a red t-shirt, brown leather jacket and jeans that looked sort of new. The second guy had a prominent bone structure, fine dark hair, and very pale skin. He wore a black suit and white shirt.

The one in the leather jacket lifted his hand and waved at Chelsea. She gave him a thumbs up without losing a beat in the mojitos she was making. Jen smiled and waved at them as well. They came directly to my end of the bar. The one in leather took the seat. The other guy stood to his right. Neither one looked at me.

They both ordered Sierra Nevada beer. Jen brought the bottles and two mugs.

"Hey, Alex," she said. "This is Chelsea's boyfriend — Rick." She gestured toward the guy in the leather jacket. "And Dan."

I smiled.

They both lifted their chins in the way of a greeting.

"Drinking alone?" Dan said.

"It looks that way." I picked up my glass and took a sip. I realized the sharp comment didn't fit my attempt to come across as a quiet little lamb. I smiled and tilted my head to the side. "Just a glass of wine. I came by to see Jen, but it's so busy, she can't even stop for a minute."

Neither one said anything. I guess there wasn't anything to be said in response to those inane comments.

Rick took a few sips of beer. "Do you live in the city?"

"Yes."

"Around here?"

"I'm house sitting right now. In Russian Hill."

"Sweet," Rick said.

"Do you?"

Both nodded. They seemed to be some sort of team, despite the difference in clothing. Maybe one just got off work and...

"Rick and Dan are detectives," Jen said. She gave them a rigid smile.

I supposed even with her change in career, her instinctive reaction to police officers hadn't changed. I wondered if the detectives were aware of her discomfort.

"Sounds interesting," I said.

They shrugged, in unison. I wanted to laugh. They were too modest, for one thing. And for another, the buddy thing was overdone. Although maybe if you spend all your working hours with one other person, you start to behave in the same way, copy each other's mannerisms. Maybe they weren't aware of how ridiculous they looked with their copycat behavior.

"What kind of crimes?" I said.

"Shouldn't really say," Rick said.

"Of course not." I smiled. Was that true? Did detectives not talk about their work in social settings? Maybe not with strangers.

"I better get busy," Jen said. "Let me know if you need another beer." She glanced at me. "Or wine, or a..."

Before she could say martini, I cut her off. "I'm good. This is perfect."

She drifted off toward the other end of the bar, wiping the counter as she went. It seemed to be a never-ending requirement and it made me think about how I'd loved dusting when I was a kid. Wiping up spilled drinks was not as appealing, with all the sticky residue from cocktails.

Rick turned his attention to Chelsea, following her like a

tracking device. Dan began asking me questions, which I batted and dodged as best I could. I got away with saying I worked in high-tech without mentioning the company name. He looked startled at that. I'm sure, standing and looking down at my unkempt roots and glancing at my tired clothes, he couldn't quite complete the picture. I steered him toward the firmer ground of movies and TV shows.

Talking to detectives in a social setting is not my first choice.

He seemed like a nice enough guy, but I wondered if people were snorting coke in the bathrooms as they sometimes do. I wondered if they knew detectives made a habit of drinking there. And I wondered if he could tell by looking at my eyes that I was mildly stoned.

CHAPTER 6

 ortland, Oregon

* * *

My parents adhered to the belief that cleanliness is next to godliness. This isn't such a bad idea. Human beings have an innate desire to be clean. It's the mentally ill people on the street who accept the inevitable filthy conditions. In other words, tolerating grime and trash and deterioration is not a normal state. Most of us go crazy when we open a cluttered closet. We don't like seeing soap scum on faucets and toothpaste smears in the sink. No one would disagree that a dirty toilet is disgusting.

It's part of why crack houses turn our stomachs when we see interior shots on the news, or scenes in movies. It's not simply the sadness of addiction, it's the filth that turns our stomachs.

We like to be clean. We like our hair washed and our fingernails scraped free of dirt and dead skin.

When looky-loos walk through model homes, ogling a

decorator's idea of idyllic living, admiring granite and tile, carpet and wood, most of what's seducing them is the pristine condition. The counters don't have dried rice glued to the surface and piles of junk mail and odds and ends that haven't been returned to their proper places. They relish the absence of any odor beyond a light almond or coconut, the total eradication of grit and finely powdered skin and hairs and missed bits of food and dust balls.

It's what we love about five-star hotel rooms. Immaculate conditions. Unless you peruse the internet and find out the dirty secrets of poorly cleaned rooms.

I couldn't object to my parents' desire for cleanliness. Maybe I was a freak of nature, but I enjoyed cleaning. The first time my mother handed me a soft cotton cloth and told me to sweep it across the tables in the living room, I was enraptured.

As the cloth ran down the length of the coffee table, leaving a clean streak of wood behind it, I was wildly satisfied with my accomplishment. Such a gentle, quick movement to change the environment. My actions had impact. I quickly polished the rest of the table and moved to the end tables, running the cloth around the bases of lamps and down the legs. The wood glowed in appreciation.

Holding the cloth up in the sunlight coming in through the living room windows made me even more content. The gray streaks of dirt now glued to the cloth were removed from the room. It glistened. My mother would toss the cloth in the wash, and it would emerge pure white.

The panic-stricken story of *The Cat in the Hat Comes Back* wasn't true after all, teaching children that cleaning up a mess simply chases it somewhere else. That cat and those kids chased that pink stain all over the house and it took an act of magic to be rid of it. The story was a lie. Grime could be removed without magic. It might reappear in a week or so, but for that day and the few days following, the living room furniture was clean.

The only thing I didn't like about the cleaning chores I was given was the fact that they were only given to me. My sister was too young, and boys did not clean house. Boys got to mow the lawn and weed the garden and rake leaves. I would have loved cleaning the outdoors as much as I liked sweeping debris out of the house.

But my father was adamant. Housecleaning was women's work.

By the time I was in high school, I was cleaning the entire house. My mother still did the laundry and the boys did the windows. My sister was old enough to take over the dusting and vacuuming hallways. But the bathroom cleaning, the kitchen floor mopping, most of the vacuuming, windowsills and doorjambs and baseboards were my responsibility. My mother cooked, and we younger *girls* set and cleared the table, loaded the dishwasher, scrubbed the pans, and wiped the counters.

I became a housecleaning dominatrix. I loved to pick up my brothers' scattered belongings and fling them into their bedrooms for sorting and organizing. I loved chasing them away from the bathroom when I was cleaning, forcing them to race up the stairs since they were in the habit of waiting until the last minute to pee. I loved informing them that the floor had been mopped and they had to stay out of the kitchen, barred from the refrigerator for the next thirty minutes.

Such power given to the cleaning goddess! The power was backed by my mother, and occasionally even my father. It was one thing, aside from my grades, that he praised me for, one thing that pleased him about the way I was growing up. He didn't like my attitude, my lack of submission, my outright defiance of god, but he loved the way the house looked when I was finished with it. He loved the sparkling porcelain in the bathrooms and the evenly spaced tracks in the carpet and the lack of clutter.

Nice job.

Well done, Alexandra. A godly woman looks after her home.

The house looks beautiful. I'm proud to have company.

His praise was genuine, although I didn't let it entice me into letting down my guard around him. He might be thrilled with one facet, but it didn't mean he'd cut me slack anywhere else. Still, between my housecleaning expertise and my report cards, he was pleased with two aspects of my otherwise uncontrollable and troubling personality.

The power I'd been given was something I thought about quite a lot as the vacuum roared and I pushed it across the carpet, focused on keeping the path straight, making sure I overlapped each section so not a single thread or piece of fuzz or broken fingernail escaped its growling, sucking force.

In most situations, my brothers had the upper hand. They had more freedom, they were allowed to dominate dinner table conversations, and they were allowed to run around with their friends without having to account for every move. Their freedom infuriated me, and they acted as if they were superior because I had to clean up their shit, literally.

There had to be a way to use my power as the designated queen of clean to take control of them.

CHAPTER 7

*S*an Francisco

* * *

It had been nearly two weeks since Tess's announcement that she was staying in Australia. Meanwhile, I'd been avoiding all but the bare minimum of my responsibilities at CoastalCreative, feeding Damien, and changing my appearance. Damien hadn't commented on my new look, although he angled his head slightly when I first came into his room smelling of patchouli and sporting my blonde hair and dark roots. I suppose it was the odor more than anything.

I abandoned the patchouli the second day. It was overpowering and reeked of trying too hard, and not something I could wear to work.

While I'd waited for Tess to get in touch, I hadn't made much progress on my vow to figure out my own next steps, as she so casually put it. I scrolled through career planning websites, trying to figure out what I might want to do while also trying to find some magically perfect career path that would get me on a faster trajectory to the kind of income I desired. I guess if it were that easy, everyone would have their dream job and a dream paycheck.

My phone buzzed. I was shocked to see her name appear on the screen. I'd started to wonder whether she'd gone on a soul-cleansing trip to the outback. I'd once suggested she might try some sort of wilderness head-clearing experience, but she'd dismissed the idea. The angst that troubled her so deeply at the time had never come up again — career versus marriage and motherhood. Mostly motherhood, had been my take. But like a desire for a new pair of shoes that you later decide you don't really need, the motherhood thing had flitted briefly through her life and disappeared. At least as far as I knew.

I picked up my phone.

Tess: *Here's the deal.*

Alex: *Yes?*

Tess: *I'm going to stay for a while longer.*

Alex: *What about work?*

Tess: *I asked for an extended leave.*

Alex: *How extended? It's already been six weeks.*

Tess: *Three more months.*

Alex: *Are you resigning?*

Tess: *What gave you that idea?*

I didn't want to mention Steve's suggestions that she had fallen out of favor with the senior management team. I wasn't even sure it was true, so I pretended my own concerns. *Aren't you losing momentum? Or credibility? Or something?*

Tess: *I believe that time away makes for more creative, effective employees.*

Alex: *Does exec management also believe that??*

Tess: *We're off topic here. Is it a problem for you to stay at my place another three months?*

Of course it wasn't a problem. I loved her condo. I could

stay there forever, even with Damien and his chatter. The views were spectacular. Every room was filled with natural light and beautifully decorated, giving it an atmosphere of tranquility. The mattress and pillows and comforter on the guest bed allowed me to fall into the most peaceful sleep I'd ever experienced. Helped by the absolute silence, I never woke during the night. In the mornings, I was so well-rested, I nearly danced out of bed.

Tess: *U there?*

Alex: *Yes, I can stay.*

She replied with a smiling yellow face wearing dark glasses. Then she sent an image of the Australian flag.

The flag made me think I'd missed something important. If you're vacationing in Australia, don't you send emojis of fish and crocodiles? Even spiders, hinting at some of the nasty eight-legged creatures that populate that strange continent. Why a flag? There was something she wasn't saying. I scrolled back through her messages. She'd provided minimal information, only what was absolutely required to assure that her house and bird were taken care of.

She hadn't said a word about why she was staying. Had she met a man? Found a new job? Become a tanned, glittery girl strutting on Bondi Beach?

I didn't feel used. The luxury compensated for any irritation regarding being beholden to the bird, my time not fully my own, since he had to eat on a regular schedule. But she was seriously interfering with my sex life. As far as she knew, no one else was coming into the condo. Even though I'd broken that rule, bringing Isaiah and Jen for a nice dinner, I hadn't asked him to stay over, or visit a second time. I didn't want to push my luck too far. And it wasn't Tess's doing, but my sex life was also hampered by inviting Jen to enjoy free rent along with Isaiah in my studio apartment. I ached for him. I pulled out my phone.

Alex: *Kind of needing my guy, so I'm going to have him over. I hope that's not a problem.*

Two hours later, she responded by sending an emoji rolling its eyes. I took that as a *yes*. I messaged her back that she needed to let the security people in her lobby and parking garage know about the exception to her hardline *no guests* rule. I texted Isaiah and told him we didn't have any more worries about breaking her rules.

There were two slices of leftover pizza in the fridge. I stuck them in the microwave. While they rotated, softening, cheese starting to bubble, mushrooms sizzling, I opened a bottle of Cab.

From the other room, Damien shouted — *Chardonnay time!* He laughed with a suggestion of mockery. I wasn't sure whether the mocking was due to the Cab rather than Chardonnay, or something completely unrelated. He too often acted as if he knew what I was thinking.

I poured some wine into a glass and took one of Tess's linen napkins out of the drawer. I sat at the bar sideways so I could look out the enormous window.

While I chewed pizza, I thought about my new look. I wasn't sure Isaiah would be thrilled with it. My hair definitely did not look sexy. Well, maybe it did in a kind of free-spirit, open-to-anything kind of way, but not what he was used to. I hadn't been around him long enough to know how he felt about sudden change. He wasn't the type that tried to tell me how to dress, or how to wear my hair — long or short, dyed unnatural colors or not. But this was a bit different. It was very in-your-face, and the main thing about him was that he was so easy going, just super nice, and never in anyone's face.

Alongside that tiny Australian flag, it started to niggle at me that he wouldn't find my new look charming and fun.

CHAPTER 8

*J*saiah put one foot into Tess's spacious foyer and stopped. "Uh, that's different."

I smiled. "A bit outside the norm, I know, but..."

"I guess that's your signature. Outside the norm." He laughed, but didn't take another step forward.

"True."

"What's with...your hair looks..."

"I'm going for a hippie look."

"You went all out." He didn't smile.

I turned around, showing him the back of my halter top and the tie-dyed skirt that hugged my hip bones. My feet were bare and I had more rings than usual on my toes, including one with a heart charm attached.

"That's very nice."

I felt him move closer. He touched my back and ran his finger down my spine. I sighed and shivered at the same time.

"I guess I could get into a hippie chick," he said. "Although your hair..."

I turned back to face him.

"To be honest..."

"I wouldn't expect anything less," I said.

"It looks a little skanky."

"Perfect."

"Why? I don't get it."

"I get bored."

He touched my face, pushing my hair off my cheeks. "It feels soft."

"I don't cut corners on my hair."

"Then why?"

"Like I said, bored."

"Whatever. I hope this isn't a passive-aggressive message about widespread boredom."

"Absolutely not."

"How will your hair go over at work?"

"Not sure. But I don't have to worry about Tess for a while, obviously."

He glanced down the hallway toward the bedrooms, as if he expected her to appear and chase him out for daring to tread on her Amish hand-scraped wood floors.

It wasn't clear why he'd reverted to concern over breaking her rules when he'd been perfectly happy cooking dinner in her kitchen against her wishes. Maybe, despite all his protesting over not wanting to defy her rules, he got a thrill from doing just that. Now that he was welcome, it was no longer fun.

He slipped off his backpack and set it on the floor, handed a reusable bag full of groceries to me, and shoved his hands in his pockets. "This is weird."

"Why?"

He shrugged. "How's Damien?"

"Fine."

The bird's voice, sharp and quite clear, came from his room a few yards down the hallway. *Dangerous woman.*

Isaiah laughed. "He's not going to mimic us having sex,

is he?"

"I hope not."

Dangerous woman! The bird's voice was louder, more insistent.

Isaiah smiled, but it didn't seem genuine.

I picked up the grocery bag. We went into the kitchen and I set the bag on the counter. I pulled out vine-ripened tomatoes, garlic, green onions, a half carton of eggs, two kinds of cheese, basil, two avocados, fresh pasta, fresh clams, sourdough bread — of which San Francisco has the absolute best — unsalted butter, and two bottles of Chardonnay. "I can't wait for your dinner."

"Something simple. And easy," he said.

"Sounds perfect."

I got out two glasses while he uncorked the wine. He filled the glasses and put the bottle in the fridge. We went out to the balcony and pushed the lounge chairs close to each other.

We reclined, holding hands across the space between us. We didn't talk while we sipped wine and watched the sun slowly move toward the horizon. Once it got close, a strong breeze sprang up, whipping around the balcony and blowing my hair across my face. With my bare feet and partially exposed midriff and bare shoulders and arms, I got cold fast. I resisted shivering because I wanted to watch the sun go down completely. My skin grew hard, goosebumps sprouting along my arms and on my legs under the thin skirt.

I drank my wine faster, hoping for some warmth, but of course chilled Chardonnay doesn't really do that, at least not right away.

When the sun touched the tops of the buildings, I slipped my hand out of Isaiah's. "Let's go inside."

He stood. He handed me his glass and pulled the canvas covers over the chairs.

While he steamed the clams and cooked pasta with an

avocado, basil, and lemon sauce, I sat at the bar and watched, sipping wine and listening to the bird repeat *Chardonnay time* until I wanted to close the door to his room. We ate at Tess's dining room table for twelve, sitting at opposite ends. We pretended we were a wealthy couple, which was easy in the luxurious condo. Suppressing our smiles so we wouldn't spoil the fantasy, we acted as if we had a relationship that had grown so cold and bitter over the years, we ate our meals without speaking to each other.

After dinner, he continued the game, seducing me as if we hadn't had sex in two years. It was fun, even though my hippie outfit and hair were all wrong for a wealthy woman with a frosty shield around her. Eventually, I forgot about my appearance. I'm sure Isaiah was very aware.

Lying in bed, he ran his fingers through my hair. "I just don't get the dark roots. Don't most women try to make sure their roots never show?"

"That's the point."

"What point?"

"My look. Someone without a lot of money."

"And yet your clothes look rather expensive. Shabby chic."

I laughed. "That's an interior design look, not clothes."

"Why do you need a look? Especially one that tries to pretend you don't have much money? Is this some trick to get a raise? I don't think it will work." He touched my earlobe and held it between his thumb and index finger.

"Are you worried I'll lose my job and you won't have a free apartment for the next six months?"

"No." He sounded offended. He let go of my earlobe. "We should go to The Chimera tomorrow night. Say *hi* to Jen. Leave her a big fat tip."

I turned onto my back. "I'd rather not."

"Why?"

"It's not my kind of place."

"Not your kind of place for hippie chick Alex, or not your kind of place because there's something wrong with it?"

"She's working. We shouldn't bother her. Especially on a Saturday night."

He ran his hand down my leg and rested it just below my knee. "We won't bother her, just show our support."

"There are other ways to do that."

"Such as?"

"I don't know. Let me think about it." I'd shown quite a bit of support. I'd given her a place to live. Wasn't that enough? I'd showed up once. That was more than enough.

I did not want to run into those detectives again. When you've committed more than one murder, you have a different relationship with law enforcement. Even the most casual encounter is risky, landmines scattered in the most mundane conversations. The guy in the suit had been very intense. He stared into my eyes with the determination of an optometrist, trying to see past the surface, deep into the cornea. I was sure he knew I was a little bit high. Cops have a way of sniffing those things out, even if I didn't actually have the odor of pot smoke on me.

Getting to know a couple of police detectives was not in my plan for moving my life forward. They had no way of ever knowing anything about me, but why bother? There was no reason to let it turn into something. What if, in some extreme freak chance, they talked to the detectives working on the murders of the Clayton family? What if they mentioned a woman who lived in the area? And...

There was no connecting point. I knew that.

I'm not paranoid. But I'm very careful. And that's why I've never had a problem.

Isaiah put his lips close to my ear. "Do you know what chimera means?"

I sighed under the warm touch of his breath. My *no* came out in another sigh.

"It's from Greek mythology. A fire-breathing female monster."

"Is that right." I turned into him and began kissing him.

CHAPTER 9

Of course Isaiah and I ended up going to The Chimera on Saturday night. Knowing what the name meant pushed me over the edge.

A female fire-breathing monster, indeed. I couldn't stop smiling inside.

I wanted to experience the atmosphere with that image in mind. What had made the owner decide chimera was the perfect name for a bar? Of course, a chimera is also something illusory. Maybe that was her intention and Isaiah focused on the female monster because he knew it would intrigue me.

A bar is a very illusory place. It suggests good times, lots of laughing and meeting new people, relaxing and feeling good, the freedom and pleasure of lowered inhibitions. Instead, there are many times that a bar offers too much alcohol, vomiting, and sexual assault. It's unlikely that was the owner's intention, a hidden message that women should stay away. Still, I couldn't help my thoughts wandering in that direction, because it's true.

It wasn't that I expected Chelsea's boyfriend and his buddy to be there every night of the week. The odds of seeing them again were slim. Besides, Isaiah would be sitting next to me. They wouldn't give me a second look. But the possibility, however slight, whispered that I should avoid the illusion of a fun evening. I'd end up looking over my shoulder, then censoring what I said if we did happen to meet up.

I wore jeans with rips in the knees and a green peasant blouse. The evening spring temperature falling into the fifties forced me to wear a coat. I was annoyed with myself for not buying a poncho to complete the look. But really, how far did I want to take this? I was acting like a child playing dress-up, having far too much fun with it. I did my hair in a French braid, which failed to cover up the roots. In fact, it drew them into furrows that made them more prominent.

The Chimera had seemed packed to capacity when I was there on Thursday, but when we opened the door this time, I realized that hadn't been the case. Wall-to-wall people, drinking, their elbows brushing against the arms of strangers as they lifted glasses to their mouths. The owner was raking in money. Three bartenders were on duty. And Jen.

There was no way we would find room at the bar. We managed to scope out a sliver of space near a cluster of tall tables. I waited while Isaiah went to the bar to order drinks and leave Jen her big fat tip. I asked him to order me a glass of Zin. He looked surprised, but didn't say anything.

After fifteen minutes, I was still standing there. I could barely make out the back of Isaiah's head in the crowd. It looked as if there were still two or three people ahead of him, trying to push their way into a small opening where they could flag down a bartender.

"Is this your go-to place?"

I turned. Dan stood a few inches away. He was wearing the same dark suit and white shirt, or at least *a* white shirt, hopefully not the same one.

He smiled. "I never got your name."

I shook my head slightly, and mouthed *hello* so he'd have the impression it was louder than it really was.

He raised his voice. "You look different. Your eyes. More..." He laughed.

"I'm here with my boyfriend," I said.

He didn't seem fazed and didn't move away, which made my antenna perk up. He wasn't hitting on me, so what was on his mind? Had he noticed I was stoned that night? Was he vigilant in his job, searching for illegal drug use during his off hours? Even though pot was recently legalized in California, the rules were confusing. Selling it was still illegal unless you were licensed, and then there was the whole tangled coil of federal laws. I imagined someone who'd made a career of chasing it down might find it hard to let go.

I took a step away from him and turned slightly.

He moved so he was directly facing me. He looked down, his chin almost touching his collarbone to emphasize our height difference. Too bad I was missing my high-heeled booster advantage. "Do I make you nervous?" he said.

"Not at all."

"You've been standing here a long time. I haven't seen any boyfriend." He actually made air quotes to accompany his challenge.

Did he think I'd lie about something so easily disprovable? I shrugged.

"It looks like you need a drink." He lifted his beer bottle in my direction.

"I'm not in a hurry." I wanted to check on Isaiah's progress, but turning my head would appear anxious. Dan's weird blend of subtle police intimidation and hitting on me in a rather ineffective way, mostly rude and mildly insulting, left me unsure what to say.

"So how do you know Chelsea?" he said.

"I know Jen."

He nodded. "Which one is Jen?"

Jen had introduced us. Had he really forgotten her, or was he trying to unsettle me? Even though he'd switched to quasi friendly, there was a tone that wouldn't let me stop thinking there was more to this. Time to put him on the back foot. Fire-breathing monster that I am. "Are you lost without your buddy?"

"Rick?"

"Yes."

"We aren't joined at the hip."

"That wasn't my impression. Are you vice, homicide, or...?"

He studied my face as if waiting for me to say more.

We stood without speaking, hardly looking at each other. He put the beer bottle to his mouth and tipped his head back. His Adam's apple moved like a boat bobbing along a flooded creek.

"Do you come here to see Chelsea, or you just like it?" I said.

"It's a nice place."

"I agree." I did. If it weren't for him and Rick, I'd definitely want to enjoy it on a regular basis. "I assume you're not work-ing. Since you're drinking."

"I'm always working. In my job, it's hard to turn it off."

"Makes sense," I said.

"What did you say you do?"

"Project manager."

"That's generic."

I smiled.

"And you said you work in high-tech?" he said.

I nodded, longing for my wine and Isaiah, and a place to sit. I shifted my feet and tucked my fingertips in my pockets. It was also getting warm from swarms of bodies. My wool coat was heavy on my shoulders. I took my hands out of my pockets and slid out of the coat before he could grab it in an offer to help.

"Can I hold that for you?"

"No."

He took a swig of beer. "So is that an engineering job? You're an engineer?"

I laughed. "Marketing."

"This might sound messed up, so apologies if I'm overstepping, but you don't look like you work in high-tech." He eyed my torn jeans and messy French braid. I imagined my roots were on full display under the track lighting.

Suddenly Isaiah was standing beside Dan. He held out my glass of wine. The minute it was in my hand, I took a long sip. I hoped Isaiah would feel threatened, or at least annoyed that this guy was talking to me when I'm sure my face said I didn't want him there, and get rid of him. Usually I'm perfectly good at ridding myself of unwanted men all on my own, but him being a detective put a different filter over the situation. I couldn't offend him, I couldn't do anything to make him take a closer look at me.

I'd never known a detective personally and I wasn't sure whether his chumminess and extreme curiosity were acquired traits for the profession, or an oddity that was all his own. I took another sip of wine.

"This is your boyfriend?" Dan said.

Isaiah smiled. I'd never used that word. Great. Now the guy was not only going to invade my space, he was disrupting the dynamic between me and Isaiah.

Isaiah held out his hand. "Isaiah Parker."

"Dan Vorcek." He shook Isaiah's hand.

"Dan's a detective," I said.

"Cool." Isaiah lifted his gin and tonic toward Dan as if he was toasting him for being a cop.

"I was just telling your girlfriend, who hasn't entrusted me with her name, that she doesn't look like she works in marketing."

All credit to Isaiah, not a single muscle on his face twitched in agreement. "She's looking to move into sales," he said.

I took a huge gulp of wine. So much for reading my state of mind or guessing that I might not know this cop as well as he'd implied. So much for keeping the information flow to a minor trickle. Did Isaiah offer too many personal details to every stranger he met in a bar? How had I not ever witnessed this? He wasn't busy telling servers in restaurants our life stories. Was this because the idea of a detective made him feel that he had to be *Mr. Open-and-Honest* and *we-have-nothing-to-hide*? I didn't get it. I took another sip of wine.

Isaiah glanced at me, noticed the nearly empty state of my glass and gave me a curious look.

Dan was not crude enough to comment further on my style of dress and how inappropriate it was for a sales job, but he seemed overly interested in my torn jeans, and I had the sense he couldn't stop looking at my hair. I'd had no idea it would be such a point of fascination. I knew people would judge me a certain way, stereotype me as a certain kind of woman, but I hadn't expected to meet cops in a bar. A small part of me was starting to regret the choice. It had seemed like something fun that would mess with people's heads, but the only messed up head was my own.

CHAPTER 10

*S*ydney, *Australia*

* * *

Three days before her flight back to the U.S., Tess had realized she'd wasted her entire sabbatical. First of all, she would be hard-pressed to define it as a sabbatical if asked about it by her manager and peers at CC. A sabbatical — even though a paid break of that type wasn't offered by CC, making her time away unofficial — should have some sort of career-improvement angle to it. At the very least, some accomplishment that increased her perceived value.

If she wanted them to take her seriously, she should have pursued a course or seminar or professional contacts that would benefit CoastalCreative.

Instead, she'd lounged around her hotel room in Sydney, sleeping until mid-morning, and lingering over fattening breakfasts before lurching toward early afternoon lunches featuring a glass or two or three of wine. She'd met a lot of interesting people, fun people, but within days of meeting them, wasn't sure she would recognize them if they ran into each other again.

She'd had sex twice, both times with laid back Aussies. They didn't ask for her contact info and neither did she, the purpose of their encounters clear to both partners while they were still laughing in the bar. They mostly talked about The Cricket — *The* Cricket — what was that about? No one called it *the* baseball or *the* football. Aussies were so much like Americans, but so not.

In the past, she'd taken business trips to Sydney and Melbourne several times, and met a fair number of Australians, but living among them for several weeks was quite different. She felt she missed half their jokes. It wasn't as if she couldn't make sense of the words, they were clear and precise. But the terminology was bizarre at times, making her feel slightly unintelligent. Their accents were so seductive, her own voice sounding dull, flat, and unoriginal in the forced volume required in a bar. Pub. She'd mostly hung out in pubs where locals behaved like extended family with each other. Why couldn't she remember that?

She'd gone to every movie showing in the area, taken boat trips around the harbor, and visited the Aquarium and the Harbor Bridge Museum. She'd taken a tour of the Sydney Opera House. She'd read a few political biographies, a book on the history of The Rocks — the penal colony established by the British when they first arrived in Australia. She read lots of online articles about the wildlife and sea life in and around Australia.

What she hadn't done was given more than ten minutes of thought to her career and her place at CoastalCreative, and really, if she was honest, about why she'd bolted to the other side of the world. She'd given no thought to the rest of her life.

That Sunday morning when it really lodged in her brain

that she'd accomplished nothing toward figuring out whether she wanted to stay at CC, look for a position at another company, possibly outside the Bay Area, or step away from the corporate world for a while, or... or what?...she'd spread her arms out to the side and stared at the ceiling. Her chest rose and fell with subtle movements, the rumpled sheets on top of her hardly moving. The ceiling fan rotating slowly overhead seemed more alive than she was.

Instead of ordering a sausage roll or corn frittata and potatoes which left her brain numb with carbs, she called room service for a double espresso and a bowl of strawberries. The woman taking her order tried to press her for something more — *yoghurt? A slice of toast? A muffin?* Tess said she wanted nothing on the tray but the coffee and berries.

The shock to her system from caffeine, which made her stomach scream for one of her big breakfasts and a celebratory Sunday mimosa, had allowed her to think for the first time in days. This time, she didn't shove her existential angst to the back corner of her mind or drown it with alcohol. She sat on the balcony and stared at the impossibly blue water of the harbor and the clamshell opera house. She refused to allow herself back into her room, refused to indulge in a shower or any food but the berries until she figured out what she should do next.

It came to her that her pride was greater than her desire to sort out her life. She could not go home in this condition. Everyone would ask about Australia. *Four weeks!*, they would say. *You must have seen amazing things, done amazing things, met amazing people.* How could she respond? *I saw a platypus in a pond in an Aquarium, drank myself numb, and had sex with two strangers whose accents made me silly with lust?*

She'd told Alex she might see the Great Barrier Reef, and that's what she was going to do. Now. It wasn't as if a paycheck was driving her back to work. It wasn't as if she'd miss a promotion by staying away, falling out of the loop, proving herself somewhat unnecessary. There were no more promotions for her at CC. Only engineers were invited into the executive vice president and CEO roles.

* * *

The condo she booked on Hamilton Island, part of the Whitsunday chain scattered throughout the Coral Sea near Queensland, looked out over a long swimming pool built right beside a sparkling white beach toward Dent Island. The main floor had a large balcony with a table and chairs for eight and a gas barbecue. The glass doors folded up against the wall on one side, so the interior became a living area and kitchen that was partially outdoors. The balcony was wide enough that even when a tropical storm blew across the island, no water came near the hardwood floors. The sound of rain and warm, moist air filled the room.

There was a small bedroom on the main floor and a bedroom and bathroom suite with an equally wide balcony and the same type of folding doors on the floor above.

No cars were allowed on the island. The condo was equipped with a golf cart that she drove to restaurants, a small market, beaches, and a wildlife preserve where she could have breakfast with Koalas if she desired.

There were two dive shops that ran trips to the Reef. Both offered intensive diving classes for tourists who wanted to get deep into the Reef instead of enjoying it from a glass-bottom boat, or simply floating along the surface of the water, blowing salt water out of a snorkel.

The thought of going down thirty or forty feet, nothing to preserve her life but a tank on her back and a thin tube running to her mouth was terrifying. Maybe this would shock her out of her lethargic state.

CHAPTER 11

 an Francisco

* * *

Rain pounded against the building. The overhang was less than two feet wide, providing no protection at all. Jen opened the back door leading to the storage and glass washing area of The Chimera. A gust of wind shoved her through the door into the empty room. She walked through to an adjacent room that held a few lockers and a vending machine stocked with candy bars and chips. She twisted the combination on locker number five, opened the door, and shoved her purse inside. She took off her rain jacket and hung it on a hook beside the vending machine.

Chelsea didn't use a locker. She stored her purse behind the bar, keeping her beloved journal close by. It seemed like a mistake, leaving a purse out where people might see it. No one but the employees went behind the bar, but it wasn't like it was completely impossible for a tipsy patron to wander back there. Things got hectic behind the bar during peak hours, Chelsea couldn't keep her eye on her purse while she was mixing drinks and collecting credit cards.

Jen looked in the mirror, ran her fingers through her hair to lift it away from the sides of her face, and went into the main part of the bar. It was quiet for a Thursday at three-thirty. She'd never seen it this empty — two men at the bar, four unoccupied chairs between them, and three other men sitting around a table near the front, leaning forward and talking quietly.

Jen walked toward the front end of the bar where Chelsea was slicing limes.

"Hey."

Chelsea drew the knife down the center of half a lime in a quick, clean cut. Juice dribbled onto the cutting board. She began slicing the pieces into thin wedges. "It's really quiet. Not sure we need you until later, but here you are, so..."

"Can I do that for you?"

"It's taken care of." She picked up another lime and cut it in half.

Jen nodded. "So what should I do?"

"You could get more olives. And napkins."

Jen hurried back to the storeroom. She grabbed an enormous jug of green olives and a plastic sleeve of pale-yellow napkins stamped with the bar's name in dark blue. She carried them back to the bar.

"Did you start your bullet journal?" Chelsea said. She rinsed her hands and dried them.

"No."

"Well you wrote down the drink recipes I gave you. For the Cosmo and the Apple-tini. So that's a start. And the tricks for a perfect martini. Did you write a reminder that the critical part is properly chilled glasses, shaker, and alcohol?"

"Yes."

"You don't seem very excited about the journal." Chelsea

picked up a can of cola and took a sip. She licked her lips and took another sip.

"I'm not sure it's my thing."

"Trust me, it's very powerful."

"That's what you said, but I don't have a lot of plans. I'm not sure what to write."

"That's the point. You write about what's important, about where you want to be five years from now, and figure out steps for getting there."

Chelsea was the one missing the point. Jen didn't know where she wanted to be in five years. Okay, maybe that wasn't true. She probably wanted to be married, and maybe have a child. She definitely wanted a job she was excited about, one that paid a decent amount of money. But you couldn't journal your way to those things. They were all pretty much outside of your control.

As if to prove her dedication and the supernatural power of her notebook, Chelsea reached under the bar, tugged her purse out of the cubbyhole, and pulled out her journal. The edges were worn and the elastic strap was slightly stretched. She flipped it open on the bar and rifled through the pages. She took a red pen out of her back pocket and wrote in large, loopy script.

"What are you writing?" Jen said.

"My biggest accomplishment for the day."

"What's that?"

"Encouraging you." She gave Jen a confident smile.

Jen didn't like feeling as if she was someone's project, an accomplishment for the day. And she didn't think she needed any encouragement. What she needed was to learn more about bartending so she could get a job that would allow her to rent her own apartment. Maybe if she felt in control of her life, she'd meet a nice guy. And maybe then she'd have things to write about with multi-colored pens and pencils. Chelsea was obsessed with her journal. And she seemed annoyed that Jen wasn't cherishing the gift. "I'll get to it. Maybe tonight after work."

"You'll be too tired." Chelsea closed her journal and walked toward the guy sitting near the center of the bar. "Ready for a refill?"

"Sure." He pushed the glass toward her.

Chelsea turned and took the bottle of Johnny Walker Black off the shelf. She poured a stream of shimmering gold liquid into the glass and placed it on a fresh napkin.

"How are things at work?" Chelsea said.

"Fucked."

"Nothing new there."

"Same for you?" he said.

She laughed. "No. But I work for a woman, so things are well-managed, and we're treated with respect."

"That sounds sexist." He laughed and took a sip of his drink.

"It's the truth. So that makes it not sexist."

"If you say so."

Chelsea smiled. "Why is it so awful?"

"I don't actually have a boss, I'm a therapist."

"I know, you told me."

"Didn't expect you to remember." He smiled.

"So what happened?"

"A client quit therapy. One who really needed to be there."

"Don't they all need to be there?" she said.

"To be honest, some more than others."

"Well that's too bad. I guess it's true, you can lead a horse to water..."

"We were making progress. Of course, that's when things always get rough. It happens from time to time, but in this case..." He shook his head and took a long swallow of whiskey.

"Sorry to hear that. Hopefully this takes the edge off."

"You know it. Everyone in here is taking the edge off something."

Chelsea smiled. "Maybe the client will think it over and come back."

"Aren't you the optimist."

"Not really, but I try not to assume the worst of the worst."

"Well, it feels like a defeat. That's all. As if I didn't do my job — foreseeing the rough spots coming at that phase in his therapy." He moved his glass in circles around the counter. It glided soundlessly, muffled by the napkin.

Chelsea patted the counter. "Next drink is on the house."

"Really? You can do that?" He looked up, his mouth partially open as if he'd planned to say more.

"Absolutely."

"Thanks."

Chelsea turned and moved back to where Jen stood watching.

"I don't know if I'll ever be able to do that," Jen said.

"Do what? Offer a freebie? You'll learn when it's appropriate. And Claire will start to trust your instincts." She picked up her notebook and slipped off the strap. "If you listen, you'll get a sense of who might be lured to come back more often once they're offered a free drink. You could write about that in your bullet journal. It's a feeling you get from talking to them. Listen to the cues — his surprise that I remembered what he did. That made him feel welcome and important. Now, he'll remember that feeling and the free drink. Think he'll pick another bar?"

Jen shook her head.

"Write it down."

"My book's at home."

Chelsea glared at her. "First thing tonight. I mean it. For it to work, you have to use it."

"Okay." It sounded ridiculous, but if it was that important...she needed to keep a good relationship with Chelsea.

Chelsea opened her book, turned slightly, and began writing, this time with a blue pen. Her words flowed across the
page.

"What are you writing about?" Jen said.

"I like to write down when I help people. I told you that.
I'm writing what he said, how he was feeling, and how talking
to him helped." She didn't lift her head, continuing to write
while she talked.

Jen went to the sink and filled a glass with water. She took
a sip. Chelsea was a little fanatical about the journal thing.
Her belief in it made it sound supernatural, but maybe there
was something to it. What the heck. She might as well give it a
shot.

She looked back. Chelsea was still writing.

CHAPTER 12

*L*ike most high-tech companies, CoastalCreative has a very loose dress code. I guess you wouldn't even call it a dress code. No company really has a dress code per se any more, just an unspoken expectation. Maybe it's East Coast versus California, but women on Wall Street and in national politics wear dark suits and high heels. And of course recently, if you work in the White House, a woman damn well better *dress like a woman* — meaning a dress. Skirts and dresses offer easy access. After all, isn't that why women have worn dresses throughout history? Or did dresses evolve to cover up the distracting parts of their bodies? I'm not sure. It's a little confusing because I love dresses and skirts. Do I have an inherent affection for them? In western countries, with one notable exception, men don't have any desire to wear skirts — so it has to be cultural. Was I socialized to love them before I could even walk, much less think for myself?

My heart burns when I see children in a park and the baby girls are trying to crawl, knees catching on their adorable sun dresses, pitching them forward into face plants, while boys scramble ahead of them.

In Silicon Valley, clothing style has a split personality. Engineers often dress like the creative types that they are — faded jeans, over-washed t-shirts with the names of musicians or product code names commemorating the public announcements of their creations. They wear Birkenstock sandals and occasionally display tattoos. There's a lot more facial hair. Although mostly that goes for the Anglo guys born in the United States or transplants from Europe. Engineers who were born in Asia or India tend to dress more conservatively, more like their marketing counterparts. I'm not sure what that says about cultural differences, but it definitely says something.

Quite a few female engineers choose clothes not unlike my new hippie look. Some have equally flamboyant tattoos and hair dyed shocking orange or copper or streaked with blue.

The engineering side is one half of a company's personality, and marketing and sales are the other. Sales would hate being lumped with marketing like that, but in terms of clothing choices, they're the same breed. They're an army dressed in suits and leather shoes, silk and Egyptian cotton. Expensive haircuts, super-close shaves, and buffed and manicured fingernails.

Before I dyed my hair to expose the roots and went shopping in The Haight, I fit perfectly into the corporate expectation. I had deliberately mirrored Tess's clothing style, which went above and beyond the Silicon Valley nod to a suit jacket spiffing up a pair of designer blue jeans. Dressing like Tess made her feel connected to me, made her feel she could trust me on a gut level that she wasn't fully aware of.

Maybe my change of appearance was an effort to fake out my own self. Maybe it wasn't about concealing myself from detectives looking for a killer in the vicinity of Tess's condo. Maybe, I thought, as I walked through the front doors of CoastalCreative, it was a signal from my subconscious mind that I was ready for a change. My gut telling me to shake things up.

Sometimes the subconscious brain has a mind of its own.

I admit, I was very, very curious to see how Steve Montgomery would respond to the change in my appearance. Maybe that's why I did it, to unnerve him, throw him off his game, and prove that I wasn't going to turn myself into the protégé he seemed to need so desperately.

I rode the elevator up to my floor. I walked to my cubicle without attracting any double takes. I settled at my desk and unlocked my computer display.

Lately, Steve worked at the San Francisco office on Fridays, so odds were high that I'd run into him at some point, if he didn't come looking for me. I hadn't spoken to him since he'd caught me outside of Tess's building. I wondered if he'd given second thoughts to his initial attempt at profiling me based on absolutely no information.

Because I'd been in an exclusive neighborhood and he had no idea what I was doing there, he leaped to his first conclusion that I lived there, followed by faulty conclusion number two that I must have a lot of money, and then tacked on the belief that I didn't need my job because of this supposed money. He assumed I had either a rich father, a rich husband, or a rich lover. I hadn't corrected his assumptions.

I worked through lunch, nibbling on a bag of crackers I'd tucked into my fringed leather bag that morning. My plan was to get all my work done and escape the building by two o'clock. It was a sunny day with a warm breeze. A late lunch at an outdoor cafe was all I could think about. A crab salad or a hoagie both sounded good. I hadn't made up my mind yet.

My face was inches from the computer screen, an unconscious habit that deludes me into thinking I'm improving my concentration. I was working on changing formulas in a spreadsheet so it would correctly calculate a due date for a first draft of a white paper and the timing for the interim review deadlines, based on the publication date, which was not negotiable.

"Alex?" Steve's voice was quiet, as if he were speaking inside the back of my mind, instead of his usual brash dive into the middle of whatever I was doing.

I pushed my chair away from my desk and looked up. I tilted the desk lamp toward the wall so the light wasn't glaring into my eyes.

"Has it been that long since I've seen you?" he said. "Only two weeks or so, isn't it?"

"Something like that."

"What happened to your hair?"

I shrugged.

"It looks…Well, probably not my place to say, but it looks unprofessional."

"I sit in a cubicle all day. My meetings all take place on the phone. What difference does it make?"

He tilted his chin down and raised his eyebrows, the same sort of look someone would give if he was staring over the top edge of a pair of bifocals. "It's not appropriate for the workplace. Surely you can afford…"

"You're not my boss."

"Is that your final decision, then?"

I raised my eyebrows back at him.

"Hair aside, which I assume will be fixed soon, I know we keep getting derailed, but I thought you were seriously… Look." He glanced around the group of cubicles toward the windowed offices that lined the outer edge of the floor, reserved for managers. "Do you want to grab a late lunch?"

"Sure."

He looked startled. He glanced at his watch and shoved his hands in his pockets.

I stood and locked the computer screen. I grabbed my

jacket and purse off the large metal hook near the entry to the cubicle. As I stepped into the hallway, he eyed my outfit — a paisley dress that hung to the middle of my shins and the Doc Martens. We turned toward the elevators and walked in silence to the end of the hall.

He was equally quiet during the ride to the first floor. We exited into the lobby. As he started walking toward the main doors he said, "Dim sum?"

"Sounds good."

We went outside and turned left. He didn't say a word during the entire six-block walk to the restaurant. I was starving and couldn't wait to eat, so I didn't bother with conversation. While we walked, I decided it was almost time to stop this game with him. I was never going to work for him. Thinking that was a viable plan had been pure laziness. My goal was to make a ridiculous amount of money and it wasn't going to happen at CoastalCreative, even with the acceleration provided by a sales commission. As long as I kept playing this game with him, I wasn't moving forward.

CHAPTER 13

*E*xtricating myself from Steve Montgomery would take some care. It might have been optimistic to think I could do it over one meal. First, I had to be sure there was nothing in his mind that tied me unnaturally to Tess's neighborhood, so his mischaracterization of me was something I needed to feed after all. If he thought I had a wealthy benefactor, married or not, blood relative or not, it would be better. There would be no need for him to think about why I was in that part of the city.

So possibly, making sure he understood that I didn't need the *more lucrative* job he'd offered was the way to go. I'd made a mistake seeming too interested. I'd given the impression I was pursuing him as much as he had me. He knew he was winning. If he thought I was simply working at CC to pass the time of day, or to earn discretionary spending money, the shock of seeing me in that wealthy neighborhood would fade.

But I wasn't sure of any of that. He knew CC was subsidizing apartments to lure people from Santa Cruz to work in the city. Didn't he wonder why I'd taken one of the subsidized apartments if I lived in Russian Hill? Who knew what he was aware of or what he was really up to. I still wasn't even entirely sure if his attention was about me or Tess. I know I would be good at sales, so maybe he truly was thinking about my contribution to his organization. But his fixation on denigrating Tess was somehow tied up in it. I just needed to make sure I closed all the doors before I walked away.

If he had any curiosity about where I was living and why, it was a vulnerability. A very small one. But the lines were too close for my comfort.

He held the door to the dim sum restaurant and I stepped inside. We were shown to a table in a dark corner. I wondered if he'd given some sort of signal to the maître d' since we walked past several unoccupied tables on our way to the cozy booth. We settled in and a server appeared asking to take our drink orders.

Although I love wine, good wine, I'd had enough with ordering it by the glass in a rather limp attempt to fit my drink to my adopted persona. "I'll have a vodka martini," I said. "Dry. Three olives."

The server gave me a delighted smile, as if it was his supreme pleasure to deliver martinis.

Steve ordered his usual scotch on the rocks.

When the server was gone, Steve turned to me. "So. I think I've been too reticent with you."

"How is that?"

"You're very complicated."

"Isn't everyone?"

"No." He clicked his chopsticks against each other. "What exactly are your career aspirations?"

"Since we're not being reticent, my goal is to make a lot of money."

"How much is a lot?"

"That's a personal question."

"Fair enough."

The server returned with our drinks. He placed the martini in front of me without a single drop slipping over the edge of the glass. The tray was also dry, suggesting he'd crossed the entire restaurant without spilling it. I took a sip before Steve could make a toast. It was as delicious as it looked.

He toasted me anyway, a single-sided toast with a simple raising of his glass, saying nothing. He took a sip and kept the glass in his hand, his other hand finding its way to the chopsticks for the nervous clicking. "I had the impression, after I saw you in Russian Hill, that money wasn't an issue for you. Which of course, I'd originally misread. You'd acted as if you were extremely hungry for a more lucrative opportunity."

"I am."

"You seem comfortable enough, living in a place like that."

"Can't a girl want money of her own?"

"Ah." He took two rapid sips of scotch. "Now that makes more sense."

I swirled the stick of olives around my glass. A woman wheeled a dim sum cart to our table. We ordered pork dumplings, potstickers, and shrimp with slender stalks of cilantro folded into large sheets of rice noodle. I took several sips of my drink. I moved the glass to the side and grabbed a dumpling with my chopsticks. I set it on my plate and spooned hot mustard into the tiny dish nearby.

Steve watched me. He made no move to take a dumpling of his own. "But then why do you seem to be going out of your way to sabotage your potential by dressing like a flower child, or whatever that get-up is?"

I ate my dumpling and took a few more sips of my drink. He finally began to fill his plate.

"I don't really have an answer for that," I said.

"You figure since Tess is MIA, you can do what you want?"

"I pretty much always do what I want."

"Not surprising. You don't seem to be trying very hard to impress me, if you're still pursuing a position in sales."

"Was I ever pursuing a position in sales?"

"I thought you were. We spoke about it several times."

I smiled in a very genuine way. I leaned back and nudged my plate away from me.

"Full?"

"Not yet."

In an act of perfect timing, one of the women appeared with a cart. Steve pointed to a tin of pork buns, more potstickers, and chicken dumplings.

"You can call me a dumb dude," he said. "But I have no idea what you want." As if the honesty was too much for him, he winked. "Maybe you just enjoy my company."

"Maybe I do."

His eyes widened and he picked up his glass. It was empty.

I took the last sip of my drink and ate the final olive.

"Do you want some sake?" he said.

"I'd rather have another martini."

He turned and nodded at the server, pointed at our glasses, and held up two fingers. The server disappeared into the bar area.

Without seeming to shift his position, Steve was suddenly a few inches closer to me on the curved bench. He began talking about his sales wins and golf, his second favorite topic.

By the time we started our third round of drinks, our bellies were bloated with noodles and our tongues hot with spicy mustard and chili sauce. He was sitting even closer.

The server removed our plates and we settled against the backrest. I picked up my glass and took the tiniest sip I could manage. Drinking three martinis is risky. I was glad I wasn't wearing high heels so I wouldn't wobble when we finally stood up to leave. But wobbling isn't the only risk. There's my sharp tongue. And desire. I nibbled olives and moved the martini behind my water glass and the cluster of condiment bottles so he wouldn't notice that the liquid only went down as the olives disappeared.

His leg was almost touching mine. I relaxed slightly, closing the distance.

He took a long swallow of scotch and then his hand was on my thigh. Heat ran through my body faster than the alcohol.

Clearly my ratty hair and hippie clothes didn't bother him after all.

CHAPTER 14

*W*hy are clothes, especially women's clothes, such a thing? Billions of dollars are spent on women's clothing, and billions more on the adjacent business of cosmetics, not to mention the advertising of both. Women surely aren't dressing for comfort much of the time. Why do we wear high heels? Let's start with that. They make our legs look good. But why? Because they get stretched into unnatural shapes?

Narrow high heels are difficult to walk in, they damage your feet and calf muscles. They're downright dangerous in a rainstorm or walking across a garden or down a steep flight of stairs, and don't even think about walking down some of San Francisco's hills wearing them. You could end up smashing your face on concrete.

Yet, I love high heels.

I love putting on a nice dress and a pair of well-designed, well-crafted heels. I love how I feel and I love how I look. Who am I doing it for? Me? Am I trying to send a message to other women that I look better? *My legs are nicer, my walk more*

seductive? I'll beat you in acquiring the best male animal available.
Men will look at me first, they'll choose me over you.

I don't even know the answer to those questions. I don't think that's my intention when I put on a tight, well-cut dress and super high heels. Those competitive thoughts don't form in my mind. I feel sleek and elegant, and despite the problems with walking, I just feel good. Where does that come from? The media? Is it some sort of weird group-think, like the Emperor's new clothes — an entire culture that's decided this is how a woman looks her best?

It makes me feel as if I've been brainwashed in a very insidious and deeply rooted fashion, that I've adopted the ideas of some external force without question, folding them into my very DNA. Otherwise, why would I feel so great when I certainly can't run for my life, if necessary?

No woman finds high heels comfortable for more than a few hours. And when you're walking with men, you're literally hobbled. In school, we were horrified to learn about female toddlers in China whose feet had been bound with cloth soaked in herbs and animal blood to prevent growth. As bones broke and their feet became non-functioning, these children learned to become women who took pride in this symbol of wealth. Walking wasn't a requirement. Standing and moving about was for the working class. No one would mistake one of those women for a dirty, hopeless peasant — a woman who had to work to survive, who wasn't carried from one pillow to another like a delicate blown-glass lotus.

For the rest of her life she was immobilized, and she accepted it with pleasure!

I can't stop buying new pairs of heels. I savor the chance to look through my collection when I'm going out to dinner or a club. Since starting at CoastalCreative, I'd worn high heels to work most days. Those high heels bought me respect from Tess, they told my peers who I was, and they captured Steve's attention. But they weren't simply tools, I truly loved wearing them. And even though I had to walk more slowly, more deliberately, I was thrilled with my appearance.

And what about makeup? Another critical part of my life, possibly even more than the high heels. I wouldn't mind wandering into a cosmetic shop or a department store every single week to check out new colors, admiring brushes and considering sponges, finding a must-have for my facial art kit.

Spreading expensive lotion and tinted cream or foundation across my face feels as good as a kiss on the cheek. The pressure of my fingertips on my skin, the response of the firm flesh beneath it, and the contour of my bones is an all-consuming pleasure. Shading my eyes, lining them with dark color, and stroking on mascara is fun. My face is transformed. I become more exotic, and yes, more beautiful.

But no one ever says a man isn't handsome because he hasn't altered the tone of his skin or darkened his eyes or stroked black liquid into his eyelashes. They never say he could use a bit of color. A man doesn't look in the mirror and think — *I can fix this*. A man doesn't walk up to a cosmetics counter and listen to fairy tales about regaining his youth, covering blemishes, making his eyes *pop*. I suppose they succumb to Rogaine and tanning booths, but that's the exception. Most men who lose their hair shave their heads, or carry on without a second thought. And only those pursuing careers where their appearance is judged as viciously as women's are lured to tanning booths. For women, appearance is a factor in every job on the planet. You can't even get a job in a damn daycare center if your face lacks a certain tender expression.

It's an undeniable fact that makeup enhances your appearance. I can't think of any reason why I'd stop using it.

Why do I think these things?

Why *do* I love makeup? Aside from the benefits it gives to

me specifically — changing my appearance enough to confuse people about my identity, suggesting I'm either open to anything or completely unapproachable — I like how it makes me look. I like my eyes made darker, or more shapely. I like my cheekbones more prominent and my lips the color and texture of fresh fruit.

I hate that I feel undressed without it. I love the artistry of it and the face reflected back at me in the mirror. Me, but better.

The minimal makeup on my eyes, the unkempt appearance of my hair, and my soft, undemanding clothes sent a message to men that I wasn't very interesting. I wasn't highly fuckable. I wasn't an eight, nine, or ten who would add to their social cachet. When I sat at the bar in The Chimera, giving the illusion I wasn't a very exciting woman, they left me alone. Nothing about my appearance said I was looking for a few laughs and might be open to easy sex.

Steve was a different story. To Steve, I think I gave the message, although I hadn't planned this in advance, that I was open to anything. I was no longer a prize he wanted to win, but someone he could easily take. That, and my coy white lie that I simply enjoyed his company.

CHAPTER 15

When Jen arrived at The Chimera for her shift, the bar was empty. It made no sense, especially on a Friday afternoon. Chelsea was nowhere in sight, but her bullet journal was lying on the bar, the elastic strap curled off to the side. There were two pens a few inches away.

Jen walked across the room to the front door and pressed the handle. It was locked. She glanced at the front window. The *Open* sign was unlit. She turned and looked back across the room. The dishwashing area and break room had also been empty, but the back door was unlocked, as always. From the first day, it struck her as odd that they left themselves exposed to robbery with an unattended, unlocked door. She'd meant to ask Chelsea about it, but by the time she came into the bar itself, the thought always slipped out of her mind as her thoughts shifted to making sure she was at her best — appearing cheerful, friendly, and eager to work hard.

She returned to the area behind the bar and picked up the journal. Chelsea never left it lying around, she must have left unexpectedly. There hadn't been some kind of robbery, had there? She went to the cash register, still holding the notebook.

Nothing looked out of order, but she had no way of opening it to be sure. Chelsea and the other bartenders had individual access codes. Jen wasn't allowed to ring up sales. She would be soon, hopefully, but not yet.

She glanced at the notebook and placed her palm on the hard, smooth cover. Reading it was so wrong, but the desire was overwhelming. If Chelsea returned suddenly...she could be fired. She *would* be fired. Even if Chelsea didn't have that authority on her own, she would speak to Claire and Jen would be gone. The risk was too much.

But she was so curious. The longer she held the book, the more she felt she couldn't put it down without looking inside. She could take it into the bathroom, read it, then tuck it in her locker and tell Chelsea she'd found it on the bar and didn't want anyone to take it. She glanced around the room. Where was she?

She put the notebook on the bar and stood looking at it. She touched the cover, then slid her finger over the side, running it along the soft edges of the paper that was slowly transforming to the consistency of fabric from all the touching and thumbing. She yanked her hand away as if she'd been burned.

Her cell phone buzzed. She pulled it out of her pocket.

Chelsea: *Claire wanted some kind of bullshit super urgent meeting. We're upstairs in the office. When you get here, can you put my journal away? I left it on the bar. She practically dragged me out of there bodily. I'll be there in ten minutes. Cut up some limes. Lots.*

Jen messaged back a thumbs up. She picked up the journal. What could have been so urgent?

She opened the book and skimmed the first page where Chelsea listed the contents and wrote in the appropriate page numbers. She had workout plans, yoga classes, TV shows, restaurants to try, movies to see, a five-year plan...the list when on for two pages. The last topic was *Customers*. The number sixty-three, followed by a dash and a blank space, was written in the left-hand column.

Jen flipped to page sixty-three.

The names of customers were written in red. Where Chelsea didn't seem to know the name, she'd written a brief description.

Thurs. regular, rings on middle fingers: *Thanks for listening. Can't stop talking about it cuz I've never seen the Niners score like that.*

Thurs. 2x/month guy always wears pink tie: *Never seen so many smokin' bartenders in one place.*

Joe the lawyer: *...best bagels in the city. My friend owns the place, mention me...I'll tell him to hook you up with an excellent discount. You're a good sport. I owe you.*

Kate, lawyer?: *You're sweet. Thanks for letting me yap forever about my mom's medical stuff.*

Johnny W Therapist: *You can do that? ... Thanks!*

Jen closed the book. She wasn't sure how Chelsea thought she'd helped the one going on about great-looking bartenders.

The notes gave a different impression of Chelsea. Writing down people's appreciative comments might make a person feel good, something to look back at when you were down, maybe. But there was a touch of neediness to it.

She wrapped the elastic strap around the notebook and shoved it into Chelsea's purse. She tucked the pens on top of it. The minute the journal was secured, she found herself wanting to read more. There was something fascinating about reading what another person found important. Even information as dull as a list of television shows became enticing because it was private. She wanted to read more of the quotes, and she wanted to look at Chelsea's five-year plan. She wanted all the details, wanted to know what movies she liked. She wanted to know if there was anything about herself written in the notebook.

The notebook was never lying around. This had been her one chance. But she was glad she hadn't kept going. She hadn't checked the time, and Chelsea might show up at any minute.

She took three limes out of the metal tub and put them on the cutting board. She sliced all of them in half then began cutting the required thin wedges. The book floated at the back of her mind, taunting her with a peek into Chelsea's life. It was kind of disgusting. It was no different from reading someone's diary. She felt terrible. At the same time, she tried to work out a way of getting another chance.

CHAPTER 16

*D*espite the involuntary sensation that shot through my body when Steve placed his hand on my leg, I had no intention of having sex with him. Ever. I'm not opposed to transactional sex if it gets me something worthwhile, but mostly I prefer it for pleasure. Still, the heat from his hand told me I had a brief amount of time to lead his thoughts where I wanted.

When we left the dim sum place, he touched his hand to the small of my back. A rather proprietary move after one feel, but not surprising.

By instinct, we turned back toward the CoastalCreative building. We started walking, his hand still on my back. Keeping it there forced him to move with an awkward gait rather than his usual posture and movements that announced he was the man in charge. His sense of possession was clearly more important for the time being.

"Should we..." he said.

"Get another drink?"

"You haven't had enough?"

"Have you?"

He laughed and we continued walking without looking at each other. The silence between us stretched for over a block. I was not going to answer my own question, or his. It seemed as if he wasn't sure what to say, for once. We crossed California Street headed toward Market.

"I guess we could have another," he said. "If that's what you want."

It was clearly not what he wanted, and I wondered if he was worried about his performance, three glasses of scotch into the afternoon. I wasn't worried at all. Two martinis leave me sharp, less careful about what I say, but still in control of myself. He hadn't seemed to notice I'd left the third untouched, except for the olives.

We stopped at the Irish bar where we'd had drinks twice before. It was starting to feel like our regular place, but hopefully, that would be short-lived.

Steve ordered his scotch and a vodka martini with three olives.

I looked at the bartender. "You know, I'm kind of thirsty. Will you make that a vodka tonic instead of a martini. In a tall glass."

Steve looked mildly disturbed but said nothing. He surely saw what I was doing, intending to consume more tonic water than alcohol, forcing him to drink more than he'd wanted in order to appear sociable. As if to reassure himself that we were still headed in his anticipated direction, he slipped his hand onto my leg, much higher this time. Not only had his aversion to my hippie clothes evaporated, the way his fingers moved on my leg suggested he liked the soft, thin fabric.

Our drinks arrived and I took a sip through the narrow red straw.

He knocked his glass against mine, not bothering to lift it.

He swallowed some and placed it on the bar. "I hope you're not playing some kind of game again," he said.

"Absolutely not. Haven't you ever heard of foreplay?"

That perked him right up. He sipped his drink in a failed attempt to cover the grin spreading across his cheeks. It was painful to watch, seeing him try to restrain it, to avoid giving the impression of leering.

The bar was crowded, the noise level moderate, but we were enclosed in our own bubble of alcohol and desire — his, not mine. After that first rush of my blood to meet the pressure of his hand, I had a grip on my body. There's nothing like a game plan — a far greater desire — to dampen the other.

"I do want money of my own," I said. "I don't like being dependent."

"Obviously."

"It's great, having money. But knowing you didn't earn it yourself, knowing it comes from your predecessors, or... others...is more demoralizing than you might think."

He nodded.

"Like Barker Clayton," I said.

"What do you mean?"

"He was proud of his company. But you have to wonder how it was for him, knowing that he succeeded because his family had money. He didn't get all the VC money he needed based solely on his idea. Without his mother's investment, who knows if his idea would have gotten off the ground."

"I was shocked to hear he was dead."

"I can imagine. You were friends, right?"

He shook his head, keeping his faced turned toward the bartender. "He was a customer. I wouldn't call him a friend. Not at all."

The door opened and a group of five men surged inside, a splash of sunlight pouring in with them. It fell across the shelves of alcohol. A fine sprinkling of dust on the bottles was exposed, making them look cheap, stripping away the seductive appearance they had in the darkness. The door remained open for longer than necessary. I wanted it closed, I wanted the protection of dim lighting, the hum of voices beneath mine, lulling Steve's senses so I could lead him where I wanted him to go.

He didn't seem to feel the shock of bright light, like a wave of icy water. He took a sip of his drink. I did the same. I plucked the lime off the side of the glass and squeezed the juice into the tonic and vodka. I dropped in the rind, and stirred the ice and liquid with my straw. I took another sip.

"Talking about a dead guy isn't my idea of foreplay," he said.

I laughed. "Sex and violence get equated quite often, don't you think?"

He carefully avoided looking directly into my eyes.

"Do you think it was a competitor who killed him?" I said.

"Not likely. In his mother's apartment? And her dead too." He shuddered. Ashamed of his unconscious show of weakness, he took several sips of his drink.

"It must be some weird family thing," I said. "Those families with money are crazy."

"I guess you would know. All those secrets, betrayals. The buried sexual tension."

I laughed. "You nailed it."

He didn't look uncomfortable at what I'd said, making me wonder whether he was really listening. He picked up his glass and swallowed the rest of the scotch. His whole body hummed with a tangible desire to get out of there and find a hotel room. He was so clearly trying to decide his next move.

"I was glad you introduced me to him that day," I said.

He looked defeated. "That was a little strange. Why were you so eager?" He raised his hand to the bartender and ordered another scotch.

Had he resigned himself to nothing happening today, to the first step in another very long game between the two of us? It seemed that way, but I couldn't take it for granted.

"I was close to his mother," I said. "Such a sweet woman. And so proud and independent."

He smirked. "Your criteria for friendship? Independent?"

"Yes, I think so." I put my straw between my lips but didn't draw anything into my mouth. I moved away from it again. "I was devastated. Such a tragedy. She lived such an amazing life, and to end like that…"

He nodded.

"Anyway, I was dying to meet him because she talked about him *all* the time. She was so proud of him."

"He lived right above her. Why didn't she introduce you?"

"She was a little afraid of him, I think. She was in awe of his success, very aware of how busy he was, how important, and that his time was so in demand. She didn't like to ask him for much."

Steve nodded, swallowing my bullshit like a thirty-dollar shot of scotch — smooth and full of complex flavors.

"I guess we won't ever know what happened," I said.

He shrugged. "I'm not into true crime. There's too much to do in life. But yeah, if it was some family conflict, they probably won't figure it out. Who knows. Maybe he killed her and then himself."

So, he didn't know much about the details of how they'd died. I smiled. I'd mitigated the risk as much as I could. I was confident he wouldn't draw a connection. He really didn't care. There was more narcissism in him than I'd realized.

And right now, he only had one agenda item — to get away from the subject of murder.

CHAPTER 17

*P*ortland

* * *

At first I thought I had to figure out a way to use my power position as the designated housekeeper over my brothers, but in the end, my brothers wound up trapped by their own sense of privilege.

Their desire to lord it over me gave me an idea. All I needed was my mother's willingness to give me some authority. In order to get that, I had to lure her to see my side of the situation.

She was pounding bread dough into a bowl, a very therapeutic activity that was never offered to me. Mostly, I didn't mind that she hoarded that job for herself. She needed to punch that soft white stuff, almost the color and texture of a human face, far more than I did.

I slipped up behind her and pinched off a tiny piece of dough. I popped it into my mouth and let the moist, yeasty taste flow through me.

"Don't eat that," she said, probably for the hundredth time. Maybe the thousandth.

"I like it."

"It's not good for you."

"Why not?"

"It just isn't. It's not cooked."

"So?"

She slammed her left fist into the center of the dough. Her wedding rings sat in a juice glass on the window sill. They sparkled in the late afternoon light as the sun dipped lower and the rays pierced the kitchen window with such ferocity I wanted to put on a pair of sunglasses. The bright light didn't bother my mother, she was looking down at the bowl of dough.

"I'm a little frustrated," I said.

"Why is that?" She punched the dough again. I thought it looked like it had taken all the punching it needed and was ready to be covered again with a towel so it could continue rising, but she kept at it.

"The boys get pee all over the sides of the toilet."

"That's boys for you."

"It's disgusting."

"It's a fact of life."

"I have to keep re-washing the toilets. The bathrooms look perfect, and before dad even gets home, there are yellow stains again. Sometimes they drip on the floor. If he notices..."

She took her hands out of the dough. "Will you turn on the warm water for me?"

I adjusted the faucet and moved away. She put her hands under the stream of water, rubbing them together. She picked up the bottle of dish soap and squirted a puddle into the palm of her hand. She scrubbed vigorously, lather covering her hands, bubbles dripping off her fingertips, and climbing up to her wrists. When her hands were rinsed and dried, she placed a blue and white striped towel over the bowl of dough.

"That's a woman's role. Homemaking is something that's never finished. You complete your tasks over and over, and the same things need doing again the next hour or the next day. Everyone eats dinner and they're hungry in the morning."

"Sure, for food. But why should I keep wiping up their pee?"

"Don't use that word."

"What am I supposed to call it?"

"There's no need to discuss it at all. It just needs to be done." She smiled. She walked to the opposite counter and pulled her German cookbook off the shelf. "I'm making sauerbraten for dinner. Doesn't that sound good? Then we'll have leftovers for lunch Saturday." She turned and smiled at me. "See, not everything has to be redone every day. But most of the time, that is the way it works."

"They pee five times a day!"

"Don't shout. There's satisfaction in hard work, in the doing of the job itself. You can't think about the repetition. Life is repetitious."

"It's not fair."

She flipped open the cookbook. The pages parted to the sauerbraten recipe. It made no sense that she had to study the recipe. She served it once every two or three months, and she had for as long as I could remember. Surely she knew it by heart.

"I was thinking..."

"There's nothing to think about. We all have jobs to do, cleaning the house is yours. And you do it beautifully. You'll be a wonderful wife...and mother."

I had no intention of becoming a wife, or a mother. I did like the cleaning, wiping away dirt and grime, seeing things sparkle, feeling at peace with my environment. In fact, I thought about what a beautiful home I'd have if no one else lived there. I did not like wiping up their mess — a result of pure sloppiness and laziness, and of course, a power play on their part, to show me who was at the top of the heap.

None of my brothers had said anything about it. The battle was silent. I wasn't even sure if all three of them were doing it, or if one of them was out for me more than the others. Sometimes I felt as if all three of them liked to provoke me, watching the fights between my father and me, occasionally my mother. Live entertainment.

They loved seeing me crawl around on my knees, holding my breath so I wouldn't smell it, spraying disinfectant on their sticky yellow ribbons, wiping it up, filling the basin with steaming soapy water to wash the sponge. Doing it once a week was okay. But on the days my father inspected the bathrooms, I sometimes had to do it three times, and always twice.

My mother's initial refusal to help delayed me for a while. I needed to find a way to get her on my side. For once in her life, she needed to set aside her robotic insistence that everything my father decreed was straight from the mind of god, and every suggestion or idea that I proposed was an act of rebellion.

My parents believed god put each one of us on earth for a purpose. It definitely was not my purpose to wipe up piss several times a day.

CHAPTER 18

Hamilton Island

* * *

There were five other students in the diving class — four guys and one girl. All but Tess were in their early twenties. Although she was only ten years older or so, she felt like their mother. Not that she had the first clue what motherhood felt like, so maybe it wasn't that at all. She just felt old. Questioning her life and her current path had brought that about, looking back with a tremor of fear that she'd wasted an awful lot of time was not good.

First, were their bathing suits. Her classmates were one step away from childhood and they had the same lack of concern that children have over how their bodies looked when barely covered by a few strips of fabric. Everything was firm and supple. They didn't worry about it jiggling or slipping into an unattractive sight if they sat or stood the wrong way. They didn't have to concentrate on good posture to be sure they looked good. The boys' bellies were lean, their board shorts hugging their hip bones, soft hair drawing her eyes downward. Their backs were sculpted with solid muscle and bone.

It was the undiluted advantage of young flesh. She tried to shove it out of her mind. She was by no means old or flabby in any way, but neither was she twenty. Her skin didn't have the same smooth, undamaged texture. She could see it, and she was sure they could too. A very faint softness at the tops of her inner thighs, a bit of extra flesh in the area outside her armpit on her upper back, and some roughness in the skin around her knees.

She also felt maternal when she contrasted her life with their utter lack of concern. She carried extra psychological weight in her knowledge of how the world caught you off guard, and the relentless pressing down of the life-altering decisions she was facing. Did that mean she saw motherhood as a burden? Another looming cavern in her life she still hadn't addressed. Before long, there would be no need to address it, nature would decide for her.

The others laughed and talked about music and scuba diving and drinking and all kinds of trivia. It was clear they weren't trying to prove something to a corporate entity about their worthwhile use of time. They weren't out here to test their mettle. They were learning to dive because they wanted to dive. It was so pure. So clean. She hoped some of it would rub off on her.

The course would cover five days, four hours every morning. On the last day, they would go for a dive in a cove where the water was about ten to twelve feet deep. With a certification in hand, she would be allowed to dive off a charter boat as it floated over The Great Barrier Reef. This was something most people never did. Another achievement that put her ahead of the pack. It was one of the most spectacular places on the planet, but so many only experienced it in photographs and video. They never even considered diving down to see it firsthand.

She didn't want to think of the dive as something to check off a list, bragging rights to an exciting vacation. The others in the class would help adjust her mindset. They would set her free. As long as she let go and allowed them.

So far, she'd spent far too much energy trying not to think about thirty or forty feet of water pressing down on her head. The aluminum tank strapped on her back, the large regulator in her mouth, stretching her jaw wide enough that she worried she'd have an instinctive urge to close it, shoving the hunk of plastic out of her mouth without thinking about what she was doing. The training, along with the material they were required to read after each day's class, would keep fear from creeping to the center of her mind. This was supposed to be fun. An adventure. A once-in-a-lifetime experience. Travel for sheer pleasure rather than doing it for her employer, positioning and pushing products to customers, always performing. That's why she felt old. Her scuba classmates had never had to perform, they just existed — carefree as dolphins.

The instructor had laid all the equipment out around a swimming pool at a hotel where they would first learn to use it underwater. A pool provided a safe place where a rogue wave couldn't enter in to make the situation more complex, where distress could be easily observed and quickly alleviated.

He explained how to smear their spit over the inside of the clear plastic mask to prevent it from steaming up. He went over the working of the regulator. He emphasized the importance of staying calm and signaling your buddy if you ran out of air and needed to share their tank and ascend. He talked about a hundred other things that Tess hoped would come easily to mind when she was bobbing along the ocean floor.

That night she studied the handouts like she hadn't studied

in years. Distant memories of college and graduate school drove her to pull a pen out of her purse, underlining and adding checkmarks to important points. She wanted to know it all, she wanted to make sure all the details about buoyancy and breathing and the equipment became as familiar as the various aspects of her job. Responding to every possibility without needing to think through each step was critical. Besides, there were written tests each morning.

Her dreams that night were filled with enormous schools of fish. They formed solid walls above her, blocking her way to the surface. Each time she woke and took a sip of water and returned to sleep, the fish came with her. Preparing for her time underwater, she'd stopped drinking alcohol for the week. Consuming a few drinks too many the night before a dive could become a life-threatening mistake. It was probably the lack of alcohol, after weeks of it flowing through her veins, making her dreams more intense and memorable.

The next morning, she looked at her classmates, wondering if their dreams had been filled with such obvious symbols of fear.

The group was paired off into dive buddies. Naturally Tess and the girl — Lily — were teamed up. Lily had short brown hair and large brown eyes that appeared to consume her face. She wore a bathing suit cut so high over her butt that Tess was almost embarrassed to look at her.

They dove into the pool, faces distorted by silicone masks. They practiced diving to the bottom and using hand signals to communicate *descending, low on air,* and *returning to the surface.*

After twenty minutes, they climbed out. The tropical air made sitting around in a wet bathing suit comfortable. They listened to another thirty minutes of instruction.

Their skin now dry, they shoved their limbs into nylon stinger suits, required to protect from the deadly jellyfish surrounding Australia. They buckled their weight belts and returned to the pool to experiment with the different weights required to reach deeper levels.

Lily asked Tess if she was moving to Australia or visiting on holiday. Tess said *holiday*.

As if that perfunctory and obvious question was simply an entree to her own thoughts, Lily didn't ask a single additional question about Tess's life. She launched into stories of her own, her dream of traveling all over the world, making the most spectacular dives. Her lifelong love of the water, her childhood spent snorkeling. The long hours she crewed on a sixty-foot sailboat to support herself and her diving plans. But she adored sailing too, anything around the ocean. She wasn't just doing it for money. The expense of staying on Hamilton Island was *awful*, though, even *sharing* a hotel room with two of the four guys.

Lily chattered about the *mind-blowing coolness* of sea life and sailing. Her face glowed as she talked, the whole world open before her, the sun shining on her golden skin to enhance that impression.

Tess listened and smiled and felt more maternal than ever.

On the last day, as they yanked on stinger suits, strapped on weight belts, and lifted tanks of oxygen onto their backs, she thought about Alex and her insistence that Tess should clear her head with a wilderness challenge. This certainly qualified. She imagined Alex smirking with satisfaction at how Tess had taken her advice, as if the mother-daughter illusion were reversed. Maybe you didn't need a child to have all sorts of maternal-like relationships. Besides, considering her much closer relationship with her father, the mother-daughter thing was more likely a myth for most.

"This is so awesome," Lily said. "We're living the dream, aren't we!"

Tess nodded. Lily had no idea that life developed its own momentum. It accelerated so that you hardly had time to look at the scenery. Suddenly, you woke up in your thirties, headed toward middle age at an even faster pace, the lead weights strapped to your hips pushing you deeper below the surface. You had a career that wasn't quite what you'd expected and you didn't look hot in a swimsuit and you'd spent your twenties speaking to PowerPoint slides in conference rooms and sitting on airplanes.

Maybe the same would happen to Lily. She'd wake up with leathered skin and without the vibrancy that had put her in high demand for crewing a sailboat.

CHAPTER 19

 *an Francisco*

* * *

Before Steve could finish his fifth scotch, I slid off the barstool. "I need to…"

He turned and looked at me.

I swallowed and moved my lips uncomfortably. "I…"

"You okay?"

I nodded. I turned and walked quickly toward the restrooms, moving faster as I got to the rear of the bar, trusting he was watching and inferring distress.

Inside, I locked myself in a stall. I took out my phone and set the timer for seven minutes. Standing there skimming email and Twitter, waiting for time to pass turned my knees stiff. I shifted my position as much as the narrow space would allow. I put in a request for an Uber. To Steve, I hoped those seven minutes felt like half an hour.

When the timer went off, I splashed water on my face and

patted it dry, leaving a few drops around my chin. I ran my fingers under the water and combed them through the front of my hair, creating damp furrows. I looped my purse strap over my head so it crossed over my chest and returned to the bar.

I made my way to Steve's side.

He turned. In front of him was another scotch but it didn't look like he'd had any to drink. "I wouldn't have figured you for a lightweight," he said.

I gave him a wan smile. It was a relief that I didn't have to explain. I was satisfied that my pantomime and long absence had suggested I was violently sick, maybe ashamed and feeling unappealing. "I thought I was okay with the tonic and vodka, but I guess I overdid it with the martinis."

"I never understood how anyone drinks those things. They taste like cleaning fluid."

"I don't think so at all," I said.

"I guess you'll be off them now."

I gave him another limp smile. "It did happen once before, and it didn't dampen my enthusiasm. I guess too much food, and...everything." I flipped my hand back and forth.

He smiled and put his hand on my shoulder. "It's good you're feeling back to normal."

"I wouldn't go that far." I leaned against the stool.

He picked up his drink and slammed it down in a single shot. He nodded at the bartender and pulled his wallet out of his hip pocket. He settled the bill and took my elbow, guiding me toward the door.

It was cold outside. I shivered, exaggerating my movements to give the impression of convulsing chills.

"I'll call us a cab." He pulled out his phone.

"Um...I put in a request for an Uber. I really don't feel that great." I couldn't believe he wanted to carry on with a woman who'd been spewing vomit. The thought made me sick all on its own.

"Right. Right. I can understand that. I'll call a cab for me."

I crossed my arms, hunched my shoulders, and shivered again.

"You'll be okay?"

"I think so. I just need some water. And my bed."

He made the call. When he was finished, he still gripped the phone in his fist. He looked out into the street, watching traffic. After a minute or two, he took a step away from me. "So, I guess..."

"We should..."

He turned and smiled. "Yes. How about dinner? Sunday?"

I nodded. My Uber driver pulled up to the curb. "See you."

"Where should I pick you up?"

"I'll meet you. Just text me the restaurant."

"Understood," he said.

I climbed into the car, slammed the door, and shifted sideways, resting my head on the back of the seat, facing toward the driver's side of the car. I didn't turn to wave good-bye, and I resisted the very strong impulse to look at his reaction to the puncturing of his desire.

He wasn't the sort of man I could string along forever. It was possible I could cancel one date, but very quickly, his desire would turn to anger. Winning had become easy for him, an expectation. His desire for a lengthy challenge was diminished.

I had to take this route to make sure he had no stray thoughts about why I was so very interested in Barker Clayton. But now I'd pushed myself into a corner.

The choices for escape were sex or murder.

I closed my eyes and tried to empty my mind of all thoughts. I desperately wanted a cigarette, but it was forbidden in the Uber. I sat up and ran my fingers through my hair, mussing it more than it already was. I pulled my coat collar up as high as possible around my jaw. I didn't expect to see the detectives or Jeanne Clayton outside on a cold, windy night, but I couldn't be one hundred percent sure.

When the Uber pulled to the curb, I was already clutching the door handle. Before the car came to a full stop, I thanked the driver and opened the door. She let out a noise as if to warn me, but I was out and slamming the door. I walked quickly into the lobby, ran my guest ID across the scanner, and darted to the elevator.

I didn't take a deep breath until I was inside Tess's condo with the door locked.

I went into the bedroom, sat down, and unlaced my Doc Martens.

The cockatoo shouted from his room — *Delicious mango! Bad girl! Dangerous woman! Watch out for that man.*

He ran through this series several times. The suggestion that I watch out for a man unnerved me, but Damien often said things that seemed to fit the situation. I knew they didn't. I was sure they didn't. Still.

I brushed my hair and went into the kitchen. I was stuffed with dim sum, and I really didn't need another martini. I cut up some apple and strawberries and took them into Damien's room. I put the plate on the floor and refreshed his water.

Delicious mango, the bird said.

"Not tonight. I have to buy more."

Delicious mango!

"Enjoy your dinner." I stepped out of the room. He'd have to eat dinner solo tonight.

I grabbed my purse and filled a glass with water. I put on a hat and sweater and went out to the balcony. I set the glass of water on the table to use as an ashtray and lit a cigarette.

Despite the wind, I leaned on the railing to smoke, just to

be extra cautious the odor didn't find its way into the cushions on Tess's lovely patio furniture.

The smoke calmed me. I pushed all thoughts of Steve out of my head. It was only Friday night. I didn't have to decide anything until Sunday. And my decision might be to simply reschedule our dinner.

CHAPTER 20

The crowd at The Chimera was sparse. There were a few wine-drinkers seated at tables. No one was seated at the bar. At three-thirty on a clear and balmy Saturday afternoon, it wasn't surprising. Half the city was outdoors — cycling at Golden Gate park, eating at outdoor restaurants, sailing, and walking or picnicking by the water.

Although the bar offered a warm, comfortable atmosphere, today it felt gloomy. It was too dark, a little cold compared to the temperature outside, and without a crowd, it felt lonely, with a tinge of pathetic.

It was the first time Jen didn't feel like working. Walking from the sunshine into the gloom had been depressing. The lack of customers meant a lot of standing around, aware of how slowly time was passing. When she was scurrying back and forth serving wine and beer, picking up glasses, wiping and polishing the bar, the hours went so quickly she was shocked to hear Chelsea or one of the others tell her it was time for her break.

The only thing keeping her mood from collapsing entirely was Chelsea's revelation when Jen had started her shift — *If you keep going the way you are, you'll get a code for the cash register by the end of the month. It'll be a huge help when we're super busy.*

The words left a warm puddle in the center of Jen's heart. The only thing marring the feeling was that she hadn't asked what, exactly, she was doing right. *Keep going the way you are* meant...what?

A woman from one of the tables stood and came to the bar. "Can I get three more glasses of wine? The Beringer Cab." She placed the empty glasses on the counter. Jen turned to get the wine and suddenly Chelsea was right beside her.

"Jen, I know you have it under control, but we really need to make sure the olives are stocked in case we get a surge, which could happen any minute now. Will you go get some? I'll take care of this."

Doing what she was asked without arguing was probably part of *keep going the way you are*. She walked to the end of the bar and out, headed toward the storage room.

When she returned, Chelsea had moved back to the far end of the bar. Her journal lay open in front of her. She was writing furiously. Jen stood with the jug of olives in her arms. Chelsea seemed unaware of her presence. Her hand flew across the page with quick, sharp movements. She paused and flipped the page.

The very consistency of the paper changed as Chelsea poured her thoughts out through the ink. It was an amazing thing — holding a pen and transferring the ideas inside your head or the people and buildings you saw around you onto a sheet of paper. Jen still hadn't written anything but drink recipes in her journal. The book was in her purse. She brought it to work every day now so she could record the recipes, but she still had no idea what else to write about. She wasn't sure she wanted all the things inside her head on sheets of paper where anyone could read them.

Not that anyone would. Who even cared?

She walked to the center of the bar and put the jug on the counter below. She unscrewed the lid and began scooping out olives with a slotted spoon, putting them into the tub that was nestled beside others containing sliced limes and lemons, small onions, strips of curled orange rind, and cherries. When the tub was nearly overflowing with the green egg-like fruits, she screwed the lid on the jug and took it back to the store-room, putting it inside the refrigerator now that the seal was broken.

Back in the bar, Chelsea's notebook was closed, the pen lying on top. Claire had come in and was standing on the opposite side. Jen had only been gone a minute or so, making it feel as if Claire had materialized out of thin air.

She was a tall, slender woman who dressed in flowing clothes made from expensive fabrics. She usually wore white or cream tops and charcoal gray or coffee colored skirts and slacks. Her white-blonde hair was cropped close to her head. She wore a lot of makeup and kept her nails freshly updated with a French manicure. Her perfume was a heavy, floral scent that seemed to move toward Jen. It built a dense phys-ical cloud around Claire that kept anyone from coming too close, their airflow pinched by the strong odor.

Sometimes it seemed as if women could be divided into two groups — those who thought strong perfume made them more beautiful, more alluring, and those who were at home with the scent of their own clean, mildly fruity or nutty odor, even their own bare skin. And floral wasn't even the right word. It wasn't the fresh, sweet smell that came from walking into a flower shop. It smelled as if the flowers had been smashed underfoot and soaked with chemicals to transform them into something harsh and brutal, something that wanted to crush every milder odor in the room. Of course, people were always trying to categorize the human race into two opposing groups. But in this case, Jen wondered if there wasn't something to it. Alex didn't wear perfume. Thinking over the friendships of her life, she was certain that she'd never been close with someone who was compelled to douse herself in a scent that overpowered everything in its vicinity, shouting — *notice me!*

She often wondered what men thought of perfumes like that. She'd never asked. She'd never noticed a man cringe at the smell. Maybe men had less sensitivity to perfumes and some women knew this, so they practically bathed in the stuff, knowing extreme excess was necessary to even gently prick a man's nostrils.

Claire spoke in a low voice. Jen walked slowly, not sure whether the conversation was meant to be private. They were standing in a public place, so it couldn't be that private. But they continued to murmur as if they wanted to be sure they weren't overheard.

Jen moved along behind the bar, unable to escape that feeling that she was a nuisance, eavesdropping instead of standing where she belonged. She stopped.

A moment later, both women turned and looked at her.

"Hello," Claire said. She turned back to Chelsea and said something else that Jen couldn't hear.

Chelsea stepped away from the bar.

"Will you take over?" Claire said. "Chelsea and I need to run upstairs. We'll only be a few minutes."

"What if someone wants a drink?"

"If they want something other than beer or wine, tell them I'll be right back."

"And if they're unhappy, let them know it's on the house." Claire smiled.

Claire and Chelsea walked toward the back of the bar and disappeared into the stairwell.

Chelsea's notebook was still on the bar. The red cover

seemed to stroke Jen's heart, drawing her to it. But with those women drinking wine, occasionally glancing around the room, even a quick peek would be a mistake. She walked toward the spot where it lay. She touched the cover.

The appeal of digging into someone's secret thoughts wouldn't leave her alone. She wanted to know what Chelsea dreamed about, wanted to know how often she worked out, and how she was making progress with her goals. Most of all, she wanted to read more of those sad little comments telling Chelsea she was useful or liked, or whatever it was she got out of it.

She ran her fingers over the cover, as if she could draw the words off the pages, make the book open by itself.

She laughed and took her hand away.

Her desire to read Chelsea's words, to possibly find a comment she'd written that revealed secrets about the customers, or even Chelsea, burned in her throat. She couldn't swallow. Right this minute, there wasn't anything she wanted more.

What was wrong with her? Why was she not able to think about anything else when she saw that red notebook?

CHAPTER 21

*W*hen I cancelled our date, Steve hadn't seemed annoyed. Maybe he also had other plans. Or maybe he was trying to unsettle me. Or take back control. Revealing disappointment cedes control to the other, the one who possesses the power to disappoint.

Maybe he'd lost interest.

Maybe he'd decided my subordinate role at the company made me too much of a risk.

Most of that was wishful thinking, since he texted me about thirty minutes later to let me know that on Monday, when his schedule for the week *firmed up*, he'd *shoot me* another proposed time for *dinner and...*

So subtle of him.

On Sunday afternoon, Isaiah and I went for a hike in the foothills near Stanford University, about thirty-five miles south of San Francisco. We came back to Tess's to shower and figure out dinner.

Water pounded on our heads from the rain-head shower. It sprayed our backs from nozzles set about shoulder height on either side. Isaiah rubbed body wash over my belly, sliding his hands up to my breasts, forcing a sigh out of me. I closed my eyes, tipped my head back slightly, and opened my mouth to let the hot water fall inside.

"Let's eat at that deli on Columbus, and then go hang out at The Chimera," he said.

I lowered my head and opened my eyes. I turned and rinsed off the lather. "There are a hundred other bars in San Francisco."

"I like it there."

"I've already been too many times."

"It's comfortable and classy at the same time."

"There's nothing remarkable about it."

"Jen works there."

"So? She doesn't need our daily support in order to do her job."

"I know, but she's working so hard to change her situation, it's good for her to see friendly faces."

I toweled my hair, hiding my pinched lips from him.

We dressed and went out to the kitchen, I filled two glasses with water and handed one to Isaiah. "We could go dancing."

He studied my turquoise t-shirt and tie-dyed skirt. The front of the shirt was wet where my hair touched the shoulders. A droplet of water fell and dribbled over my collarbone.

"Dancing?" He lowered his gaze to the bare skin between my shirt and the edge of the skirt. He lowered it farther to my flat leather sandals. Despite my devotion to high heels, I was loving these sandals. Wearing them felt like walking barefoot, like warm, firm hands were wrapped around my feet. I hardly took them off, except to put on the Doc Martens.

"I would change," I said. "For dancing."

"Why are you so opposed to going there?" he said.

"Why are you so hot to go there?" I sipped my water and smiled.

"That guy we met — Dan — I wouldn't mind talking to him again."

"There are interesting people in every bar. And some not so interesting. A lot more of those."

"Aren't you curious?" He drank some water and put down the glass.

"About what?"

"I've always been interested in detectives. FBI agents. The CIA. I've never known one, and talking to him was cool. Maybe he'll tell stories."

"He's not in the CIA. He's a San Francisco cop."

"I know, but the whole field is fascinating. Digging into things and finding out the truth."

"I don't think it's as interesting as you imagine," I said.

"I think it is."

"Detectives usually work nights, it was probably a fluke he was even there."

"That's not true."

"Well I'm sure he doesn't hang out at the same bar every night of the week."

"Why are you trying to talk me out of it?" he said.

"I'm not trying to talk you out of anything."

"It sounds like you are."

"You're reading into it."

"I don't think I am. So how does the deli sound?"

I thought about their Reuben sandwiches. The tangy taste of the enormous dill pickle spears they serve on the side pricked my tongue. And beer. An icy beer sounded perfect after a hike. But none of those things were a good prelude to dancing. He was using dinner to push me relentlessly toward The Chimera. The result would be an evening spent watching every word I spoke. I didn't want to arouse a detective's curiosity any more than I already had with the incongruous relationship between my appearance and my career and my dilated pupils. "The deli is good, but it's not the best pre-dancing food."

"We just spent three hours hiking. Chilling out sounds better than dancing."

"Once the music hits, you'll feel differently. We don't go dancing enough."

"I don't get why you're so opposed to The Chimera."

"I'm not opposed. It's just kind of unremarkable."

"Imagine the stories that guy could tell."

"He's not going to give you an inside scoop on San Francisco true crime." I knew about Isaiah's bent toward detective shows and thriller films. He had a steady diet of the stuff. He really didn't enjoy any other kind of movies or TV shows, but I didn't know he'd blurred the lines into real life. I did not need him becoming buddies with a detective.

"You never know." He grinned like a kid standing outside the gates of Disneyland, thinking he's going to get one-on-one time with Mickey Mouse.

I could hear my objections becoming repetitious, and I was clearly not dressed for dancing. I would have loved to go crazy, thumping music pounding conscious thoughts out of my brain. Loud music with a good beat bleeds into my bones and muscles. Dancing is like a religious experience, or at least what I imagine religious people are seeking. It's sort of the same thing as monks finding ecstasy after days of deprivation and silence, or people who face near-death experiences and their minds explode beyond the mundane thoughts of daily life. All the analytical functions fade into the background, whether slowly through fasting, or in a heartbeat as you turn and see a man with a knife, or a car is suddenly racing straight toward you, headlights blinding you. "I want to go dancing again. Soon."

"Absolutely." He didn't look smug at winning the argument. His face retained the eager look of someone who is about to have a wish fulfilled.

At the deli, we both ordered a Reuben. We split a beer since there would be more drinks coming at The Chimera.

We walked holding hands. The cold air wound around my exposed strip of skin like a belt of ice, but it felt kind of good in contrast to savory corned beef and sauerkraut and melted Swiss cheese warming my insides.

The Chimera was crowded. They were playing a mix of 70s rock and disco. The music made you want to dance, but it wasn't that kind of place.

We walked up to the bar together. There was one empty chair. Isaiah offered it to me. He stood close behind me, his hand on my shoulder. As Chelsea approached us, I was over-come with revulsion, thinking about another glass of house wine. So what if my hippie look conflicted with a martini? It's what I prefer when I'm in a bar. Besides, I was slightly unsure at this point what I hoped to accomplish with the adopted persona.

Isaiah ordered the martini, and a margarita for himself.

I turned the chair on its pedestal and surveyed the room. Neither Dan nor his buddy stood out to me, but the place was pretty full. If they were standing with their backs to us, I wouldn't be able to pick them out. Rick had struck me as somewhat proprietary, so I guessed if he was there, he'd be leaning on the bar, checking out every movement Chelsea made.

For all I knew, Dan was in a dark corner somewhere, keeping his eye on me. I know it was overly cautious to the point of paranoia, but I couldn't stop thinking about it. He seemed more interested in me than he should be, and it didn't really matter what the reason was, I wanted him to dismiss me. To find me forgettable. That had been the whole point of the new look. Instead, it seemed to have had the opposite effect.

Our drinks were placed on the bar. We clicked our glasses against each other.

"Cheers. The place where everybody knows your name," I said.

Isaiah rolled his eyes, but then he smiled.

We drank in silence for several minutes. His hand was tight on my shoulder. I could feel the movement of his arm through my body each time he turned casually, trying to locate Dan.

"He's not here," I said.

"How do you know?"

"If you just want to hang out with him, why am I even here?"

He rubbed my shoulder. "Don't get upset. I just thought..."

"I'm not upset. I'm asking a question. I could have found something else to do. Like dancing."

He took his hand off my shoulder. "What's wrong with you?" he said.

"Absolutely nothing."

He moved to my side and took a long swallow of his drink. I can't swallow all that blended ice so fast. Watching him gave me a vicarious brain freeze, but maybe his brain was already frozen.

CHAPTER 22

*H*earing Isaiah ask what was *wrong* with me shot an icy needle into my spine. He was a man who gave every indication there wasn't a single misogynistic cell in his body. I'd thought it came from being raised by a very competent single mother — a nurse. A profession known for attracting people who don't stand for a lot of fluff and who call things as they see them. They work with some of the most arrogant professionals on the planet and hold their own. Unlike so many surgeons and specialists, they see the patients as human beings, not science experiments. They'll stand up to a man, or woman, with four or five letters after their name versus the RN's lowly two, and tell them to back off and pay attention.

Although his tone hadn't sounded condescending, the words alone were enough to set my bones humming. His question implied that expressing my opinion, an opinion contrary to his, or speaking my mind, meant there was something *wrong* with me. I wasn't being *nice*. I wasn't being charming.

It's the oldest misogynistic tool there is. There is something wrong, something unfit, something despicable in a woman who doesn't soften the words she speaks. She has no right to desires or opinions that differ from the male's. Expressing her thoughts in a firm tone means something is *wrong* with the order of the world. Men speak without a flowery array of nice words crafted to undermine and soften what they say and they're considered firm and direct. Women do the same and out comes the *B* word. And I don't mean a b-girl in a bar.

I sipped my martini and considered what he was saying. I didn't want an argument. And I didn't want to assume he meant what I'd heard behind those four innocuous words. It seemed so unlike him.

Was I taking the words to mean more than they did, because they're usually inflammatory, but in his case, maybe not? It all depends on the source?

He finished his margarita in several quick gulps and ordered another. I was only one olive and a few sips into my martini. I felt his body move as he turned again to survey the room. It had become an unconscious habit, as if the constant vigilance would cause Dan to appear, lapping up Isaiah's admiration and rewarding him with stories of complicated, horrifying crimes and perplexing evidence.

I popped the second olive into my mouth.

Jen was at the far end of the bar, close to the hallway leading to the restrooms. She'd hardly glanced at us beyond her welcoming smile. She was in constant motion, running her cloth across the wood, wiping up every drop of moisture. Her left hand preceded her right, picking up discarded napkins.

When the bar was polished and dry, she filled mugs with beer, popped caps off bottles, and poured yellow or red gleaming wine into glasses that took on the appearance of small lights themselves as they reflected the lighting suspended from the ceiling by long metal rods.

She looked like she was doing just fine without Isaiah and me to cheer her on.

"I guess he's not here," Isaiah said. He moved his hand down my back. After his fingertips caressed the bones of my spine, they found the strip of skin between my skirt and the top that rose higher as I leaned forward slightly. He stroked it with soft movements. My body turned to liquid, but beneath the melted flesh was a sludge of ice, still sifting through his words in my mind, trying to decide how I was going to confront it. "So should we leave after I finish my drink?" I said.

"He might still show up."

I straightened my back and moved forward on the chair, leaving his gentle fingers suspended behind me.

He didn't seem to notice the deliberate pulling away. He moved his hand back into place. Chelsea brought his margarita. She placed it on the bar and he handed her his credit card.

Jen moved past with her swirling cloth, always dry and almost perfectly clean, even though we never noticed her swapping it out for another. Isaiah reached into the front pocket of his jeans and pulled out a twenty. He tucked it under the side of her pinky finger.

She nudged it back. "You don't have to do that. I didn't even serve you."

"But you're keeping the place clean."

Normally I'd be admiring his gentility, but now... He was patronizing her and she felt it.

"I really shouldn't," she said.

"Yes, you should."

She smiled and took the twenty. She moved down the bar, wiping and removing empty glasses, smiling at the drinkers, plucking straws out of puddles of water and stabbing them into piles of ice cubes inside empty glasses. It made me think of my mother and her comment that cleaning was satisfying and meaningful in its mindless repetition.

I turned toward him. "You shouldn't have done that."

"Why not?"

"You insulted her."

"No I didn't. She doesn't get tips and she works just as hard as the others."

"She gets a portion of their tips."

"I'm sure it's not much."

"You're missing the point."

"What point is that?" He slurped the margarita through the straw, reminding me again of a kid at Disneyland.

"It's degrading to give her money for doing nothing. You're just drawing attention to her subordinate status."

He laughed. "Money is money. She needs it and I'm not drawing attention to anything."

"People like to feel they've earned their money, not have it handed to them like they're some kind of dancing poodle."

He turned so he was looking directly at me. He moved his face closer to mine, studying my expression. It wasn't clear what he was looking for or what he saw there, but the minute he spoke, I knew he'd misread it.

"I'm not into her, if that's what you think."

I laughed. I finished my drink and ate the last olive.

"I'm going to take off now. Text me if you want to come back to Tess's." I slid off the stool and pulled a twenty out of my purse. I placed it near the base of my glass.

He put his hand on my wrist. "You're jealous."

"No, Isaiah. I'm not jealous."

"I think you are."

"Because you didn't give me a twenty?"

"No. You think I'm trying too hard to be supportive of her,

and you're taking it the wrong way. We're just friends. I promise."

"It never crossed my mind you were anything else." I stepped away from the chair.

"Then why are you leaving?"

"I finished my drink. And I never really wanted to come here to begin with. I told you that."

"So we only do what you want to do?"

"I thought we enjoyed the same things."

"We do. But I want to support Jen, and I hoped to run into that guy again. You're acting like that's a personal affront."

"We've supported Jen. And…" I wanted to say that hanging out with cops was not my idea of an exciting evening, but he might read too much into it. I wasn't clear on it myself. There was no way Dan would connect me to a double homicide in Russian Hill. Even if he was well-acquainted with the detectives investigating. It would be way beyond simple coincidence for him to mention me and them to refer to a curious neighbor, but it was just too close, too much like flirting with exposure. Weird coincidental events happen all the time.

There was no reason for me to ever see Dan Vorcek again, and without Isaiah's interfering obsession, I wouldn't. If he wanted to socialize with the guy, he didn't need me there. We weren't a couple in that way — required to join our social lives into a single entity.

"Then what is the problem?"

I smiled. "Call it a quirk, I just don't get a good vibe here. It has nothing to do with Jen, nothing to do with you supporting her, nothing to do with detectives who like to drink here."

"What's wrong with the vibe?"

"I don't know. Just a feeling. Like I said, a quirk."

"One of the things I love about you is you're always up for fun. You go with the flow. I've never seen you all irritable and difficult."

"Not liking a bar doesn't make me difficult."

"Okay, sorry."

He put his glass on the bar, the contents mostly untouched. "I'll go with you, if you really want to leave."

"Now you're patronizing *me*."

"I can't win with you tonight. Are you having your period?"

I widened my eyes. I looked into his, not blinking. I let my lips gently curve into something that wasn't truly a smile, but showed no animosity. "Pardon?"

Chelsea returned with his credit card. He scribbled a tip and his signature on the bill and slid the card into his back pocket. He put his hand on my hip. "Come on, let's go."

"I'd rather walk by myself." I turned and made my way to the door. I could feel the movement of him behind me. I wouldn't be rid of him that easily, but now, I wanted to walk for blocks. I didn't want any more conversation or any more interpretations of my behavior. I wanted to be alone.

At the door, he stepped around me and opened it. Outside, he turned as if he assumed I would walk beside him. We walked the entire way in silence.

Back at Tess's, I went into the bedroom, shed my hippie gear and dressed in running clothes and a white hoodie for reflective safety. I yanked my hair into a pony tail and grabbed my earbuds.

"You're going for a run? At night? After drinking a martini?"

"Yes."

"Wait, I'll go with you."

"Not this time." I stuffed the hard white plastic orbs into my ears and went out. I pulled up my hood and yanked the cord tight, so my face was just a small oval surrounded by white cotton, hopefully not recognizable to anyone next door.

I ran for nearly half a mile before I felt myself settle. I

continued for another four and a half miles, crisscrossing the streets of Russian Hill, circling the small park. I pounded out all thoughts of Isaiah with the finale to Tchaikovsky's 1812 Overture, playing on repeat. The 1812 Overture does it every time.

CHAPTER 23

The unplanned, urgent meetings between the bar owner and Chelsea were starting to make Jen nervous. Was it possible they were up there talking about her? Surely that was a self-absorbed, paranoid thought. There was nothing so interesting about her job that would require all these meetings, and such secret meetings. Meetings that seemed to take the front seat over customers. Claire would swoop in at the most inconvenient times and Chelsea went running after her as if someone in the business office on the second floor was dying.

The dramatic secretiveness made Jen feel like she was in elementary school. Girls were huddled on a bench, whispering, sneaking glances at Jen. She watched, not knowing what was being discussed, wondering what she was missing, and worrying it was about her. If it wasn't, why did they keeping looking at her? It was normal to think that people whispering in your presence were talking about you. Of course they also might be talking about you when you were nowhere in sight. You would never know. But having it in your face made what might be a casual conversation about a trip to the discount store cast a worrying shadow over your rational thoughts.

It usually started with Claire leaning over the bar, tucking the wisps of hair that weren't long enough behind her ears. It seemed as if the habit lingered from when she'd had longer hair and now, she couldn't stop moving it out of her face, securing it behind her ear, even though the hair was gone. Like a phantom limb itching madly.

Chelsea would approach and lean her own elbows on the bar. They spoke in low voices, not seeming to deliberately whisper, yet making sure not a single word took on a recognizable shape.

This didn't stop Jen from straining to hear. Her neck grew stiff and the base of her skull ached with the effort of trying to translate the murmuring into sounds that fit together.

After several minutes of this, Claire would look up. Her head jerked back as if she'd just that minute realized Jen was standing at the other end of the bar, trying to keep busy cleaning things that were already clean, running her soft cloth over the edges of the curved wood surface, swapping it for a sponge and wiping along the hard-to-reach crevice behind the workspace.

Claire gestured for Chelsea to follow and they walked quickly to the back hallway. A moment later, Jen heard their footsteps on the stairs.

The meetings sometimes lasted only five or six minutes. Other times, Chelsea was gone for nearly forty-five minutes. When she returned, she was distracted. Jen had to ask questions twice. Chelsea seemed to look right through her, even when she responded correctly, indicating she'd heard. But the response seemed to come from an automatic reflex, while Chelsea's mind was in a different place.

The meetings were a new development, since that day

she'd first seen Chelsea's journal open and unattended on the bar. Now, they happened almost daily. Sometimes there were two in the course of an afternoon before things got busy.

This afternoon, the bar was empty. Chelsea's purse was in its usual spot, the spine of the red journal visible through the gap in the edges of her purse.

Jen replenished the cocktail napkins and swept the floor.

Twenty minutes passed before Chelsea finally showed up.

"Inventory time," Chelsea said. She pulled a clipboard with several sheets of paper attached from behind the cash register. She handed it to Jen. "I'll go down the rows and tell you what needs to be ordered. Be sure to write down exactly what I say so we don't double order anything."

"Sure." Jen took the cap off the pen.

Chelsea dragged a step ladder to the vodka shelves and climbed to the top step. "Ready?"

"Yes."

"Absolut — yes. Skyy — yes. Stolichnaya — no. Orange Grey Goose...uhm, yes."

Jen made notes.

Chelsea moved some of the bottles, not speaking as she checked each one. She listed five more, then climbed down and moved the step ladder to the gin section. She ran her fingers through her hair, letting the white-blonde and copper and bronze strands flow over her fingers. "It's warm in here."

Jen laughed. "I'm kind of cold."

Chelsea lowered her hands. "Really?"

Jen nodded. "I was wondering, what are the meetings with Claire about?"

"Nothing much." Chelsea turned toward the shelves and put her foot on the first step of the ladder, ready to climb. She grabbed her hair and twisted it into a coil, then wrapped it around into a self-securing bun at the nape of her neck. She climbed to the top. "Ready?"

"It seems like she should meet with everyone."

"Why would you think that?"

"If it's about how things are going, or…"

"MYOB," Chelsea said.

"Sorry. I just…they always seem kind of unexpected."

"Don't be so curious. It won't help you."

"I was just worried that there are things I should know. I want to do a good job."

"You know everything you need to. I'm the supervisor, more or less. She talks to me and I'll tell you anything else you need to know."

Jen nodded. "Does she not trust me?"

"Why would you ask that?"

"It seems like when you're whispering, talking, I mean, she looks at me. Like she thinks I'm trying to listen, or she wants to make sure I can't hear."

"Don't read into it." Chelsea's hair collapsed out of the bun. She grabbed her hair. Lifting her elbows, she worked her hands furiously down the length of it, weaving it into a loose braid. She lowered her hands. "There, that's better. Ready for the gin?"

"Yes."

She began reading off names while Jen printed them carefully. "If there's anything I could do better, you'd tell me, right?"

"Of course."

"Do you think she trusts me?"

"You have to earn trust. It's not a given."

"I get that."

Chelsea turned and smiled. "Stop worrying. But don't be snooping where you don't belong." She turned back and adjusted two bottles so the labels faced directly forward.

The thought of snooping tightened around Jen's stomach. The journal was so enticing. Even with the knot in her gut, she knew she would read it again, if she got the chance. She drew tiny circles at the bottom of the sheet of paper, waiting for Chelsea to speak. It was several minutes before she did.

CHAPTER 24

*T*hat Sunday after my standoff with Isaiah bled from the bar over to Tess's condo, he spent the night. We had fantastic sex, aided by the adrenaline pulsing through me from my five-mile run. We seemed to slip into our easy, uncomplicated rhythm, but there was something between us now. I wasn't sure whether or not he noticed it. A sheer cloth that distorted his appearance slightly, a sensation that my ears were clogged.

I think he assumed my run had exorcised all the *PMS* out of my bloodstream. There was no longer anything *wrong* with me. I think he assumed that since I didn't say anything more about it, all was good between us.

It wasn't.

He looked different to me, not the person I'd thought he was. I should have talked about it, should have asked what he meant and why he'd used the ridiculous cliché of a woman on her period to define my behavior. But I wanted to let it play out a bit. I didn't want a big, complicated conversation, arguing about tone of voice and the meaning behind words.

On Monday he went back to my studio apartment. We

didn't make any plans for the following weekend. It was just as well. I couldn't delay Steve forever, and I needed the extra psychological space to figure out the next steps with him.

On Tuesday, Steve texted me while I was at the gym. Four messages in a row without waiting for a response.

Steve Montgomery: *When are you free for dinner?*

Steve Montgomery: *We have some unfinished business.*

This was followed by a winking emoji.

Steve Montgomery: *I thought you would be in touch.*

Steve Montgomery: *How does Saturday look? Steak?*

Technically, that was five messages without waiting for my response.

After my shower, I texted back — *Saturday night is good. I love steak.*

He sent back a foolishly grinning emoji. I hoped he wasn't reading eagerness into the word, *love*. It was a simple statement — I love steak. There were no layers in what I wrote and no double entendres.

The disruption in the flow with Isaiah was already making it easier to deal with Steve. My focus was sharp. And although I was still planning on never, Isaiah wouldn't intrude into my thoughts if sex with Steve became necessary.

I didn't want to, even though he was attractive enough. There was no mental connection. I didn't imagine he was very creative. And he was a Senior VP at the company. He never let me forget that and I was surprised that it didn't seem to worry him. Despite all his flirting and games, I truly thought he would realize it was a mistake to sleep with me. I thought he would wake up from the alcohol-flirting buzz and remove himself from my life.

There were no rules between Isaiah and me. We'd never said there was any sort of agreement regarding seeing other people. I assumed he liked things the way they were. I'd never noticed a suggestion he was sleeping with other women, but it wasn't as if I followed him around, or sniffed out odors on his clothes.

Still, I thought he might be troubled if he found out I'd had sex with Steve.

It's not considered normal to be spending most of your social time with one guy and then go off and have sex with another. And it's definitely not considered acceptable, or nice, to have sex with a man because you're trying to distract him from thinking too much about the other parts of your life, asking questions you'd rather not answer.

I know these are considered antisocial views. But they're anti-social because they go against rules that were set up by religions and governments. And let's face it, most governments were either set up by, or hugely influenced by religion. Which is fine, we need rules. Laws. Guidelines.

But the rules apply disproportionately to women.

If Isaiah even discovered what I'd done, which he probably wouldn't, things might change. He'd never suggested he adhered to all kinds of boundaries and descriptions for the thing between the two of us, but just because he hadn't said it didn't mean he wasn't thinking it. I didn't want what we had to end, and if he had unspoken beliefs about us, I might be risking that. I just didn't *know*. I hate not knowing.

I preferred not to sleep with Steve, but I had no plan, and I'd taken steps in that direction that were difficult to reverse. I could simply tell him I'd changed my mind. Unfortunately, I'd made it quite clear I was suggesting sex and he'd made it quite clear he was interested in following the suggestion. Frustration oozed out of his pores, prickled along the stubble on his chin after my faux vomiting. Cancelling dinner had not nudged him to view me as a tease, it made him more determined to get what he wanted. If he did believe I was just a tease, he clearly was not going to let me get away with it easily.

My phone buzzed with another text.

Steve Montgomery: *Six-thirty?*

Alexandra Mallory: *Yes.*

Steve Montgomery: *The Epicurean. On Jackson.*

Alexandra Mallory: *Got it.*

Steve Montgomery: *btw, don't tell your "boss" about our date.*

I laughed. The laugh was loud enough to spur the cockatoo into an accurate imitation of the sound. Steve had it backwards. *Date* should have been in quotes, not *boss*. And what did that mean? Was he implying Tess no longer mattered because she was drifting around Australia? Was he suggesting it was a done deal that I was going to work for him? Or was he one of those people who randomly adds quotation marks where they're meaningless?

Alexandra Mallory: *What does it matter?*

Steve Montgomery: *She doesn't need to know.*

He hadn't answered the question.

Alexandra Mallory: *Why not?*

Steve Montgomery: *Why can't you take anything at face value?*

Alexandra Mallory: *Do you?*

Steve Montgomery: *Fair enough.*

I sent a few question marks, still wanting an answer to my question, but he didn't respond. Two hours later, another message appeared, telling me to wear something sexy. He didn't clarify whether he meant upscale-sexy or hippie-sexy, so I decided I would retain my current look.

I took a plate of cut-up cantaloupe into the cockatoo's room. I sat in the armchair and sipped a glass of Pinot Noir while he ate. He seemed to accept the cantaloupe. Mangos weren't mentioned. He picked up a piece of fruit and looked at me, lowering his crown feathers slightly. He began eating, murmuring with satisfaction over each bite of fruit. I didn't feel the same over each drop of wine.

The walls were closing around me. I absolutely had to divert Steve from thinking about seeing me in that neighborhood, but I'd backed myself neatly into a corner. I was tired of his arrogance and privilege and condescension. The way to be rid of him once and for all was obvious, but strings of text messages on our company-provided smart phones made it difficult to consider that option.

CHAPTER 25

 ortland

* * *

My mother had made it clear she wasn't going to back me up in my attempt to exert power over my brother, or brothers. I still wasn't sure if all three were spraying their pee to illustrate their superior positions, or if one was doing it deliberately and the others were just sloppy. There were multiple possibilities.

I couldn't tell whether she'd seen through me. Maybe I was too intense and she felt, even if she couldn't see it on my face, my desire to get the upper hand. She spent a fair amount of time teaching me about the directive to women that they submit to their husbands. I think she wanted me to learn that fact of life as a child, paving the way for a pleasant marriage.

My parents, and many like them, take instructions from the Bible meant for specific situations, and expand them to other arenas. The Bible insisted women should submit to their husbands and to male authority in church. The Bible proclaimed males were the head of the household. It came close to suggesting they were stand-ins for god himself. Therefore, since it's clear god gave men the reigns to the world, women should adopt that submissive attitude in all parts of life. Most don't say it directly, but they would advise women to avoid debating with a professor, to accept the unwanted attention of a colleague or boss, to put up with boys being boys, yielding to their superior intelligence. They never said that either, but it's implied.

My mother knew I wasn't submitting to the idea of mopping up piss multiple times a day, and it wasn't much of a leap to recognize that I wanted to carry my rebellion further. She was usually so mild and focused on the face value of things, it wasn't always clear what she understood about me. I continued to believe I could get her on my side. I believed this with the fierce intensity they wanted me to bring to Sunday morning services and Bible study classes. I believed in my skill at getting what I wanted. Getting what I needed.

About three weeks after my failed attempt at persuading my mother to agree I shouldn't be required to clean the toilets several times in one day, I decided enough time had passed, and our conversation had slipped to the far corners of her mind. I approached her again while she was cooking, the best time to get a distracted response. She was making oatmeal cookies. I didn't even steal a bit of raw dough, I wanted something else so much more.

I pulled out a chair and sat at the kitchen table.

"Is something on your mind?" She lowered the head of the mixer, shoving the blade into the stiff dough.

"Nothing important," I said.

"If it's on your mind, it's important. All your thoughts are important to me." She smiled. She reached into the bowl and pinched out a bit of dough. She put it in her mouth and chewed with tiny movements of her teeth and jaw.

I closed my eyes and counted to fifteen. When I opened them, she was finished chewing. "The shower curtain in the upstairs bathroom smells like it's gone off."

"Mildew? That's surprising. You're so good about keeping it clean." She smiled and flicked the switch on the mixer. The motor hummed and the blade circled the bowl slowly.

"I think they get old, no matter how much you clean them."

"I suppose."

"Bacteria collects in the seam..."

She nodded. She turned off the mixer, raised the head, and began scraping the rubber spatula around the sides of the bowl.

"Can I pick out the new one? I saw something really nice in the Target catalog."

"I don't see why not. You've certainly earned it. You do enough cleaning, the hard part of keeping a home. Decorating is the fun part."

I smiled and tipped my head to the side. I tucked my hair behind my ear.

"As long as it matches the rest of the room," she said. "We're not going to start buying new towels and other accessories just to match a shower curtain."

"The one I like is dark blue."

"Dark blue?"

"Blue and green. It's a little dramatic, but it has an abstract ocean look to it."

"I've never seen those colors in a shower curtain."

"It's not plastic, it's fabric. There's a water-repellent liner. That way, if this happens again, you only have to replace the liner."

"It sounds expensive."

"What do you consider expensive?"

"More than fifteen dollars."

"It's twenty-nine-ninety-nine."

"I don't know...that's a lot. For a shower curtain."

"But you only have to replace the liner next time."

"How much is that?"

She acted as if our family were destitute. We lived in a six-bedroom Victorian house in a suburb filled with mature trees, and wide, quiet streets, featuring huge backyards without fences. We could afford new shower curtains for all the bathrooms. "I'm not sure. But it will really make the room look nice. Fresher."

"That's probably true. Let me think about it."

I couldn't believe a shower curtain required so much scrutiny, but I shouldn't have been surprised. Still, I knew she didn't want mildew smells wafting through the house. Eventually she would take me shopping for the shower curtain of my dreams.

CHAPTER 26

S *an Francisco*

The red journal had turned into a flag waved in front of an amped up bull. Jen could not stop thinking about it. She'd thought about talking to Alex about the journal, hoping that hearing Alex's reaction would help her figure out why it had become so important. It seemed like something girlfriends would discuss, but if she mentioned it, she'd have to say what she'd done. Alex had some weird ideas, she definitely did not think like other people, but Jen wasn't sure she would forgive reading something private without permission. Alex was a very private person.

Besides, once she mentioned that she'd read the journal, the thrill of doing something she shouldn't might fade. Right now, it was her secret. It made her feel powerful, knowing that she possessed information she shouldn't. As far as she knew, she was the only person on earth who knew what was inside Chelsea's head.

Alex was also the sort of person who might be sitting at the bar one night and suddenly and very casually tell Chelsea she'd been betrayed.

Why was it so important to know Chelsea's private thoughts? Most of them weren't even that interesting. It was kind of pathetic to be so obsessed with seeing whether or not Chelsea met her workout goals or what TV shows she wanted to watch.

The journal was hidden inside Chelsea's purse. She had a new purse — teal-dyed leather with stiff sides and two short straps for looping over her forearm. Small brass nubs on the bottom protected the leather when the purse was sitting down. A tag hung off a gold chain, with a gold ring noting the designer's name. Jen couldn't read the name from where she stood.

The purse was zipped all the way closed, a new habit to go with the new bag. It was an expensive-looking purse to keep stuffed in a cubbyhole under a bar.

Jen grabbed the dustpan and broom from the narrow cabinet beside the cash register. She knelt and brushed grit that had been tracked in behind the bar, pushing it into the pan. She carried it to the trash and watched dirt and pebbles and a tiny shard of glass slide off the hard plastic. She walked along the length of the bar, looking for other areas that needed to be swept up. She thought about the journal and the secured zipper, and wondered how long Chelsea would remain upstairs this time.

As if an outside force were rescuing her from getting caught in the act, Chelsea appeared at the back of the bar. She walked to the cash register and tapped in her code. "Everything okay?"

"Sure. Why not?"

"You had a strange look on your face."

"Did I?"

"Yes, you did."

Jen shoved her hands in her back pockets. "Maybe I'm jealous."

"Of what?"

"Your new purse. I love it."

"Sweet, isn't it?"

"Is it rude to ask what it cost?"

"Yes."

"So, I guess that means it's expensive."

Chelsea laughed. "You know what they say…if you have to ask…"

Jen laughed alongside her, prolonging the laugh while she tried to think about what she should say next. "I really don't think it's safe, sitting out here where anyone can see it."

"No one comes behind the bar but us."

"You never know."

"One of us is always here."

Jen swallowed. She'd gone too far. If she made too big a deal out of it, and anything happened to the purse, or the journal, Chelsea would immediately think of Jen.

She changed the subject to the cramped conditions of the three hundred square foot studio apartment she was sharing with Isaiah. He was a fairly tidy guy with minimal possessions, but with most of Alex's clothes overflowing the closet, and all of Jen's stuff, it was beginning to feel like they lived in a storage shed.

When Jen mentioned the boxes stacked on the balcony, Chelsea's laugh was a short burst of sound, almost as if she was speaking the word — *ha* — instead of being honestly amused. Her back was to Jen, her long, multi-colored hair woven into a fishtail braid that looked like a work of art. It was soft and silken, like a carefully painted design on the wall of an ancient cave, or the soft lines of a henna tattoo. Jen had the feeling Chelsea wasn't really laughing at the storage boxes, but something playing out inside her own head.

They worked in silence after that.

At quarter to five, Chelsea's phone chimed. Jen knew it was quarter to five because one of the regulars, regular in his timing as well as the days of the week, pushed open the door and stepped inside. He was tall and thin, always dressed in jeans that were too loose around the hips, a white dress shirt, and a black suit jacket. It wasn't a sport coat. It was half of a nice suit, almost in the class of a tuxedo. It sat forward on his bony shoulders, hitching it up in the back so it looked like it didn't fit him at all.

He took a seat at the bar. Chelsea served him a Corona with a wedge of lime. He always shoved the lime down the neck of the bottle in a way that struck Jen as mildly violent. His fingertip went deep into the neck, and the lime smeared its juice along the inside of the glass before plunging into the yellow liquid.

Jen had listened to many of his diatribes directed at Chelsea's pleasant, welcoming smile. He only had one topic of conversation — complaining about a woman he worked with — a *ball-buster and a cunt*. Chelsea tried to offer sympathetic noises, but they sounded more like a puppy trying to get its master's attention. The man went on and on about this woman. She couldn't do anything right.

"She acts like she owns me. She's not my fucking boss. We're *peers*." Everything this woman said, every nasty expression was up for dissection at the bar of The Chimera — four-forty-five, Monday through Friday.

"Her perfume reeks. She smells like a fucking funeral parlor." He scowled at his beer. "It stinks up the room and attaches itself to your clothes so you can still smell her three hours later. She's like a dog marking her space. But the pay is good, so what are you gonna do?" He slammed down some beer and glanced toward the door.

As far as Jen could tell, Chelsea added nothing to the conversation. She listened, and even that was halfhearted. The guy always left her the barest tip. Apparently he didn't value her listening even as much as he valued the unfortunate limes that drowned in his beer.

"She's so superior. We're almost *partners!*" He hardly looked at Chelsea when he talked, gazing instead at the floating lime as it soaked itself to death in beer, turning pale — bloated and limp as a dead fish.

The bottle was empty. Chelsea had the next one ready. Her phone chimed. She pulled it out of her back pocket and studied the screen. "Jen. Can you look after Matt? Make sure he doesn't run out of beer?" She smiled at Matt who didn't look up at her, although he did pause in his list of complaints.

Chelsea grabbed her purse from the cubbyhole and hurried to the end of the bar. She disappeared down the hallway.

It was at least ten minutes before she returned. She shoved the purse into its spot, the zipper only partially closed. Holding her phone in her left hand, she signaled to Jen. "I need to talk to Claire. Can you keep an eye on things a bit longer?"

"I should learn how to make more drinks," Jen said. Her request sounded uncertain and out of place. She gritted her teeth and shoved forward, trying not to hear the echo of her abrupt comments. "And how to use the cash register. It would really help, don't you think?"

Chelsea nodded. "You got it covered?" She was already retreating to the end of the bar again.

"Yes." Jen wasn't sure Chelsea even heard.

After a while, Jen served Matt his third beer, wedging the lime in the top of the bottle so it poked out like a groundhog surveying the landscape. He seemed to have wound down in his list of complaints. He accepted the beer silently, shoved in the lime, and took a long, gulping swallow. He slid off the chair. "Don't toss this, just taking a piss."

Jen nodded. When his back was turned, she inched toward the end where Chelsea's purse hadn't been pushed all the way inside the cubbyhole. She poked it with her toe and it moved out farther. She bent quickly, yanked the zipper and spread the two sides. The red journal wasn't there. She yanked the zipper closed and nudged the purse back into a more secure position.

CHAPTER 27

*a*t seven, Chelsea told Jen to take her break.

Jen hated break time. There was nothing to do but stuff her face. After she'd eaten half a sandwich, peed, and washed her hands, another ten minutes remained of the twenty-minute forced rest. The area with the lockers had two chairs and a vending machine, but it wasn't exactly a nice place to hang out, surrounded by a wall of metal on one side, and nothing but tan paint covering the other blank walls. She could browse through her phone, but it was easy to lose track of time, and then she'd receive a message from Chelsea, asking where she was. Better to stare at the clock, watching the second hand move, the minute hand lurch forward, until it was time for her scheduled return.

Tonight she had ham and cheddar cheese with mayonnaise on sourdough bread. She sat in one of the chairs and nibbled at it, trying to make it last. She thought about Chelsea's journal, and her own identical, but almost completely blank notebook. It looked like Chelsea had decided not to risk bringing her notebook to work any more. Although she was willing to risk an envy-inducing purse that cost two or three hundred dollars. Chelsea didn't make *that* much mixing and serving drinks and playing at friendship with the bar patrons. Or, maybe tips were more than Jen realized and they were sharing a smaller percentage than they'd promised.

The sandwich was gone. Usually half was more than enough, but not tonight. She eyed the snack machine. Cheetos. Doritos. Regular potato chips. Fritos. Why did they all end with O? Was it a subliminal message that suggested the O-shape of an open mouth?

She went to her locker, took out her purse, and removed a dollar bill. It was a total rip-off — a dollar and twenty-five cents for the smallest bags of chips imaginable, but she had to stop the gnawing in her gut. She fed the money into the machine and removed the orange bag that dropped into the well. She tore it open.

The bag was empty before she was satisfied, but she wasn't wasting another dollar on puffed, dyed carbs and fat and salt. She finished her bottle of water and went into the women's bathroom. It was a single occupant restroom, which was adequate most of the time. Occasionally there would be a few women waiting in the hallway. As always, the men's was less in demand, and occasionally Jen was forced to use it if she had to get back to work immediately.

The bathrooms were spacious, the scent of peach potpourri softening the air. The paper towels and toilet paper were always well-stocked, and the bottles of anti-bacterial almond-scented hand soap were never more than half empty. In both restrooms, a leafy plant in a blue ceramic pot sat on the counter by the sink. The mirrors and coffee-colored tile floors were glistening clean. She had no idea who maintained them. Thankfully it wasn't her job.

The trash can was a tall wicker basket with a lid that made her think of a hat. It was tucked under the counter, which was an awkward place for it. With the lid on, it just fit. She tugged on the handle, pulling the basket toward her. It resisted, then lurched forward and there was a thud as something fell off the lid.

She bent down to look under the counter. Chelsea's red journal.

She stood, washed the orange dye off her fingers, dried her hands, and picked up the journal.

It was as if the book had dropped out of the sky right into her lap. Maybe someone up there was telling her she should read it. If the thing — writing down goals and making colorful plans — was so powerful it could change your life, maybe spending more time really studying Chelsea's would help her figure out what she was supposed to write in her own book. Reading it would give her ideas for planning her life. Chelsea insisted writing in the notebook was the secret to getting what she wanted, to moving her life in the right direction — absolute magic. And now, this had been given to her, like magic.

Deep beneath the desire to explore Chelsea's life was a slightly ill feeling, churning around the knowledge that it was wrong. But that feeling wasn't strong enough. She had to read more, she had to know what else Chelsea wrote about The Chimera. Maybe descriptions of the secret meetings were now included, and maybe there were comments about things Jen had said, compliments about how well she was doing, and dates noting when Chelsea would train her to become a bartender.

She took the lid off the wicker basket and buried the journal beneath ten or twelve crumpled and only slightly damp paper towels. She hurried back to the break room, got her purse out of the locker, and returned to the bathroom. After locking the door, she dug the journal out of the basket, tucked it inside her purse, and zipped it shut. Her phone buzzed in her back pocket.

Chelsea: *Where are you? Break time is OVER.*

She yanked open the door, darted into the break room, and shoved her purse into the locker.

Returning the journal was going to be much more difficult than taking it. At some point, Chelsea would remember she'd left it in the bathroom. Dozens of customers used the restrooms every night. There was no reason Chelsea would suspect Jen. At the same time, she couldn't return it to the bathroom hoping Chelsea would find it before someone else did. Putting it inside Chelsea's purse would be even more difficult than taking it out, but she'd figure that out later. It wasn't impossible.

Right now, all she could think about was curling up beneath the covers, sipping a glass of wine or a Bailey's White Russian, and devouring the secrets inside of Chelsea's mind.

CHAPTER 28

*a*t two-forty in the morning when Jen unlocked the door, the apartment was empty. She didn't think Isaiah was spending the weekend with Alex. He must have gone out with friends, or maybe he had some sort of cooking marathon for an exam at his school. It happened, although he'd never been out this late for something like that.

It was Jen's week to have the bed. Isaiah was using his sleeping bag in the space near the floor-to-ceiling window that looked down ten stories to Harrison Street. The bag was rolled up and secured with the elastic strap.

There wasn't any Bailey's in the cabinet after all. She opened the fridge. A full bottle of cranberry juice stood on the top shelf. Tea would be healthier, and the warmth more comforting, but her nerves were raw and jittery and the vodka was more necessary than heat, and in the end, more soothing. She poured a shot of vodka into a glass and added ice and cranberry juice.

She changed into sweat pants and a long-sleeved t-shirt. She wriggled into bed, propped up the pillows, and opened Chelsea's journal. She put it face down on the bed and turned to the side table for her drink. She needed to be super careful not to spill on the pages. Not that a drop of red or a coffee stain or a few bread crumbs would point to her, but it was better if Chelsea thought the book was simply misplaced, not that someone was reading it.

She took several sips and put the glass down.

She flipped through the pages, looking for additions since the last time. It was so much easier reading it like this, without constantly looking up, watching for Chelsea. The edgy feeling of doing something she shouldn't, something terribly wrong, wasn't nearly as unnerving as keeping her eyes half on the pages and half on the back of the bar, expecting Chelsea to round the corner any minute, worried she couldn't put the book away in time, worried that even if she did, she would still give off an anxious vibe.

There didn't appear to be any new sections. Nothing was written about Jen, and there weren't any notes on Chelsea's meetings with Claire, although it wasn't really the kind of book used for recording meeting notes. Did that mean the meetings had nothing to do with Chelsea's responsibilities at the bar? Or maybe those were things she didn't care about. She had bigger career goals.

The problem was, those goals were spelled out in some sort of code. Not a real code, but in a series of letters that couldn't be interpreted. *Career Momentum* was written in fat purple letters at the top of the page. Most of the space was filled with a not-too-subtle staircase. Beneath each step she'd written a letter or several letters, all upper case. The three bottom steps were colored in with pale blue pencil, still dimly exposing the red ink of the letters. The letters on the other steps were bright and glossy, the lines drawn multiple times to thicken the letters.

There were ten steps in the staircase...it didn't look like a career at The Chimera, or any bar. One of the steps contained the letters CD. That could mean college degree. But it could mean fifty other things as well.

The following pages had nothing about The Chimera or any other clues on what the career with ten steps might be.

A key clicked inside the deadbolt. She closed the book and shoved it under the covers.

As the door opened, she picked up her glass and took a few sips.

Isaiah stepped inside. "You're awake."

"I am." She took another sip of her drink. "I was too wired."

"What were you doing?" He closed the door and shrugged his way out of his jacket.

"Just relaxing."

"It seemed like you shoved something under the covers." He walked toward the bed. "Come on, let me see."

"Nothing. You surprised me, so I must have jumped."

"You're hiding something."

There was no way Isaiah would approve of what she was doing. In fact, she wouldn't be surprised if he showed up at the bar the next day, handed the red notebook to Chelsea and apologized for Jen's lack of discretion. He was a very ethical guy. Or maybe he just cared about people. He wanted everyone to be treated with respect, wanted everyone to get along, and he would go out of his way to make sure Chelsea and her private thoughts got the respect they deserved.

She crawled out of bed, yanking the covers up to the pillows. She picked up her glass. "It's vodka and cranberry. Want one?"

"Sure, why not? It's Friday...Saturday, now. We can sleep all day."

"Well I have to go to work at three."

"Okay, half the day. I'll get some chips."

Jen got out the vodka and measured a shot. She filled the

rest of the glass with cranberry juice and stirred the ice cubes and liquid with a fork.

They sat on the bed, legs crossed, facing each other. Isaiah talked about cooking, which made Jen want more than potato chips. Her half a ham sandwich and the bag of Cheetos seemed like ages ago. It was almost time to think about breakfast.

She told him about the secret meetings at the bar.

"It's probably something boring. Most things are, right?"

"Then why won't she tell me what they talk about?"

"Maybe they want to sell the place. Or remodel. It could be a lot of things. But I doubt they're huddled in the office every day discussing you, if that's what you're worried about."

"Not really." She sipped her drink.

"Yes, you are." He laughed. "I can see it all across your forehead in those little lines." He wrinkled his nose to crease the skin of his forehead, trying to mimic her. He moved to the side, re-crossing his legs. His shin was within a few inches of the notebook, if he moved again, the book might press up against his bones, or make itself known as a hard surface beneath his ankle and the side of his foot. She wished she'd put it under the pillow.

"How are things going, other than the meetings?" he said.

"Good. I told you Chelsea was teaching me to mix drinks."

He nodded.

"I'm really hoping…"

"Before you know it you'll be the main bartender, raking in tips from all those guys. Trust me."

"How can you be so sure? You don't know Claire. You don't know how Chelsea is."

He got up off the bed. She realized she'd been holding her breath slightly, staring at the spot where the notebook lay covered. He yawned. "I'm tired. Thanks for the drink, but I'm gonna crash."

"Sure."

"I don't mind the light, if you still need to wind down."

"Thanks." She smiled and pretended to sip her drink, wanting it to last until he was asleep.

He dumped the rest of his drink down the drain, used the bathroom, and crawled into his sleeping bag, turning his back to the room. She waited another ten minutes before she slid the journal out from under the covers.

* * *

A drawing had been added to the first page of the section that contained snippets of Chelsea's conversations with customers. Two large, heavily outlined eyeballs, complete with thick black lashes, stared out from the top margin of the page. They were so life-like, staring into Jen's eyes as if they knew what was inside, as if there was intelligence behind the green irises. Maybe Chelsea's dream was becoming an artist. Despite being rendered in colored pencil, there was a shimmer to the eyeballs and a three-dimensional quality.

The names and physical descriptions she'd seen before were repeated with new comments. Most of them were lame — chats about alcohol, sports, work. She still couldn't see why Chelsea was compelled to write them down. It was all rather boring, and the compliments were thin. If Chelsea believed she was making customers' lives better or having some sort of glowing effect on the world, she was deluding herself.

* * *

❖ ❖ ❖

* * *

Thurs. 2x/month guy always wears pink tie: *You work too hard.*
We don't mind waiting for the next round.

Kate, lawyer: *You definitely earned your tip tonight.*

* * *

* * *

It went on like that for pages. In some cases, the descriptions
were more detailed than the pieces of conversation. It seemed
that she didn't want to forget a single thing about what these
people looked like and what they'd said to her.

Was this really the purpose of a bullet journal? Jen couldn't
see how it related to Chelsea's goals at all. Maybe despite her
confident appearance and her sense of ease behind the bar,
she was deeply insecure. How neurotic did you have to be to
write down offhand things customers said to you?

The last entry was her exchange with Matt earlier that
evening.

Jen felt her eyelids starting to fall closed as she skimmed
the pages. She reached for her glass. The ice rattled and she
moved her focus to her drink. The glass was empty. No
wonder she was falling asleep. She put it back on the table.
She re-read the quotation of what Matt had said. Something
seemed off about it. She couldn't figure out what it was, but it
read differently than what she remembered him saying.

The words wove and blurred on the page.

She'd figure it out later. She tucked the book under the
pillow just in case Isaiah got up and happened to notice it. She
turned off the light and went to sleep.

CHAPTER 29

*I*saiah had gone off to meet a friend for lunch, leaving a huge pot of fresh coffee for Jen. It was quarter to twelve already. This had been her first good night's sleep in a week. She re-filled her mug and sat at the counter. She opened the journal and studied what Chelsea had written about Matt.

The problem with what she'd written was perfectly clear in the light of day and the clarity of caffeine. First, there was no compliment paid to Chelsea like there was in the others. Second, and more important, Chelsea had changed Matt's words. She deleted his comments about the perfume and left out the cursing, writing that he'd said *work was a bitch, but the pay was good.*

It didn't make any sense. His daily complaining had nothing to do with Chelsea, it was just his ongoing loathing and sense of outrage about some woman he worked with.

She thought about it while she scrambled eggs and made toast.

It was funny how much better she was eating now that she

shared living space with Isaiah. His adoration of good food, simple and healthy ingredients cooked to perfection, must have rubbed off on her. She didn't recall scrambling eggs the entire time she'd worked as a call girl. It went along with her new life. Healthier habits all around.

She scooped the egg onto a plate and spread a thin smear of butter across the toast — real butter. Isaiah looked physically ill the one time Jen had purchased a butter substitute.

She sat at the bar, still trying to make sense of Chelsea's adjustment to Matt's words. Her head ached from trying to think of an explanation.

Overall, she was disappointed with the journal. It was actually quite boring. Reading it, she realized she'd truly expected to find something about herself. She wasn't that interested in Chelsea's secrets after all. She didn't even care what her career plan was. All she cared about was figuring out how to move her own career forward, if you could call it that. She needed a better income and a better sense that she was headed somewhere stable. The clock was ticking on her time freeloading off Alex, actually Alex's employer, for this apartment.

Maybe she should talk directly to Claire. She could ask Alex or Isaiah, or both of them, to give her ideas on how to make a pitch for becoming a bartender without any training. Now that she thought about it, Chelsea was deliberately holding her back. Chelsea acted all friendly, taught her how to make a few drinks to fool her into thinking she had a chance. Then, she treated Jen like she was nothing but a clean-up girl, someone to do her bidding — a project, even though she wasn't an important enough project to make it into Chelsea's bullet journal. Chelsea had claimed she was writing about Jen, but her name didn't appear on any of the pages.

Jen didn't need a stupid notebook to figure out her life.

She needed to do something, not draw pictures with colored pencils and dream about it. But before she made a decision about trying to get Claire's attention, she needed Alex's help in getting the journal back to Chelsea. She picked up her phone and sent a text to Alex.

Jen: *Do you mind coming to The Chimera tonight? I need your help.*

Alex: *Can't. Dinner plans.*

Jen: *After dinner?*

Alex: *Too hard to predict the evening.*

Jen: *Tomorrow?*

Alex: *What do you need?*

Jen: *It's easier to explain in person.*

Alex: *Text me tomorrow.*

Jen sent a thumbs up, but her stomach felt suddenly swollen with too much egg. And coffee. She had to pee. She slid off the stool. She'd assumed Alex would be able to help today. The longer she waited to return it, the more nervous she would be. Why on earth had she decided to take the journal home? Still, there was no way Chelsea would focus on her. It could have been anyone. She needed to relax and stay cool.

The Chimera was filling up when she arrived for her shift. Most of the seats at the bar were taken. Chelsea and Maggie were both working. Maggie was an average looking girl with wildly curly brown hair and a perfect smile that smothered all of her average features. She mostly kept to herself. She looked up, said *hi*, and flashed her smile at Jen. The smile was so enticing, Jen's lips were forced to mirror it every time.

Chelsea said nothing.

Jen took a deep breath. It was only the missing journal putting that awful look on Chelsea's face. It had nothing to do with Jen. She knew that was it, but she still felt uneasy, as if

Chelsea was scrutinizing every expression and gesture. No matter how she tried to keep her nerves inside, all kinds of passive, pleading words were going to pour out of her. She could feel them coming.

She moved closer and smiled at Chelsea. "How are things? Looks busy. That should be good for tips." Her stomach tightened. What a stupid thing to say.

Chelsea picked up a beer glass and shoved it at her. "The guy with the Giants hat wants a Stella. He wants a glass but don't pour it. He was very specific." She turned away.

Jen sighed. She never filled the glasses with bottled beer unless the customer asked. It was the normal procedure. She got the beer and set the glass and beer in front of the guy. She proceeded to follow Chelsea and Maggie up and down the length of the bar, picking up the beer and wine orders.

"Don't be so pushy," Chelsea said. "You don't have to serve every damn beer. Especially on a Saturday. It's more important for you to keep the counter wiped. And there's some spilled wine over there. It needs to be cleaned up before one of us slips."

"Sure. Okay." Jen mopped up the spill. She got a rag and went to the end of the bar, working her way back toward Chelsea, wiping up the sheen of water that was sweating off glasses filled with ice. She grabbed discarded straws and napkins and dropped them in the trash.

They worked without a letup for two hours before Chelsea announced she was taking her break. "Can you come with me for a minute." She looked at Jen. It wasn't a question.

Jen followed her out and into the break room.

"I can't find my fucking bullet journal! Have you seen it?"

"That's terrible." Jen held Chelsea's gaze. It was important to keep from looking anxious, from letting Chelsea intimidate her.

"Have you seen it?"

"No."

Chelsea's eyes filled with tears.

Jen stared. She'd never guessed Chelsea was a girl who cried easily. Maybe it wasn't easily, the notebook was obviously very important to her, but god, it wasn't like it was worth money. She could re-write all her TV shows and goals in a new book.

Tears spilled over Chelsea's lashes. "I'm so dead without it. I can't believe this is happening."

"Where did you have it the last time you used it?"

"My purse. It's *always* in my purse."

"I've seen it on the bar, when you had to run out to meet with Claire."

"Okay, I guess. But it wasn't this time. I always put it back in my purse. Which is why I'm kind of curious about you. And Maggie." The tears were gone as quickly as they'd appeared.

"Come on, we would never take it. How can you think that?"

"Really?"

"Of course not. You're sure you weren't writing in it somewhere else?"

Chelsea closed her eyes, nibbling on her bottom lip.

Jen willed her to remember the bathroom. *Think, Chelsea. Remember. You took it in the bathroom. That way, you can blame the customers.*

Chelsea opened her eyes. "You're sure you haven't seen it?"

"Nope."

"I'm serious. I am so fucking dead without it. Dead. Do you understand?"

"I wish I could help."

"So do I."

Jen badly wanted to suggest the bathroom, but she

couldn't. Chelsea would know she'd seen it. Until she remem-bered, Chelsea's mind would be stuck on her insistence to herself that the book was never out of her purse or off the bar. Chelsea needed to get a grip. She wasn't *dead* without it. She could draw new eyeballs and staircases to coded dream jobs.

CHAPTER 30

The steak house Steve chose was loud. It featured a fifty-six inch TV over the bar, visible from every table. Even the booths along the back wall that were supposedly secluded, like the one he'd reserved for us, weren't immune from the distracting flicker of rapidly changing images. It was almost worse than the noise because you wanted to see what was happening. You *had* to know what was happening.

Colored images dancing at the corners of your eyes are so much more alluring than a human being at your side. Their digital, electrifying, insistent demand for your retinas and the adrenaline-seeking part of your brain are impossible for any flesh and blood person to compete with. It isn't just televisions. All digital devices have a way of stroking the surface of your eyes, easing their way into your brain, promising instant pleasure in the form of something new. They offer to stir your emotions, whether it's the thrill of a fast-paced game or the blood-thirsty offering of a scandal or a political fight filled with whip-sharp words and smackdowns. Jokes and videos and photos from friends all offer immediate dopamine releases, unlike listening to someone complain about work or share their meandering thoughts about weekend plans.

I turned slightly so I was facing Steve, putting most of the flicker behind me. The move put my leg closer to his and his left hand found it easily without him even shifting his gaze away from my face.

I needed to keep focused on my goal — I was absolutely not having sex with him. Not this evening, not ever.

What was not clear was how I was going to shift our positions so that not having sex was his idea, at least for now, and that I would be allowed a few more days or weeks to decide how to remove him firmly from my life without consequences. It was the *without consequences* part that was difficult.

He ordered a bottle of Cabernet and we opened our menus. I always think ordering in a steak house is going to be rather quick and simplistic. There are your basic five or six cuts of beef, a few sauces, and sides. But it always takes longer. I'm not quite sure why. Maybe it's the whole atmosphere of beef-worship, wanting to carefully read each description, consider your mood, think about whether a sauce will enhance or if you should just go with bloody, unadorned meat.

I happen to like the sauces, but my bet was that Steve didn't.

As if I'd spoken my thought, he closed his menu. "That's easy. Filet Mignon, the truffled mac and cheese, and a Caesar salad. How about you?"

"I'm still thinking."

He picked up his wine glass and drank some, but not before a flash of irritation passed across his lips and wound its way along his jaw, tightening it like an iron-toothed bear trap.

After a few more minutes, I decided on the cauliflower with fried shallots as my side dish to share. I chose a spinach salad with pine nuts. "And the New York strip."

CATHRYN GRANT

"Really?"

"Yes." I closed my menu. His obvious distress over my poor choice in steak made me want to play with him. "And the Bordelaise sauce."

"You might as well dump ketchup on it."

I smiled.

He relaxed, but only slightly. "With a New York, I guess I can see why you want the sauce."

"Can you?" I picked up my wine glass and took a sip.

"How do you like the wine?" he said.

"Very good."

He squeezed my leg. I hoped he didn't plan on leaving his hand there all through dinner.

He talked and massaged my leg with one hand and held onto his wine glass with the other. The salads arrived and he slowly let his fingers trail away from my skin.

He ate his salad in the same way he had the last time — some of the lettuce and all of the croutons. I wondered why he bothered with a salad at all, he could just order an extra serving of bread.

It wasn't until he ran his knife across the steak, cleanly removing a tender, juicy strip ready to be speared with his fork, that he addressed the thing between us.

"I was thinking we would go to my place. After."

I sipped my wine and said nothing.

"Don't start that shit." He shoved the slice of meat into his mouth and cut another.

I ate a few bites of macaroni bathing in gruyere, mozzarella, and cheddar. "This is so good. I always forget. Total comfort food."

"I mean it, Alex."

"I'm not sure what you're referring to." I dipped a piece of meat in the Bordelaise. He turned away, as if he found the sight repulsive.

148

"Staring at me with those eyes, instead of holding up your end of the conversation."

I nodded. I picked up my wine glass. I tipped it and moved it in a gentle arc, letting the wine swirl up the sides like silk cascading over skin. I took a small drink of it. The wine was so good. He really had excellent taste, or at least a very good education in how to choose great red wine.

I put down the glass. "I was caught off guard."

"Bullshit."

I smiled and pushed a loose section of hair away from my face, tucking it behind my ear.

"By the way, I appreciate you fixing your hair, and wearing normal clothes instead of that hippie shit you're suddenly fond of."

"You asked."

He laughed. "I never expect to get anything I ask for from you."

I'd worn a simple black dress, not very low cut but silky and clingy. I had on black, four-inch heels and my hair was up in a loose bun which covered the unsightly roots, for the most part. I'd worn a lot of makeup — thick, dark eyeliner, lots of mascara — and long silver earrings.

We ate in silence for a few minutes. He ate the Filet Mignon as quickly as if he were devouring a hamburger. He consumed a few bites of mac and cheese and none of the cauliflower.

I held out the dish to him. "You didn't take any."

"I'm a meat and potatoes kind of guy. Or meat and macaroni." He chuckled, mostly to himself.

I served myself another helping of cauliflower and shallots.

He pushed his plate away, a small piece of steak still sitting in its juice, surrounded by a few forgotten pieces of creamy macaroni. He refilled both our wine glasses. The server who had just appeared at our table, ready to take care of it, backed away slowly.

"No worries," Steve said. He shot the guy a smile. "I have it covered."

The server nodded and turned to another table.

"You always have to have the upper hand, don't you," he said.

He didn't say it as a question and didn't seem to notice the irony.

"I'm not sure how to answer that," I said.

"It doesn't require an answer. You think you're smarter than I am."

"Do I?"

He sipped his wine and studied me. One hand was on the stem of the glass, the other on the unused spoon beside his plate. His finger stroked the bowl of the spoon. "You think you have me all figured out."

"That is definitely not true."

He laughed. "So are you coming to my place, or not?"

"I assumed..."

"What, that I'd drop five or six hundred bucks on a hotel room?"

"I didn't think of the cost, but yes."

"It's not a problem, the expense. But I prefer to go to my place."

This was starting to feel rather transactional. I wondered if it was deliberate. I was getting the sense that he wanted me to feel like a hooker, or at least his piece of property. Something owned by the company and, by default, belonging to him.

"You think you can outsmart me with your little games and your body. I genuinely wanted to help you, but at this point, I'm wondering if you're just another fucked up female. No wonder you and Tess get along."

I pushed my plate away. I wasn't sure where he was headed and I was starting to worry I truly had underestimated him and did not have him figured out at all. Maybe he wasn't just an entitled guy who wanted to have sex with me because he liked the way I looked, and because he could.

CHAPTER 31

*S*teve ordered a second bottle of wine. I wasn't sure I wanted any more, and I was very surprised he did, given his goal for the evening. But it meant more time to acquire information. It's always better to be prepared with as much information as possible before making a move. I learned that when I was a child, and it's proven to be true over and over again.

After the wine was open, tasted, and poured, he lifted his glass in a wordless toast. He took a sip. "I'm going to be very blunt, because honestly, I'm tired of the repartee. If you can even call it that."

"You don't like flirting?"

"I don't think that's what this is."

"How can you be sure?"

He closed his eyes. His expression was one of a parent dealing with a three-year-old who has just learned the power of repetition to drive an adult to madness. He opened his eyes. "I'm a straight-forward guy."

I nodded.

"First, what do you want for dessert?" he said.

"The chocolate éclair."

"Okay." He signaled the server and ordered the éclair and a crème brûlée. Without asking my opinion, he rejected the suggestion of coffee.

"You gave me the impression you were attracted to me," he said. "You implied you wanted to have sex. Do you or don't you?"

"Wow. That is very straight up."

"You should have known that, from a guy who drinks scotch."

I would have, if he drank it neat. But the ice confused the issue. Just like he confused the entire interaction with elusive job offers, mind games, and blatant misogyny mixed with a weird kind of respect. "I don't think that's true. I don't get the sense you've been straight with me at all. Suggesting Tess is stabbing me in the back. Yanking my chain regarding a job in sales..."

"It's yours if you want it."

"I wasn't finished."

"You never are." He topped off our wine.

The server removed our plates and scraped the tablecloth of non-existent crumbs in preparation for the arrival of our desserts.

"You've insulted me by assuming things about my life, you've implied that Tess bad-mouths me, that she lied about pushing to get me a pay increase. Not just implied, you said it, although you managed to say it in a way that suggested you might be kidding and left it to me to decide whether I was going to be paranoid."

He sipped his wine. "Go on."

"I'm just not sure what's going on."

"And you don't like that at all, do you."

"No one does."

Our desserts arrived. He tapped his spoon on the top of

the crème brûlée, testing the consistency of the caramelized top. He stuck in his spoon and lifted the custard and cracked pieces of shell to his mouth.

"So if you want to be a straight up guy, maybe tell me what exactly is going on with you and Tess. Or, Tess and the executive team at CC, for that matter."

He drank half his wine and topped off his glass again before he responded. "Tess is a flake. Honestly, this is the problem with women getting promoted to higher levels. They don't take it seriously. When we hire them, the company is forbidden to ask any questions about intentions regarding pregnancy or marriage or any of that. But females wind up their biological clocks and drop out at any moment. All the time. You don't see men just walking away to play with babies or find themselves or explore an *agrarian lifestyle*."

It took all my will power to keep silent, but I wanted to find out what his deal was with Tess. Maybe it would explain his behavior. Maybe none of this had been about me at all, until he believed I was interested in sex, and then he figured, *what the hell*, and changed course.

"You would have been better off in my organization. This long-term leave of hers is proving my point. You don't just walk away for a month, and then three days before you're due back in the office, disappear entirely."

That was news to me. I hadn't realized she wasn't communicating with anyone at CoastalCreative. Maybe she'd decided not to return, ever. But then, why hadn't she told them?

"Do you think that's executive behavior? Doing whatever the hell you want and screw the company?" he said.

"I think a lot of men do whatever the hell they want." I spoke slowly, carefully, suggesting I wasn't quite sure about this. I didn't want to slow down his rant.

"Not like this. It's a dereliction of duty."

"This isn't the military."

"There are similarities. Chain of command. Loyalty. For a company to do well, it needs to function like the military."

"If you say so."

"Before she left, she was already unstable."

"I've never had that sense."

"You're a subordinate. You didn't see her in critical decision-making meetings. Half the time, her feelings were written all over her face. She sulked if anyone disagreed with her point of view. She held grudges. That's not how you behave in business. She…"

"You sound angry."

"Do I?"

"She didn't hurt your paycheck."

"It hurts the company. I care about the company. I care about our reputation and long-term success."

"It's not like she did any of that in front of customers, whatever *that* is, I'm still not really sure." I took a bite of my éclair, letting the cream and pastry and chocolate saturate my tongue. I felt my throat sigh. I pressed my fork down and pulled off another piece. "So why are you really angry at her?"

"I'm not angry."

"You sure sound like you are."

"You got it wrong."

"Even now, you sound angry. Did she do something to damage you personally?"

He picked up his glass and took several sips. He dug back into the crème brûlée.

"Didn't you have a thing with her?" The question was a huge risk, but it was the only way I could see to turning things in a different direction, and the only way to find out what was really going on between him and Tess. My future sort of depended on it. If he was telling the truth and she wasn't coming back, I was in a difficult position.

"She told you?"

"Yes."

He took three more large scoops of his dessert and then the dish was empty. He pushed it away and poured a bit of wine into his glass. At the rate he was going, he would consume nearly the entire bottle himself. "What did she say?"

"Why don't you tell me your view?"

He proceeded to tell me a story that was so completely unrelated to Tess, I had to look away several times to keep from laughing. From his perspective, she'd been his protégé. Of course she was. That had been his generous and condescending offer to me as well. Were all women automatically relegated to the position of protégé, assumed to be inferior and in need of guidance and support?

According to Steve, she dressed *provocatively* and gave off signals that she wanted him. They dated for a while, were forming a relationship, and she suddenly went non-linear. She was so emotional and upset that their relationship wasn't proceeding to her satisfaction, he became concerned she was going to drag the whole thing through the company. The fact that she'd told me about it confirmed his fears. He wondered who else she'd told. He wondered if she would take it to HR.

They hadn't done anything wrong, but employees were supposed to report relationships to HR, there were transparency requirements, especially for people at their level.

To be honest, he was worried she might damage his career. She hadn't yet, but she was *so fucking emotional and unpredictable.*

He felt in his pocket and pulled out his phone. The screen was lit with an incoming call. "I need to take this." He eased himself out of the booth and walked quickly toward the entrance. He disappeared into the vestibule.

I poured myself a healthy glass of wine. I pulled my phone out of my purse.

I texted Tess. *Steve said he wouldn't agree to the committed relationship you wanted, and you went nuts.*

Tess Turner: *Au contraire.*

It was odd that she answered right away...early afternoon in Australia. I wondered what she was doing.

I texted back: *That's what I thought.*

She sent a winking emoji and then nothing. She didn't even ask why I was talking to Steve, or why I was discussing their dead relationship with him. She didn't wonder why I was talking to him at nine on a Saturday night. Nothing. She didn't care.

I believed her. Although she sometimes held things close to her, and could be evasive, I'd never caught her outright lying. Her casual response said everything. There was no drama. No attempt to convince me of her side of the story.

So.

She'd dumped him and he was pissed. His ego badly bruised. The more a person wins, the more tender the ego. And maybe he really liked her. Maybe he loved her. People who get dumped either mope and crawl into a hole of misery, or they get angry. He'd obviously opted for the latter.

CHAPTER 32

I was not thrilled that helping Jen required me to show up at The Chimera again. But at least I was doing it without Isaiah panting after the detective, hungry for a vicarious crime thrill, or whatever it was he was looking for.

I suppose it's common — that desire to know the inner secrets of crimes and their detection.

There's a ghoulish, vampire-like fascination with the dark side of human nature, despite everyone crowing about how despicable that dark side is, how regrettable, how difficult to eradicate, how much it must be destroyed. People want to know the details of how someone was murdered, even though they cringe in the face of those details. Most of all, they want to know *why*. They want to know what failures and secrets and ugly behavior drove a human being to that point, what horrible set of circumstances put the victim in that spot.

I suppose part of it is the same fascination that draws audiences to horror movies — confronting a debilitating fear. Unlike horror, a fascination with crime brings with it the feeling of one's own goodness and superiority. Another line to separate *us* from *them*. But fear dominates.

No one, even the biggest, toughest guy, walks alone in an area known for crime without the hair on the back of his neck standing up in anticipation of assault. Women, many women, most women, walk terrified everywhere they go. For a woman, a nightclub brings that prick of anxiety and so does walking along a city street. Too often, even her own office or bedroom forces her to confront that fear.

Hearing the details of a crime gives a sense of power, a sense that you're smart enough to get insight into the *criminal* mind, and with that supposed insight comes a sense that you can outwit the other. It will never happen to you because you know all the ins and outs.

And there's also the sheer pleasure of the mental puzzle. Isaiah wanted to know how they discovered crimes, and the process they followed to uncover criminal missteps, and the evidence carelessly left behind, and the tools for eliciting the telling details that could be woven together into a cord that ran directly to the culprit.

* * *

The Chimera was crowded. What else was new? A quick glance around the room suggested Dan was not there. His sidekick wasn't at the bar, keeping an eye on his girl. Even after only a single, casual meeting, I knew he was the kind of guy who wanted to watch over his partner. Intensity oozed out of Rick's pores. It was surprising he wasn't planted there every night of the week, watching. She was fairly hot, I could see that. And he was clearly the type whose main criteria is hotness, along with a constant edginess that other guys will notice she's hot — of course they will — and try to invade his territory.

I didn't see how she could deal with it — having a guy's psyche hovering around her like that. And I do mean hover —

it was like having a swarm of flies attracted to your sweat, filling the space where your body heat percolates in the air around you.

Being a bartender puts you on stage enough, who needs someone scrutinizing every pour of liquor, each flick of your wrist, every straw stabbed into a pile of ice cubes?

And being a female bartender attracted even more attention. All those guys coming in alone, many of them believing she was there to listen to their jokes and soothe their egos and marvel over their successes.

I wore my hair in a French braid again, not much makeup, the Doc Marten boots, and a brown knit dress. It was so comfortable. I was getting to love these clothes. I could see the appeal of dressing for comfort instead of eye-catching style. Wearing expensive fabrics, well-cut, with flamboyant shoes is nice, it feels good in its own way, but going out in clothes that feel like you're lounging on your sofa, eating snacks and watching a fantastic movie is really very nice.

I sat at the bar, waiting for Jen's signal. The journal she wanted me to return was in my fringed bag, and the bag was hanging off my shoulder so I wouldn't waste time lifting it off the back of the chair. She wanted me to take the notebook to the restroom right before Chelsea slipped out for a break, leaving it nestled on top of used paper towels in the trash container.

It was a risky move. The timing had to be perfect. And besides that, Chelsea wasn't dumb. She would take one look at the planted journal and know it hadn't been sitting in the trash for two days. To me, this pointed to someone who worked there as the obvious culprit. But Jen insisted. It was the only way. And it didn't matter if Chelsea was suspicious, she couldn't prove anything. She just needed her book. She would forget all about who took it, once it was safely back with her.

It was baffling that Jen had taken it to begin with. She didn't have a good explanation. She'd been *curious*. Well why hadn't she locked the bathroom door and read the book on the spot, if she had to read it so badly? Which I didn't understand either. So what if she was late getting back to work? It was far worse to make Chelsea distrust her, whisper something to the owner, and Jen would be out of the job Isaiah had so kindly worked her into. I didn't get it.

I took a sip of my martini and watched Jen and Chelsea work with perfectly harmonized movements. Jen seemed to know where Chelsea was going before she took a step, anticipating every gesture. Maybe reading Chelsea's private thoughts had put her inside Chelsea's head in a way that simply working together hadn't.

A man spoke from just over my left shoulder. "Hey. Good to see you again."

I didn't have to turn to know who it was. Friendly Dan the detective. I ate one of my olives and turned my head slightly to look at him.

He slid in beside me, standing too close, equally touchy with the woman on his other side, but she didn't seem bothered.

The martini glass was nearly empty when Jen signaled me by sliding a cocktail napkin across the bar, touching the edge against the base of my glass. She gave me a look and I could tell she felt very clandestine giving this clever signal, unrecognizable to anyone but me.

I swallowed the rest of my drink and popped the olive in my mouth. I slid off the chair to the right, avoiding contact with Dan who was coddling his beer bottle and staring into the opening as if he could find a pick-up line swimming in the foam.

"You're leaving?" He looked up.

I gave him a half smile.

"Why don't you let me buy you another drink. I'll save your seat." He grinned.

"I suppose."

"Not very gracious of you."

"You didn't buy it yet." I turned and headed toward the back of the bar, moving more quickly than I should, possibly attracting too much attention. I needed to make sure I got in there before Chelsea showed up. And there was no way of knowing whether it was already occupied, possibly further complicated with a line of women waiting their turns.

It struck me again what a poor plan this was.

The door was indeed locked, but no one was waiting. I put my hand in my purse and gripped the notebook.

A minute or two later, the door opened. I pushed my way inside without any of the usual niceties women exchange when one is exiting and another entering a public restroom.

I locked the door and took out the notebook. I placed it on the counter. I took the lid off the wicker trash can.

The container was filled with paper towels, some sopping wet, tissues smeared with lip gloss and mascara. There were torn foil packets for hand sanitizer and small tubes that had contained pain killers. There was even a straight-edged razor blade. It had been wrapped in a damp paper towel, but the towel had slowly unfolded itself.

I set the notebook on top of the toxic pile.

As I reached for the trash cover, my purse swung away from my side and knocked it on the floor, the inside facing up. Tucked between the woven strands of wicker was a piece of paper folded into a small envelope. I pulled it out. I placed a dry paper towel on the counter and unfolded the little packet like it was a piece of origami. Inside was white powder speckled with light brown granules. I carefully re-did the folds, tucking the flap into the packet. Either coke or heroin. The brown spots as well as the current mood of the country tending toward opioids, I was betting on the latter. I slipped it into the pocket inside my purse, zipped the pocket closed, and replaced the trashcan lid.

Now, I had no interest in avoiding The Chimera. I wanted to see if I could scope out the seller and the buyer of the packet. The Chimera had certainly lived up to its name — if heroin isn't a fire-breathing monster, I don't know what is.

Returning the notebook to the trash can had been a stupid idea. I didn't care if Chelsea found it sitting on top of crumpled paper towels. Clearly it hadn't sat inside for the past thirty or forty hours. I took the notebook out of the trash, opened it to the spot where one of the ribbons marked the place. There was an intricate drawing of two eyeballs ringed by huge feathery lashes. I tore out that page and the next.

This needed to look a bit more real and Jen had not thought it through.

I pulled a few paper towels out of the dispenser and wiped the front, back, and spine of the notebook. After all, Chelsea's boyfriend was a cop, who knew what she'd do when she found the book. I pushed it to the back of the counter, put some clean paper towels on top of it, but left part of it exposed. I replaced the trash cover.

In case Chelsea was outside in the hallway, I flushed the toilet and ran the faucet for a few seconds. I studied my reflection and decided nothing needed touching up.

I opened the door and went out. No one was waiting.

CHAPTER 33

When I returned to the bar, Chelsea was gone. She must have slipped out while I was weaving through the crowd. I should have walked directly to the door and gone home, but now my curiosity was aroused. I wanted to see what Chelsea did when she returned, clutching her precious notebook.

Dan was seated in the chair I'd left empty, his head turned, searching the back of the room to ensure he saw me before I saw him. He didn't. That pale face and fine hair and nondescript mouth, almost the stereotypical look of a serial killer, shone like a beacon in my direction.

It's a horrid stereotype, the chalky-to-the-point-of-bloodless, meek-appearing man, someone who doesn't have social confidence and therefore substitutes extreme niceness, niceness that's clearly trying too hard, and failing because it feels stiff and awkward and extremely creepy. A man lusting for death, pretending at a desire for human connection. And underneath, a current of anger and aggression toward anyone perceived as a threat, which is almost anyone.

But I'm just guessing.

THE WOMAN IN THE BAR

I couldn't figure out what Dan wanted. He didn't really give off a vibe of hitting on me. But neither did it seem like he wanted to pick at my life and try to find something wrong, as if everyone he met had some sort of tiny or egregious crime in their life and he was on a quest to uncover that, no matter whether he was working or on his own time.

There was only one way to get more information. "Are you going to buy me that drink?" I used a casual tone, suggesting I didn't care all that much.

"Certainly. A glass of wine?"

"Another martini. Grey Goose. With three olives, please." I smiled.

He caught Jen's attention and ordered the martini and another beer. She hurried off to tell Maggie, her head jerking to the side every fifteen seconds, checking to see whether Chelsea had returned.

Maggie finished the mojitos she was making for three women a few seats down. She moved to the spot in front of us and began preparing the martini. She smiled at Dan. "A night off, finally?"

"Yep."

"Any plans for the evening?" She shook the vodka and vermouth and strained the liquid into a glass.

"Just another beer."

"You have minimal requirements for happiness. That's good."

He didn't respond.

She stabbed three olives, settled them into the glass, bringing the liquid to the perfect line below the rim. She placed it in front of me. She gave him the bottle of beer and a clean glass. She ran his credit card and put the receipt and card in an empty whiskey glass in front of him.

Dan barely turned as he held his beer toward me. "Cheers."

"To minimal requirements for happiness," I said.

"Agreed." He didn't smile.

"Where's your partner?"

"Working."

"You don't work the same shifts?"

"We're not actually partners."

"I thought..."

"We work together a lot, but not partners. I'm a detective. He's a street cop."

"He wasn't wearing a uniform."

"Off duty."

Something about his tone suggested a detective, in contrast to a cop, was never truly off duty. That told me something about Dan, but it didn't get me any closer to figuring out why he was so interested in me. There was still no suggestion of desire coming from him. Maybe he was lonely. It was possible. Again with the stereotypes, but he had that look. And I don't imagine you have a raging social life when you're a detective. At least that's the impression given by TV and movies — always working, always obsessed with getting to the truth, executing justice. They shut everyone out of their lives in their single-minded pursuit of catching the bad guys. Always the bad guys, rarely bad girls.

I felt a smirk pushing at my cheeks. I forced it back so it didn't spread to my lips. Such a different connotation between bad guys and bad girls. I moved the stick of olives around the glass. "Do you like being a detective?"

"I could never do anything else."

I sipped my drink. "What's the best case you ever solved?"

"Human trafficking. The enslavement of nine runaway girls. Most were hooked into a prostitution ring, but not all."

I softened toward him. Law enforcement isn't really there just to curtail my activities. I know they would never support what I do, but in some ways, at least from my perspective, we were on the same team. Trying to get rid of the scum and occasionally looking out for people who couldn't quite manage looking out for themselves, for whatever reason.

"How did you catch the guy?"

"Nothing exciting and dramatic, if that's what you're thinking."

I couldn't imagine what would be exciting and dramatic. Wasn't it always just a matter of collecting hairs and fibers and conducting interviews until a certain person stood out from the rest? "I wasn't thinking anything specific."

"Descriptions of him began to emerge from several people who had seen him talking to young girls that hung out around a homeless camp."

I nodded. "Do you feel like you saved lives? Of other girls you'll never see or know?"

"Absolutely." He swallowed some of his beer.

He still didn't turn to look at me. "Why are you so unwilling to talk about where you work? Just careful what you say to strange men in bars?"

"Maybe."

"What else?"

I took another sip of my drink.

"Okay. I get it. How do you know Jen? Or is that also off limits?"

"We live in the same building."

He waited several minutes, I think expecting me to provide more details. Maybe to explain why I'd told him before that I lived in Russian Hill. He poured his beer into the glass and took several sips. "Look, if you're not interested in talking about yourself, just tell me to get lost. I will."

"No, it's fine."

"Don't put yourself out."

"Don't get so easily offended."

I could feel him bristle at that, but he didn't say anything.

I'm sure he didn't consider himself easily offended. He probably thought he was being sensitive to my boundaries.

After sliding his bottle in circles on the bar, he finally pushed it away. "Is this your regular place?"

"I don't have a regular place."

He was quiet again.

"I prefer bars with food," I said.

"It's surprising this place is so popular, without food."

"I agree. If you're going to have several drinks, you get hungry. And even if you don't feel particularly hungry, mixing food with drinks keeps you sober."

"That's a myth."

"Is it?"

"Yes. Inebriation isn't mitigated by coffee or food, or even water. It might happen more slowly, but that's it."

He seemed quite positive about it, but I still thought food with alcohol was a good idea.

"So you only come here because you know Jen?"

"Pretty much."

"How many times have you been in?"

Weird question. Suddenly he felt a lot more detective-like. He was looking for something after all. But it was unlikely it had to do with me. It was just my over-active caution. I took a long, slow breath. "I don't know, three or four times."

"Do you know other people who hang out here?"

"No. Just Isaiah."

He picked up his glass and swallowed the rest of the beer. "Well, good talking to you. Enjoy your drink." He stuffed a ten in the whiskey glass. I hadn't even seen him take it out of his pocket. Maybe he'd been holding it since he'd placed the order. He removed his credit card and receipt from the glass, turned, and walked to the door. I didn't see him put the card away either. He was very subtle, after all.

CHAPTER 34

I stayed in my spot at The Chimera for another hour or more, drinking my martini as slowly as I could manage. I saw a wide variety of people walk into the back hallway headed toward the restrooms, but there was nothing remarkable about any of them. Not that I expected them to be grasping cocktail napkins to noses pouring out cups of blood, or to be sporting filthy hair and rotted teeth and yellow skin.

Smack isn't the kind of drug that's used occasionally. Once you start that relationship, my understanding is you're in it for life, unless a superhero emerges from your inner resources.

No one heading down the hallway to the restrooms looked furtive or anxious. No one looked like a gangster with gold chains draped around his neck, or whatever it was I expected. I buy my roofies online, and pot is available almost anywhere. That's the extent of my personal drug knowledge.

Disappointed that I couldn't pinpoint the intended recipient of the packet hidden in my purse, I drained the last of the martini, paid, and slid off the stool. Before I could leave, Jen approached me. She leaned over the bar, taking my glass and wiping at the counter.

She spoke quietly. "Did you do it?"

"Of course. Ages ago."

"Okay, good. I hope she found it."

"We can't control that."

She sighed. "I know. I didn't see her when she came back, so I'm not sure."

"Don't worry, it's all good."

As I walked home, I sent a message to Isaiah — *Just left The Chimera. Turns out, it's no fun without you.*

I figured that would sooth any upset feelings he had from our last go-around, although he'd be cranky that I went there without him. I couldn't have him there because Jen demanded I keep her journal theft a secret. In fact, she mentioned Isaiah by name when I asked who on earth I would tell.

I'd decided not to hold on to his comments about something being wrong with me, and the added insult of a male tendency to attribute everything they don't like to PMS. To some, a woman is never in a justifiably bad mood unless her period is involved. He'd never said things like that before. It was an isolated incident, I was sure.

Isaiah texted back that he missed me. I invited him to spend the night and he said he'd be at Tess's condo in forty minutes.

I took a long shower and put on a camisole and Capri leggings. I touched up my burgundy toenail polish. I blew my hair dry and brushed it into a ponytail that mostly hid the ugly roots. It was the least I could do for him. Isaiah and I were very compatible in a lot of ways and being a little more accommodating and welcoming was a good idea. I didn't want to push him out of my life, and I thought that changing my off-putting appearance would make for a more relaxing evening.

I was right.

The next day was Monday. He didn't have any classes and suggested I take the afternoon off work. "There's an exhibit at MOMA I want to see."

"What's that?"

"Victorian-era crime photos."

I smiled. Better Victorian crime than getting too friendly with a San Francisco Police Detective, snooping into crimes from our own era. "Sure. Sounds interesting."

"They're mug shots."

"That sounds less interesting."

"So you don't want to go?"

"I didn't say that." I kissed his neck. One thing lead to another and we were back in bed.

We woke just before noon, and without any further discussion about my interest in sepia-toned mug shots, we showered and got dressed. I'd finally bought mangos for Damien. He was very appreciative and didn't say a word when we left the condo, he was too busy eating. We ate our own lunch at a bistro where I had crab bisque and sourdough bread with perfectly softened butter, and Isaiah had a pastrami sandwich. We each had a glass of Chardonnay. We took a cable car to California and Market, then walked to the Museum of Modern Art on Third Street.

We climbed the majestic staircase and wandered around looking at paintings for a while, then took the elevator to the seventh floor.

The premise of the show was a Victorian belief that criminals were born with distinctly different brains from the rest of the population, their destiny a life of robbery, murder and other illegal activity. Even petty thieves who swiped the iconic loaf of bread to feed their empty bellies were born that way. There were criminal types and there were godly people.

I suppose much of their view of criminal minds came out

of the prevailing religious beliefs at that time — those going to heaven were specifically chosen by god and all people were pre-destined from birth to either heaven or hell. A rather harsh, and quite self-satisfied view which puts some current fanatical beliefs in a bit of a better light. Although not much.

Certain psychologists and law enforcement types came to believe this criminal tendency could be determined by a person's appearance, especially the shape and structure of the head. They took careful photographs and studied skull sizes and formations, hoping to better classify the features that would presumably allow them to sweep the streets for criminals, locking them up before they could commit murder or burglary or arson, or steal a loaf of bread.

"It was profiling on steroids," I said. We walked through the entrance and turned into the first small room that displayed cameras, and provided information about photography and photo development techniques.

"Profiling isn't always a bad thing," Isaiah said.

"Since when?"

"I don't mean racial profiling. But that's what the FBI does, to get a sense of what type of person they're looking for when they're after a serial killer or a mass murderer."

"Isn't that kind of narrow minded, thinking you can define a type of person?"

"Not at all," Isaiah said.

We walked around the room, reading the tags in front of each display. I didn't answer until we entered the next room. It was much larger, with nicely spaced kiosks, all of them containing old photographs. Each one was labeled with a description of the crime committed and the features of the perpetrators' jaw, nose, and the back of the skull and size and shape of the forehead, as if the mind inside had formed an enclosure that suited it.

"What I meant was that the profiling I've heard about

always describes the same type of person. So what are they really figuring out that's unique to each killer? They all get identified as loners, meticulously clean, with mommy issues. At least the men. Maybe that's why you don't hear about many female serial killers being caught. They can't figure out a stereotype."

"Are there female serial killers?"

I shrugged and turned away from him. I didn't like the way he was studying my eyes.

"Anyway, there are subtle variations in the profiles," he said. "It's all about details."

I took a deep breath to slow down my suddenly thrumming heart. "How do you know so much about it?"

"I'm interested. I've read some books by FBI profilers." After a brief pause, he said, "It's a valid science."

"Well the Victorians thought this was a valid science." I swept my arm out to indicate all the poor souls, the petty criminals and the wrongfully accused, long dead. Their photographs had remained to help ignorant cops try to screw up the lives of those who had the misfortune to be born with receding foreheads, large eye sockets, fleshy lower lips, small or weak chins, thin necks, sloping shoulders, long arms, protuberances on their heads, and other nonsense.

"Fair point," he said.

I took his arm and leaned my head against his shoulder. "It's more interesting than I expected when you said *mug shots*. The old photos are cool. And it is interesting to see how much humanity changes its beliefs, and how much it doesn't." I regretted those words too. I wanted to get off the topic of profiling altogether.

We walked through several more rooms, talking about the information provided on the thick white cards, but keeping our interpretations to ourselves.

When we finished looking at the exhibit, we went to a cafe

a few buildings up the street and ordered two glasses of Pinot Noir and a cheese plate.

Isaiah took a few sips of wine. He put down his glass and rested his forearms on the table. "I graduate from culinary school at the end of May. Did you know that?"

I'd had a vague idea this was coming, but he hadn't mentioned it recently. I smiled. "I knew it was soon."

"Next week, it's time to start applying for jobs."

"And then how long until you open your own restaurant?"

He laughed. "In San Francisco? Anywhere in the Bay Area? I told you what that costs."

"Half a million."

"For starters."

"So what kind of jobs?"

"Ideally, sous-chef. I hope. If I'm lucky. It's a little optimistic, but depends on the restaurant. If I'm in the right place at the right time and there's a good fit and all of that. I'll be able to afford an apartment now, although I still need a roommate. I appreciate what you've done, letting me stay in your place. But I'm sure Tess will be home soon, and..."

"I have no idea what she's doing."

"Well she's not planning to stay in Australia forever."

"Maybe she is," I said.

"Then she'll rent or sell her condo."

"She has the bird..."

He stroked the stem of his glass. "My point is, I'm not sure what's happening with you and me."

"What do you mean?"

"We're sort of...undefined."

"I like it that way. I thought you did too."

"I did."

"But now?"

"Finishing my training makes me think about life, about the next steps."

"I suppose." I'd never finished school, technically. I finished in the way that he meant — starting a new chapter. But not with the finality of a degree. Maybe you think differently if you complete something that will change your course. My course has always been a bit more about letting the spinning planet carry me wherever. Stopping when it looks interesting, or, more often, being forced to change direction because of what I've done.

He smiled, but without giving off an air of neediness, or wanting something from me. I relaxed my shoulders.

He picked up his wine glass and settled back in his chair, as if he were already putting space between us. "I just thought it should be said."

"Okay."

"So you want things to stay as they are?"

"I don't see a reason to change. Do you?"

"I thought you were also making plans...regarding your job? And no matter what Tess does, you won't have your subsidized place for too much longer."

I spread blue cheese on a slice of apple. I ate it and took a sip of wine. "I should probably give some thought to that."

"You aren't going to tell me where your head's at?"

I smiled.

He studied me with his head tipped slightly to the left. I wondered if he was assessing the shape of my skull, trying to decide whether I had criminal tendencies.

CHAPTER 35

*S*teve and I had not gone to his condo or to a hotel after our steak dinner that Saturday night. I'd been given a reprieve by outside forces — the phone call that pulled his attention away from me and the fabulous wine, and drove him outside to talk in private. After that, he ended our evening quickly and said he'd be in touch. He hardly looked at me.

The reprieve was temporary, I wasn't kidding myself about that. He was not going to let go of whatever he had in mind, whether it was just sex, or some attempt to get Tess under control by using me. Or pure revenge. Or...he just liked messing with women's heads. I could see how a career in sales might nurture that desire. There are so many techniques they learn for telling people what they want to hear, speaking to customers' often unrecognized emotions and egos, manipulating conversations to get to the *yes* needed for a multi-million-dollar sale.

I had to decide what to do with him. If Tess wasn't coming back, as he seemed to believe, I had to figure out my future income. And those things were woven into a single piece. I couldn't rush into something and not consider the unintended consequences.

The first requirement was more information from Tess. She was obviously no longer worried about Steve and no longer interested in a relationship with him, whatever that had consisted of. Her messages gave off a cool, unconcerned attitude, but I had to know more than Steve knew that I knew.

Since I had no idea where she was, except presumably still on the continent of Australia, and no idea how she was spending her days, there was no way to time my message appropriately, so I charged ahead.

Alex: *I'm in a situation with Steve, and I have a few questions, if you don't mind.*

It was a day and a half before she responded.

Tess: *What situation?*

Alex: *He's sort of hitting on me.*

Tess: *So what's the question?*

Alex: *If it's not too personal, exactly what was the deal with you and him?*

Tess: *We were in a relationship.*

Alex: *I know that. And it was...?*

Tess: *Sex. Dinners, lunches.*

Alex: *Heading anywhere?*

Tess: *Not in my mind, but in his, yes.*

Alex: *What happened?*

Tess: *I knew he wasn't the right man for me.*

Alex: *Sounds momentous.*

Tess: *It wasn't. I knew from the get-go.*

Alex: *How did he take it?*

Tess: *Bruised ego.*

Alex: *How bruised? And you're sure his heart wasn't also bruised?*

Tess: *It's hard to know. It was a very combative relationship.*

Alex: *Do you think he's hitting on me to get back at you?*

Tess: *Of course.*

She seemed quite sure of herself. I'd expected the opposite answer. I'd expected her to tell me he wasn't that childish, he wasn't a territorial, vindictive barbarian.

Alex: *Seems like a weird reason to have sex. For someone like him.*

Tess: *People have sex for all kinds of weird reasons.*

I smiled at the phone. Did she think she was offering new information? I wanted to know specifically about Steve, not the human race in general. This wasn't a philosophical conversation.

Tess: *You're a moron if you sleep with him. I can't believe you're thinking about it.*

Alex: *What makes you think I am? Thinking about it?*

Tess: *Why else are you asking?*

Alex: *He keeps dangling this job in front of me.*

Tess: *I already told you working for him is a bad idea.*

Alex: *I would be good in sales.*

Tess: *I have no doubt. But you don't have the background for that.*

Alex: *I have natural talent.*

Tess: *Is that your inflated ego or bullshit from Steve talking?*

My ego was not inflated. It was accurate most of the time. Was it Steve's bullshit talking through me? I wasn't one hundred percent sure it wasn't.

Tess: *Don't be naïve.*

I bristled and typed back: *Never.*

Tess: *I think you are.*

Alex: *How so?*

Tess: *This has never been about you. It was always about me. He felt threatened by me. His admiration of your skills, his "offers" without ever following through — not about you. And whatever is going on now, and I don't need to know the icky details...it's. Not. About. You.*

Alex: *Message received.*

Tess: *Good. Now I'm going back to my holiday.*

So she'd taken to the Australian term of *holiday* rather than vacation…alongside that little Australian flag she'd sent previously, she seemed to be hinting at something. Or maybe I was reading into it.

If she was right, and I had no reason to doubt her, Steve had manipulated me rather than the reverse. I'd never doubted he was playing some sort of game, but I had believed he truly wanted to hire me. I'd believed I could make a lot more money in sales. I believed I unsettled him. And maybe I did, but not enough. I had swallowed his bullshit because it was expertly laced with just enough truth.

I wouldn't say I had a bruised ego, but I felt bruised by the corporate battle. And I reacted in a way similar to Steve's — a desire to equalize the situation. It wasn't simply revenge. He was a threat to my relationship with Tess. He had stalker potential and still might get it into his head to wander the Russian Hill neighborhood looking for me. He might talk to the detectives investigating Barker Clayton's murder. He might do a lot of things I hadn't even considered.

The tricky part with Steve was that usually when I kill someone, I rely on disappearing from the place I was occupying in the world, becoming slippery and invisible. And most often, I tried to remain in the shadows to begin with — someone not easily identified as a significant part of the victim's world. With Steve, I had digital records that were like handcuffs locking me to his life. There were phone records and text messages with him, and with Tess. Possibly, he'd had conversations with HR about hiring me. And possibly, there was a whole list of things I wasn't even aware of.

His death absolutely had to appear accidental, no room for any doubt. Accidental, or self-inflicted.

CHAPTER 36

*H*amilton Island

* * *

Tess sat on the upper deck of the boat that would carry them fifty miles out to the Reef. The boat felt small for a vessel that would lose sight of land for hours at a time. It had an enclosed lower deck with seating for up to forty passengers, and a central storage area containing oxygen tanks, flippers, and stinger suits. There were two toilets in what were little more than closets. The boat was open to the rear with large picture windows on either side. Forward from that was a cabin with a built-in table where lunch was served.

The controls were on the upper deck in a covered area. Behind that, the boat was open with a waist-high railing and bench seating. There were about twenty-five people seated below, including an extended family of eight. Only Tess and six others had chosen to enjoy the two-hour ride on the upper deck. It baffled her that most wanted to remain enclosed below, inhaling the odors of too much skin and moist human breath.

Tess wanted to breathe in every splash of the waves and shift in the clouds. She wanted to feel the boat rising and falling over large swells. Alex had been right, damn her. Tess's entire psyche was being cleansed by the limitless stretch of ocean and sky, the confident movement of the boat through the water.

She leaned back and tipped her face up, closing her eyes for a moment. Forty-five minutes out, they'd lost sight of land. She'd taken a cruise once, but the lack of land mass hadn't seemed as edgy on board a ship as large as a resort. In this relatively small boat, they were bobbing alone, with minimal resources, in the middle of an endless sea. There was only enough to keep them alive for twenty-four hours at best. No place to sleep, a single meal, some bottled water. There was nothing anywhere but open sea. If something happened to the boat...She imagined how it would feel to be adrift after a shipwreck or a plane crash, tens of thousands of creatures lurking out of sight below the surface and birds drifting overhead, watching.

She twisted on the bench, gazing out across the water, hoping to see a whale, or at least a few dolphins. The sky was thick with pale gray clouds, but even if it rained, she planned to remain on the open deck. She'd be wet one way or the other, so what did it matter? She was only going below to get her food when they served lunch.

A man with blonde hair, wearing swim trunks and a sleeveless gray tank, his feet bare, appeared at the top of the narrow stairs that led to the upper deck. He walked to the opposite side of the boat and leaned against the railing, gazing out at the water for a few minutes. Finally, he turned and took a seat near the center on a bench facing Tess. "G'day, beauty. What brings you down under?"

She grimaced. "Cliché much?" It sounded unforgivably rude, he was only trying to be friendly, but it was too much. *Beauty?* Really? She wasn't a twelve-year-old fantasizing herself into a fairy tale.

He laughed. He extended his hand. "Sean. Pleased to meet you."

"Tess." She took his hand. His grip was firm, his skin surprisingly soft despite his dark tan.

"Diver or snorkeler?" he said.

"Diver."

"Very good."

She was pleased he didn't ask whether she was alone, which she obviously was, or offer to be a dive buddy. It took the stain off his mildly sleazy introduction. As always, the languid but crisp, clear Aussie accent charmed her.

"Have you been to the Reef before?" he said.

"This is my first time."

"It's one of the greatest, and most splendid natural treasures the world possesses."

"That's a gorgeous way of describing it."

"Can't take credit. The great David Attenborough said it. Our little Reef is one of the seven natural wonders of the world."

"I know." She shifted and crossed her legs. She smiled. "What else?"

He leaned back and crossed his arms. "It's visible from space — 344,400 square kilometers. That's the size of about seventy million American football fields or the size of Japan or Italy. And it's the biggest coral reef on the planet. It extends twenty-three-hundred kilometers along the Queensland coastline."

"Amazing."

"The inshore waters are about thirty-five meters deep, on average. The outer reefs are more than two thousand."

"I'm only certified to forty feet. I'm not sure what that is in meters."

He shrugged. "No one dives anywhere close to two thousand meters."

"I know. I was just saying…"

"How long have you been certified?" he said.

Her face grew warm beneath the cool, damp air blowing across her skin. "This is my first real dive."

"Quite bold. Although the distance from shore is what unnerves most people, not the dive itself. The conditions are fairly basic."

"That's what I heard."

He stood and crossed the deck. He settled beside her and stretched out his legs. On his left foot was a tattoo of a shark, the tail reaching toward his toes, and the dorsal fin over his metatarsal bone. The head looked up his ankle. The eyes were beady and brilliant blue.

"Want to hear her stats?" he said.

"Sure."

"There are sixteen-hundred-twenty-five species of fish, which is ten percent of the world's total species. Six hundred types of hard and soft coral and two-hundred-fifteen species of birds. One-hundred-thirty-three varieties of sharks and rays, thirty kinds of whales and dolphins, fourteen species of sea snakes, and seven out of eight of the world's species of sea turtles."

"You have a good memory."

"Birthed and raised in Queensland. I've loved the Reef since before I could write my own name."

"I'm so excited to see it."

He smiled as if she were complimenting his child. His smile disappeared after half a second. "It's under threat, you know."

"Yes, I know."

"It's like the human race has become a giant flesh-eating disease, destroying its own body."

She nodded. "Climate change."

"That's the worst. Also illegal fishing. Poaching. Land development. Runoff of contaminated water. But you're right climate change is the sleeping dragon. Bleaching from rising temperatures is killing off the coral. The rest of the planet is killing us. They're starting to wear a hole in our part of the ozone. That's why you need better quality sunscreen down here."

They rode in silence for a while, each brooding about the filth creeping over the surface of the earth, water saturated with chemicals and sludge. Carcinogens filling human and animal lungs, eating away from the inside, the ice caps melting, the extinction of so much exotic wildlife, it was hard to keep track. She felt like crying when she thought of it.

Occasionally you heard about a reversal — the return of red-legged frogs gleefully discovered in Southern California. They used to populate the state all over and slowly were destroyed by non-native bullfrogs and over-building. Now, they were back. But mostly, things disappeared.

Tess turned so she was facing the water. It was so beautiful, the damage hidden, for now. She didn't want to think about any of that. It was too depressing and too impossible for any one person to fix. If she were more passionate, she would take public transportation, do more to minimize her carbon footprint. But work got hectic, and international travel with its resulting impact to the planet was a given...She sighed. She was out here to have the experience of a lifetime, not to think about the relentless decay of the planet. She wanted to be free from all thoughts, to absorb the physical experience. She hoped he wouldn't say any more about it.

CHAPTER 37

*S*an Francisco

* * *

I was curled up in Tess's sun room, eating a bowl of popcorn and sipping Pinot Grigio. The bird was happy with his mango, murmuring from his room. He'd become acclimated to me. He no longer shrieked and mocked me as often as he had when I first started living there, although he continued shouting about Chardonnay when I opened a bottle of wine or mixed a martini, and he constantly reminded me I was dangerous.

I'd become used to him, and spent a little time trying to teach him some new phrases — *nice to see you* — for one.

There were six text messages from Jen sitting on my phone, searching for a step-by-step explanation of what I'd done with Chelsea's notebook. The messages had an increasingly anxious and pissed off tone, demanding to know why I was ignoring her.

Then, the tone of the messages lightened somewhat.

Chelsea had let Jen know that she'd found her journal. All was good, but she still wanted to know the details. She wanted reassurance no one had seen me with the notebook. It sounded to Jen as if I hadn't quite followed her guidelines. She worried my improvisation had pointed a finger at her.

I sent a message back. *Just got your messages.*

Jen: *I have to know exactly what happened. She said pages were torn out! She had a weird look, like she was watching for me to act guilty.*

Alex: *Don't worry so much.*

Jen: *Can you come to The Chimera for a drink before I start?*

Alex: *That makes no sense. Won't she be there?*

Jen: *She's off.*

Alex: *Maggie will hear us.*

Jen: *No time to meet somewhere else. We can sit at a table, she won't hear.*

Alex: *You're allowed to drink before your shift?*

Jen: *I'll have soda. Stop making excuses.*

Alex: *Okay. But I can explain it in a text, if you give me a minute.*

Jen: *I have to talk to you.*

Alex: *What time?*

Jen: *Three-thirty.*

I showed up at The Chimera at three-thirty-four. Jen acted as if I was four hours late instead of four minutes.

"I have to start work. I said three-thirty."

"Okay, let's not waste more time arguing about it."

I settled at the table farthest from the bar. Jen brought over a glass of Syrah and a soda. I sipped the wine while she reviewed her list of worries for what seemed like the tenth time. When she finally wound down, I took another sip of wine. "So why did you do it, if you're afraid it could risk your job?"

"I don't know." She put her mouth over the long, narrow

straw and sucked lemon lime soda without putting her hand on the glass. It made her look like a little kid. She stopped drinking and shifted in her chair. She glanced at the bar. Maggie wasn't even looking at us, but still, Jen lowered her voice. "It was like she was waving it in front of my face. And she writes weird stuff in there. I read it once before and it made me curious. I couldn't stop thinking about it."

"The conversations?"

"You read them?"

"Not really. But I saw them. I tore out the page with the eyeballs."

"Yeah. Why did you do that?"

"To make it look more real, as if a stranger had borrowed it, or stolen it and changed her mind."

"How does that make it more real?"

I shrugged. "It seemed like the right thing to do at the time."

"I feel like she knows."

"That's paranoia. You keep worrying she knows and the worrying changes your feelings and you start imagining all kinds of bad outcomes. She probably wasn't even thinking about you. She's just relieved to have it back."

"Do you think it looks suspicious that it was gone for a few days and then magically came back?"

"I honestly think she's just glad to have it. If it's that important to her."

"Maybe."

"So what are the conversations about?"

Jen lowered her voice to a whisper. "She writes down what customers say. Mostly flattering things they say to her. It's like she's super insecure or something and has to have reminders every day that she's so important to them. That they think she's doing a good job."

"That's strange."

"She doesn't usually seem insecure, but then I read these things, things that aren't even important. Just offhand comments about how nice she is, or something. Aren't the tips enough to make her feel important?"

"Lots of people who don't seem like it, are insecure. They fake it — looking confident."

"I guess."

"Well it's all taken care of. If you stop thinking about it, the whole thing will fade away. If you keep acting nervous, she might pick up on something."

Jen nodded.

I lifted my glass to my mouth and took several sips of wine. I put down the glass and pushed my chair away from the table.

"Are you leaving already?"

"I thought you were starting work?"

"A few more minutes. There's something else."

I settled back in my chair. "What's up?"

"I think it would be easy for me to train as a bartender."

"Seems easy enough." I took another sip of wine, letting the smooth, mellow taste wrap itself around my throat, my mind wandering off to the shaky status of my own job. Jen's situation seemed simple in comparison.

"I think Chelsea is trying to hold me back."

"Why would she do that?"

She fished an ice cube out of her glass and put it in her mouth. "I don't know. Because I took her book?"

"Not likely."

"It's the only reason I can think of. At first she was teaching me how to make drinks, and then she stopped."

"There could be a lot of reasons for that."

She picked up her glass and took a long sip of her drink. She glanced at the bar. "I'm thinking I should talk to Claire. Instead of letting Chelsea be in the middle."

"Isn't Chelsea your supervisor?"

"It's not really clear. I don't think she would decide about me being a bartender. I thought she was trying to help me, to impress Claire with what a team player she is. That's all."

"Then, yes, talk to Claire."

"I know they did a favor even hiring me. But I learn fast. And sometimes it seems like having me just wiping counters and serving beer slows things down. When people give me their cards and I can't ring them up, sometimes they get annoyed. Or they wonder why they have to wait for their drinks when I'm just wiping the counter. Chelsea knows that, but she doesn't do anything."

"Then tell Claire all of that."

"I'm nervous."

"About what?"

"That she'll get pissed that I didn't go through Chelsea, or say no because I don't have experience. And then I won't have another chance."

"Just go for it."

She nodded.

"There's nothing to lose."

"Except my job." She put down her glass and pushed her bangs off her face.

"There are other jobs."

"Not for someone like me."

"I'm sure Isaiah would help again. He knows a lot of people. And they all find him charming." I smiled.

"He is."

"Yes. Very."

She studied me for several minutes. It seemed as if she wanted to say something more, but she couldn't figure out exactly what that was. She stood and picked up her glass. "I should get to work."

"They aren't going to fire you just because you ask for more responsibility. Don't worry so much."

"Easy for you to say. Are you done with your wine?"

I took one more sip and handed the glass to her.

"They have all these secret meetings. I think that's what's making me nervous."

"Ignore it. They probably have nothing to do with you."

She nodded.

I stood. "Maybe they're concerned about drugs."

"What do you mean?"

"Someone, or several someones, are handing off drugs in the bathrooms."

"Why do you think that?"

"I saw something…"

"What was it?"

"I shouldn't say. Just a thought. Maybe that's why the detective hangs out here all the time."

"Oh. I don't think so. Rick is a little possessive of Chelsea. And he and Dan are buddies." She moved away. "I'll let you know what happens. Thanks."

"Any time." I grabbed my purse and left. I hadn't considered that was why Dan was there until the words came out of my mouth.

CHAPTER 38

 *ortland*

* * *

The new shower curtain made the bathroom look so much nicer. The dark colors transformed the pale-yellow tile. It appeared muted and not quite so dated. The towels were all mismatched, acquired over nineteen years of marriage and five children, so it was impossible to make the room look completely pulled together. Still, my mother was pleased, and agreed that a fabric curtain created a richer, warmer feeling.

The rest of my plan was quite simple. The next time I cleaned the bathroom, a Saturday morning in July when the day was already growing hot, and my brothers would be drinking lots of iced tea and lemonade and using the bath-room more than usual, I would find out who was adding to the most disgusting part of my chores.

I mopped the floor last and put away the cleaning supplies in the downstairs utility closet. I crept back up the stairs, went into my room, and put on a pair of thick socks. I preferred to be barefoot when I cleaned, it just seemed easier. I closed my bedroom door to give the impression I was inside, and went into the hall bathroom. I climbed into the tub, pulled the shower curtain partially closed and sat a few inches from the drain, just far enough toward the center so the faucet didn't stab me in the chest.

Near the wall where the faucet was, the curtain was pulled slightly away from the wall, giving me a slender strip of space through which I could easily see the toilet. I only had to wait for fifteen or twenty minutes, although it felt like an hour.

Footsteps pounded up the stairs, already proving my point. I hadn't yet cleaned the downstairs bath, and that was clearly the more convenient one. My nemesis had chosen this bathroom because, through whatever surveillance techniques he had of his own, he knew I'd just finished cleaning it.

The temptation was to hold my breath. I resisted, to be sure I didn't suddenly suck in air with a noisy explosion. I took quiet, shallow breaths and waited.

The bathroom door closed. Through the crack, I saw Jake step up to the toilet.

I waited. His presence wasn't proof of his guilt, I had to catch him in the act.

He unzipped his fly and a moment later urine splattered into the bowl of water. Then, it stopped. He took a step back and began moving his hips, decorating the edge of the bowl and the floor around it with pale-yellow liquid. I continued biding my time. Although coming up with a plan to identify the culprit had been simple, figuring out a punishment, since I wasn't likely to get my mother's help on this one, would be more difficult.

I'd been thinking about it for weeks and still hadn't come up with a solid idea. I'd tried to think of things to startle him — coiled pop-up snakes or something similar — but I couldn't figure out a way to make them jump out of the toilet. I'd thought of something in the water that might fill the room with a horrid stench when it made contact with urine. I'd also considered and discarded the old standby of plastic wrap across the bowl so the pee ran down the sides. It wasn't likely he'd even care. He'd realize he'd been found out, but it would still be my mess to clean up.

Jake was sixteen. The middle of three boys. The middle among differing sexes isn't so tough, but when you have a brother like Eric, tall and full of confidence, the chief of the herd, and a younger brother like Tom who was the best looking and the most witty and charming of the three, you get lost. Tom earned superb grades, hit home runs like he was swatting flies, and broke school records in the high jump. What was left for a guy like Jake?

He was nice looking, with light brown hair and brown eyes. His nose was a little large for his face, and his thin lips made his smile appear slightly needy, but overall he was average and not the kind of kid that got picked on or isolated from the crowd. He had a soft voice, which meant Eric and Tom were always talking over him. Eric corrected him, like he did all of us, and Tom teased him. Not in a cruel way, but he managed to make Jake the butt of his jokes. Jake also did well in school, but not well enough to outshine the competition above and below. He was useless at sports, although he did like to run for the sheer pleasure of it, and by high school he was running eight to ten miles a day.

Even my twelve-year-old brain could see Jake was tormenting me because it was easy — I was younger, a girl, unable to fight back because of my assigned chores.

Still. He had no right to make me clean up his pee. He was trying to get me in trouble and trying to upset me, trying to make sure I knew my place. He picked the wrong girl to mess with.

As I sprayed disinfectant and wiped up his urine, my brain

cycled through all kinds of possibilities for how I might punish him. I'd considered simply telling my father about the pee all over the toilet and the floor. I had no doubt he'd be horrified, but I was fairly sure that wouldn't change the fact that it was the girl's job to mop it up. Jake might get in trouble, but I wouldn't get anything out of it.

Ideally, I would use this to get the upper hand with all my brothers. Even though Jake was doing it deliberately, I suspected the others were doing it carelessly. I decided to keep watching. The more information, the better.

CHAPTER 39

 *an Francisco*

* * *

Jen knew the only way to get Claire's attention without Chelsea noticing was to show up at The Chimera well before her shift and go immediately to the second-floor offices, hoping Claire was at her desk.

She didn't want to wait too long. There was an electrified feeling in the air that worried her. Maybe they were thinking of hiring more bartenders. When she saw Claire and Chelsea together — Claire leaning over the bar, her flowing clothes draped seductively across the polished wood — she felt a tightness between the two of them. As if a solid wall surrounded them, something no one else could break through.

Claire was old. Easily seventy. Maybe she was planning to sell the bar to Chelsea. That would explain the stair steps in Chelsea's notebook — maybe the letters *CD* meant *Claire Deposit*, or *Claire Down payment*. It would explain, maybe a little, why she wrote down all the nice things customers said to her. But it was hard to believe Chelsea had that kind of money. And surely Claire wouldn't just hand over The Chimera like a stupidly extravagant gift.

The day she planned to go uninvited to Claire's office, Jen wore ballet slipper flats to work. They looked more professional, even though her feet would ache by the end of her shift. She wore a skirt, not too short, and a white t-shirt with a wide scooped neck that looked dramatic with her dark hair. She covered it with a short black jacket and put on a little extra make-up, hoping it would make her face appear confident and assertive. Claire would value an assertive attitude.

She arrived at three-fifteen. Her shift started at four. Better to hang around than to run into Chelsea. It might backfire later, but for now, it was important to go behind Chelsea's back on this.

Chelsea no longer asked about the bullet journal notebook she'd bought for Jen. Had she given up caring, since Jen was so obviously unenthused about it? Had she forgotten? Either way, it added to the sense that things between them were awkward, heading toward unfriendly. Chelsea was no longer excited to get Jen planning out her life, sharing glimpses of her decorated pages filled with large, thick cursive letters, diagrams for tracking your whole fucking life. It was dumb. She wished she'd had the courage to say that the minute Chelsea had handed the notebook to her.

She walked through the storage room into the break room. She put her purse in her locker, closing the metal door carefully to avoid a clang that echoed through the building, rattling across the concrete floors in the back. She climbed the stairs slowly, keeping her footsteps soft, then worried it was a mistake. She didn't want to go clomping up, but neither did she want to startle Claire and start off with an apology.

At the top of the stairs were three doors, two facing each

other. The one on the left had a black plastic sign nailed to it that read *office*. She knocked. The door wasn't latched and it moved an inch or two under the force of her knuckles.

Through the narrow opening, she could see a small couch with a coffee table in front of it. Above the couch was a long narrow window with mini blinds pulled down and angled closed. She heard someone moving about, but there was no response to her knock.

If she knocked harder, the door would swing open and she might appear to be sneaking up on Claire, assuming it was Claire who was inside. If she waited, Claire might see the partially opened door, walk over to close it, and find Jen appearing to spy on her.

She tapped gently. The sound was barely audible to her, it was unlikely Claire heard. She took a deep breath and gave two solid raps on the door. It moved open and as it did a strong odor of perfume wafted over her. The flowery acrid scent caused her sinuses to spasm.

Claire turned. Her short white hair glistened in the dimly lit room. She wore a long pale gray sweater with sleeves that covered the upper parts of her hands, giving her a waif-like appearance. Her leggings were the same shade of gray and she wore black ankle boots.

"This isn't a public place," Claire said.

"I wondered if I could talk to you for a minute?" Jen put her hand over her nose, hoping to clear her lungs of the over-powering odor.

Claire stood and took a few steps toward the door. "Who are you?"

"Jen? Jen Miller. I work in the bar. I help clean, keep things stocked." She smiled hopefully and tried to relax into the smell of the perfume instead of fighting it.

"Oh. Yes. My mind was elsewhere. I couldn't place you."

Jen smiled. "It's okay."

Claire lowered her head slightly and held Jen's gaze. "Well what is it?"

Jen had been hoping Claire would offer her a seat. She took a step into the office. "I wanted to talk to you about my role here."

"What about it?" Claire folded her arms. She didn't sound harsh, but she sounded as if she didn't have time for a vague discussion of Jens' *role*.

"It will just take a few minutes."

"Then get to the point."

"I've been here almost eight weeks. I guess you know that."

"I didn't, but go on."

"Chelsea was teaching me to mix drinks. I'm a fast learner, and I was wondering if you'd consider letting me work my way into being a bartender. I don't need more money, at least not until I learn everything. But I'd be more useful, I could ring up sales, help out more when things are hectic, and..."

"I don't need any more bartenders. If I did, we would have hired one."

"Sometimes it really gets crazy. I guess you know that, but I think people get frustrated when they tell me what they want and I can't make it right away."

"Then we need a better process so it's clear who is responsible for what." She smiled.

The smile didn't make Jen feel any better. Claire had slammed the door on Jen's idea before it could even be fully explained. Jen had thought that a woman running a bar that was completely staffed by females might be more open to helping a woman move forward in her life. Of course, Claire knew nothing about Jen, so maybe she didn't realize...

"Anything else?"

Jen glanced at the other side of the room, searching her mind for something to say that would extend the conversation, possibly get Claire to offer her a seat on the couch after all. The opposite wall was lined with photographs in narrow black frames. There were pictures of the bar, various bartenders over the years, customers with their arms around each other, holding drinks and laughing. As she studied the photographs, she wondered if Claire didn't actually know how busy things got. She'd owned the place forever, and maybe she didn't realize that the crowds were so huge on weekend evenings that people got tired of waiting and left. They needed another bartender, whether Claire recognized that or not.

She glanced again at the couch, one last longing thought that Claire would be interested in her assessment of customer satisfaction and the mood in the bar. If there was one thing Jen had learned in her previous *career*, it was how to read moods, especially those of male customers.

On the coffee table in front of the couch was a stack of National Geographic magazines. It looked like there were fifteen or twenty magazines, quite a lot for casual reading. Some of them had pages torn loose, sticking out at odd angles from the rest of the pages. Claire must be quite an intellectual, or something. Maybe she liked to travel virtually, since she was always working.

"Is there anything else?" Claire said.

Jen looked at her. "I don't want to tell you how to do things in your bar. You've owned it for so long, I'm sure you know…"

"Then don't tell me. You're being a little presumptuous, do you know that?"

"Yes. But I think I have a lot to offer. And…"

"I'll speak to Chelsea about it. And see if she thinks we're under-staffed."

"Okay." Jen's voice came out in a croaking whisper, as she thought about how Chelsea would react.

"That's all I can do. Don't get upset about it."

"I'm not upset."

Claire lowered her chin again, letting her pupils roll up toward her upper eyelids. "I need to get back to work."

"Sure." Jen went to the door. "Thanks for your time."

"Please close the door," Claire said. "Securely."

Jen nodded. She stepped into the space at the top of the stairs and pulled the door closed. She felt as if bags of cement hung from her shoulders, making her neck ache, tugging her spine into a slump. She didn't think she even had the energy to walk down the stairs, certainly not for spending a ten-hour shift smiling and wiping up spills.

CHAPTER 40

*H*amilton Island

* * *

Tess was encased in the stinger suit. It was quite comfortable, made of thick nylon and spandex. The fabric clung to her body like yoga clothes, so much nicer than the relentless grip of a rubber wet suit. She felt she could move as easily as if she were wearing only her bikini.

The flippers were another story. When she shoved her feet into them, they resisted, pulling at her skin. Once they were in place, her feet felt claustrophobic. The experienced divers, Sean included, had their own flippers which looked much more flexible. Although hers had been thoroughly disinfected, she couldn't stop wondering whether bits of dead skin from a hundred previous newbie divers had become embedded in the rubber. She shook off the thought.

Walking in flippers was an exercise in absurdity. They forced her to lift her feet eight or nine inches off the deck with each step, turning her knees at awkward angles, keeping her eyes on her destination while also scanning a much larger area for obstacles, including other divers with their enormous flippers.

Sean appeared to be on his own. She took a slow, easy breath and flapped and waddled her way to where he was sitting on a backless bench, adding lead bricks to his weight belt.

"Do you have a dive partner?" she said.

"Not until you showed up." He pulled his mask over his face, covering his brow to his mouth, grinning with a frightening expression as the mask pulled his upper lip into a distorted shape, not unlike a fish himself.

She laughed.

They lifted the tanks onto each other's shoulders, strapped them in place, and settled the weight belts around their hip bones.

Despite the sleek suit covering even the backs of her hands with a strap around her thumb, she shivered. She looked out at the horizon. Nothing. In every direction, nothing but rolling water. The swells appeared gentle but their impact on the boat was rougher than she would have guessed. She had no idea where she'd gotten the idea that the ocean, far from shore, was smooth and glassy. Maybe because from the height of a cruise ship deck, it looked calm.

Sean moved toward the small platform and ladder at the back of the boat, where others waited for the go-ahead to jump in.

Snorkelers lined up at the ladder on the opposite side. They were handed bright pink foam noodle floats to provide a way to rest if they got tired. Tess had nothing but a belt filled with lead and an aluminum oxygen tank ready to drag her to the ocean floor.

The ten scuba divers entered the water first. Lily was the only person from Tess's class who was on the trip. The black stinger suits turned out to be equalizers for their bodies. Their forms were not all that different, molded by the taught nylon. In fact, Tess felt she looked better — she was taller, her legs longer, her movements more confident. It was funny how she'd thought Lily's display of her body was something that gave the younger girl some sort of vague advantage. That wasn't the case at all.

It bothered her that she was so fixated on Lily's swimsuit and her young body. It was bad enough that men judged and graded women's bodies. When women started doing it to each other, how perverted was that? But she couldn't help it. She hated the desire, but at the same time, wanted her body to be admired. She didn't even know her own mind — she wanted men to look at her body and she wanted them to keep their eyes to themselves and treat her like a peer. She wasn't sure whether it was learned behavior, instilled through years of television and media images, mannequins and magazines and men's blatant assessments, but she too often found herself comparing her appearance to other women.

Maybe men did it too, they could certainly be vain. But it didn't seem to be as pathological as it was with women.

And did she really want to compete and attract attention by showing more of her ass, more of her breasts? That wasn't the kind of attention she wanted at all. So why did she even think about it?

Was it biological? A feeling that her fertility was declining and the slowly shifting appearance of her body indicated that? Lily had nearly all her fertile years ahead of her, Tess had a handful, possibly less.

She stood behind Sean who was behind Lily. He turned and gave Tess a thumbs up.

For no particular reason, she considered her accomplishments. If there was some cosmic grading system, her experience and financial security, enhanced by an attractive appearance put her way ahead of Lily. And who was comparing anyway? This was all inside her head, a flashing array of images and self-criticism and irrelevant details.

Her sense of power bloomed, which was exactly what she needed before she plunged into eighty feet of water.

The current carried her quickly away from the boat. Sean was just ahead of her and they descended together.

When they reached a depth of about fifty feet, they swam toward a section of coral that hosted three large, cobalt blue starfish. Already she was overwhelmed with the spectacular nature of this place. Unique on the planet. She'd never seen starfish that color. She hadn't even known they existed.

In her experience, starfish were the size of her hand, the color not unlike her own skin tone. Interesting to look at, pretty because of their shape. These were enormous — like something from another planet. As if they'd fallen off a passing asteroid and sunk down into this perfect spot where they remained hidden from human sight. Unless you were bold enough to step out of an office building and explore the natural world, putting away thoughts of career advancement and winning and acquiring all the symbols of security.

They swam closer to the coral. Her breath was like a soft wind in her ears, hissing in and out through the regulator and the connecting tubes.

She felt more comfortable than she would have guessed. The sound of her breath was having the strange effect of calming her. She'd thought it would drive her mad, thinking about the narrow tube that was the only thing preventing her from suffocating. If something happened to the regulator, or her tank emptied too quickly and Sean wasn't close enough with the emergency oxygen support that all divers had, it wasn't likely she'd make it to the top. If she did, she'd certainly become ill with everything from joint pain to vomiting and rashes from the too-rapid ascent. Instead, her breath was reassuring because the sound filled the inside of her head. Her body was taking care of itself, automatically doing what was required, without her having to pay attention to each contraction and expansion of her lungs.

She pushed herself closer to take in the beauty of the starfish. Several fish moved past her. So far, the fish weren't as colorful as those she'd seen in pictures and videos. Rather average, but they were so large, and so calm and at peace in their silent world, seemingly unconcerned by her intrusion, she marveled at their soothing presence.

Something bumped her shoulder. Panic shot through her before she realized it was Sean. He pointed to another coral shelf below the one she'd been looking at.

Nestled in a crevice was a clam the size of a truck wheel. She felt her lungs contract in surprise, but her breathing remained steady and her mouth firmly closed around the regulator. She let Sean guide her lower to take in the enormous scalloped edge of a shell that was easily five or six inches thick. It was partially opened, revealing a bluish interior. The dive guide had said some of the clams were a hundred years old. They had a slight resemblance to a woman's genitals, although the dive guide had not mentioned that.

It was like entering a fantasy — everything larger than life, and so calmly keeping its place, unaware an entire universe existed above the surface of the water. She felt a swell of emotion, thinking about all the creatures making their home in this place, all the beauty that most people would never see firsthand. Her eyes blurred.

She wanted to stay down here forever. She didn't care if she never ate again or had another human conversation. Observing the life around her was enough to give meaning and purpose to her existence. She felt an inexplicable connection to the creatures living on and around the coral. It seemed as if they were all silently connected to each other, sharing a peaceful existence, and the supposedly magnificent human brain was not that important after all.

Sean turned and gestured for her to follow him around the outcropping of coral in front of them. They glided through the water, their legs moving in rhythmic coordination, streams of bubbles rising up and disappearing. She couldn't even see the surface from here, although there was sufficient filtered light, despite the heavy clouds spread out toward the horizon in all directions.

On the other side of the coral shelf was a cove filled with yellow and blue fish. The fish swam in precise synchronization with each other, turning as a single being, as if directed by identical internal clocks. They darted up and down, waves of brilliant color. Tess and Sean watched for a few minutes, and then the fish rushed through an opening in the coral and disappeared.

She turned. Staring directly at her was a sea turtle. It moved its head, inspecting her shape, trying to figure out what she was doing in its home. She had the feeling it had never seen a diver before that moment. She and the turtle hung suspended in the water, studying each other, neither smiling or making any move beyond a gentle fluttering of flippers. The creature hardly blinked. There was no fear in its eyes or in the way it remained so close to her.

She ached to touch the shell, to feel the hard, smooth ridges. She wanted to stay there forever, communicating something beyond words.

Finally, she looked away. She was alone. Sean was nowhere in sight. When she turned back, the turtle was swimming away.

CHAPTER 41

 *an Francisco*

* * *

Wiping the counter continuously was making Jen's arm feel like it might crack at the shoulder and fall away from her body. She wasn't so far out of touch with herself that she didn't see what was happening. Now that her one chance at getting Claire's attention was gone, all of her enthusiasm to do a good job, all of the optimism that made her put in more effort than was required, had evaporated. She had no hope, as far as she could see right now, of doing something worthwhile, something that used her brain, not just her muscles, something that actually paid money she could live on. She would make more money cleaning expensive homes, if she set up her own business. But that also required money.

She rinsed the cloth and wrung it out. It was time to replace it, but she didn't feel like walking to the end of the bar. She didn't want to ease her way around Chelsea as she performed what looked like a dance, pouring long lines of liquid out of silver spouts into waiting glasses, stirring and adding mixers and garnishes.

Jen wiped up a bit of foam that had bubbled out the top of a beer bottle. The edge of her hand nudged the beer bottle to the left. The owner of the bottle moved it quickly and irritably back to its original position.

"Sorry," Jen said.

"Is it really necessary to clean up right now? We're trying to enjoy our drinks," he said.

"You wouldn't like it if the whole bar was covered with spills." She smiled.

"Well don't knock my beer the next time and it won't *spill*."

Some had dribbled out when he tossed it back too quickly, causing the foam to rise up through the neck. She wasn't the one who had caused the mess. She forced a wider smile before she turned away.

It was hard to concentrate. All she could think about was how she might have said different things to Claire, started from a different position. If she'd managed the conversation better, Claire would have seen immediately why she should make Jen a bartender.

And now, Chelsea.

Instead of slipping around Chelsea, she'd made the situation worse. Should she apologize right away? Or later? Definitely later. There was no point bringing it up before Chelsea even knew what Jen had done. Claire might forget and Chelsea would never know.

Was Chelsea her manager? She wasn't clear about that. No one had ever said. Her weekly paychecks were signed by Claire, the envelope handed to her by Chelsea. Chelsea told her what to do during each shift, but that didn't mean she was in charge of everything related to the bar.

Jen tossed the rag into the sink and took out a clean cloth.

Chelsea went to the sink and turned on the tap. "Jen.

Come get this rag. It will get soaked with mixers and stuff and get all nasty."

Jen took the rag, wrung it out, and carried it out of the bar to the storage room. She threw it into the plastic garbage can with others waiting for laundry pick-up.

When she returned to the bar, Rick was sitting in the last seat near the back hallway.

"Hi," she said.

"Hey there. How about a beer?"

"Sierra Nevada?"

"Good memory. You should be a bartender, not just a mop-up girl."

Her face grew warm and slightly damp. Was he mocking her? Her body had read it that way and automatically responded with embarrassment. Maybe because it felt as if he'd seen what she was thinking. Did she look needy and too eager? No, it was just a passing comment. She was making too much of it.

She took the beer out of the cooler, pried off the cap, and put it beside a chilled beer glass.

"On the house?" he said.

She laughed. "I don't think so."

"Just kidding." He handed her a twenty. "Tell Chelsea I need to talk to her."

"I think she's kind of busy."

"It's important. It won't take long."

She went to the opposite end of the bar and handed the twenty to Chelsea. "From Rick. Sierra Nevada. And he wants to talk to you."

"Tell him I can't."

Jen wanted to inform Chelsea to tell him herself. She might be required to pick up soggy, sometimes mucous-laden napkins, but she was not the delivery girl for messages between Chelsea and her boyfriend. "He seemed like he really..."

"Tell him firmly. I'm working."

"Okay."

Jen returned to the end of the bar. "She can't talk right now. Sorry about that. It's kind of busy."

"She'll talk to me. Did you tell her?"

"She said she can't."

He raised his eyebrows, but didn't look directly at her. "It's important. I shouldn't have to tell her that."

"She said..."

"Will you please tell her it's important. Thank you." He took a sip of his beer. He moved his mouth around the opening of the bottle, sucking it like a pacifier he was trying to situate firmly between his lips.

Jen walked slowly back toward Chelsea. This was not going to end well. One of them was likely to get angry, and if she knew anything about couples, they'd make up later and then talk about her, both of them agreeing she was a pain in the ass.

She moved up behind Chelsea. The man sitting in front of Chelsea smiled. "You two are pretty as a picture."

Chelsea turned suddenly, jerking her shoulders. "Don't sneak up on me like that."

"Be nice," the man said.

"I didn't sneak up, I...Rick..."

"I didn't see you there, so you absolutely did sneak up. Don't do it again."

"I'm getting thirsty," the man said, clearly no longer interested in the pretty picture.

"Almost done," Chelsea said. She poured two shots of whiskey into a mixing glass that already contained sweet vermouth. She stirred the contents. She strained the liquid into a glass, added a splash of bitters, and topped it with a maraschino cherry. She put it on a napkin and placed it in front of him.

He yanked the cherry out of the drink, dropped it on the bar, and lifted the glass. "That's better. Cheers." He grinned and swallowed half the drink.

Jen picked up the cherry. "You don't want this?"

He shook his head and took another long swallow of his drink.

She walked to the trashcan a few feet away and dropped the cherry in. She rinsed her hands and dried them, and straightened a stack of napkins, not that it was important. The bartenders, and Jen, handed out the napkins with each drink. The stack wasn't visible to the customers and didn't need to be tidy. She moved along the bar, checking for damp spots.

"Jen."

She turned. Rick was curling his index finger like a hook, drawing her to him. "It's Jen, right?"

"Yes."

"Come here."

She moved closer. He leaned over the bar. "Do you know what's up with Chelsea?"

"What do you mean?"

"She's blowing me off."

"She's busy."

"She's never been too busy before."

"I don't know, maybe she thinks she should pay attention to the customers. That guy she just served is kind of tightly wound."

Rick nodded. "Yup. But she's been acting…aloof. All the time."

So maybe it wasn't just Jen who felt paranoid and worried that Chelsea was treating her oddly. Guilt over taking the journal, and reading it, was distorting her feelings.

"Ever since someone swiped her notebook," Rick said.

Jen nodded, hoping it seemed noncommittal.

"She sure was upset," he said.

"She got it back."

"Do you know who took it?"

Her jaw tightened. She could hardly open her mouth. His gaze was level and unemotional, there didn't seem to be anything behind his words, but he was a cop. Who knew what tricks he had for appearing disinterested while he led you gracefully into a trap. Had Chelsea asked him to question her? She shook her head.

"It was strange," he said. "To have it go missing and then reappear. Don't you think?"

"I guess."

"You never saw anyone with it?"

She straightened her shoulders. "Nope." She hadn't seen anyone with it, so the half-truth came easily, boldly.

"Well she seems wound up and she's blowing me off."

"That's what you said."

"I don't like it."

"Maybe there's a lot on her mind."

"The question is, was it really stolen? Her *bullet* journal." He laughed. "Such a girly idea."

"Why would she make up a story like that?"

"You tell me."

"I have no idea. I should get back to work."

"So it wasn't a story? So she forgot that she left her beloved book in the bathroom? And someone took a notebook filled with her little drawings and to-do lists, which why anyone would be interested, I have no idea. And then, instead of chucking it, they bring it back and leave it in the bathroom? And a bunch of other customers go in and out and no one touches it? Doesn't that seem odd to you?"

Jen shrugged. "That's what she said." She took a few steps away from him.

"Do me a favor, sweetie. See if you can find out the real story."

"I think that is the real story."

"Well I don't."

"Okay. I guess, if she says anything else about it…"

"Thanks." He raised his beer toward her and took a sip. "How about another one of these?"

She turned and went to the beer cooler. Was there anything else she could do to make her life more complicated? Why didn't these sorts of things happen to Alex? Or Isaiah?

CHAPTER 42

*I*saiah was lying on his back on Tess's living room couch, his feet propped up on a pillow that was balanced on the armrest. He'd just cooked a meal of swordfish with Moroccan quinoa, and an arugula, feta cheese, Greek olive, and delicately sliced yellow pepper salad. He'd loaded the dishwasher, scrubbed the pans, and refilled my wine glass while I scrolled through news updates and watched the Twitter feed flow past my eyes, spilling over with rage and laughter and pithy quotes offering advice for a better life. Why anyone would take advice from the internet for improving their wellbeing is beyond me, but it doesn't stop thousands of people from dispensing it with a great deal of self-appointed authority.

Isaiah sat up. "Let's go to The Chimera."

"I'd rather not. You know that."

"You can be very selfish," he said.

"Can't we all."

He looked at me over the top of his wine glass and said nothing.

"I'd rather try a new place."

THE WOMAN IN THE BAR

"Such as?"

"Let me look." I picked up my tablet and opened a search window.

"I thought you already had some place in mind…"

"Just give me a minute."

"Then what's wrong with The Chimera? I'd like to take my own fire-breathing female monster there." He smiled.

I wasn't sure if I was expected to laugh or drop my objection to going there. Probably both. "I really don't want to."

"So you can go there whenever you feel like it, and I can't?"

"You can go whenever. Just not with me."

"If you hate it so much, why did you go the other day?"

I shrugged, still tapping around, reading reviews of bars, looking for something unique, preferably a place that wasn't crawling with detectives. Even in my own mind, that was an extreme overstatement, but that was the impression I was left with — a cop breathing down my neck every time I approached the bar.

He stood and picked up his jacket off the armchair.

"Why do we need to go out?"

"I like the energy of other people."

"In moderation. You hope we'll run into the detective. You want to hear true crime stories. Why don't we listen to one of those true crime podcasts?"

"What's your objection to this guy? Was he hitting on you?"

"No."

"Then what?"

"Nothing."

"Yes, there is. The resistance is coming out of you like heat from an oven."

I took a deep breath. I pushed my wine glass to the middle of the table.

"Did you have a bad experience with cops once? Guilty conscience?"

"Definitely not."

"Then what the fuck is the problem?"

I stood. "You're right. I'm being selfish. Let me fix my hair."

"It's a hopeless cause with that weird dye job," he said.

"Why are you so angry?"

"Because after making a rather amazing dinner, I thought…"

"It was amazing. I told you that."

"And cleaning up the kitchen…I thought it would be fun to go out for a drink, socialize a bit, and you act like you're in a witness protection program."

I wasn't sure whether that referred to my not wanting to go out, or my hair, but either way, I had pushed it too far. There's nothing like violently avoiding something to make other people curious about the intensity of your reaction. I needed to chill about The Chimera. If we went there a few times too many, he'd grow bored himself. The odds were in my favor that the detective wasn't going to be there every time. And so what if he was? He knew nothing about me. I was so focused on keeping an unobtrusive presence, I'd forgotten that unless they're given a reason, no one really cared who I was or anything about my background.

I walked over to Isaiah and slid my hands up inside his shirt. "You're right. We should get out and absorb some energy. Get out of our own heads." I moved my fingertips along his spine until he allowed a slight shiver to overcome his annoyance.

I moved my hands along his ribs, bringing them together on his chest, letting them drift through the blend of soft hair, brushing them across the hard buttons of his nipples. He shivered again. I stood on my tiptoes and put my mouth close to his ear. "Thank you for a delicious dinner."

He took my head in his hands and kissed me. We stayed like that for several minutes, my mind racing all the while, wondering whether he was checking the shape of my head for criminal tendencies.

He pulled away slightly.

"Still want to go out?" I said.

"Actually I do, but not for too long." He reached down and pinched my butt. "Go do whatever you think is needed for your hair. You're still hot, even with your cheap hair."

When we stepped inside The Chimera, my gaze went immediately to the bar. Dan and Rick sat beside each other at the end near the back. I sighed. Apparently the odds were against me.

Following Isaiah, I walked to where they were seated. We all said hello. Dan slid off his chair and gestured for me to take it. I put one hip on the edge of the seat, not wanting to give him the pleasure of doing something chivalrous for me. I wished I'd been more aggressive with Isaiah. I'd been a few breaths from enticing him into bed.

Isaiah ordered a mojito and I ordered a glass of Syrah. He looked at me with a surprised lift of his eyebrows, but said nothing. He put his hand on the back of my neck, his fingers extended up toward the base of my skull. Maybe he really was checking the back of my skull.

I still thought Dan had a criminal look — not the receding forehead and fleshy lower lip of the Victorian age, but the thin hair and pasty skin tone of the modern psychopath. Maybe that's why I was wary around him. Maybe he was a serial killer using a badge as cover. It's not unheard of. Possibly something dark in me was noticing the same inside of him. Or, he was simply watching for drug deals. It was the more likely explanation, rather than my fanciful amateur profiling based on absolutely nothing but stereotypes and urban legend.

The four of us toasted nothing in particular.

Rick moved to my left, Isaiah was still behind me, gripping my skull, and Dan was on my right. I felt surrounded.

CHAPTER 43

*A*fter a few minutes of holding this tableau — me, surrounded by two detectives and a guy getting too curious — drinking in relative and somewhat un-companionable silence, or maybe that was just me, Isaiah released his grip on my head. He moved to my right and asked Dan what was new on the investigation front.

Unlike his rather terse, *sorry-I-can't-talk-about-it* attitude he'd taken with me, Dan began chatting to Isaiah. He had no qualms about telling Isaiah he was in vice and that meant a combo of illegal gambling investigations and drug enforcement. Sometimes they dealt with solicitation, when it was tied to those other activities.

As they chatted on, my shoulders relaxed and settled into a comfortable position. There was no mention of murder, so I guessed if drug enforcement turned deadly, they hand it off to someone else. I thought about his pride and joy case with the runaways. It didn't sound like vice, but what did I know? Maybe he'd recently changed assignments. Or maybe it was one of those stories from fifteen years ago that people tell over and over, because looking back, they see it was the pinnacle of their career, or their life. It's like the football player who can't stop referring to an interception that ended in a touchdown when he was in freakin' high school. Like anyone cares about that ten or twelve years after. Like they care two years after.

I sensed Rick leaning closer. "How do you know Jen?" he said.

I would have thought Dan had mentioned it to him, but maybe not. Or maybe Rick couldn't think of anything else to say. He was one of those guys who didn't know how to converse, only to tell stories. Like that interception in high school, and he simply needed to probe for an opening where he could insert his stock of stories.

"We live in the same building," I said.

He nodded. He picked up his beer and took a long swallow.

"Where is that?"

"Near The Embarcadero."

"Didn't you say you were in Russian Hill?"

"House sitting."

He picked at his beer label and said nothing.

I told him about Damien and described some of his antics. Rick laughed. My glass of wine was already empty. I wasn't sure why I'd ordered it. I really wanted a martini.

More than a martini, I wanted a cigarette. Avoiding the detectives who were investigating the Clayton murders had forced me to abandon my habit of smoking on the bench across from their building. I could smoke on Tess's balcony again, but if I did it too often, the odor would gradually seep into the very expensive cushions of her lounge chairs. Once that smell settles in, it stays forever.

"You seem like your mind is somewhere else," Rick said.

"Just thinking I could go for a smoke right now."

"What kind of smoke?" He grinned.

Did he really think I was going to inhale a little weed with a cop? Even with it being legal? There are some things that just don't quite work.

"A cigarette," I said.

"Yeah, bars lost something when they banned smoking."

"You aren't old enough to remember being allowed to smoke in a bar," I said.

"I'm not. But movies."

I nodded.

"I don't mind the occasional cigarette either," he said. After several beats, without looking at me, he said, "Wanna go grab one?"

"Sure."

"Will your boyfriend mind?"

"No." I didn't want to stand around smoking with a cop, but the craving was growing with each sip of wine, and each thought of how long it had been, and each imprinted physical recollection of the pleasure.

He took a sip of beer and slid off the stool.

I nudged Isaiah and told him I was going out for a smoke. He nodded, too busy wallowing in his vicarious thrills. He and Dan moved onto the stools that Rick and I had vacated. We made our way to the door and went out.

I pulled a pack out of my bag, removed two cigarettes, and lit them both.

"I've never had a lady light my cigarette." He laughed and took a drag.

"There's a first time for everything."

He seemed to enjoy the cliché because his grin lingered and he shifted so he was slightly closer to me.

"So. Jen and you. Same building. How well do you know her?"

"Is this an interrogation?"

"Why would you think that?"

"Because we're smoking and relaxing outside a bar, and suddenly you're asking invasive questions. We just met."

"I met you weeks ago."

"Okay. Someone you don't know beyond being a fellow San Franciscan."

"Fair enough. But what's her story? I'm just curious."

"Why?"

"She's a good looking gal."

The smoke seemed to freeze inside my lungs. Dan had said detectives were always working. Apparently it was the same for all of them, even when they were drinking and smoking cigarettes, they were prying into other people's lives.

"I'm just saying." He took a drag and turned away to release it immediately. It hung in the air to his right.

I put the cigarette to my lips and slowly drew in smoke. Were these two hanging around because they were looking at Jen's previous career as a hooker? That part of her life wasn't terribly far in the past. Less than three months, maybe not even two. How awful for her to be arrested when she was finally starting over. But they couldn't arrest her for the past, could they? Didn't they have to catch her soliciting? Had management at our apartment complex reported her? Someone from one of the four- or five-star hotels she used? Or maybe that woman in our building with the shitty boyfriend that Jen had gotten into it with.

I exhaled carefully. "Yes, she is good looking."

"Don't be put out. So are you, under those floppy clothes."

I laughed.

"What's so funny?"

"I couldn't care less what you think of my appearance."

"Good."

"So why is she doing shit work like mopping up bars when she's so good looking? And obviously intelligent."

"You've talked to her?"

"Once or twice. But you can usually gauge intelligence by looking, don't you think?"

He was right, for the most part. But I didn't want to be agreeing with him. "If you want to know her story, ask her. I don't talk about people behind their backs."

"Excuse *me*." He laughed.

I pulled smoke into my lungs and let it glide out again. "So, did you always want to be a cop?"

"Changing the subject?"

"The other subject is over."

He tapped ash off his cigarette. He stared at the tip as if he was considering dropping it on the ground, stepping on it, and ending the conversation, now that I wasn't forthcoming.

"If you're interested, we pay cash to informants."

"So I've heard."

"Is that the offer you were hoping for? Is that why you rushed out here for a smoke?" he said.

"I didn't rush out here."

"It would stay between us. Entirely confidential. And I absolutely mean confidential. Even Dan and I don't know each other's informants."

"How nice that you look out for individuals' privacy. Even in vice."

He laughed. "You're funny. I hope the boyfriend won't be a problem." He made air quotes around the word boyfriend.

"I'm not interested in being an informant."

"You look like the type."

"Do I?"

"Needing a bit of extra cash. Hanging around the bar waiting for men to buy you drinks."

"Is that what I do?"

"It was my impression when I first saw you, sitting there alone."

I smiled. I inhaled smoke, blew it out, and dropped my

cigarette into a sand-filled container about ten feet from the door of The Chimera.

He followed me to the side of the building and did the same. "If you change your mind, the offer stands."

I smiled again and opened the door. I nodded for him to enter before me. I couldn't wait to get back to my seat at the bar and order a martini. I was done with the illusion of meek, possibly needy hippie girl. At least when I was at The Chimera.

CHAPTER 44

 ortland

* * *

For over a month, I hid out behind the new shower curtain each time I cleaned the upstairs hall bathroom. During that time, Jake was the only one who came in to paint his urine-colored designs on the toilet seat and the surrounding tile. I watched him spray sticky trails that glistened like the slime left by a snail moving along the pavement. Of course, it wasn't as if all three of my brothers would come in together, but I'd assumed it was more than one.

It wasn't only the second story bathroom where they were pissing all over the place. They did it on the first floor as well, but there was no shower in that bathroom, so I still couldn't be sure about whether the others were participating.

I don't know why I suspected all of them. There was something about the way they ganged up on me in other things, something about their smirks when they left the house on their bikes and I was punished for acting out because I couldn't do the same. There was something about the looks they gave me when they saw me on my knees scrubbing the base of the toilet and something about their shouts of pure pleasure when they were raking leaves or weeding the yard that made me think they considered themselves privileged, lucky to be males. They foresaw their entire lives without ever having to encounter the reality of human filth. They got to work with clean soil and dry crisp leaves and sweet-smelling blades of grass. They got to squeegee streaks of rain water off windows.

After several weeks, I began to consider whether Jake might be the front man. Maybe Eric and Tom hadn't actually pissed on the floor, but they'd put Jake up to it. Did that mean he wasn't fully on their team? A weak spot?

I rearranged the contents of the closet a few feet down and across from the first-floor guest bathroom. I hid inside with the door cracked a fraction of an inch. I didn't have to catch them in the act, I only had to watch who used the bathroom and make sure I got in there immediately after he finished.

It only took a week to confirm that Jake was the only one working overtime to create a bio-hazardous mess for me.

During this time, I was getting interested in dreams. I'd read a few books about dream interpretations, and started writing down my dreams every morning, when I remembered them, which wasn't often.

The things I wrote didn't always make sense, but it was fun to see what I remembered and to figure out what events from the previous days had shaped each dream. I liked reading up on symbols, trying to decipher what my subconscious was gnawing on.

Then I hit on the suggestion that people can deliberately shape their dreams. I wasn't sure what the benefit of that was overall, but I liked the idea of my conscious self talking to my unconscious self and seeing whether they could carry on a conversation.

Before I went to sleep, I wrote in my spiral notebook about the peeing situation. I told my hidden self to come up with an idea for how I might get back at Jake and get power over my brothers and their obnoxious male superiority. I told myself that since my parents would do nothing, I needed an idea for putting them in their place. Turning their maleness against them, maybe.

The first night, I didn't dream at all.

The second night I had a dream about taking a math test and not being able to remember the difference between addition, subtraction, multiplication, and division. I sat at my desk, a pencil in my hand, but no idea where to start, the unfamiliar symbols taunting me from the page.

For several nights after that, I didn't dream at all.

The next night before bed, I wrote down a list of all the unfair rules in our family that allowed boys to do things that were forbidden for girls.

I got on the floor and did a backbend, holding it as long as I could, with a perfect arch, hoping it would stretch my muscles, send blood racing throughout my body, pouring more blood into my brain, or whatever it was that made it so active some nights and deathly silent on others.

That night I had a nightmare. It was filled with a disturbing array of monsters, hideous faces opening their mouths and lunging at me as if they meant to tear off my head. Vivid sounds of growling and shrieking filled my ears, piercing the soft stuff of my brain. I wasn't sure if the shrieks were mine or something coming out of the monsters' throats. I was running and stumbling, I felt like I'd been running forever. I could hardly breathe and still they were after me.

Razor sharp teeth scraped at my flesh, drawing blood.

When I woke, it was still dark. I couldn't remember what

day it was and I'd forgotten completely about the list in my dream notebook. I didn't even want to look up the scenes in my dream dictionaries. I didn't want to know what it all meant.

And then, after lying there for an hour or more in the darkness, watching the sky outside my window grow lighter, it came to me that the dream was giving me a plan for getting power over my smug brothers. I shivered as I thought about how easy it would be.

The two levels of my mind were talking to each other after all.

I smiled and sat up in bed and watched the sunlight slowly creep across the sky.

CHAPTER 45

 an Francisco

* * *

The day after I, the most unlikely person in the city of San Francisco, was propositioned to become a police informant, Jen sent me a text message at five a.m. Not so early for me, but Jen's shifts at The Chimera ended at two, and then there was clean-up and closing.

Jen: *I've been thinking about starting to run.*

Alex: *Cool.*

Jen: *Want to meet me at The Embarcadero? Give me some tips on stretching and building up my stamina? We could run together, if that's okay.*

Alex: *I like to run alone.*

Jen: *I know, I don't mean as a regular thing. Just to start.*

Alex: *Today?*

Jen: *Yes.*

Alex: *Did you even sleep?*

Jen: *A little. But I'm wired.*

I sent an emoji with a dazed, wide-eyed look.

Jen: *I have some stuff I want to talk to you about.*

Alex: *Running and talking don't go well together. If you're just starting, you'll get about four sentences out before you have to use all your energy just to breathe.*

Then, I remembered the time she'd used the treadmill at my gym. She ran for over forty-five minutes, at more or less full speed, and I didn't recall her being winded.

Alex: *Maybe you're already in good shape.*

Jen: *I think I am. I just want to start running for the mental aspects. The feel-good part.*

Alex: *It can take a while to get to the euphoric stage.*

Jen: *I have time.* Beside her words was a smiley face.

Alex: *I'll meet you at six-thirty. Does that work?*

Jen: *Yes. THANKS!!!*

I volleyed back my own smiley face.

I took my car instead of using an Uber since I had my work clothes and gym bag in the trunk. As I pulled up to the entrance to the garage where CoastalCreative had discount rates for employees, I saw Jen waiting near a bench about thirty feet away. I waved but she didn't see me.

I parked and left the garage.

First, I showed her the stretches I liked and explained why it was critical and to not cut corners on it. We started at a slow jog, headed toward the ferry building. We ran for about half a mile and she wasn't even breathing hard.

"I tried talking to Claire about becoming a bartender and she blew me off," Jen said as we passed a bench where two seagulls were trying to get inside a crumpled potato chip bag.

"Why?"

"I don't know. I think I messed up. Going to Claire instead of talking to Chelsea."

We dodged around two homeless guys digging through trash containers for cans and bottles.

"Things are weird there. I don't know what to do. I really, really need to make more money."

I knew what that was like. Of course, in her eyes I was making huge sums already, but the sense of needing more persists at every step up the ladder, and we all want to skip a few rungs. "What seems weird? Just Chelsea? Are you worried about those cops always hanging around?"

"No. It's Chelsea. I feel..." She paused and slowed her pace. Still jogging she began peeling off her sweatshirt. There was a low fog and no breeze. Despite the damp cold when we'd started, the air now had a thick, muggy quality.

"I feel like I'm caught in the middle of everything. Rick, the cop with the..."

"I know which one he is."

"He wants me to keep an eye on Chelsea, whatever that means. And I'm waiting for the shoe to drop with Claire telling Chelsea I went behind her back. And I don't even know if it's behind her back. Chelsea isn't my boss, not really. She tells me what to do, but Claire is the one who hired me. But she doesn't even know me. She forgot who I was. She hired me because Isaiah's friend went on and on about me, but..."

"Slow down."

"Sorry." She slowed her pace again and fell behind me a few steps.

"I meant your words, not your running. Your cardiovascular system is in amazing condition."

"For someone who spent the last two years sitting on her ass all day and lying on her back half the night?" She laughed with an almost giddy tone.

"No. For anyone. Most people, even in good shape, can't run and talk."

"I guess I have extra lung capacity or something."

"What are you asking me?"

"I don't know what to do."

"I can't tell you what to do."

"Why would Rick want me to keep an eye on her? An eye for what?"

At least he hadn't been asking about Jen's story because of her vice-like behavior in the past. It sounded like he might be recruiting her as an informant as well. What was with the guy? Did the San Francisco police department have so much spare cash lying around they could pay people in every bar in the city to become lookouts for them? It was a creepy way to get extra money — spying on your fellow partiers.

It made me wonder who else at the bar he had working for him. If your average person knew this was going on, they might not feel like they could go to a bar to unwind and let go of their worries. "I don't know why. Maybe just keep doing what you're doing. Things have a way of changing around you when you least expect it."

I thought about my previously secure position that was in the process of dissolving into nothing. I'd worked to cultivate Tess as an ally, someone who trusted me, someone who would reward me for being her right-hand gal, or whatever you want to call it. I thought Steve genuinely believed I had natural skill in sales, and wanted to offer me a position with its fantastic pay structure that rewards people who are cold and efficient and charming, like me.

Well...charming when I want to be. I doubt Rick or Dan thought I was all that charming.

Lately, neither did Isaiah. I reached around to the back of my head, pressing my fingers into the soft spot at the base of my skull. It had become an unconscious habit since we'd seen the exhibit and I'd felt his hands on my head so many times. It was possible he'd always held my head when he kissed me, massaged my scalp, but suddenly those gestures had a sinister quality.

Just like Jen reading into a few odd situations and thinking she was in trouble.

"Maybe it's a simple answer. It usually is. Maybe he thinks Chelsea is cheating on him."

"That wasn't my impression."

"Then what was your impression?"

"I'm not sure." She slowed. "Okay, now I'm getting a little tired. Should we turn back?"

I reversed direction and we jogged at a slower pace. The sidewalk was filling up with people heading out for croissants and coffee, the gym, and some go-getters aiming directly for their offices. We dodged traffic, our conversation interrupted in the process.

"He was asking about her notebook. He didn't believe it disappeared and reappeared. So he thinks she's lying to him about it. But why would he care? It's a fancy to-do list. That's all."

"Maybe she's doing things for him." I considered this. Was Chelsea an informant too? What the hell?

CHAPTER 46

*F*our men were seated at the bar, scattered along its length, each leaving a safety zone of one or two chairs between him and the next guy. In the chair closest to the front door was a woman with blonde hair. She wore it swept up into a floppy loop that was a cross between a bun and a ponytail. A fringe of thick bangs covered her brows and brushed across the tops of her eyelids.

She was partially turned so Jen couldn't see much of her face. She wore a black sleeveless dress with a wide scooped neck. On the bar in front of her was a martini. The drink looked untouched.

Jen squinted as if narrowing her eyes might provide more light in the dimly lit room. The woman was familiar. Was it Alex, fooling around with her appearance again? It was silly to assume that any woman drinking a martini was Alex. The association between the drink and her strange, prickly friend was so strong, it was her gut response. But the woman looked nothing like Alex. Her lips were plump with an exaggerated pout, very much like Chelsea's.

Jen stepped behind the bar and walked slowly toward the

front. She stopped midway. None of the men looked at her or gave any indication they were ready for refills.

"Hey, I'm on tonight."

She turned. Maggie, one of the bartenders usually only working Saturday and Sunday nights, was standing at the opening to the bar area. She scooted into the enclosure, walked to the cash register, and entered her code.

Jen turned back to the familiar-looking woman, trying to figure out what was creating such a strong echo inside her mind. She took several steps closer. The woman turned. She picked up her drink and took a sip. The alcohol barely touched her lips.

Jen moved toward the woman. "Chelsea?"

Chelsea gave a single, dismissive nod of her head and placed the drink on the bar, leaving her fingers touching the stem.

"Why'd you dye your hair? The bangs look good. I hardly recognized you."

Chelsea put a finger to her lips.

"What's going on?"

Chelsea crooked a finger at her. Jen walked to where she sat. Chelsea moved her glass to the side and leaned forward. "Market research, you could call it. Claire wants to get some customer perspective."

"But why did you dye your hair?"

"It was sort of distinctive. Right? All those colors. People recognize me."

"You don't think they won't recognize you just because you changed your hair?"

"You didn't. People glom onto one feature of a person and it's all they see. Unless a customer I know really well sits right next to me, I doubt anyone will notice. Claire is counting on it."

Jen nodded. It seemed a bit cloak and dagger, but maybe

CATHRYN GRANT

this was how Claire kept The Chimera's cutting edge.

"Just ignore me."

"Okay."

"Unless I order a drink, of course. But that's Maggie's job."

"What are you watching for?"

"Nothing specific. Just getting a sense of the customer experience. Seeing it from the opposite side of the bar, so-to-speak." She laughed. "Better not to hang around me."

"Okay. Sure." Jen turned.

Maggie assigned re-stocking duty to Jen — nothing new about that. She moved quickly, letting the upbeat music fuel her. She scurried back and forth to the supply room, carrying bottles of mixer, condiments, straws and stir sticks, and napkins. By the time she finished, every seat at the bar was taken and the noise level in the room had swollen to a comforting roar.

No one talked to Chelsea, but she kept herself partially turned on the chair, the back of her bare shoulder facing the guy next to her. No one approached her on the other side, seeming to read her pout as a request to be left alone.

The night moved relentlessly forward. The Chimera was busy and Jen didn't have time to look at Chelsea or wonder any more about what Claire hoped Chelsea would accomplish with her phony research. The situation was irritating, and when she saw Maggie deliver a second martini to the bar in front of Chelsea, it struck her why she was so upset, almost angry, at what Chelsea was doing.

It should have been Jen! Understanding what it was like for customers had been her idea. Claire had taken the suggestion after all.

It wasn't fair. Chelsea could mix drinks and make a lot of money. Jen was left mopping up and cutting limes and re-filling the olive and onion tubs. She would have been a much better choice — almost invisible to most of the customers.

236

They hardly noticed Jen and wouldn't remember her face. Surely anyone looking at Chelsea for more than two minutes would recognize her, despite the blonde hair, the flashy up-do, and the dress. She'd worked there for years and it wasn't as if she could change the shape of her mouth or her nose. When she smiled, it was obviously Chelsea. Her hair wasn't *that* different.

Of course, Claire trusted Chelsea. And after all their secret meetings, Chelsea knew what Claire was trying to accomplish with The Chimera. She knew all the ins and outs of the bar and how to entice customers to return, making sure they felt comfortable, subtly increasing the quantity of alcohol they purchased. Jen was left in the dark, a faceless, unimportant, and easily replaceable employee.

There must be a way to change that, but if there was, she couldn't see it.

While she wiped the counters and scooped up the wadded paper from labels peeled off beer bottles that some customers compulsively picked into shreds, she kept one eye on Chelsea. Without having planned it, she was doing what Rick had asked. Not that she would report back to him. Did he know about Chelsea's new gig? It would be interesting to see what happened if he came in. She smiled. Keeping one eye on Chelsea made her think of the eyeballs Chelsea had drawn in her notebook. They were really very well-done. It was too bad Alex had chosen those pages to tear out.

She wiped along the edge of the bar, rubbing hard to buff the wood.

Chelsea took a sip of her drink. An involuntary spasm ran across her face. It looked like she didn't care much for martinis. If that was the case, why had she chosen a martini? It certainly fit with her image. There was something about a fitted, short black dress that went with a martini. It might be the whole Audrey Hepburn thing.

A man slipped into the space between Chelsea and the man seated to her left.

The new man was a regular, but Jen couldn't remember his usual drink.

He said something to Chelsea and she smiled, although her smile looked like she felt rather nauseous instead of alert to picking up on customer cues. He said something else and she laughed unenthusiastically. The man grinned. Clearly her lukewarm response was lost on him. He began talking more. Chelsea turned slightly to face the bar and took another sip of her drink.

The man raised his hand and Maggie made her way toward them. He ordered and Maggie began mixing a martini. She used the most expensive gin.

Was Chelsea really there to check on customer satisfaction, or was she just there to entice men into spending a bit more than originally planned? One additional drink, top shelf liquor, and then, a larger than usual tip to Maggie.

Maybe Claire had nothing at all to do with this. It could be some sort of scam cooked up by Chelsea and Maggie.

CHAPTER 47

*D*espite his enormous blind spots, Steve was an intelligent man. Getting him into a position where I had the psychological — and physical — upper hand was not going to be as easy as it had been with some men in the past. He already mistrusted me.

Using me in his vengeful power struggle with Tess was unforgivable. Deep in my subconscious mind, I'd been aware of it all along — his back and forth with the job offer, trying to keep me panting after him. His steady invites to drinks and dinner, working to get me on his side, trying to get inside my head so he could figure out how to sabotage Tess by using me as his weapon.

Even his insistence that the glass ceiling had already been shattered now felt like an attempt to manipulate me into dismissing her experience of the business world, subtly working to turn me against her. He had no idea that every woman trying to build a career knows damn good and well that the glass ceiling is thicker than ever. A few women in the upper echelons, a handful of female senators, the occasional world leader, doesn't change that fact. Their very oddity in those roles proves it.

Explaining away their underpaid status as something a woman can correct with *better* negotiation skills, therefore not a valid issue, and characterizing their complaints to HR as whiny, the very pitch of their voices labeled shrill.

The attacks continue, even louder now, more vicious as women *resist*. Not an insignificant percentage of men, and even women themselves, love telling women how they should dress, how they should think, how they should interpret their own experiences, blaming them for their own god damn rapes.

What man, ever, had his *outfit* criticized by the media? Too flamboyant, too drab. Too thin, too fat. Too sexy, too dykey. Too much makeup, she should fix herself up. Too bitchy, too meek.

In all fairness, at a technology company like CoastalCreative, it wasn't simply the glass ceiling over Tess's head, and therefore mine. CC was an engineering company, run by engineers. Neither Steve nor Tess were engineers, so maybe that's why the battle got so bloody between them. It wasn't just gender and desire, it was knowing they'd both hit a visible ceiling in their quest for more...whatever.

I didn't like being used.

I was seated in my cubicle, poking away at spreadsheets, realizing my job had shrunk to very little without Tess. I needed to get that sorted out soon, but it wasn't going to get fixed by going to work for Steve. I would deal with him first.

At ten minutes to twelve, I locked my computer screen and stood up. I stretched my arms overhead, which had the effect of pulling my white t-shirt up, exposing skin. I adjusted my skirt slightly — the same tie-dyed one Isaiah loved. I arranged it so there was a suggestion of skin between top and skirt, ready to reveal itself at any minute, even a deep breath bringing it into play. I ran my fingers through my hair. I grabbed my purse and strolled down the hallway.

The largest, nicest conference rooms in the building were on my floor and the one below. Steve would be in one of those four rooms for his Friday sales executive meeting. When they broke for lunch, my odds of seeing him were good.

I didn't even have to go downstairs. As I passed the Presidio Heights conference room, a spacious, window-lined haven with royal blue carpet, an enormous oval table, and enough chairs for thirty people to sit around it, Steve stepped out into the hallway.

His greeting was a tight grimace.

"Hi," I said. "I haven't seen you around."

"Were you looking for me?"

"Sort of."

He sighed. "What do you want?"

"We have some unfinished business," I said.

"Do we?"

"Is there an empty conference room where we can talk?"

He shrugged.

"That small one downstairs — the Sausalito Room?"

Without answering, he walked toward the elevators. We rode down in silence and he followed me to the conference room, closing the door behind us.

We sat across the table from each other. I waited for him to speak first. I had no doubt he was doing the same.

"What's up?" he said.

I smiled with a suggestion of coyness. "Well…"

"You are one fucked up woman," he said.

"Like Tess?"

"Maybe that's why you two get along so well."

"So you've said." I smiled.

"See? Why are you smiling? It's not a compliment. I wonder if you're certifiably insane."

"You know I'm not."

"You change your story every week. First, you dress like you work on Wall Street. You want a better career path, then you don't. You live in a very pricey area with some benefactor keeping you in style. Now, you dress like a… You flirt with me and then fake being sick to get out of fucking me. It's insulting."

"I didn't fake being sick."

"I'm not stupid."

"I never thought you were."

"So what's the deal?"

I lowered my head. I folded my hands on the table in front of me. "I'm nervous. I do want a more exciting job. I think I'd be good in sales…"

"Not with that look. I thought you had class."

"It's just dye."

"It proves you're mentally unbalanced."

"You know I'd be good in sales. My hair is an easy fix. And I do want to, um, have sex with you. The martinis went to my head, I didn't mean to let you see how I felt, but now that it's out there…"

He smiled, a very satisfied look.

"I'm worried it's inappropriate," I said.

He laughed. "You're the last person to worry about inappropriate."

I pouted. "That's not very nice."

He settled back. "I'm not sure anymore. I don't like crazy chicks."

"You still want me."

His cheeks flushed. He clenched his jaw, as if doing so would force the betraying rush of blood back where it belonged.

"I've realized you're the type that will run to HR," he said.

"Is that really what you think?"

"I honestly don't know. I thought I had assessed you correctly. I'm pretty good at that. But now I just think you're one step from bat-shit crazy. If not half a step."

"But you know I'm not."

"True. I've known crazy chicks. You're...different. A whole other league of mental."

He was closer to the truth than he realized. I don't define it as crazy. I'm not mentally ill, I'm not disturbed. I'm...Well, we're born how we're born. DNA dictates nearly everything, and then the world starts shaping you with its random forces — the indiscriminate assignment of parents and siblings, socioeconomic position, childhood experiences, tragedy and success.

He folded his hands and pressed his forearms against the edge of the table. It looked painful, even with his suit jacket providing some padding. "When I saw you near Barker Clayton's place, I knew you were acting out some kind of charade. I don't know what it is, and I don't care."

I pushed my chair away from the table. I wriggled forward on the seat and watched his response. He wasn't quite as done as he wanted me to believe. I could feel his eyes on my clingy t-shirt and the hint of skin near my hips.

"You act like a rich bitch. Entitled."

I smiled.

"Again, not a compliment. For all I know, you were hooked up with Clayton, sitting there staring at his building like that. Stalking him. That's what it felt like. The begging for an introduction was a game too. It felt like you didn't really belong there."

I shivered.

If there was a shred of doubt in my mind about what had to be done with him, the look on his face pushed me fully into moving forward with the inevitable outcome. His eyes glittered like a mountain lion's, eyeing his prey in the darkness.

His lips were moist with saliva, and even though I was pretty sure he didn't know what he'd stumbled upon, I couldn't risk him giving one more moment of thought to me and Barker, to why I'd been hanging around that neighborhood.

"You have me all wrong. I really want to work for you. It's just, I'm loyal to Tess, and..."

"Misplaced loyalty."

"I don't want to sabotage my chance to move ahead here."

His eyes widened. "And yet." He gestured at me, sweeping his hand in the direction of my knees to my forehead.

I nodded.

"So, what's it gonna be?"

"I'm drawn to you," I said in a soft, low voice. I crossed my legs, letting my skirt hitch up to show my leg between the top of the Doc Marten boots and the hem.

He smirked. "How can those boots be so damn ugly and so sexy?"

I smiled.

"Look. Do you want to come to my place tomorrow? I'll order in dinner, or maybe barbecue steaks."

"Steak is good."

"I knew you'd like that."

I straightened in the chair and leaned forward slightly. "And this won't jeopardize my chances? On the sales team?"

"Not at all."

What a fucking liar. I smiled. "I'll bring a bottle of wine."

"I have that covered."

"Okay. Can I bring something?"

"Just you."

I waited for several seconds, staring down at my hands in my lap. "Ever tried coke? It's quite the..."

"I think there's enough with just you and me."

"I could bring some. It's supposed to..."

"I know the effects." He stood. "Whatever. I suppose it could be enjoyable. If you think it's necessary."

"Not necessary, but it will stop me from being nervous."

He gave me a smile that was very close to benevolent. "Just bringing yourself is fine, but if you want that, I have no objections. You're right, it can be wild. And I guess you're kind of wild. When you're not so nervous."

I laughed and he joined me.

Step one.

CHAPTER 48

*H*amilton Island

* * *

Tess felt as if her skin was being ripped off as she followed the dive leader's instructions to climb out of the water. A sob heaved its way up through her chest. After two dives at different segments of the Reef, she'd seen only a fraction. Less than a fraction, a micro fraction. What were the chances she'd ever return? She couldn't spend her entire life in Queensland, renting vacation condos, taking regular trips out to the middle of the ocean.

It might be doable for a few years, but not forever. Then what? If she drained her bank account, she'd then be a nearly forty-year-old woman with a huge inexplicable gap in her résumé. Sure, some younger companies, firms started by millennials, valued people who took their own paths, who lived on the edge for a while, who invested in life experiences as much as they did in education. But did those companies want middle-aged employees? Not many of them. Not likely.

You didn't acquire an excellent college education, devote time and enormous amounts of money to grad school, work your way up to Senior Vice President of Marketing, and then walk away to spend a few years hanging out in a silent world, watching fish and imagining you were having supernatural experiences communicating with sea turtles. Did you?

Life was short. That's what everyone knew on some deep level but failed to factor into their plans.

You were only young once. *YOLO.*

She pulled off the face mask and put it beside her on the bench. Despite the magic underneath the water, it felt good to breathe without the tiny sliver of fear deep inside her brain whispering that she needed to be careful, to keep her mouth closed around the regulator, to remember to avoid breathing through her nose, to trust there was truly plenty of oxygen in the tank. To trust her own self.

Sean flopped beside her. "How was it?" He pulled one foot onto his thigh and peeled off the flipper. He switched feet and dropped the huge rubber things, so sleek and powerful in the water, but a bone-breaking threat walking around a boat cluttered with people and diving gear.

"Stunning." She didn't want to say much. It was too overwhelming, too indescribable. Talking about it might make it seem less than it was. There were no words to express how she felt, no adequate enthusiastic phrases that would allow her to communicate the experience to another human being. She longed for the unblinking eyes of the sea turtle. The turtle understood. The turtle knew her thoughts. She laughed. Maybe she'd had a shortage of oxygen after all, maybe she'd risen too fast and this was what they warned about — visual abnormalities and altered sensation and the meltdown of your mind.

"It's impossible to describe. I know," Sean said.

She turned to him and smiled.

"Should we go to the upper deck for the ride back?" he said.

She nodded, still afraid of speaking. Soon, the experience would begin to slip into the background, it would feel like something she'd imagined, something that happened a long time ago, maybe never. Tears filled her eyes. She bent down and tugged off her flippers. She sat up and pulled the elastic tie out of her hair. She re-did her ponytail, aware of how much her hair had grown since she'd left the states. Her bangs were so long she'd started styling them off to the side. It seemed symbolic, maybe a letting go…of something.

Sean followed her up the stairs to the top deck. When they were settled on the bench along the starboard side, he handed her a bottle of water. They removed the caps and each drank half of their bottle in silence.

She stared out across the water. It was easy to imagine she'd never see a land formation again. Everywhere she looked there was nothing but undulating water. She was a good swimmer, but she'd never make it to shore. The water was so deep and filled with all kinds of creatures who saw her as either food or a threat.

"There are other charters that take you to different locations," he said.

"I saw that."

"Do you think you'll be back someday?"

"I hope I can go once more while I'm here."

"And that's it? Forever?"

Why was he being so dramatic? He was acting like a salesman for the Reef, someone who got commission for articulating its value and ensuring a constant flow of visitors.

"What do you do? For a living?" she said.

He smiled. "Nothing right now. I worked for an American start-up. The company was acquired, and I got a short-term window of freedom."

"That's nice."

"You?"

"I work for a software company, based in San Francisco."

He nodded. "Are you a developer?"

She laughed. "Do I look like a developer?"

"No. Do I?"

"Yes."

He raised his water bottle in a silent toast and took a sip.

She turned and looked out across the water again. Less than a hundred feet away, the dorsal fins of seven or eight dolphins broke the surface of the water. "Dolphins," she said.

He turned.

"I hope they jump," she said.

"They might. It's more common out here than close to shore."

She kept her gaze fixed on them, taking small sips of her water. She was parched. Maybe all the canned air in her lungs, or the salt water.

"When do you have to be back at work?" he said.

"I'm taking extended time off."

"We're in the same boat." He laughed.

She giggled. Then, it wouldn't stop. She laughed harder, soon she was nearly shrieking.

"It's a high," he said.

She nodded. She removed her sun glasses, necessary to block the glare of so much water, even though it was still overcast. She wiped her eyes and after another minute or so, the hysterics subsided.

"Do you like what you do?" he said.

As if she truly was high, on speed, not pot or something that made you stupid with apathy, but a chemical that animated her mind and caused incessant talking, she began telling him everything. She talked about the awful death of her father and her self-blame, her advancement and success at

CoastalCreative, her conflicted feelings about always moving higher to ever more powerful and lucrative positions, as if there were no other choice but to keep climbing. Climb or fall.

She told him about feeling she'd missed most of her twenties and was well on her way to doing the same with her thirties. She told him about wanting a child, but not, about wanting a relationship but not wanting to settle, always afraid she was missing something in life. There was so much, so many choices. Every choice eliminated other possibilities.

How could you do it all? Travel and make money and find success? Have a satisfying social life, cultivating lifelong friends that were true friends? Develop hobbies, keep learning, spend time outdoors? Find love? Leave a mark on the world?

CHAPTER 49

 *an Francisco*

* * *

When I suggested to Steve that I bring a few lines of coke to enhance our evening activities, my voice sounded off key in my own ears, but he didn't seem overly startled by the unexpected suggestion. It's not something most people would propose for their first time together. Luckily for me, he was thinking about steak and me, already convinced I was way off balance, although not so far off that he wouldn't risk sex with me.

I wasn't sure which of his drives had the upper hand — sex or the desire to hurt Tess. Either way, watching him fool himself that she would be hurt was amusing. She was worried about me, not him.

Cocaine does have a reputation as an aphrodisiac. I think the only reason he found my suggestion off-putting, was because his ego refused to consider that I might need assistance to stimulate my interest in him. He was insulted and yet, he'd obviously experienced the effects. It hadn't been much of a leap to think that a guy who'd spent his career traveling to almost every country in the world would have a fair amount of experimentation in his past.

Cocaine reportedly brings out the animalistic side, creating a sense of invincibility. Neither of those qualities were far below the surface of his skin, and I suppose he agreed because he wanted more, always more. I absolutely understand that craving. I also want more — so much more. It's human nature, but in some people, it burns away every other desire.

Even those who say they're satisfied with their lives want just a tiny bit more. They try to hide it, they proclaim their utter happiness while taking a second glance at a newer, flashier car. Or maybe just a cuter car, a roomier car. They stop at store windows and admire the latest style of boots, the sleeker coat, the better cut diamond ring. They want more friends and more social activities. They want pay raises, even if their sights are set on two percent a year. They want the prestige of a promotion and more success for their children. It never stops.

Until you die.

I would put Steve out of his misery of wanting more.

I took my usual trip to South San Francisco to buy supplies. I stocked up on duct tape, a new pair of heavy-duty scissors, and clothesline-weight rope. I hate that rough, fibrous rope. It's too thick to tie securely, but easy to delude yourself into thinking it has superior strength. It does, if you plan to fortify a tree that's facing fifty-mile-an-hour winds. But for the tightest knots, and easy maneuverability, clothesline rope is the best.

Next into the cart was a box of black plastic trash bags, bleach, sponges, rubber gloves, and three packages of rags. I wasn't sure I needed all that stuff, but I was facing the most challenging murder I'd ever committed and the extra supplies made me certain I wouldn't be caught unprepared. By anything.

Making my way through the stores that had supplied what I needed in the past, I bought two candles and small cheap plates to hold them, steel handcuffs, two red silk scarves, and lingerie — a one-piece thong and bustier. Steve had seen my red patent leather high heels when he informed me the glass ceiling had already been shattered. It would be a nice walk down memory lane for him.

My plan for Steve was a show that would so occupy him with surprises that he wouldn't ask questions. I planned to walk all over his intelligence and psychological insight skills, numbing his brain. We would see who was the best sales person in the room.

I bought a syringe for dispensing liquid medicine, a disposable cell phone, a black wig with decent-looking synthetic hair that hung to the middle of my back, and a pair of cheap running shoes.

It was three-thirty by the time I got back to Tess's place. I was due at Steve's condo at six, so I had enough time, but still a lot to do.

I showered and spent forty-five minutes putting on makeup. I wore the lingerie under a pair of black leggings and a black cotton turtleneck shirt. I pulled my hair up tightly and secured it under the wig. I put on the running shoes.

All the supplies and my red high heels went into an over-sized purse. I couldn't be seen with a duffel bag. The purse was bulging, so I had to take the garbage bags out of the box. I decided I only needed three, not the entire box. I probably wouldn't need any. I hoped I wouldn't. Also inside the large bag was one of my regular purses. A very small one. Secured inside a ziplock bag inside a makeup pouch was the packet of heroin I'd found at The Chimera.

The only problem I hadn't solved was the inevitable security guard in the lobby of Steve's building. Steve would have to provide my name to the guard on duty so I could check in before I was allowed to enter the building.

I settled on the love seat in the sun room with a glass of water.

As if the tranquil atmosphere of the room had molded my mind in a different direction, the solution came to me after three sips of water. I finished the water, took off the leggings and running shoes and stuffed them into the bulging bag. I put on a knee-length black wool coat over the lingerie, smoothed the wig hair over my shoulders, and slipped my feet into the red high heels.

I activated the phone and sent a message to Steve.

415-555-6127: *Hey. Looking forward to tonight.*

Steve: *Who is this?*

415-555-6127: *Are you expecting someone else?*

I added a semi-colon and the right sided parenthesis.

Steve: *Ha ha.*

415-555-6127: *Are you up for a bit of fantasy?*

Steve: *What is with you? Why all the props?*

415-555-6127: *Where's your sense of adventure?*

Steve: *Buried under all your games.*

415-555-6127: *Well dig it out. Let's meet at a bar near your house.*

Steve: *The steaks.*

415-555-6127: *You shouldn't start them before I get there anyway. They'll be overdone.*

Steve: *Ok. Torrey's. On Union, two blocks west of Gough. This better be good.*

I sent a punctuation smiley face. Now I had him. He would escort me into his building, no name required.

Step two.

CHAPTER 50

*R*ick was already sitting in his usual spot at the end of the bar when Jen arrived for work. There was no way to slip behind the bar without walking right past him. She had no interest in talking to him. He was going to ask about Chelsea, and she couldn't understand why he wanted to put her in such an impossible position. He knew she was the lowest one on the totem pole. He knew Chelsea had power over her, that Jen was the one being watched.

He'd been deliberately vague about what he wanted her to keep an eye out for anyway. What was she supposed to tell him? Chelsea is moody? She dyed her hair so she could pretend to be a customer? She doesn't write in her bullet journal any more? It seems as though she's lost her motivation, despite all the colorful pages and charts keeping her on track?

She couldn't even be sure that Rick and Chelsea were still a couple. Rick stared at Chelsea as if he couldn't look at anything else, as if he wanted to leap over the bar and grab her. Was it the kind of grabbing where he wanted to slap her, or the kind where he wanted to carry her away to something magical, believing himself to be her knight in shining armor?

It wasn't as if being a bartender was all that glamorous. It looked fun, mixing drinks, socializing. But it was hard work, and messy. And you were forced to be friendly with people you didn't like, smiling at men who were rude and aggressive and horny, saying *thank you* to women who treated you like scum.

"Hi, Jen."

She smiled and kept walking.

"What's the rush?" he said.

"I need to get to work."

"You have time to talk to a good customer."

"I guess." She paused.

"Any news for me?"

"Not really."

"Are you sure?"

She turned to face him fully. "I don't know what I'm supposed to be watching for. Besides, I feel uncomfortable gossiping about her."

"Since when does a girl feel uncomfortable gossiping? In my experience, women can't even stop from talking about their besties behind their backs."

"Not me."

"Yeah, right."

"She's sort of my boss."

"But isn't it good to have a cop in your corner? That can never hurt, right?" He smiled.

She glanced at the other end of the bar. Maggie and Chelsea were both mixing drinks, talking to customers. Maggie laughed and patted a guy's hand.

"I should get busy," Jen said.

"Here's something to keep you busy." He pushed his almost empty beer bottle toward her. "I'll have another beer."

"Okay." She backed away from him, turned and walked to the beer cooler. She pulled out a Sierra Nevada, removed the cap, and took a glass from the shelf. She carried them to where Rick sat, pulled out two napkins, and settled the bottle on one, the glass on the other.

"Thanks." He put a twenty on the bar. She picked it up and turned to go.

"That's yours. No change necessary."

"It's kind of a lot."

"Not really."

She smiled. "Okay. Thanks. But it still has to get rung up. I'll give it to…"

"Maggie. Give it to Maggie, okay?"

"Sure."

"So nothing out of order is going on here?" he said.

"I honestly don't know what you mean."

"Look, can I trust you?"

"I think so."

"You think so?" He laughed. "That doesn't build confidence."

"Yes, you can. As long as it doesn't have to do with getting in trouble with Chelsea."

"Never." He leaned forward. She moved closer. "Do you ever see drug deals going down here?"

"No."

"Do you know what to look for?"

She knew quite a lot, but she couldn't tell him that. She smiled. She brushed her bangs away from her forehead, hoping she looked a little bit surprised and inexperienced. "No. I don't think so."

"So how can you say you've never seen anything?"

"Do people sell drugs in nice bars?" She knew damn well they did, but he seemed to believe she knew nothing about the subject, so she might as well keep it going.

"Anyone come in here more often than normal?"

"We have quite a few people who come in every single day."

"Do they stay a long time and not drink much? Or the opposite — pop in and not order a drink at all?"

She shook her head. "Not that I've noticed. But I'm usually pretty busy."

He took a sip of his beer.

"Do you think that's happening here?" she said.

"I know it is. You can't tell Dan I told you this."

"Why would I?"

"Just covering my bases."

She glanced toward the end of the bar. Chelsea and Maggie were busy with drinks. The place was filling up. "I should…"

"Can I tell you a secret?" he said.

"I don't know if…"

"I think I can trust you. There's something sweet and very honest about you."

She smiled. "Thank you."

"I'm trying to get a win here. I'm not really a detective. Sorry if I gave that impression. I'm a street cop."

"Okay."

"If I could get a line on something big…Dan's looking for the same, and I'd like to beat him to it."

She laughed. "Really? Is it a contest?"

"In a way, yes. So can you help me?"

"Is that what the big tip is for?"

"The tip is because you're nice. And you work hard. They should make you a bartender, not have you wiping counters all night."

"I hope so. I really, really need to get busy."

"Sure. But now that you know what I'm looking for, you'll keep your eyes open? And on Chelsea?"

"For drugs? I don't think she's into that. Not at all."

"No, I don't think so. It's just…she's acting strange."

"Do you think she's cheating on you or something?"

"Maybe. She's just…well, I already told you."

She folded the twenty. "I'll bring you the receipt."

"Good talking to you," he said.

She smiled. She hurried to the end of the bar. When Maggie finished mixing a Cosmo, Jen handed the twenty to her. "For Rick's Sierra Nevada."

"Thanks." Maggie entered it in the cash register and handed the change and the receipt to Jen.

Jen shoved the ten and a single into her pocket.

Chelsea turned suddenly. "What are you doing?" She moved closer. "Are you pocketing the change? What the fuck?"

Jen swallowed. "He…" She glanced at Rick. He was watching. How had this happened? He'd asked her to avoid giving the money to Chelsea and now she'd created something worse. She should have acted as if she was returning the change to him. "I'm not! It's just easier. Since I have to grab the rag, it's easier to carry his change in my pocket."

Chelsea glowered at her. "I'm not sure I believe you."

Shit. Shit, shit, shit. The lie screwed it up more. She should have explained the large tip. Even if Chelsea was pissed, it was better than having her go to Rick and find out she'd lied.

"You look like a deer in the headlights," Chelsea said.

"I don't know why you don't believe me."

"Let it go," Maggie said. "Big deal. Why are you so tightly wound?"

"I'm not," Chelsea said.

Jen turned and walked to the end of the bar. She pulled the bills out of her pocket. "I can't take this. She thinks I was stealing it, and I…you have to take it back." She placed the bills near his glass.

Rick shrugged. "Just keep your eyes open." He took a sip of beer. "You know what would be a home run?"

She tried to swallow, but it seemed like an impossible task. "What?"

"If you could get your hands on her notebook, so I can take a peek." He raised his bottle toward her and took a long swallow, then turned away to study the crowd behind him.

She took a clean cloth off the shelf. Working was tiring enough, with all of these delicate steps she had to take around Rick and Chelsea and Claire. She was exhausted. And now this. She wanted to go home and sleep for a week.

CHAPTER 51

 ortland

* * *

Even as a pre-teen, I was very resourceful.

I wasn't allowed to leave the house on my own. Walking to the next block to visit a classmate required the supervision of one of my brothers. When I wanted to go for a bike ride, one or sometimes all three brothers accompanied me. My mother drove all of us to school and picked us up until we were in high school. And then, I was only allowed to walk home with at least one other girl, and my mother called her mother to confirm that was happening. Every day.

There are still ways to escape adult scrutiny. They think they can read your mind. I don't understand why so many adults never consider that children's minds are filled with as many independent thoughts as their own heads, thoughts that adults know nothing about and didn't provide source material for.

It seems counter-intuitive that in high school, when I

could really get into trouble, the chains were loosened somewhat. Maybe they got tired of fighting. Maybe they became complacent. Or maybe my father left me in my mother's less fanatical hands, unsure what to do with a woman who was his own flesh and blood but didn't have a shred of himself in her personality. Or so he thought.

I couldn't figure out a way to run my errand without being caught. And I needed to keep the transaction to myself. Hiding my purchase afterwards would be hard enough.

The dream of those monstrous jaws had remained vivid in my mind for several days. The faces of the beasts were pointed and lightly covered with fur. Their noses were wriggling points of pink flesh, and their teeth were white razors.

They lacked the soft furry tails that make other rodents seem adorable to us. Those fleshy, naked, serpentine tails gave them away. It wasn't that my subconscious delivered up this image on its own. There were plenty of rats that occasionally scampered through the wooded green belt behind our house. Roof rats sometimes ran along the edges of gutters and leapt from one house to another at dusk. Because most people were focused on the bats that were prevalent in our outer suburban neighborhood, they ignored the rats. If rats got into your roof, an exterminator was called. But the rats always returned.

I enlisted the help of a girl in my math class. She was the smartest in my section, in all her subjects, really. She was friendly but in a very reserved way, as if she didn't see the need for friendship. Another sign that she thought things through. She didn't have a lot of friends and no best friend, just people she ate lunch with. Other smart people. It was easy to get her interested in my project. Tasks interested her more than people did.

Once I explained that I wanted to surprise my parents with an entry into the science fair, she agreed to take the thirty-five dollars I'd saved up and buy a small cage, some food, a water bottle, and a black rat. Not the enormous roof rat kind, something small, about the size of a hamster. I asked her to keep it at her house until I was ready.

Three days later, I told her to leave it on her back porch so I could pick it up that night. She didn't question this odd exchange. She was too overcome with pleasure that she was helping me become more interested in science.

At two o'clock that morning, when I was sure my parents had been asleep for a good three hours, I snuck out the back door, darted down the slope of our yard, and into the protection of the greenbelt. I crossed two houses over into her yard and retrieved the cage from her back porch.

The most exposed part of my trip was crossing the yard for the return home. I couldn't run holding a wire cage. I stayed near the edge of the yard and when I reached the house, I left the cage beside the back steps. I did a slow, silent walk through the house to make sure everyone was still asleep — no bathroom doors closed, no pre-dawn trips for a sip of water.

I went back outside and carried the cage up to my room.

My mother had made it a habit to dig through my room from time to time, looking for who knows what. Possibly she was already worried already about pot or condoms. Since she'd done her periodic snooping about a week earlier, the rat would be safe and undetected for at least two weeks.

The next part of my plan, to scare the piss out of Jake, was more difficult.

On Saturday morning, I scooped water out of the toilet tank and lowered the weight so it would deem itself full with only a gallon. I flushed until there were only a few cups bubbling up from the very bottom of the bowl. I wadded up some paper towels and pushed them into the hole, hoping no one flushed without opening the lid. Clogging the pipes would likely get me into more trouble than the rat.

I put the rat in the toilet. She settled uneasily onto the wet paper towels, using them to keep herself from sliding around the slick porcelain. She didn't look happy, but she wasn't frantic. I closed the lid, assured that she had plenty of air coming through the gaps between the bowl and the toilet seat.

Because my brothers knew it was cleaning day, Jake was guaranteed to appear in the upstairs bathroom within the next hour. I climbed into the bathtub and pulled the curtain into place.

CHAPTER 52

*S*an Francisco

* * *

While Steve was texting me the name of the bar near his place, I was already closing the front door of Tess's condo. The bird was shouting after me — *Dangerous Woman! Dangerous Woman!*

I smiled and called out that I'd see him again soon.

Confident that Steve's desire and curiosity would win, I'd already ordered an Uber. The car was waiting when I got to the lobby.

Inside the bar, I settled myself on a stool near the door. My coat was still buttoned. I ordered a martini and faced the entrance.

He arrived about five minutes later. I was holding the martini, inhaling the aroma but resisting the urge to take a sip. I watched as he scanned the people sitting at the bar and then surveyed the rest of the room. He took another step and turned his attention to the bar again. I'm sure he thought he'd pick me out instantly based on my horrific blonde hair with its unsightly roots.

I kept my gaze on him. Soon, he would feel the intensity. You always do, when someone is staring at you. It's their lack of movement. It's the vibe they give off that they aren't behaving with the normal shifts in posture and adjustments to facial expressions, which makes them stand out in a crowd.

He glanced at me. I lifted the glass a fraction of an inch and smiled.

He scrunched up his face in a half scowl. Then, he relaxed and laughed. He walked toward me.

"Hi," I said.

"What's with…"

"You look lonely. Can I buy you a drink?"

He laughed.

The guy had no imagination whatsoever. How did he enchant customers if he didn't possess at least a thin streak of playfulness? Of course, maybe I'd pushed him too far, making the game more tiring than he was used to. It might be that I'd squashed his playfulness.

"I'll take that as a *yes*," I said. "You look like a scotch drinker."

"Well done." He swallowed and seemed to find some resources to hit the re-set button. "Your hair is remarkable."

I smiled.

"Aren't you a little warm in that coat?"

At least he figured that part out — the oldest fantasy in the book.

"I get cold easily." I shivered. "I need someone to warm me up."

"Not a problem." He settled in on the stool beside me.

I ordered a scotch for him. I turned to face him and picked up my stir stick. I closed my teeth around one of the olives and slowly drew it off the plastic stick. I rolled it around in my mouth and then chewed it, keeping my eyes on his face.

He laughed.

The scotch came and he took a sip. "You're quite a drinker."

"It's society's lubricant," I said. Why did he have to make this so difficult? Maybe it felt more difficult because I was tense, plans racing through my mind, reminding myself to take each step carefully, and in the correct order.

We focused on our drinks for several minutes.

He leaned toward me and touched my hair tentatively, moving it off my left shoulder. "You look very exotic."

"Thank you."

He inserted his finger into the neck of his black t-shirt. "It's stuffy in here. You're sure you're not too warm?"

I put my drink on the bar and unbuttoned the top two buttons of my coat.

He stared at the narrow V formed by the soft wool fabric. "There's sweat on your skin," he said.

"Really? I don't feel it."

"It's there." He smiled, and finally, I had the sense he was being drawn in.

I unbuttoned the third button and moved the side of the coat enough to show some red lace and the tops of my breasts.

"Why are we still here?" He picked up his drink and swallowed the rest in one gulp.

"It is getting noisy. And crowded."

"Let's go," he said.

"Sure." I drew the last two olives off the stick and left the rest of the martini in the glass. I needed a clear head and I would be required to drink some wine with dinner.

We walked out and I buttoned my coat.

As he took my arm, he glanced down at my shoes. "I remember those."

"Of course you do."

We walked the two blocks to his condo. We entered and crossed the lobby. He nodded at the security guard but said nothing. We rode the elevator up and he unlocked his front door.

In some ways, the interior was as much of a cliché as he was. The living room was stark, but not in the white, sunlit way of Tess's. The dark hardwood floor was covered with a black and forest-green carpet. The furniture was black leather and the occasional tables and lamps were all glass and aluminum and straight, sharp lines.

He had a nice view of the city lights, and when I stood close to the picture window, a portion of the Golden Gate Bridge was visible.

"Can I take your coat?"

"Won't you be barbecuing the steaks outside?"

"It only takes a few minutes. You can relax in here." He grinned.

I placed my oversized bag behind an armchair and slowly unfastened the buttons. He took a few steps closer, holding out his hand for the coat.

I slid it off my shoulders and then removed it completely. I glanced down at his fly. He definitely liked the outfit.

"You hid quite a lot under those flower child clothes," he said. It was supposed to be a compliment, but I guess he always needed to express his disapproval at the same time.

I gave him a limp smile.

He poured two glasses of wine. As I'd expected, it was a delicious, obviously expensive Cab. Resisting the urge to match him glass for glass was going to be difficult, and disappointing. Maybe I'd cork the bottle and take it with me.

I settled on the couch with my glass of wine.

"I'm putting the steaks on." He leaned over me and ran his finger up my breastbone to my throat.

I shivered appropriately, and not in a completely phony way.

"We're having baked potatoes with our steak. I picked up some chocolate-frosted brownies. But maybe we won't need any dessert." He disappeared into the kitchen and a moment later the balcony door opened and closed.

I sipped my wine and put the glass on the table. The timing of all this was going to be far trickier than barbecuing steaks.

The ribeye was perfect. Dark brown on the outside, a nice crispness to the thin strip of fat that ran along one edge. The inside was a luscious shade of red — moist and tender. I decided to view it as an omen that my timing would also be ideal.

While we devoured steak and potatoes filled with butter and sour cream, he talked about work. He didn't mention my job change, which was just as well. I was tired of keeping up that charade along with everything else.

He offered dessert, but I declined. We stood and he led me toward his bedroom. It was furnished with a simple mahogany dresser and two bedside tables, all of which matched the most enormous bed I'd ever seen. It had a huge thick headboard and footboard and reminded me of something that might be at home in a medieval castle.

"Let me get the coke," I said.

"Is that really necessary?"

"It's not necessary, but it's fun. I like it." I smiled.

"Well, then. Whatever the lady likes."

"Why don't you bring the wine," I said.

He went into the dining room to open a second bottle and collect our glasses.

I set out the two squat candles on the dresser, lit them, and turned out the overhead light. I opened the makeup bag as he returned with the wine.

He poured two half glasses and stripped off his clothes. Very seductive of him.

I placed a small mirror on the dresser, took out a straight-edged razor blade, chopped the heroin, and spread out two lines. "Do you mind getting me a glass of water?"

He groaned. "You know how to drag things out, I'll give you that."

"Thanks."

After he left the room, I made a little pile of baking soda flecked with cinnamon, leaving quite a bit of space between it and the lines of heroin. This was the riskiest part. It looked similar enough, if you didn't look too closely. I wasn't sure whether he'd agree to inhaling his own lines first. I hoped my cooking ingredients didn't make me sneeze, or that he didn't taste my pile, or even try to take more than his fair share. There were so many variables.

He returned and put the glass of water on the dresser. He came to my side. He slid the red satin straps off my shoulders and lowered his head to suck on my breast. I was more disgusted than I'd expected. I put my hand on the back of his head for a moment and took a slow, deep breath. "Let's take it nice and easy."

He sighed.

I rolled up a one-hundred-dollar bill, a touch I thought he'd appreciate.

He smiled and took it. He leaned over the mirror and paused. He lifted his head and squinted slightly. "It looks brown."

I looked at my feet. I giggled awkwardly and glanced up at him. "It's partly the candlelight...but I hoped you wouldn't notice."

"What?" The rolled bill was still inserted in his nostril.

I giggled. "I feel like such an idiot. I dropped it. I'm lucky it didn't all blow away. I got some dirt in it, but it's fine."

"If you say so."

It was too late, he wanted it. He was hoping the coke would puncture my aloof attitude, rip away my hesitation and delay. He leaned forward and snorted one line then the other without pausing. He ran his finger over the residue and rubbed it on his upper gum.

I spread out my placebo lines as thinly as I could make them and carefully inhaled the first. He went to the bed and flung himself onto the mattress. "Here we go." He sounded like he was crowing.

"Here we go, indeed!" I remained by the dresser, watching. Expectant.

Step three.

CHAPTER 53

*J*en didn't like it that Rick remained at the end of the bar, full-on staring at her and Chelsea and Maggie. It seemed as if there was something specific he was watching for, but she couldn't figure out what it was. Surely he didn't think Chelsea or Maggie was selling drugs. Did he? And why did he want Chelsea's notebook? It had been almost impossible trying to return it without being found out. Jen couldn't imagine how she would sneak it out of Chelsea's zippered designer bag while Chelsea was right there.

She would be risking everything. But he was a cop, she couldn't just tell him to fuck off.

There was a tension in all their movements. Even Maggie wasn't as mellow as usual. There was a hard line to her lips and a stiffness in her shoulders that made her back look like it was made of molded plastic.

At ten minutes to eight, Chelsea wiped her hands on a towel. She tapped Maggie's shoulder and said something. She walked to the end of the bar. Without stopping to talk to Rick, or even glancing at him, she slipped out and disappeared down the hallway.

Maggie went to the register. She picked up a scrap of paper and scribbled on it. She walked toward Jen, holding out the slip of paper. "This is such bullshit."

"What's wrong?"

Maggie handed her the slip of paper. "This is Chelsea's register code. Can you at least ring up cash purchases? I can't do all this myself." She waved her hand toward the crowded room. "Cash is easy, just enter the code before each transaction. Punch in the amount they gave you and hit this button, then the cost of the drink, then total. Easy."

"Where did she go?"

"To change into her little black dress. She's going to sit at the bar again."

Jen glanced at Rick. He wasn't looking in their direction. "Why?"

"Claire wants her to do it. But on a Saturday night when we're mobbed? It's nuts. And it's not fair. I can't keep up and people get pissed and I'm the one losing tips."

So Chelsea had been telling the truth, maybe. She and Maggie certainly weren't working together on some sort of deal to get bigger tips. "I don't see the point," Jen said.

"Neither do I. But Claire gets weird ideas. And if she thinks it's important, then everything has to work around it."

"I wonder why she didn't ask one of the others to come in."

"I think it was a last-minute thing."

"She could still call and see if someone can make it."

Maggie shrugged her shoulders, moving them in the way that made Jen think of a jazz dancer. "I don't care if we get in trouble. Just ring up the cash sales, okay?"

"Sure." Jen glanced at the spot under the counter where Chelsea stored her purse. It was still there. "Doesn't she need her purse?"

"Why? She doesn't pay for drinks. She keeps her dress and makeup in her locker."

Jen could imagine customers lining up to use the restroom, waiting while Chelsea put on a dress, re-did her makeup, and combed her hair into that floppy retro bun.

A few minutes later, Chelsea was seated near the front of the bar, turned at an angle on the stool, her legs crossed, signaling to Maggie for a martini.

Jen walked along the length of the bar, checking the status of everyone drinking beer or wine. They all looked fine for now. She wiped up moisture from a gin and tonic and scooped up several dropped straws.

When she drew close to the end of the bar, she felt Rick's gaze like a blow torch on the side of her neck. She looked up. He gestured for her to come over. "What's Chelsea up to?"

"The owner wants her to test the customer experience or something. It's stupid, because the customer experience is going downhill fast with only one bartender."

"A perfect time for you to grab her notebook."

"I can't. Not with all these people. Not with her sitting right there."

"Sure you can."

Jen shook her head. "No."

"She's not even looking. I know you can do it."

"If she catches me, I'll get fired."

"If you do this for me, I'll have your back. Always."

"Why do I need you to have my back? I need a job."

"And I could help you get one, so don't worry. I know a lot of people. And you're not gonna get caught."

"You seem pretty sure about it."

"Her head is somewhere else. Come on. This is perfect. Maggie is running her ass off, she won't notice."

"And I should be too."

"While you are, stop by her purse, grab the book and…"

"I can't walk all this way carrying it."

He nodded at the counter behind her. "Get that tray. Hold it underneath."

"You sure thought all of this out."

"I need to see it."

"Why?"

"I just do."

"It's an invasion of her privacy."

He rolled his eyes. "She shows her workout schedule and lists of movies to everyone. It's no big deal."

"Why do you want to see it then? If there's nothing important?"

"Just do it. I'm tired of talking about it and you're going to lose your chance."

"Tell me why, and maybe I will." She glanced down the length of the bar. No one seemed to be looking for a beer, but she couldn't be standing here talking.

"*Maybe*? Aren't you ballsy." He leaned forward and lowered his voice. "She was taking some notes for me. Okay?" He sat up. "And now she's gotten all protective of it. But they belong to me."

Jen didn't remember any notes, but she hadn't looked at every single page, she'd gotten too caught up in the flattery log. She didn't see how something in Chelsea's notebook could belong to him at all, but she wasn't going to keep arguing with a cop. She didn't need to wind up on his bad side. There was no choice. And he was probably right, no one would notice. Chelsea was in her imaginary world, watching customers and shivering her way through a martini. Maggie hardly had time to breathe.

She walked back, refilled three wine glasses, served five beers to three men and two women, and took two twenties from another guy. She entered his bill into the cash register and took out the change. Her chest felt full and warm. Surely

Maggie would tell Claire what a great job she was doing, how helpful she was.

She moved toward the shelf where the purse was. She bent over and with a flick of her hand, unzipped it. She straightened and glanced around. No one was looking at her. She took a few steps to her left, picked up a small tray and turned back. She bent down, plunged her fingers into the purse and pushed the two sides apart. She grabbed the notebook and slid it beneath the tray. She walked quickly to where Rick was seated.

She put the tray and notebook on the bar and walked away without looking back.

As soon as Chelsea finished her performance with the martini, she would discover the missing notebook. Rick damn well better help if Chelsea got her fired. It wasn't her experience that cops were helpful. It was all about you helping them and giving them respect. But as Isaiah had insisted, her views of men were distorted. Maybe cops only seemed that way when you were doing something illegal.

CHAPTER 54

$\mathcal{H}$amilton Island

* * *

Tess was surprised at how she felt after pouring out so many intimate details of her life to Sean. Some of the things she'd told him, she'd never mentioned to another living being, except Damien.

She was a private person. What had caused this unexpected flood, and why wasn't she immediately regretting it? Was it the endless water surrounding them? Feeling as if the rest of the human race didn't exist? Would her feelings change once the islands came into view, her shame deepening as they stepped off the boat onto the pier?

"Thanks for listening," she said. She meant it. She felt light and pleasantly empty. The vacant feeling didn't bother her at all. Was this what death felt like? Releasing everything and knowing you could no longer control what was said or thought about you? As if that were ever possible to begin with.

"You're a talented woman," Sean said.

She shrugged. "I was privileged. I had a good education. It gives you a leg up."

"It does."

"What's your story?" she said.

He stood. "Let me go get some water. And I think there are a few bags of crisps left. I'm famished." He walked away without waiting for an answer.

When he returned, he had a paper bag containing four bottles of water, two bags of plain potato chips, and a bag of Cheetos. He handed a water bottle to her.

"Thanks."

"My story isn't as interesting as yours."

"I don't believe that," she said.

"I do want to run something by you, though."

"What's that?"

"Hearing about your life, at a crossroads, so to speak… your uncertainty about taking the right fork in the road… Anyway, I have an app I'm working on. I'm pretty excited about it, and…"

She laughed. She hadn't meant to. Everyone had an app. How many people actually made money with their apps? But she felt open and relaxed. What did it matter? She shouldn't be so dismissive. He'd already gone through a complete life-cycle with one successful company, maybe he wasn't like every developer, thinking their app would tip the world on its side. "Are you pitching me?" She smiled kindly, trying to erase the laugh.

"Not at all. I want your thoughts, as a person facing some life decisions."

"Market research," she said.

He grinned. "Don't categorize everything."

"Okay. Tell me."

"You know there are apps to track physiology — your

heart rate and respiration. This is a blend of bio feedback tools and the technology that measures your body functions."

"Okay." She drank some water and put the bottle beside her. She tore open one of the bags of potato chips.

"There are lots of apps to help you make decisions, but they're all basically decision trees, or other types of analytical tools. My app measures your breathing and heart rate as you answer questions about your choices and the things you're trying to get clear about. It would basically give you insight into what your body is telling you about your deepest desires."

"Listening to your gut?"

"Exactly."

"That's interesting."

"Just interesting?"

"Are there any similar apps on the market?"

"Not that we've been able to uncover."

So. There was a *we*. He had a team working on this, perhaps a small company already in the works.

"We don't always know our own minds. Like you described."

"I'm not sure I'd be willing to allow an app to decide whether I should quit my job." She slid a chip out of the bag and put it in her mouth. The comfort of salt and fat flooded her mouth. She chewed slowly. Why was the crunch of fried chips so satisfying? The crunch was part of their addictive quality.

"It would provide you insight though. Help you figure out your next steps, help you get clear on what you really wanted, things you might be lying to yourself about."

"I don't lie to myself."

"I didn't mean you specifically. And I think lying wasn't the right word. Letting other authoritative voices and societal pressures obscure your own instincts."

"Are you suggesting people aren't intelligent enough to

make decisions? That we're really only listening to other people?" A small part of her thought it could be revolutionary to have a tool that told her what her instinct was really saying. Another, much larger part of her, was hugely insulted. He hadn't said it, but was he suggesting that women couldn't make up their minds? That this app would haul in millions of dollars from tens or hundreds of millions of women paying $2.99 to get help making a decision? Not to mention the revenue from the companion device required to read your heart rate and other physiological responses.

"I thought you'd be more intrigued," he said.

"I am intrigued."

"But you seem hesitant."

"And you picked up on that without the use of an app."

He laughed. "If you think it's ridiculous, just say so."

"I'm conflicted," she said.

"About what?"

She opened her water and took a sip. Despite the ease with which she'd revealed all her flaws and missteps along with her successes, she now felt exposed. She didn't want to tell him she was insulted, that he seemed to be implying she would be interested in the idea, would praise the concept and see its money-making potential because she was female and indecisive and couldn't even see her way to knowing whether or not she wanted a child.

Or was she projecting all of that? Maybe she was too hard on herself for being indecisive about such important things. They were huge decisions. Anyone would be hesitant. In her working life, she'd never had trouble making decisions. She looked at data, weighed pros and cons and assessed risk and the decisions, most of the time, felt easy after that. But the thing troubling her now was she didn't recall choosing her career at all. Looking back, she had the impression she'd been on automatic pilot.

After setting your course in one direction when you were fifteen years old, to now question all of that...well it was deeply unsettling. And it was simplistic to think an app could ease that horrifying sense that she'd misdirected her life, or was in danger of misdirecting it going forward.

CHAPTER 55

 ortland

* * *

As I sat hidden behind the luxurious green and blue fabric shower curtain and its water-repellent liner, I took slow deep breaths. I had to make sure I stayed calm when Jake had his predictable reaction to the rat. The impact would be lost if I laughed or scrambled to help the rat, or did anything to reveal my presence.

He would figure out I'd planted it, but not in the midst of his first moments of panic. Once he escaped, he would realize it hadn't found its way into the toilet bowl all by itself. But I didn't want him catching me in the act. I didn't want him to know I'd been watching him pee and decorate the floor. I didn't want his terror to subside sooner than necessary.

Sitting on porcelain makes your bones ache, but it was worth the reward coming my way. I settled into a cross-legged position, determined to stay that way until he arrived. If I shifted again and he suddenly appeared, he would hear me wiggling around, my shoulder touching the curtain liner with its telltale rustle. Even though the pressure on my ankle bones was intense, I remained still.

It was almost twenty-five minutes before I heard footsteps, followed by the bathroom door closing and the lock turning. The door was as old as the house — it wasn't the kind that automatically unlocked when the knob was turned. If he panicked, *when* he panicked, I hoped he wouldn't lose his presence of mind and start rattling the knob, so scared he forgot he'd locked it. If all he got was a fright, it would stay between my brothers and me, but if he hurt himself, or the door, my father would get dragged into the situation. Although I'd still experience a small victory, I'd have to face punishment of my own.

The toilet lid and seat banged as he flipped them up.

The rat didn't make a sound that I could hear.

Jake screamed, his voice high-pitched, and ear-piercing. The seat and lid slammed closed. I heard the sound of him zipping his fly, groaning from the pressure of the urine that was rebelling at being held inside his bladder when he'd thought he was moments from relief.

He rattled the door and fumbled with the lock, still whimpering. The lock clicked and the door swung open.

I heard him lunge down the hallway and stop. He pounded on my bedroom door. He shouted my name several times, then pounded repeatedly as if he were hammering Martin Luther's ninety-five theses into the wood. Finally he stopped and a moment later I heard his feet thudding down the stairs.

I climbed out of the tub and closed and locked the bathroom door.

I opened the toilet lid and scooped out the rat. She glared at me, angry at being shut up in such an inhospitable place. I lifted her close to my face, stroking the top of her head with my finger. "Sitting in the tub was almost as bad," I whispered.

She continued wiggling her nose at me, trembling slightly. My bellowing brother and the slamming of plastic on porcelain had terrified her as much as she'd frightened him. I stroked her head for a few more minutes and she seemed to calm down.

I put her in the bathtub, scooped the paper towels out of the toilet, and dropped the soggy mess in the trash. I took a bucket I'd left under the sink and re-filled the tank. I cleaned and flushed the toilet and washed my hands with hot water and anti-bacterial soap.

Holding the rat close to my chest, I opened the door and peered into the hallway. It was empty. I hurried to my room and put her in the cage, pushing it back inside my closet. "I'll find a better home for you soon, I promise." She went straight for her food dish, ignoring me completely. I didn't blame her.

When I went to the downstairs bathroom, the toilet and surrounding area were sparkling clean, as I'd left them. Either Jake had learned his lesson, or been so scared that he forgot about tormenting me.

The next few days were tense. I felt my brothers constantly looking at me. I had no doubt he'd told them what happened. I knew he knew it was me, and I felt all three of them going out of their way to avoid passing me in the hallway or sitting anywhere near me in the living room after dinner.

I figuratively held my breath. I wasn't sure whether to expect payback in the form of my own fright show, or ratting me out, so to speak, and the resulting punishment from my father. I didn't want his punishment to fall onto the rat's shoulders. I was getting used to having her around. I loved watching her scurry around my bedroom floor checking out all the smells, enjoying the challenge of climbing my comforter or experiencing the thrill of leaping from my bed to my desk.

THE WOMAN IN THE BAR

She couldn't stay in my room forever, especially buried in the closet. She needed sunlight. And she needed a better quality of life, a chance to run around outdoors.

The response from Jake came in the form of a note under my pillow.

You could have scarred me for life, or given me bubonic plague with your dumb trick. There's something wrong with you.

I wasn't sure what I thought about his words. I'd wanted power over him, all of them. Instead, I think he was afraid of me. I couldn't decide whether fear was the same as power. I suppose it's the ultimate form of power. Maybe fear automatically gives you power, but it wasn't quite what I'd expected.

Hanging out with my brothers was fun. I didn't want them to be terrified of me.

Maybe I hadn't taken control after all. None of them were speaking to me.

CHAPTER 56

 an Francisco

* * *

Steve's eyes were closed. I approached the bed.

"Hey," I said softly.

His eyelids remained motionless. His voice was soft and lazy. "I'm not feeling the rush."

"You will."

I slipped off the high heels and walked quickly and quietly into the living room and dug the scarves and handcuffs out of my bag. I picked up Steve's smart phone. When I returned, he was in the same position, eyes still closed.

I moved close to the side of the enormous bed. "I forgot my phone and I need to check that something was uploaded to the product documentation page for the four-dot-three product update. Can I check yours? It'll only take a second." I sat on the side of the bed and tucked the scarves and handcuffs underneath.

He opened his eyes partially, exposing only narrow slits so I couldn't tell if he was actually looking at me. "Are you kidding? You're thinking about work right now?" He gave me a lethargic smile.

"I really need to take care of it. Only a second. I promise."

"Are you feeling the rush?" he said.

"A little. After I check your phone, I think I'll have another line." I smiled and cocked my hip slightly, promising I wasn't deliberately delaying.

He sighed. He pushed himself up to a sitting position and took the phone from my hand. He pressed his thumb on the home button, handed it to me, and slid back down until his head was on the pillow.

I turned slightly and tapped quickly to his settings. I opened the display controls and set the automatic screen lock to *never*. I checked to make sure it was on vibrate and placed the phone face down on the carpet where any sound from an incoming call would be muffled. I spread out another very delicate, barely visible line of baking powder and cinnamon. I inhaled it and turned to face the bed. "Wow." I sniffed hard. "Woo!"

"Really? Did you get a rush?" His eyes were closed. "I got something, very, very nice, but I feel...off."

"You do?"

He didn't respond.

"Steve?"

"It's good, extremely good, just...off. Not what I was expecting."

"I have something for you."

He smiled without opening his eyes. I walked toward the bed. I reached down and pulled out the scarves. I brushed one across his chest, then down the center of his body and across his struggling erection.

"How about I tie your wrists?" I said.

"You really are fucked up." He said it calmly. His eyes remained closed.

I waited a few more seconds. I gently moved his upper body so he was lying on his left shoulder. I adjusted his arms behind his back and tied the scarf around his wrists.

"I don't like that," he said.

"It's fun."

"Why does every fucking thing have to be a game?"

I love games. Life itself is a game, and before this, I thought he agreed with that view. Possibly he only thought business was a game.

I picked up the other scarf and tied his ankles, not too tightly, just enough that he couldn't move his feet. He didn't seem to notice.

I bent over him and put my mouth close to his ear, barely touching my lips to his skin, letting my breath flow inside of his head. I spoke in a whisper. "Are you feeling a rush?"

"I feel excellent. But it's not like usual. To be honest, I don't think I've ever had a high this good, from anything, but I'm tired. I don't get it."

"Maybe a bit more?"

"Give me a minute."

I went to the dresser and removed the syringe from the makeup bag. I took out a small bottle of artificial tears that I'd mixed with some of the heroin. I removed the cap and drew the contents into the syringe. I placed the syringe on the nightstand.

A smile moved across his lips. He opened his eyes but didn't seem to focus on me. I reached under the bed and pulled out the handcuffs.

"Do you want another line? I can bring it over here."

"I don't think so. I'm pretty spaced, flying high." He laughed. "Very high. Soaring."

I sat on the edge of the bed and waited. After several minutes, I took his wrists and snapped the cuffs in place.

"Hey. What're you doing?" His voice was slow and deeper than normal, coming from some other place in his mind that he hadn't accessed recently, if ever.

"Just more fun and games," I said.

He chuckled.

Step four.

I moved him so his head was flat on the pillow, his upper body arched awkwardly with his bound hands beneath him. I wedged the pillow under his neck, tipping his forehead back. His mouth opened. I put the syringe inside his right nostril. He tried to twist his head away, but I pressed firmly on his forehead with my left hand and released the contents of the syringe with my right thumb. He snorted and coughed. His eyes opened, but he didn't see me at all this time.

Step five.

Heroin, I'm told, takes you on a crazy drifting trip that feels utterly divine. But then, you fall asleep, and then, your tripped up mind gently informs your brain that you absolutely must sleep, it whispers the terrible words — *breathing is no longer necessary.*

Thirty minutes later, his eyes were still closed, his mouth partially open. When I held the mirror over his mouth, there was no condensation. I couldn't feel a pulse in his neck. I would wait a bit longer, just to be sure.

In the meantime, I stripped off the red lingerie and wig. I put on underwear and my leggings and long-sleeved t-shirt. I washed the dinner dishes, polishing the wine glasses for several minutes with a soft linen towel, careful not to touch the glass directly with my fingers. Pushing away the temptation to keep it, I polished and corked that delicious, nearly full bottle of Cabernet. I put everything away and stuffed the bag from the trash compactor inside one of my garbage bags. I added the lingerie, wig, syringe, and scarves.

I returned to the bedroom. Steve was lying motionless on the bed. It looked like I wouldn't need all the extra trash bags, the rope, or the duct tape. They were simple security props, but over-preparation is always good. I went into the bathroom and washed the makeup off my face. I brushed my hair back tightly into a ponytail, adding some of his hair gel to slick it close to my scalp.

I washed the sink and floor, toilet and faucets and dried it with the hand towel I'd used. The sponge and damp towel also went into the black trash bag sitting open in the entryway until I was ready to leave.

The small mirror was still on the dresser. I polished it with glass cleaner, wiped it thoroughly, and then drew out two lines of heroin. I smudged one of the lines to make it look used. The little envelope was made of slick magazine paper which I thought might have the potential to retain fingerprints, so I dumped the rest of the drug in a pile on the mirror. I left the razor blade beside it, on top of the hundred dollar bill — my most expensive murder thus far. It was worth the money. It needed to look good, and I wanted to do everything I could to make it clear that he liked to experiment.

It seemed safe now to remove the handcuffs and scarves. I took them into the entryway and dropped them into the trash bag. It's wasteful to constantly purchase scarves and handcuffs and throw them away, but with all the guests in my studio apartment, and living in Tess's condo, those weren't things I wanted to leave where someone might find them. Of course they'd just think I was into kinky sex, but better not to have people thinking of you at all, speculating about the unknown parts of your life.

I packed my bag, made one last sweep through the condo

and then settled in the living room with his phone resting on my left thigh. I was thirsty, but it was too late. The cleaning was done so I'd have to bear with it for another hour or so. I pulled my phone out of my purse, unlocked the display, and placed it on my right leg.

CHAPTER 57

I found the thread containing Steve's string of text message exchanges with me. It did no good to delete them, because if his overdose was identified as suspicious, the records on his CoastalCreative-owned smart phone would surely be checked.

Our last exchange from my real phone was about our "date" and his directive that I not tell Tess. It was unfortunate that anything suggesting a relationship was on there at all, but I could fix it. First, I tapped out of that thread and deleted all the messages from the anonymous number. They would show up on a search of his records, but deleting them from his phone would at least stop the first level inquiry. If it went so far that they did pull records, my identity was concealed. I was pretty sure it could be explained as a meeting with a fancy call girl for whom he cooked dinner, or possibly, a dealer using extremely weird codes to cover the purpose of their meeting, although that was a stretch.

The next part would take over an hour in order to create a trail of semi-natural-looking time stamps.

I started with my phone.

Alexandra Mallory: *I need you to stop calling me.*

I sent a message to myself from Steve's phone: *I thought you were interested in a JOB in sales?*

I waited eight minutes and sent another message from my phone.

Alexandra Mallory: *It's not going to be a good fit. I told you that.*

Steve Montgomery: *You don't know until you try.*

I waited fifteen minutes.

Alexandra Mallory: *Stop calling! This is starting to feel a little bit like harassment.*

This time I waited twenty-three minutes before typing a message from Steve's phone.

Steve Montgomery: *Whoa. What is your problem? I offered you a fucking job.*

Alexandra Mallory: *And I told you, several times! It isn't the right position for me.*

Steve Montgomery: *Whatever.*

I waited twelve minutes.

Alexandra Mallory: *Thanks for all the dinners to discuss my career, though. No hard feelings?*

Steve Montgomery: *No problemo.*

I stared at the two phones on my lap. This seemed like a solid enough ending. The mild threat of workplace harassment was better than a full melt-down from "Steve" and an intense smackdown from me.

I peeled off the leather case off his phone. I opened the package of rubber gloves and put them on. I wiped down the entire phone with glass cleaner, replaced the case, and wiped that down too.

Step six.

By three a.m., I was certain he was dead. No pulse, no breath for several hours.

I stuffed the rubber gloves into the trash bag. It was

bulkier than I wanted. I couldn't go walking past the security desk with a trash bag this huge. I took the second pair of gloves out of the package. I went into the guest room and opened the closet. It was filled with suits and shoes, an overflow from the walk-in closet in the master bedroom. Very impressive. His extensive wardrobe beat out mine.

In the office, the closet was packed with sports equipment. After another wasted fifteen minutes combing through the condo, I finally found a storage cabinet, in the pantry of all places. Inside were two garment bags and a set of luggage. I took the smallest suitcase, the size that fits in an airplane's overhead bin. I extended the handle and wheeled it to the entryway. I stuffed the trash and my wool coat into the suitcase and yanked the zipper closed. I put on the cheap running shoes and a black hoodie, making sure all but a few strands of blonde hair were hidden. I took one last look through every room, standing in each doorway with my eyes closed to settle my mind and make sure I noticed every detail when I opened them.

With my bag over my shoulder and the suitcase handle in the opposite hand I went out the front door and let it close and lock behind me.

Done.

I breezed through the lobby without a second glance from the security guard. Outside, I walked five blocks before I hailed a cab. I eased myself back against the seat and let my neck and shoulders relax. I wouldn't fully release the tension until I'd gotten rid of the trash bag and was settled in Tess's condo. I doubted I would sleep that night. I desperately wanted to go for a long, strenuous run.

CHAPTER 58

*S*unday evening, Isaiah and I met at The Chimera. I'd
ignored him all day Friday and Saturday, utterly
consumed with taking care of Steve. Adopting an easy-going,
compliant response to Isaiah's love of hanging out at The
Chimera would ease me back into a more normal state of
mind, if such a thing exists.

Isaiah had three days' worth of stubble on his cheeks and
chin. He wore a black Giants hat which, sitting on top of the
dark shadow on his jaw, made him look slightly sinister. I'd let
my hair dry naturally. I hadn't used conditioner or combed
out the waves, so it was quite wild and tangled. I wore my
new brown leather sandals and all five toe rings along with an
ankle bracelet. I put on a short dark brown skirt and a pale
pink short-sleeved t-shirt, and covered both my forearms
with bangles.

I was mildly curious whether our different appearances
would elicit a comment from Dan or Rick, if they showed up.
This time, I sort of hoped they did. Now that my thoughts
were cleared of Steve, I was more interested in figuring out
what they were after. I also sort of hoped they would prove

they weren't simply being friendly. If they had an agenda, it might show Isaiah that friendships with cops were not really possible, and not a good idea.

It wasn't as though Isaiah had anything to hide. At least not that I was aware of, so maybe for him, a cop friendship was a good idea. He smokes pot, but that was suddenly not an issue, thanks to California voters. I'm sure Dan and Rick were not approving of the legality, and it probably made them irritated and itching to find something else wrong with all these people gleefully blowing clouds of marijuana smoke in their faces, as if to say — *catch me now, dude!*

It's possible my antagonism and caution around law enforcement was making me assume all sorts of bad attitudes on their part, when I really had no idea how they viewed the legalization.

I was also eager to spend time at The Chimera because I was curious about the heroin. It had come in so handy, like a little miracle, falling from heaven just when I needed it, giving me the idea and means to provide an accidental scenario for Steve's death.

How often was someone, or several someones, leaving packets of the drug in the women's restroom? Was the same thing happening in the men's room?

Talking to Dan had taken on a whole new perspective. Not that I wanted to get involved, but curiosity has a way of swelling to mammoth proportions the more you mull something over. All that time spent fixated on Dan and wondering what he was after, along with my lucky find, had made the thing grow into something living inside me, wanting to be fed. Maybe I could understand why Jen was so fixated on the journal after all.

Isaiah and I settled at the bar. This time, I was the one twisting around every few minutes to see whether Dan and Rick would show up. The fourth time I turned, I caught a glimpse of Rick at the far end of the bar. His back was partially turned toward us, which was why I hadn't seen him earlier.

Isaiah and I had both ordered martinis. Isaiah didn't seem put out that he hadn't heard from me for over forty-eight hours until my sudden text suggesting we meet at the bar. He didn't ask what I'd done over the rest of the weekend and he didn't mention what he'd been up to. He seemed to deliberately avoid those topics, sticking to comments about the political scene and his final months of culinary school. He also didn't mention his job search. Neither did I. The only job taking my attention was my own, but I'd still done nothing about it. Maybe I would see my way clearly, now that Steve wasn't handing out vaporous offers. I needed to put some pressure on Tess. As soon as I heard the official details around the discovery of Steve's body, and knew how that was going to play out, I'd ask her to video chat with me.

I sipped my martini and turned again, searching the crowd. The cops didn't appear to have noticed us. I slid off my stool. "I'll be right back."

"Where are you going?"

"To the restroom."

Isaiah nodded and pulled my drink closer to his, keeping it safe. I wove through the crowd to the back hallway. One woman was waiting for the restroom. The door to the men's stood partially open.

"Are you going to use that?" I gestured at the men's.

She shook her head. "God, no."

When restrooms are single use, the idea of splitting them male and female is absurd. What does it matter? They both have the same toilet, same sink. Sure, as I'd experienced, more than most, men can be messy, but so can women. Besides, no matter how clean, all public restrooms are infested with bacteria. The entire world is infested. People are constantly touching chairs and tables, railings and doorknobs with germ-riddled hands. A restroom isn't necessarily worse than any other place that gets a lot of traffic. People touch fruits and vegetables in supermarkets, and try on shoes and clothing that others have put on their bodies, some of those bodies crawling with skin diseases.

If you stopped to really consider it, you might never leave your house for all the secondary contact you have with the cold and flu and much more disgusting and life-threatening organisms carried by the rest of the human race, and their billions of pets.

I shrugged and went into the men's. I locked the door and pulled the wicker trashcan from under the counter. I lifted off the lid and looked inside. A tiny envelope folded from a razor-cut page of a magazine was tucked into the wicker strands. I pulled it out.

It stunned me for a minute. I hadn't expected to find anything.

I tucked it in my purse, replaced the trash can, flushed the toilet, and washed my hands.

When I stepped out, the hallway was empty.

I hurried down the hallway, hoping the intended recipient of the packet hadn't seen me coming out. Hopefully if he had, he wouldn't immediately assume I'd been using the incorrect restroom.

I wove my way toward the bar. Dan and Rick were standing behind Isaiah. We exchanged greetings and I settled on my chair. The two of them had ordered their beers. As Jen handed the beer to Rick, he winked at her. It was subtle. I don't think anyone else noticed, but Jen looked away.

Rick and Isaiah talked about baseball, Dan and I listened, and all four of us sipped our drinks. After about fifteen minutes, I excused myself and headed back toward the restrooms. They were both empty. I locked myself in the

THE WOMAN IN THE BAR

women's first, and then the men's. There were no heroin packets in either one.

I returned to the bar in time to hear the conversation turning to video games, something in which I have absolutely no interest. I let their words flow around me while I nursed my martini and nibbled at the olives. My lack of interest in the game discussion made the minutes tick slowly.

Isaiah ordered another round for the two of us, and I slid off the chair again.

"Where are you going?" Dan said.

"Restroom."

"Didn't you just..." A touch of pink washed across his cheeks. He took a sip of beer and looked away.

I came back a few minutes later, no additional packages of heroin in my purse. I hadn't noticed anyone coming out of the hallway with a distressed look on their face, but I hadn't been able to watch non-stop, so maybe I'd missed it.

Dan was beside my barstool now and Rick was on the opposite side of Isaiah, their heads close together as they talked. Dan stepped aside so I could sit down. "I don't mean to be rude," he said, "But there's something not quite right about you."

"What's that?" I picked up my fresh drink and took a sip.

"I can't put my finger on it." He looked down, studying my ringed toes. His eyes flicked up to the bangles tinkling along my arms.

I smiled. I was sure he thought I was dealing drugs. And suddenly the packet of heroin inside my purse seemed like an incredibly stupid impulse. I took another sip of my drink and ate one of the olives.

"Where do you work, again?" he said.

"That's the third time you've asked me that."

"And it's the third time you've dodged the question."

"Are you asking as a guy in a bar? If you're asking as a cop, checking into something?"

"No. Just curious because you've made such an effort to avoid telling me. It feels like you're hiding something."

"Which is it? Guy in bar or cop?"

"Guy in bar." He smiled.

"Then it's none of your business."

We drank in silence. I positioned myself so I could see the entrance to the hallway. There was a steady trickle of people going in and out, but no one looked furtive or glanced around, worried about being watched. No one looked upset about losing their evening's entertainment.

Now I was torn. Part of me wanted to get out of there and take that heroin out of my purse before Dan found some premise for searching it. Another part still wanted to discover a man going to the restroom, looking as if he had more than a biological interest in his destination.

CHAPTER 59

*H*amilton Island

* * *

Telling her whole life story to Sean, without any self censorship, had felt so freeing. Tess honestly hadn't cared what he thought. Why did other people's opinions matter at all? Her life was her life. Her choices her choices, some perfect, some insignificant, and some regrettable, but that was part of the process, wasn't it?

Why had his suggestion that she was indecisive made her bristle? She'd pulled herself inside like a sea turtle into its shell. She smiled at the memory of the turtle's utter lack of fear, belying its nature.

"At least you're smiling," Sean said.

He'd been sitting there for what seemed like twenty minutes, but was probably five or ten, watching her think. It must have been exciting for him. She gave him credit for keeping silent while she thought through his app and the implications, and how she wanted to explain her conflicted response. He was a good sales guy. So many of them talked too much, especially sales engineers who felt compelled to explain the intricate technical wonders of their products, thinking they had to sell, sell, sell, forgetting that the customer needs time to consider what's been said. If the seller can't stop talking, the buyer has no time to make a buying decision.

"I wonder if your app is sexist," she said.

"Why would you think that?"

"Maybe I'm projecting, but I get the feeling you think I'm a good test case because I'm an indecisive female. Maybe you see a huge female audience for this."

"No, I don't think so. I don't think women are more indecisive at all. I think they have more choices, which makes for more complex decisions. Men tend to get shoved down a narrow path from an early age."

She fiddled with the hem of her swimsuit coverup, keeping her gaze directed away from his face. He was an unusual guy, with his devotion to the Reef, his ability to listen, his dramatic tattoo. Of course his accent was compelling. It made them all sound so much better educated, more intelligent. Americans sounded gruff and crass in comparison. She could listen to Australians talk all day long, it didn't matter what they said.

So, women had more choices? Was that true? She thought maybe it was. It was rare that a man got to decide he wanted to drop out of the workforce to focus solely on raising children. Men were ostracized if they didn't love sports. They weren't free to choose any hobby from knitting to journaling to sky diving. Now, women had all those choices. Men could take up knitting, but they'd be hassled about it all the time, especially if they chose to do it in public. They were judged for the books they read and the movies they watched.

"Besides," he said. "I don't know how many men you're

close to, but they might be more indecisive than you realize. They put on a front more than women. Gotta look like you're leading the pack, right?" He grinned.

"Do you have a prototype?"

"I do."

"Have you already launched a company?"

"I have a partner — another developer. But it's all quite informal at this point."

She nodded.

"When you said you were a marketing executive...well, I had to ask."

"Looking for a bit of free consulting?" She smiled.

"I'm thinking I want to ask you to become part of our venture."

She laughed.

"I'm serious."

"You met me on a boat in the middle of the ocean. You don't even know me."

"You can know someone for twenty years and not know the truth about them. People work for companies for decades and turn out to be disloyal. Traitors. Embezzlers. They can sabotage a company with their sheer inertia. I can tell we're simpatico. And your background speaks for itself."

"You seem to have a lot of experience with people disappointing you."

He winked.

"So when can I try the app?"

"We could meet for dinner. Are you available tonight?"

She shrugged. "I'm alone on the island. My social life is with fish."

He laughed.

"I'm curious to see what it's like," she said.

"And then you'll consider my offer?"

"I didn't realize it was a serious offer."

"Of course there would be salary and role discussions, but those are details. The offer is solid."

"I'll have to see whether the app gives me any indication." She smiled. She twisted off the cap on the plastic bottle and drank the remainder of the water. What did they say about something seeming too good to be true? He was awfully confident in her interest as well as her value to whatever direction he planned to take his fledgling idea. Too confident. Too…yet, she'd always followed logic and how well had that worked out? Yes, she was extremely comfortable financially. But that was it. Decreasing job satisfaction, a stunted social life, and a perverted love life.

On the horizon, the first of the Whitsunday Islands was now a green blur. They still had another hour to go until they touched land. She wanted to be alone. She wanted to drink in every moment, gazing at the endless sea, watching for jumping dolphins, not thinking or trying to make decisions.

Until she tried the app, there was nothing else to talk about.

Even if the app wasn't perfect, it might still be viable. There were a lot of apps that were more for entertainment than practicality. If it provided you a different way of thinking about your choices, that would be interesting to a lot of people.

And he was right. Her choices had doubled. Working for his company, or even being a partner, which was what she would demand, meant moving out of the country. She would have to sell her condo. She'd have to find a way to transport Damien. Could you import a cockatoo back to its country of origin?

Without the app, she'd already known she was finished with CoastalCreative. Staying there meant another fifteen or twenty years running like a hamster on her exercise wheel. The same meetings, the same characters, the same conversations. Steve and his relentless effort to undermine her. An effort that she suspected was going to become more aggressive and more targeted at damaging her reputation rather than simply undermining her credibility. It was exhausting. Not that you couldn't end up with a nemesis at a smaller company, a new company. Or in another country. But she needed a change.

Did she want to live outside the US? It wasn't as if Australia was all that foreign. If any country was similar to home, it was Australia. And she loved the climate. Loved the feeling of spaciousness and the feeling of being distanced from some of the chaos on the rest of the planet. Although the rest of the planet was doing its best to sabotage the fantastically beautiful, exotic place, teeming with life, bleaching and smothering the breath out of their Reef. The thought made her eyes fill with tears.

What she really wanted was to leave a mark on the world. Silly, maybe, but honest. Would his app confirm that? And was that the whole drive behind her periodic thoughts of motherhood? Maybe she only wanted a child so she could leave something behind, to have an impact, to make sure the world was different when she left. Strange thoughts for a woman as young as she was, but they'd plagued her more and more since her thirtieth birthday, a date that was beginning to look farther away than the fuzzy island on the horizon.

CHAPTER 60

 ortland

* * *

None of my brothers spoke to me for nearly three weeks. There was no more piss on the sides of the toilets or the floor. Not a single drop. If they accidentally missed, they obviously wiped up their own mess with a few squares of toilet paper.

I'd never experienced such isolation. They didn't invite me to play basketball in the driveway, and of course, I was too proud to ask. They refused to accompany me on bike rides. I stayed in my room and read. They wouldn't look me in the eye during dinner and they gushed over my sister, to emphasize to me that they were cutting me off — all of them standing together.

The car was silent during our rides to school. No arguments, no complaining. My mother never turned on the radio when she was driving us to school, letting us chatter without fighting for air space. Now, she seemed oblivious to the chilling lack of sound. I suspected she enjoyed the quiet, with the background buzz of traffic around us, the hum of the engine.

I may be self sufficient, and very happy in my own company. But I do enjoy other people. I like the games, of course, the thrill of eliciting admiration and friendship and respect, or the much more exciting game of putting people off balance. I like conversations and the sheer physical presence of another human being living through the same experience at the same time — eating terrific food or hiking or watching a movie. But not running. I like to run alone.

Without my brothers, I had only my classmates to satisfy my need for games, for getting other people to bend to my will. And those opportunities were less frequent. Life at home became boring. My sister was still a child, not old enough to challenge me.

I certainly didn't regret what I'd done, it was entertaining and satisfying and had accomplished my goal of pee-free toilets. But they still knew without a doubt, thanks to my father and our church, with my mother as an accessory, that men had the upper hand.

I gave the rat to Lori, the girl who had purchased her for me. I'd named the rat Miss Oregon, since she was very beautiful and had proven herself useful. Lori was thrilled to have a pet, her parents were willing, and she never asked about the science fair.

The power I'd acquired was the wrong kind. I didn't simply want a clean bathroom floor and a reduction in my hours spent scrubbing and wiping, I'd wanted leverage. Respect. Or, maybe I just wanted to punish them. I was no longer sure.

I kept my eye on them, trying to figure out who was the most likely to back down first. I was pretty sure it would be Jake. Always Jake. Eric knew he was the head of the pack, and he was almost on his way out the door to college anyway.

Tom was too busy basking in his own glow of wonderfulness. Jake, I think, had lost some of their attention now that he was no longer getting pats on the back for messing up the bathrooms. Once again, he was the forgotten guy in the middle. I turned my focus to him. I made sure I sat beside him in the car. I walked next to him when we entered church and sat beside him there as well. I made sure I was the one who passed food to him. Anything within reach, I grabbed before one of the others could get it.

Everything finally changed on a Sunday night. Jake asked for the green beans which were about three feet to my left in the center of the table. I lunged for them before Eric could touch the bowl. I knocked over my milk. It ran all over the table, saturated the cloth, and dripped on Tom's legs.

My father sighed and asked me to clean it up. My mother suggested I was a little old to be spilling my milk and I needed better manners. But as I pushed out my chair to go get a sponge and some rags, Jake looked at me and grinned. He started to laugh, then bit his lip and looked at his plate.

He never said what he found so funny, but the next day he asked me why I stayed in my room all the time.

"Where am I going to go?" I said.

He shrugged. "Ride your bike to a friend's. Or the park. Or just around."

"You know I'm not allowed. Unless one of you goes with me."

He definitely knew this, so I'm not sure why he asked. Maybe he just wanted to start a conversation and it was the best he could come up with.

"Don't you get tired of sitting in your room?" he said.

"Yes."

"You should go running with me. It really helps."

"Helps what?"

"It clears your head. Makes all the stuff..." He waved his

hand around over his head as if he expected to conjure up physical manifestations of the things that he didn't like in his life. "It makes it seem not important. Helps you shrug it off... when someone pisses all over your life." He grinned.

I laughed. He started laughing with me and soon we were both shrieking, edging toward hysteria.

He pointed out that a rat baring its sharp teeth at his *private parts* is pretty much the worst thing a guy can imagine. Not the absolute worst, but right up there. I pointed out that I knew that.

He stared at me as if our moment of laughter had turned right back to fear, swelling to outright terror. "Why are you like this?" he said.

"Like what?"

He shook his head. "Forget it. I can't explain. "Do you want to go running?"

"Yes."

We agreed to meet on the front porch the next morning.

I wore my gym shorts and a t-shirt and put my hair in a ponytail.

As I tiptoed down the hall just before five a.m., the only other person awake was my father. He was alone in the living room, drinking the cup of coffee he liked to have while he read his Bible and prayed every single day of the week. His head was bowed, eyes presumably closed when I passed the living room on my way out the door.

Jake showed me the stretches he did to get ready. That first day, we ran a mile, which wasn't too difficult. I was used to running during PE for track and field activities, softball games, field hockey, soccer.

Each day, we increased the distance by a quarter of a mile. Soon I was keeping up with him for five miles most days, and seven or eight on Saturdays.

Running during PE had never felt like this. I wasn't sure if going in circles, or ovals to be more precise, made it dull, or if it was the forced regimen, or the other girls, or the teachers and their whistles, but I never felt that wild freedom — and overwhelming sense of power — when I ran at school.

I felt like I could out-run anyone. Not that someone was chasing, but it's a great feeling. I was limber and full of energy and in control of my body.

We didn't talk while we ran, which I liked. The only sounds were our athletic shoes on concrete, the birds, an occasional dog, upset that we were passing too close to its territory. As the sky grew lighter, we heard the soft purr of an occasional car driving slowly through the suburbs on its way to a main thoroughfare.

I never stopped running.

CHAPTER 61

 *an Francisco*

* * *

When Jen had given Rick the bullet journal, she hadn't lingered to watch whether he was cautious about looking through its pages. She hoped he was smart enough not to splay it open on the counter, but she couldn't watch. She couldn't keep hanging around him or Chelsea would notice something was up.

Earlier, Alex and Isaiah had come in and ordered martinis. Not long after, Dan showed up, and the next time she looked, Dan and Rick were drinking with Alex and Isaiah. There was no sign of the notebook. Her knees felt wobbly. Sweat formed across the back of her neck and under her arms. She tried to take a deep breath, but the air didn't seem to want to move into her lungs. She took another breath and coughed. Thick slightly damp heat filled the entire room, but no one else seemed to be uncomfortable.

"Are you okay?" Maggie said.

She nodded and went to the sink for a glass of water.

Rick needed to get that notebook back to her right now. Where had he put it? The space where he'd been sitting was empty, the tray that she'd used to cover the notebook pushed to the side. He'd taken his beer when he joined the others, leaving the clean glass behind.

It was possible he'd stuck it in the back waist of his pants, covered by his jacket, but how the hell was he going to return it to her? The place where he'd been sitting was occupied. Every seat at the bar was taken.

She'd made so many stupid mistakes. Isaiah had landed her this amazing job and she'd managed to alienate Chelsea, she'd made herself awkward and uncertain by prying into some-one's secret thoughts, becoming obsessed with having to know what was inside that notebook. She'd pissed off Chelsea and Claire both, pushing for a bartending position before she was ready, before she'd proven herself valuable, before they'd gotten to know her. It was only two months since she'd started. Who got promoted, and to something she was completely unqualified for, after only *two* months?

And now...Rick. She wasn't even sure where she'd taken her first wrong step, but he was using her. And he was going to get her fired. There was no way he could help her get another job. No matter how many *people* he knew.

She'd had a chance to fix her life and she was now on the way to making it worse than ever.

First, she had to get that notebook back. But she couldn't leave the bar, she couldn't go tapping Rick on the shoulder when there was a huge crowd, everyone watching. He and Chelsea were a couple. If she had notes in there for him, why didn't he just ask her for it? She was furious at herself for not thinking it through earlier. He was so intense, he made her feel she had to react the moment he made a request. It felt like she was still a call girl, terrified of cops, doing whatever they asked in a ridiculous effort to appear innocent.

Cops were used to having people obey instantly, and most people, herself at the top of that list, were too anxious to object. She was too aware of her recent past and too aware of his power to have the courage to say no. Besides, people who did have the courage to say no usually ended up thrown to the ground, handcuffed, and stuffed in the back of a car.

She kept herself busy. The activity was frantic. Her eyes ached from darting between Chelsea drinking her martini and pretending to be a customer, Maggie racing between actual customers with a pinched angry expression, and Rick, laughing it up with Alex as if he didn't have a thing to worry about.

Standing around brooding, watching all of them, waiting for someone else to make the first move wasn't going to her get out of this. She needed to take a deep breath and try to fix things.

She moved over to where Alex and the others were clustered in a tight huddle. "Any more beers?"

No one looked at her. She raised her voice, "Rick, Dan? Do you need another beer?"

Without turning, Dan set his bottle on the counter. "Yeah, thanks."

Rick placed his nearly empty bottle beside Dan's.

Even though they wouldn't use them, she placed two clean glasses on the bar. She got two more beers and brought them over. She pried off the caps and held out one of the bottles, forcing Dan to turn and take it out of her hand. He reached for the other bottle. She moved it out of his reach. "Rick."

Rick glanced at her. She raised the beer. He moved around closer to the bar. She pulled it back slightly. "Where is it?"

He patted his lower back.

"I need to put it away."

"Later."

"No. I'm in…"

He lowered his brow and glared at her. "This isn't a good time to talk about it."

"It is for me."

"Can I have my beer?"

"I need to talk to you."

"Aren't you supposed to be working?"

"This is important."

"Are you gonna give me that beer, or not?"

"I need to talk to you. Two minutes." Copying his approach to demanding attention seemed to work. He moved to his left. "Where?"

She nodded toward the back hallway. Hopefully with the crowd, and her absorption with her performance art, or whatever it was, Chelsea wouldn't notice. If she did, Jen would think of an excuse. Maybe she knew a friend who'd had a break-in…the cops weren't doing anything, she was asking Rick for a favor…

They walked in parallel to the end of the bar. Jen slipped out of the opening and went to the entrance to the hallway. Rick came up beside her.

"If she finds it missing, I'm in a lot of trouble. Please don't do this to me." The beer was slippery in her hand, the condensation turning slick from the heat of her skin. She moved her fingers lower, using the label as a grip.

He put his hand on her shoulder.

"Please don't touch me. Just give me the notebook."

"You could really help me out."

"I already did." She felt her throat tightening, her eyes getting watery. She gritted her teeth. She wasn't going to cry. She could fix this.

"I'm working on something. A case. Okay?"

"What does her notebook have to do with it?"

"Someone who comes in regularly is dealing smack. Heroin."

The tears disappeared. She took a quick breath.

"There have been three overdoses in the immediate vicinity," he said. "One of them had a card from this bar in his pocket. And there's someone here whose behavior is...a concern."

"Oh." She let out a sigh. This was sad. It was such a great bar. "Here? Doesn't that kind of thing happen mostly at dive bars?" She knew better. Look at the things that went on in five-star hotels.

"You'd be surprised."

"So why do you need the notebook?"

"I'm just saying I need your help, I need you to be quiet. And to keep an eye on Chelsea, like I asked."

"You think it's her?"

"Don't jump to conclusions. I can't say any more. But can you keep quiet? And if you see something, there's a small cash payment for our informants."

She wanted to laugh. A few months ago, she'd been arranging her whole life to avoid even seeing a police officer, and now the police wanted her to help them? Had they paid people to keep an eye on her, in the past? "Okay. I guess. But I need to put the notebook back in her purse."

"Quit worrying about it. She won't know it's you."

"Her purse is behind the bar. She'll know it's me or Maggie."

"She's not even looking at it. Anyone could go back there."

"But they don't."

"Just maintain your innocence. There's no proof. Don't waver. Don't look guilty."

"What if she knows, even if it's not for sure, and she tells Claire and I lose my job?"

"I don't think that will happen. Trust me."

She nodded.

"I'll get this back to you tomorrow," he said.

"I don't work on Mondays."

"When?"

"Wednesday."

He gave her a thumbs up.

"But what if she…"

"Stop worrying. I have your back."

CHAPTER 62

Hamilton Island

* * *

The restaurant Sean took her to was a lovely fusion place. The lobby featured a low fountain with gently bubbling water surrounded by a bench. Two small dining rooms opened to a patio bathed in warm tropical air. The tables and chairs were teak, smooth and contoured for comfort.

They were seated at a small table at the outer edge of the patio, tropical plants leaning close as if to listen to Tess and Sean as they conversed in low voices.

For several minutes, they studied the menus silently. Sean closed his and suggested the prix fixe four-course dinner. Tess said it sounded delicious. He ordered wine. When the server left, he pulled out his phone and a small thick disk.

"You can try the app on mine. It's easier than having me load it onto your phone."

"Or you don't want me to run off with it?" She smiled.

"I trust you."

"I have no idea why."

"Are you not to be trusted?"

"Of course I am. But…"

"I don't know you. Right?" He smiled. "I told you, I have a gut instinct."

"So you said, but you're arguing against the need for your app."

"How do you know I didn't run my thoughts about you through the app?"

"Because you offered the opportunity to me while we were still on the boat."

He handed the phone and device to her. "It's very intuitive."

The server came and opened and poured their wine.

They lifted their glasses. "To human instinct," Tess said.

"To human instinct," he said.

She took a sip and put down her glass.

"Make sure at least two fingers are touching the device. Then enter a question and walk through the responding questions it provides."

Angling the phone on the table so he couldn't read it, she tapped into the dialog box: *Should I pursue this opportunity?*

The app loaded five screens of questions, ranging from a rating of her current job satisfaction, to her sleep habits, her diet and exercise, her sex life — that got a zero — and her sense of security with her financial situation. There were other questions about her interests, her dreams, even questions about activities she enjoyed. Altogether it took her about fifteen minutes. The appetizers arrived while she was still tapping away, making sure she didn't release the pressure of her fingers on the device.

Slowly, she found herself getting pulled deep inside her own mind. There wasn't a flicker of indecision as she answered the questions. Of course she knew herself. Several questions were quite thought-provoking regarding her philosophy on various matters, and still she answered them without hesitation.

Sean remained silent. She let him polish off the entire plate of spring rolls wrapped in delicate rice paper and drizzled with squid ink.

"Be sure to keep your fingers pressed to the disk until you get the results," Sean said.

She nodded, not wanting to talk and produce a change in her heart rate.

Finally, a digital image of the moon came onto the screen, sunlight slowly sweeping across as the app made its calculations.

When it was finished. The response came up.

Tess — you have an open heart and mind. You crave the experience of knowing you have multiple paths available to you at any time. You're the most satisfied when there are an abundance of choices. You relish the feeling of not knowing. You enjoy indecision — possibility itself.

She nearly dropped the disk.

She felt like a teenager walking out of a fortunetelling booth at a county fair. The answer was extremely generic and absolutely right. Just like a horoscope, or the Myers-Briggs and other personality assessments. She'd been through many of those personality tests, but nothing had made her feel like this.

She placed the phone face down on the table between them and the disk beside it. She took a sip of wine and studied the empty plate smeared with squid ink. She was glad he'd eaten them. Despite her apparent desire for a wide variety of choices, the idea of ink oozing out of such a hideous creature didn't stir her appetite.

"Well?"

"It feels a little horoscope-like."

He laughed. "People love horoscopes."

"But it's supposed to be genuine. Not a game."

"Maybe you feel that way because you don't trust anything outside of yourself."

She nodded. He seemed to be as intuitive as his app. No wonder he'd developed the idea.

"Are you surprised at the feedback?" he said.

She shrugged.

The next course arrived — corn fritters with delicate strands of cilantro lying across the top and a whipped arrangement of spicy avocado dip.

She was starving. She cut a small piece off a fritter and lifted it to her mouth. "It's both entirely true, but also feels a bit too easy, and like I said, generic."

"How so?"

"It didn't answer the specific question. It was more an assessment of the kind of person I am. That's why I said it felt like a horoscope. Very accurate, and yet it could easily apply to a lot of people. I don't feel that it read my deeper thoughts."

"Is it incorrect?"

"No."

"The questions will become more refined. The AI will develop over time, and the device will read more bodily functions."

She chewed the fritter and took a sip of wine.

"So what do you think of it?" he said.

"I think people would find it useful, and entertaining. Mostly the latter."

"I have no doubt it's useful," he said. "The entertainment value is secondary."

"You're very confident."

"Everyone is fascinated with themselves. Any app that helps you know more of yourself, measures your activity, your accomplishments, your weight, your workouts, is appealing."

She smiled.

"So are you joining the team?" he said.

She picked up the phone. "How do I delete my results?"

"Go back to the main screen, look for your name, and swipe it off."

She removed her name and handed the phone to him. "Do the answers change, if you ask the same question a second time?"

"Yes. Because it's reading your body. Next time, I can load it onto your phone. You'll be able to input your respiration with each question, and it will also take your temperature in micro degrees when the monitoring device is available."

"So if I'm feeling differently about a question, it would presumably be different each time?"

He nodded.

"Well, for now, I'm intrigued, although I'm not sure how you can get to a final answer."

"So you're ready to discuss your role? Money?" He winked.

She smiled and took another bite of fritter.

"What's your hesitation?" he said.

"Moving out of the country. Being in business at all. Working with such a small team. Walking away from a great deal of respect and power, to be honest."

"All things to investigate."

"Well the first two aren't something to investigate with you."

"But they're something for the app to assist with. So you can further realize its value."

"Maybe, yes."

The server refilled their wine glasses and the main course arrived — Barramundi, a wildly common fish in Australia. She loved it, but felt a little guilty eating it after spending time in the world of sea life and thinking about the havoc over-fishing was bringing to the Reef. It was delicious, and she liked it. She'd ordered it frequently over the past weeks. This time it was prepared with cumin, turmeric, and cayenne pepper.

Dessert was a chocolate cake that melted like butter, a thin enough slice that she was more than satisfied without feeling ill and numbed by sugar.

She was also satisfied with the answer to her question. She liked where she was right at this moment, an array of choices. Not knowing.

CHAPTER 63

 an Francisco

* * *

The week after Steve died of a heroin overdose, I planned to be in my cubicle from eight to six every day. I had no way of predicting when his death would be discovered or how the company would communicate to the employees, if it all. I doubted they would send a mass email, so being in my seat increased my chances of knowing as soon as the news began to spread.

Before work on Monday, I ran four miles along The Embarcadero. Alone.

I went to the gym and lifted weights, a bit weakened from too much time away. As I set the bench press load at 120 pounds instead of my last weight of 137, I vowed not to let it happen again. It's amazing how quickly muscles deteriorate from lack of use. I showered and dressed in a cotton jumper with a white long-sleeved, waffle-textured t-shirt underneath. I wore my sandals. Unlike the Santa Cruz office where sandals were almost a dress code, no one in the San Francisco office wore them, but they were more subdued than the Doc Marten boots and I didn't want unnecessary attention.

The news about Steve spread quickly.

It turned out his housekeeper cleaned on Monday mornings, arriving at his condo by eight-thirty. She immediately took the elevator back to the lobby and told the security guard he was dead in a breathless, hysterical voice, trembling from the sight of a naked man, his body cold and lifeless for more than a day. The guard called the police. At an address with that kind of prestige, the police arrived so fast the housekeeper was still standing at the lobby desk, sobbing and battling waves of nausea.

Detectives were in his apartment and digging through his wallet by eight-fifty-five a.m. The death was reported to CoastalCreative, and then it burst into flames and everyone on my floor knew by nine-twenty.

The human connection is still faster than the internet, although the speed of gossip is certainly enhanced by technology. A few women whose cubicles were near mine got a bit teary, so I followed their lead, unsure whether this was about grief over losing an eligible bachelor, Steve as an individual, or pure shock and human sadness.

By late in the day on Tuesday, everyone knew he'd died from an overdose of heroin. There wasn't any discussion of murder.

If the detectives suspected anything wasn't quite right, they might not share that information with CoastalCreative. I felt mildly confident, but my senses were still sharpened, waiting for anything that might force me to construct some distractions, or leave the city, wiping away as much of my existence as possible. In the past, leaving a job or a living situation had been fairly quick and simple. But now, I had a lot more things restraining me. Isaiah, for one. And responsibility for Tess's bird. The condo could sit empty, but the bird had to be looked after. It was too beautiful and clever to just walk away from it. I had a company phone filled with pieces of my life and a bank account tied to my name.

The gossip chain was saying a woman had gone into the building with Steve the night he died. The guard had never seen her before. She was young. Good looking, with long dark hair, but there wasn't much else the guard had to offer. The woman wore a coat and red patent leather shoes — those were unforgettable. But he hadn't wanted to be staring at a guest. He hadn't wanted to be making judgments about Steve's age versus the woman's. She seemed quite young, that was his impression.

He'd never seen her leave, but it might have been after the shift change.

No, the guard who came on after hadn't seen a woman who fit that description. He'd seen a few women leave the building, but there was nothing remarkable about any of them.

I wondered if I'd hear from Tess. Surely someone had texted her the news. But the silence from Australia was profound. Maybe she was out of range. Maybe she'd simply turned off her phone.

By Thursday, there was still no talk of murder or any whispering about the kind of women Steve liked to bring home. There were no rumors of him having *too many* women. Everyone saw him as a rather stable guy, *kept his private life private*. There was no suggestion he used hookers or picked up women in bars for a night or two. *A good guy*, they all agreed. *Very successful at what he does...did. An effective leader. Passionate about the company. Always seemed in a good mood. A world-class salesman.*

There was no reason for them to assume murder. I suppose finding a guy with his kind of money dead and naked in his own bedroom raises questions no matter what. But heroin has had a resurgence. And it doesn't limit itself to street people and gangs and others who have lost their way. Plenty of people with money get into it. They say the high is superb. But why upscale users, supposedly educated people, don't consider what will happen is difficult to understand. Everyone knows it sinks its claws into you forever. Are they really so arrogant they think they'll escape? That they'll be the one in charge, more powerful than the monster coursing through their veins, burning through their brain tissue?

I began to relax. I thought about working from home on Friday, but then decided to keep up my streak, just to be sure.

Everything seemed to be settling down. I invited Isaiah to spend the weekend, but then, I heard from Tess.

Her message unnerved me. It was maddening in its lack of information. At the same time it was intriguing, and surprises always add to the fun of the game.

Reading her message, I decided I'd better not have Isaiah over after all. I needed to talk to her without any listening ears, just in case. He was pleasant enough when I suggested he come over on Saturday and stay through until Monday morning. He didn't ask why.

Then, it got more complicated. Jen asked me to go running again. She had something *super important* to tell me. We weren't even done stretching when she blurted out that Rick was trying to get her to help him uncover drug sales they suspected were taking place at The Chimera. She felt trapped and scared and worried about her job.

We started off with a slow jog, but quickly picked up our pace.

"They think someone who's a regular at The Chimera is selling heroin! Can you believe that?"

"I guess so."

"Really? I can't. But he said a few people have died of overdoses recently, all within a few blocks of the bar. One of them had a business card from The Chimera. So they're looking into whether all of them might have bought it there. It's so awful."

I ran faster. She kept up and I ran faster still, not trying to shake her off, but trying to stop her talking so I could think.

This was both fantastic news in that Steve's death would likely be confirmed as an overdose without questions. It was awful in that I had a detective who thought there was something off about me. And I had another detective who thought I looked like the type who needed cash.

CHAPTER 64

*H*amilton Island

* * *

Alex seemed more eager to video chat than Tess had expected. Was it possible her extended absence was felt at CoastalCreative? By Alex, if no one else? Or was Alex eager because she'd done something stupid with Steve, fucked him, and then accepted a job offer? She probably couldn't wait to announce she was making a job change, over-confident that she'd double her income through sales commissions and a better bonus plan.

Their chat time was scheduled for Friday night in America, Saturday morning in Australia.

When the video connected and Tess saw the icy night sky with its brittle lights through the sunroom windows behind Alex, she settled more comfortably into the lounge chair and let the warm, moist air of Queensland lay itself across her skin. The east coast of Australia had such a soothing climate, so much gentler, most of the time. That alone made her want to stay, made the prospect of working there seem less stressful. Of course, she'd only been here in late summer and early fall. Still, she didn't miss San Francisco at all.

The windows and walls and furniture of her sunroom looked unfamiliar. Alex even more so. She'd died her hair blonde again, but it was growing out. The track lighting accentuated the pale color and the harsh dark roots.

Tess adjusted the screen. With the computer on her lap and her head back against the lounge chair, the camera grabbed her face at an unattractive angle but she didn't really care. She was comfortable. And so relaxed. She smiled.

"Hi," Alex said. "You look good. Time off agrees with you."

Tess smiled. "It's been life changing."

Alex laughed. "That sounds dramatic." She looked edgy, glancing to her left repeatedly, as if someone else was in the room with her. Tess could hear Damien laughing in the distance.

"Are you alone?" Tess said.

"Yes."

"What are you looking at?"

Alex moved closer to the camera. "Nothing. So what's up? What's so important that a text message wouldn't do?"

Tess smiled. "I have some news."

"You're moving to Australia?"

Tess laughed. "I guess it wasn't too hard to figure out."

"Seriously?"

She nodded.

"But what about CC? What about Damien? Your condo?"

"All details to be worked out," Tess said.

"Have you told anyone at CC?"

"You're the first."

"Does this mean you're resigning?"

"Yes." Without mentioning where they'd met, without even telling Alex she was on an island surrounded by impossibly blue water, she gave a vague mention of Sean's app — *a personal management tool*, she called it — and his offer.

He'd spoken without a suggestion of doubt when he agreed to her acceptance on the condition she would become a principal of the company. He was confident her background and the things she'd done for CC would make the difference between global success and a ho-hum appearance on the market for his clever, fascinating smart phone app.

She'd met his other partner, who had no interest in being anything but a developer. He liked writing code and surfing. Sean wanted to keep the company small. There were no plans to develop more products, not right now, so they only needed a handful of people, but they did need world-class marketing, and Tess clearly offered that.

She disagreed that they would only have the one product. She was sure there were ancillary apps begging to be developed around it. Not that she wanted to build a huge company either. Small was nice. Private was nice. Everything they earned would come from their effort, not floating the company on the stock market, turning it into a roulette wheel.

Alex stared into the camera, her face composed into an expression that Tess couldn't read. Was she worried about her own job? If she'd already signed on with Steve, what did it matter?

Alex's face shifted to an expression of boredom, or maybe she was trying to hide fear. It was difficult to tell. She leaned closer to the camera. "When, exactly, are you resigning? Are you coming back to do it in person?"

"I don't think that's necessary. It's a five-minute conversation. All the hand-off is already in place with the acting Marketing VP. So..."

"And Damien?"

"I said I haven't worked out all the details yet."

"It sounds like you've made a major decision without thinking about *any* details."

"This is the first step. Everything will fall into place."

"Aren't you Ms. Tranquility. *No worries, mate*, and all that." Alex grinned.

Tess smiled. "I suppose. I was going to…"

"I guess you haven't heard what happened," Alex said.

"I don't know. What is it?"

"Steve Montgomery died."

Tess felt the skin of her face go slack. There was a faint ringing tone in her ears. The words sounded almost senseless. Steve? Dead?

Again, Alex's expression was unreadable. She didn't look upset. She sounded slightly self-important delivering the news, but at the same time, there was no suggestion of smugness in the curve of her mouth.

"I…how?"

"It's a shock, isn't it?" Alex said.

Tess nodded. She tried to think. She wasn't even sure how she felt. Deep inside, making her feel ashamed, she realized there was a slender vein of relief. "How?"

"I'm surprised no one was in touch with you."

"I haven't been reading my email. And I guess I wasn't very good at responding to text messages, so they've tapered off to nothing the past few weeks. So, how did it happen?"

"Drug overdose."

"What?"

"His housekeeper found him. Naked." Alex's upper lip twitched slightly.

Tess wasn't sure if Alex was suppressing a laugh or nervous. "That doesn't sound right."

Alex shrugged. "That's what they're saying."

"What kind of drugs?"

"Heroin."

"No way."

"What?"

"There is no way Steve would use heroin."

"How do you know?" Alex said.

"I know. He just wouldn't."

"That's not an answer."

"He didn't even drink all that much."

Alex lifted her eyebrows.

"You don't believe me?" Tess said.

"Not drinking *all that much* hasn't been my experience."

"Okay, maybe he drank the same as anyone else, but he absolutely is not into drugs. I think he tried coke a few times. He hated pot, said it made him feel like an idiot and made him eat too much."

"Well I don't know about that, the police were pretty definite it was heroin."

"You talked to them?"

"No, but that's what everyone is saying."

"Was there an official announcement? When did this happen?"

"A few days ago. I think he died early Monday."

"Was there a memorial?"

"There's still the autopsy. Then I think cremation. That's what I'm hearing."

"How do they know it was heroin, if they haven't done an autopsy?"

"I don't know, Tess. I'm just telling you what everyone is saying. And I heard the detective was definite that it was heroin. The autopsy is a formality, to know how it killed him — whether he had a heart attack or just stopped breathing — and all that. Or if there were other drugs."

"I just don't believe this." Tess swung her legs over the side of the lounge chair. She lifted the computer off her lap and stood. She walked to the railing of the balcony and balanced the laptop on it, looking out over the water, not caring if the camera was displaying nothing but her collarbone and neck.

"I'm sorry to upset you."

"I'm not upset. I'm shocked."

Alex smiled. "That's cold."

"Not in that way. Any death is upsetting. And he was a colleague. I knew him, and it's not believable to me that he would use heroin. Was there a party? Was he coerced?"

"I haven't heard that, but maybe there was a small party. A woman went up to his apartment with him. Maybe a hooker."

"Well. I think I'm going to head out for a swim. I need to process this."

"Okay. Just so you know, I don't mind staying here longer."

"Thank you. I'll probably end up selling it, at some point. And I need to look into getting Damien shipped here."

"So you're really making this permanent?"

"Nothing's permanent."

"True."

"Moving here doesn't mean I'd never return. But for now, I feel good about it."

"I don't mean to be selfish, with Steve dead, and all the things on your mind, but this leaves my future hanging," Alex said.

"I know. Why don't we plan to video chat again. Does Sunday afternoon, your time, work?"

"Isaiah will be here."

"Whatever's good for you."

"I'll text you," Alex said.

Tess nodded. She lifted the laptop so Alex could see her head. "Talk soon."

Alex smiled. "Damien says *hi*."

Tess laughed. "I'm sure he does."

They said good-bye and she closed the laptop. All she wanted was to dive into the long narrow pool beside the beach. She would swim until her mind went silent.

CHAPTER 65

*S*an Francisco

* * *

As soon as I was done talking to Tess, I flipped the cover over my tablet. Her reaction to Steve's death was milder than I'd expected. Although her abrupt end to our call suggested she was keeping her thoughts to herself. Hopefully she would continue that course and not push her *Steve would never* theory to the police. It had been difficult paying attention to her. I was distracted by thoughts of how closely I'd been watched at The Chimera. Tess meddling in Steve's death seemed a lesser concern, for now.

I hurried into the bedroom. I put on skinny jeans, high heels, and an off-the-shoulders black top. I brushed my hair up in a ponytail and pulled out some strands to drift around my cheeks and jaw and hug the back of my neck. I did my makeup, stuffed my things into a normal purse instead of the fringed suede, and headed out to The Chimera.

Knowledge is power. It's always better to avoid being left

out of the loop. You can't evaluate your risk if you don't have all the details. I had no idea how carefully Dan and Rick had been watching traffic in and out of the hallway leading to the restrooms. For all I knew, they had a surveillance camera in there. Even if they hadn't gone that far, I had to know where their heads were — what they knew, or thought they knew, or suspected, or just hoped because they wanted to solve a drug trafficking problem.

When I walked in, Chelsea was seated at the bar, staring at the entrance as if she was waiting for someone. She wore a short black dress and four-inch heels. The streaks of color in her hair were gone, and it was swept into a loopy half-bun, half-ponytail style. I sat beside her and ordered a martini. She turned away from me.

If anyone knew what Rick was up to, it should be her. I took a sip of my drink. I leaned over the bar, twisting around to my left to get her attention.

She moved ever so slightly and gave me a barely-there smile.

"You love this place so much that you hang out when you're not working?" I said.

She shrugged and picked up her glass.

"Are you a b-girl or something?"

"I don't know what that is."

"A girl who sits at a bar and lures men to buy more drinks. She entices them to order more top shelf alcohol so the bar will be more profitable."

"Never heard of it."

"It's from the early nineteen hundreds, I wouldn't expect you would have."

"Then why did you ask?"

"It came to mind."

She didn't answer.

"Not in a talking mood?" I said.

"I'm busy," she said.

"Busy doing what?"

She sighed and moved the olives around inside her glass, still not drinking. "Market research, or customer research, I guess you call it. I'm trying to experience the bar from a customer's perspective."

"That's bullshit," I said.

She shrugged more elaborately and put her mouth to the glass. She took a tiny sip, the liquid glancing across her upper lip. She shivered.

"Not a martini drinker?"

"Please leave me alone. I don't want to talk."

"That's not very good customer research. I'm a real live customer." I smiled. "But I don't see why you think it's required. The Chimera has the best martini in San Francisco."

"And you must know that's all marketing," she said. "There is no *best* martini. A hundred bars serve first class martinis."

I took a long sip of my drink. I slowed my voice down and exaggerated each word — "And what else are you known for?"

"What's that supposed to mean?"

"Nothing, just making conversation."

"No, you're not." Her voice was pinched. Her fingers trembled slightly as she tried to maintain a firm, elegant grip on the sides of her glass.

"I am. Do you think I'm accusing you of something?"

She turned and stared at me. "Please talk to someone else."

"You're awfully edgy."

"Because I'm working and you're distracting me."

"It doesn't seem like you're paying much attention to how long it takes to get a drink, or the general mood of the place — for your customer research."

"How would you know?"

"I like to watch people. That detective for example. Do you think it makes people comfortable, knowing there's a vice detective hanging out here, watching everyone? Eavesdropping on their conversations?"

She sipped her drink, her shoulders trembling in response to her obvious distaste.

"I'm really interested," I said. "Do you think it puts people off, knowing cops like to hang out here?"

"There are only two. And one is my boyfriend. It's not like the place is a police hangout."

"Good to know," I said.

She glared at me.

I felt a hand on my shoulder. I turned.

Rick grinned at me. His other hand rested on Chelsea's shoulder. "Two of my favorite girls." He grinned and raised his hand to signal Jen. As she approached, he said, "And here's my third. A Sierra Nevada."

Jen nodded and turned away so quickly I thought she might trip and fall.

"So what's new with you two lovelies?"

"Not much," I said.

"I told you not to bug me when I'm sitting here." Chelsea shrugged his hand off her shoulder. She didn't move enough to dislodge his fingers, stroking her bare skin, but he took the hint and let go. She slid off the stool. "Later." She turned and walked quickly toward the back of the bar and disappeared down the hallway.

"What were you talking about?" Rick said.

"Not much. Just her customer research."

"Bullshit," he said.

"Is that for me or the customer research?"

He laughed.

Jen placed his beer and glass on two napkins and pushed them toward him. He handed her a twenty and she left.

"Bars don't do market research," he said. "They serve

drinks, they take cash. It's bullshit. I don't know what her game is."

"She's your girlfriend, why don't you ask her?"

"Can't get a straight answer. But something isn't right."

Did cops spend their whole lives being suspicious, thinking something wasn't right just because they didn't understand it, or because they didn't know the whole story?

"Her boss put her up to something," he said. "It's not fucking customer research, but I can't figure out what it is. Did she say anything to you?"

"Nothing more than that."

He put the beer to his mouth and gulped it down. He moved it away. "Damn."

"Too much?"

"No." He took another long swallow to prove his macho skill with beer. "Just frustrated."

"About?"

He lowered his voice and leaned closer. "Someone here is dealing smack. There have been three overdoses within two blocks in the past two months. And probably more before this particular bar came to our attention."

I relaxed slightly. But only slightly. He didn't assume my need for cash meant I was a candidate for his scrutiny after all. Maybe only Dan was unduly curious about me. Despite their constant togetherness, they were working in isolation, each chasing whatever scenario they'd devised inside their own heads.

"Have you seen anything?" he said.

"Not that I recall." I picked up my martini and took a sip. I stared into the liquid. If he knew about heroin delivered through the wicker trashcans, maybe the owner knew. And maybe she had Chelsea doing her own *undercover* observation. Getting known as a place for heroin connections would certainly change a bar's reputation from *best martini* to *dive bar.* Although, if Chelsea observed something odd, what could she do about it? It made more sense than customer research, but it still didn't make sense.

In the end, none of that mattered. As long as they weren't focusing on me, it was all good. And I could find a new place to hang out. It was time for a lot of changes in my life.

Rick took a sip of beer and leaned against the bar. His leather jacket sagged on the other side as he hitched up his shoulder. The room was warm, too warm for a leather jacket. He was trying hard to be so cool, to project some kind of regular guy appearance, he stood out even more. If I hadn't been introduced to him as a detective, would I have guessed he was a cop?

I smiled, widened my eyes, and raised the pitch of my voice. "How exciting, if there was a drug bust here."

He took a sip of beer.

His effort to appear disinterested was over-done, just like the jacket.

"If you see anything, anything at all. Will you let me know?" He pulled a business card out of his pocket and placed it beside my glass. The card was bent from the curve of his ass, slightly worn around the edges.

I stared at it.

"It's your duty to help."

"Is it?" I tucked the card in my purse. It was not my duty to do anything.

CHAPTER 66

*R*ick had finally returned Chelsea's bullet journal, but Jen realized having it in her possession didn't solve anything. The journal was tucked inside Jen's locker, which was supposedly secure, but how did she know Chelsea didn't have the combinations to all the lockers? How did she know Chelsea hadn't used Rick to set her up? Maybe she wanted to see whether Jen had taken the notebook. Her thoughts were pure nerves, nothing else. There was a constant trembling in her fingers and a similar feeling in her heart, shuddering erratically every few minutes.

When Chelsea asked about the notebook, which she did almost continuously, Jen's skin took on the consistency of a wet sponge. When the notebook had been in Rick's possession, lying was easy — *I haven't seen it. I hope it turns up.* She had *no idea where it could be*...in her mind she always added, *right this minute*, because right at that moment, she truly didn't know.

He'd returned it as she left for her break yesterday, handing it to her without a word, his eyes avoiding meeting hers. She'd shoved it in her purse and taken it home. Instead of using the table of contents to jump around to the sections that looked interesting, this time she'd gone through every page. There wasn't a single line that looked like a note for Rick. So what was he talking about? Did he lie, only checking the notebook to find out if Chelsea had written about another guy?

But he'd seemed straight-forward and casual when he said she was taking notes for him.

Was it possible the quotes from customers were for him? Maybe the comments weren't a pathetic need for flattery. Maybe there was something in what they'd said that told Rick they were buying drugs, or looking to buy. It sounded foolish inside her own head. Too much drama and intrigue. But what else? He'd insisted Chelsea was taking notes for him, and it surely wasn't a list of TV shows or a record of how many minutes she spent doing cardio that interested him.

She re-read each comment, sipping a glass of water to keep her head clear so she didn't miss a single word, even though she'd memorized half of them. The words seemed meaningless — everyday conversations, the normal, uninteresting things people said all the time.

The comments played in her mind while she worked and while she waited for an Uber ride at two-thirty in the morning. She woke thinking about them, and she spent every unoccupied moment at the bar looking for the customers who had been described but left unnamed.

Now, Chelsea had finally stopped accusing her of taking the notebook. She still wore an angry expression every time she looked at Jen, but her face took on the same expression when she talked to Maggie or spoke to customers.

The bar was about half full, a little unusual for a Friday afternoon. Any minute, Matt would show up. The moment the thought passed through her mind, the door opened and he stepped inside. Jen smiled. The regulars were like that.

He scooted onto a chair at the center of the bar. Jen gave him a friendly smile. He seemed to look through her. He wore the same black suit jacket in the same skewed position on his bony shoulders. She wedged a lime into the open top of a Corona and placed it in front of him.

He grimaced.

She turned away.

"What a bitch."

She turned back. "Excuse me?"

"Not you." He shoved the lime into the beer and it lodged itself in the long neck. He stuck his finger in farther but the lime wouldn't move into the beer. "Aw shit."

She handed him a straw.

He shoved the straw into the bottle, pushed the lime down, and took a long swallow of beer. "I hate women like that," he said.

"Like what?"

"Always have to be right."

Jen nodded.

"And that smell."

"Smell?"

He nodded. He pinched his nostrils together. "Perfume. Does she think it's sexy?"

So, men did notice. And they didn't all find it sexy. She smiled, satisfied that her assessment of the world had been mostly right.

He swallowed some beer. He put down the bottle and closed his eyes, rubbing his hairline with his index finger.

Jen grabbed a cloth and walked to the other end of the bar. She began wiping the already clean counter with small, careful strokes. She thought back over the things Chelsea had written about Matt, intentionally leaving out his complaints about the perfume. Matt went on and on about how he hated that perfume, but Chelsea didn't write about it. She'd been very detailed with everyone else's comments.

Jen walked over and tapped Chelsea's shoulder. "I'm not feeling that great. I need to go sit down for a minute."

Chelsea sighed and rolled her eyes.

"Sorry," Jen said.

"Let me know if you have to go home." Chelsea turned back to the woman seated across from her, leaning on the bar so she could continue their quiet conversation.

Jen grabbed her purse from her locker. She went out through the storage room and stood a few feet from the door in the alley behind The Chimera. She took out the card Rick had given her and entered his number into her phone. He answered before she heard it ring on her side.

"DeMarche here."

"This is Jen Miller."

"Yes."

"I have a thought."

"Do you, now."

She took a deep breath. "There's something missing in the notes."

"What?"

"The customer comments she writes down, those are for you, right? Trying to figure out who's looking to buy?"

"Yes. A little clumsy, but I thought it would be easier for her to keep track. She uses code words, that was her idea — *score, hooking up...*"

"One of the things she wrote isn't correct."

"What does that mean?"

"She changes what people say. Well, she did for one guy, so maybe she did for others."

"Why would she do that?"

"I wonder if Claire knows you and Dan are watching."

"Okay. Could be. That would explain why she's playing that dumb game sitting at the bar."

"And I think Claire's maybe the one selling heroin."

"Why would you think that?"

"This guy...he complains all the time about a woman he works with who has obnoxious perfume. He hates her. He's here every weekday at the same time. And he always goes into the back, saying he's using the restroom, but that's how you go up to the office also."

"Could mean anything."

"Claire has really obnoxious perfume. It makes you feel sick. You can hardly breathe in her office."

"What does he look like?"

She described Matt, the bony shoulders and suit jacket that didn't seem to fit.

"Okay. I've seen that guy. I asked her to take notes on him."

"But she didn't write down that he complained about the perfume. He went on and on about it and it's been bugging me...why she would change what he said. Maybe she changed it so you wouldn't think any more about him."

"It just sunk in what you said...you read her notebook?" He laughed. He mimicked a female voice — *I don't gossip about my friends. Oh, but I do read their private thoughts.* He laughed.

"I know, I'm a terrible person. But is that important right now?"

He stopped laughing.

* * *

After that, it all happened fast.

Fifteen minutes after Jen started her shift, Rick and four other police officers showed up. Before they even spoke, Chelsea began trembling so violently, Jen thought she might be having a seizure. Two of the officers went upstairs and returned with Claire. Her perfume filled the bar. She kept her lips pressed together, the color gone so they were almost as pale as her hair. She shot fiery looks at Chelsea, but didn't speak. Chelsea continued to tremble as they read the charges and their rights.

In the end, the police put handcuffs on Claire and Chelsea and led them out of the building. Chelsea's body looked as if everything had been drained out of it, all of her flesh melting off her hunched posture. Claire looked as fierce and in charge as always.

One of the cops said he understood Jen had a notebook that belonged to Chelsea. He asked her to get it. They put it in a plastic bag, sealed it, and wrote on the outside with permanent marker. He told Jen she should go home. Apparently she no longer had a job, or even a final paycheck.

Rick stood near the back of the bar, writing in his notebook.

Jen walked over slowly. "Hi."

"You can leave. Thanks for your help." He glanced up and returned to the notebook.

"I was right."

"You were. The loser in the suit jacket had two grams ripped off from his classy distribution point in the bathroom. He tried passing some right at the bar and we grabbed him when he left yesterday. We think that's why Chelsea was playing that dumb game sitting at the bar...trying to find out who was swiping it."

"Oh. Wow."

"Yep."

"So Claire...?"

He closed the notebook and looked up. "I can't say too much. But yeah. Her and Chelsea. Matt came in every day, picked up from Claire what was ordered, slipped it into the wicker in the toilets. Chelsea told Claire who was interested, anyone who mentioned *hooking up, scoring, smokin'*... Very clever. Matt wasn't the smartest tool...Maybe the gals are smarter than the guys when it comes to games and lies and business." He laughed.

He went to the front and switched off the *Open* light.

* * *

Back in the apartment, Jen wondered whether she should feel ashamed for ratting out Chelsea. They were supposed to be friends — Chelsea teaching her how to make drinks, bonding over those stupid bullet journals. Rick had pushed her into it, taking advantage of her natural submission to authority. He must have sensed it, that she'd be easy to persuade. But heroin was a terrible thing, he didn't have to convince her of that. He was doing his job, and she'd actually helped. She smiled.

She glanced at Isaiah's laptop and several cookbooks piled on a box in the corner. She still wondered what he would have said if he'd caught her reading Chelsea's notebook. The first time he would have disapproved. But maybe now...

No. She'd done the right thing. She was sure of it. Part of turning her life back into something normal meant not seeing every single man as a likely verbal abuser, a potential rapist, or a possible killer. Someone to not be trusted. At all. Ever.

For the first time in two years, she'd decided to believe a man could be a stand-up guy.

CHAPTER 67

The Chimera was closed indefinitely. No more fire-breathing female monster, unless you counted its legacy of heroin highs and the death in its wake.

All that wonderful girl power, over thirty years of people enjoying their cocktails and finding comfort in crowds, always hoping to meet someone new, looking for a thrilling and satisfying conversation, all brought down by the woman who conceived it.

The heroin crept into Claire's psyche as insidiously as it creeps into the veins of a junkie, whether it's through a needle directly to her bloodstream, or up through his nostrils, sent on its relentless path by mucous and the body's natural desire to try to process whatever comes its way.

Jen sat across from me on Tess's balcony, smoking a cigarette. *Only the third in her entire life*, she felt compelled to remind me with every other puff. *But sometimes, a girl needs a cigarette.*

I sat across from her. We were drinking Chardonnay and eating from a bowl of pistachio nuts. It was a warm, sunny afternoon.

"Rick promised to have my back, and I guess he did. He's arranged three interviews for me."

"Or Isaiah could do that." I preferred to think of classy Isaiah finding her another job where she could sneak in with the unfortunate two-year gap in her résumé. Rick was just so…I couldn't find the word.

"I'm still scared." She took a drag and blew out a thin stream of smoke, like a ribbon unraveling from her tongue.

"It will work out."

"How can you say that?"

"Most things do."

She took another drag on her cigarette and dropped the ash into a jar beside the lounge chair.

"You look great sitting there," I said.

Her dark hair was moving in the breeze, her eyes bright with a mixture of pride from figuring out what was going on at The Chimera, and fear — the energizing kind of fear — regarding her income and her future.

"A lot of good that does," she said.

"You belong here. In a luxury condo."

She laughed.

Hearing us through the open doors, Damien mimicked her laughter, but not in a mocking tone. He sounded as if he was making an effort to be friendly.

"I know it will work out, that he'll find me something. But what sort of something? I put in a lot of effort at The Chimera, showing what I have to offer, and now I have to go back to the starting line."

"I know how that is," I said.

"I don't think you do."

I told her about Tess's plan to resign, and Steve's untimely death.

"Do you think he got the heroin from Claire? That would be weird."

"I doubt it."

"He was their kind of customer."

"I don't think he'd be that public about it. I'm sure he had his own, private supplier."

She narrowed her eyes. She put the cigarette to her lips and glanced to her left, staring at nothing, really. She turned back. "Anyway, you still have an employer. It's not like you have to go looking, and convince someone to hire you, to give you a chance."

"Isaiah would do that for you."

"Or Rick. But…starting all over. For the third time. All I do is start over. When is my life actually going to start and keep going, instead of breaking into a hundred pieces?"

"I don't think it's a hundred pieces. Maybe just one or two."

She lifted her face to let the wind move her hair off to the side.

"So what was Chelsea up to, sitting at the bar?" I said.

"They think she might have been scoping out potential customers for the side business. Or maybe, which is what I told Rick, Claire knew there were two cops were hanging around and Chelsea was supposed to figure out who they were."

"I think it's the second thing you said. She was very grouchy. She must have felt ridiculous, and nervous, pretending to be looking for cops when she knew all along who they were."

"Yes."

"Or not. I told her she was a b-girl." I smiled over my wineglass. "She was trying to get people to spend more money — on something that wasn't on the menu."

"Whatever, she's in deep shit. Writing down her goals didn't help her improve her life at all."

"And I suppose Rick is happy that he got the scoop on Dan."

Jen took several sips of wine. "Well he did put more effort and creativity into it."

I laughed. "It's sad to see The Chimera close," I said. "A very cool name. And all female. I don't see why Claire had to go down that road when she was so successful already. And the impact to her other restaurants. A lot of people will be out of work."

"She has a son, so maybe he'll take over the other places."

I nodded. "There will still be cops crawling all over the finances."

"It's not the same, though. For The Chimera, if it ever reopens. A man running it," she said.

"No, it's not. So why did she do it?"

"Why does any of us do anything? Money."

"But she has plenty. She's a huge success. She's seventy-two years old."

"Maybe she doesn't have plenty. Just because lots is coming in, doesn't mean there isn't almost as much going out. And maybe you never have enough," Jen said. "At least some people."

I want a lot of money, large sums of money, millions, probably tens of millions. But I don't need endless supplies. I want it for the peace of mind. And I want a house and property and more nice clothes and great food and good wine... but there's a limit. At least for me. I don't need a billion dollars. I don't even think I need a hundred million. I wondered what the right number was. I wondered if Jen had a number in mind, or if she was too busy trying to figure out how to rent an apartment. "But heroin? It's so low class."

She laughed. "That's the worst thing you can think of? Low class?"

I laughed.

She tapped her cigarette on the jar again and took a sip of wine. She looked right at home. Part of it might have been the contrast to the pale blue sky behind her — dark hair, thick bangs, elaborately shadowed and outlined eyes, but there was also something about the way she moved. Graceful. Classy.

"If you could have any job in the world, what would it be?" I said.

"I honestly don't know. Once I have money coming in and I'm doing something more interesting than wiping up spills, I'll think about that. I have quite a lot saved from when I was hooking." She pressed her lips together. "But I don't like always taking it out and never putting anything back. Once I have to move out of your place, my account will drain itself like a flushing toilet." She giggled.

"I feel the same." I wasn't taking anything out. The subsidized apartment helped, but I was not moving fast enough in the direction I wanted to go.

"What kind of job would you want?" she said.

"I really have no idea either. I get bored easily, so that's a problem."

"I guess we're both in the same spot," she said.

I took a drag on my cigarette and dropped it into the jar by my lounge chair. I blew out the smoke. "I have no idea what I'm going to do."

"It'll work out," she smiled. "Things usually do."

Easy for her to say. I wasn't thrilled about her throwing my cliché back in my face.

CHAPTER 68

*a*fter Jen left, I was scheduled to video chat with Tess. She'd been texting me every day, several times a day, trying to get it set up. I wasn't sure why she was so impatient, but the more she hounded me, the less I wanted to talk to her.

My guess was that she had all kinds of tasks outlined for me regarding her bird, or, more concerning, she wanted to stick her nose into Steve's death. I didn't think I'd be implicated in his death. I'd cleaned as meticulously as ever. But I didn't want her stirring things up, leading to having his phone records scrutinized. He had tons of text messages to me, and no matter how well I'd tried to divert that thread into something that made him look bad, I wasn't sure how a detective would perceive it. I wasn't sure if the timing of the messages was as perfect as it could have been, especially since it was so close to the time of his death. And no matter what, it would involve police questioning. I wanted it all to fade into the background, ruled an overdose and the case closed.

Tess had no idea whether Steve used drugs. She hadn't been seeing him for at least three months, and people can change. It wasn't as if she'd lived with him. I don't think they even spent weekends together. She had no clue what he was doing when she wasn't around. How did she know he hadn't tried heroin? Used cocaine regularly? Anything. She acted like she knew all about him. I didn't want her telling the execs at CoastalCreative that she had some kind of close and special relationship and therefore her word on the matter should be accepted. She didn't.

It felt as if each piece of my life was hanging by a very slender thread. A heavy wind would rip everything loose and send it crashing to the ground.

If Tess was putting her condo on the market, I'd have to move back to the studio, either living in sardine conditions, or shoving Isaiah and Jen out into sub-standard housing. My job, my life, was evaporating in front of me.

The dull tone of the video chat ringer filled the room. A window appeared with an image of Tess's face — very stark and serious, the photo from her employee badge.

I clicked the answer icon and settled back. A martini sat beside my propped up tablet, outside of her viewing range. I'd taken a single sip after I made it, and now it simply glowed in all its alluring perfection.

"Glad we finally connected," Tess said.

"What's the big emergency? Changed your mind about moving to Australia?" I smiled.

"Of course not." She did not smile back at me.

"Too bad."

"Don't be a bitch," she said.

I kept the smile in place, trying to ease it out of a frozen state. I looked at my drink, longing to take a sip, but it wasn't the right time to move out of range of the camera. Then she'd start querying me on where I was. "So what did you want to talk about?"

"First, I let HR know that Steve was not a drug user. No way. So I feel better about that." She gnawed gently on her lower lip. "Hopefully they'll take my input seriously and insist the police find out what the hell happened."

"Good for you."

She sighed. "You can be difficult."

I moved away from the tablet and reached for my glass. I took a very small sip.

"Even so, I trust you. I think it's because you're so unvarnished."

I smiled. I don't think I'm unvarnished, with all that implies — rough, unattractive. I just don't lie unless it benefits me in a concrete way. Without concealing what I was doing, I took another sip from my drink. I held it toward the screen in a silent toast.

She rolled her eyes. "As a partner in this company I'm joining..."

"What's it called?"

"That hasn't been decided yet. Stop interrupting."

She acted as if I'd interrupted more than once. She was the one interrupting herself.

"I want to offer you a job."

"In Australia?"

"Yes."

My very first thought was my passport, rather my passports — I have two. I keep one as a backup, in case I need immediate and far-reaching escape from my crimes. I'd never used either. I'd never left the continental United States. I'd rarely gone anywhere beyond the West Coast. I'd probably have to use the one that corresponded to the name on my employment profile, but I'd never made a definite plan as to which I'd use first. Still, knowing there are two was something that's impossible not to think about when faced with international travel.

"You look less than thrilled," Tess said.

"Just thinking."

"Are you interested?"

"What's involved?"

"To be honest, I'm not sure yet. Marketing, obviously. It will be very fluid, to some extent, you can probably define it yourself. But we'll talk about it."

"Write my own ticket?" I smiled, remembering Steve's ridiculous suggestion that I could do that if I worked for him.

"Whatever you want to call it. My point is, I do trust you. I'm excited to do something different, live in a different country, and you immediately came to mind. You're always straining after something different."

"This is true."

"You can take some time to think about it. You would earn more than at CC, although I can't spell out the details yet. The cost of living is higher here, but your salary would take that into account."

"What about your condo? What about the bird?"

Her nose turned a faint shade of pink. "The bird is more important than a building, don't you think?"

I was sure Damien would be pleased to hear that.

"I will need you to look into what's required in terms of getting him transported, quarantine, and all of that. No matter what you decide."

"Okay. And the condo?"

The color on the tip of her nose darkened. "I'm very excited about this opportunity, and living in Australia." She grinned. "But a condo in Russian Hill…I realized I'm not ready to let it go."

"So I need to take care of getting a rental and all that crap?"

"Our HOA forbids renting."

"Oh."

We were silent for several minutes, both of us looking off screen. I ate one of my olives. "I have an idea."

"Yes?"

"Isaiah. And Jen. If I leave CC, my studio goes away. They've been staying there. Isaiah's just finishing up school. And Jen...it's a long story right now, but they would be perfect. You know they'd take good care. In fact, you could even leave Damien here for a while..."

Her eyes widened. "I don't know. I don't know Isaiah at all. I only met Jen a few times. And she..."

"Come on, Tess. Doesn't your instinct tell you immediately who is unlikely to disappoint you? Didn't you have Steve's number from the start?"

"And yours..." She lifted her eyebrows slightly.

I waited for nearly a minute. She still didn't speak. "You know what your gut's saying, don't you?" I said.

She laughed, rather on the edge of hysterical, I thought.

"Let me think about it. While you think about my offer, obviously."

"Agreed."

She chattered about getting a work Visa and then told me a bit about her dives at the Great Barrier Reef and then we signed off. I'd already made my decision — more money, and a chance to divert Tess from following up on Steve's death. I was also certain she had already made her decision about Isaiah and Jen.

CHAPTER 69

$\mathcal{I}$t was a gorgeous Sunday morning. Isaiah and I were in bed, our limbs wrapped around each other, two flutes of champagne on the dresser, the puddles left in the bottom of each now getting warm. A plate that had held buttered English muffins sat beside the glasses, empty except for a few pale crumbs. Any minute he was going to start planning a hike. Or a movie, but on this kind of day, a hike was the better bet. He might want to rent bicycles, he'd talked about it before. I was willing, but first, I had to tell him.

Many women, most women, would invite a guy like Isaiah to move out of the country with them. In fact, quite a few women would have discussed the job offer first, debated the pros and cons, tried to feel him out regarding his willingness to relocate to the other side of the planet. A lot of women would turn down the job offer, putting a relationship at the top of her priority list. Some women would take off and hope he'd follow. Others would manipulate him into going.

I'm none of those women.

I'm flexible and I can enjoy the company of a lot of people. If Isaiah decided all on his own that his dream included opening a restaurant in Australia, I would have been happy to hook up there. I am happy to hook up there, if that were to happen.

But the things I want in this world — all-consuming challenges, experiences to tease and occupy my mind, people I can work to maneuver into a place where I want them, finding quite a lot of satisfaction in ruling the chess board, if you want to call it that — don't require the steady, devoted attention of a man.

I propped my head on my elbow and gripped his bicep as if to pin him to the bed, although not in an aggressive way. Just to feel the meat and the strength and the solid essence of him.

Before I could speak, he lurched into the empty verbal space between us. "You know, Dan was sure you were selling it. The heroin."

I smiled. Dan had been too interested in me, so busy studying me and trying to create a profile of my personality, and my place at the bar, drawing conclusions that were very close to the truth, yet very far away.

Isaiah looked confused by my expression.

"But you know me better than that," I said.

He pulled back slightly. I kept a firm grip on his round, full bicep.

In turn, he placed his hand on the back of my head, first massaging the indent below the skull where the tendons of the neck meet up with it, pushing hard, which releases a very pleasant sense of well-being across the scalp, seeping into the brain. He moved his hand up, prodding his fingertips against the bone. "Actually, no. I don't. That's the thing. I know your body and what it wants. I know your favorite movies, and how you swing your arms when you hike, and the bliss on your face when you're running. I know the food you crave, down to the smallest detail of when you want pepper and when you don't, and how the olives should be arranged for a martini. But I don't know *you*."

He continued to rub the back of my head as he talked, his eyes closed, as if he were speaking from some other place, as if another person was telling me these things and he had to close his eyes and compose his face for this other to speak from inside of him.

"Is that why you're always feeling my skull?" I said.

He opened his eyes. "What?"

"Lately, you're always massaging my head, as if you're looking for something."

He closed his eyes. "I don't know."

I think that was exactly what he was doing, trying to find his way inside my brain. But of course that's impossible. No one can ever find their way into the mind of another. That's why relationships are so impossible and frustrating, and playing word and mind games with other human beings is so endlessly entertaining.

He released my head and whispered. "I'm sorry to see you go. But I think the time is right for this to end."

"I agree." I leaned into him. We didn't make any plans for the day after all, but we did spend quite a bit more time together, mostly saying good-bye to each other's bodies.

CHAPTER 70

$\mathcal{I}$ walked toward the front door of Tess's condo. I was very full of myself, knowing I'd given two fascinating people a home beyond what they could have dreamed for the near future. Not just me. It wasn't mine to give, but I'd paved the way.

Of course Tess had agreed with my suggestion. I couldn't tell whether she had faint reservations, but with the HOA restrictions and her refusal to let go of her place in the United States, her options were limited.

A new job. A new country. New people. I was a snake shedding her skin.

I opened the door. Jen and Isaiah stepped inside. Both of them looked like contestants on a game show, eyes wide and filled with anticipation, looking around as if possibly their names had been called by mistake.

Jen seemed more accepting of her good fortune, ready to take what she could get when it was offered. She wore the confident smile that seemed to hug her face all the time recently, the knowledge that a former call girl had escaped notice and morphed into a police informant. And she got a job out of it, a much better job — three weeks of training and then bartending Tuesday through Thursday, to start, at a place un-ironically named, The Best Bar.

Jen said. "I really cannot believe this, Tess is so generous."

"She is," I said.

"Thank you so much for suggesting us." She glanced at Isaiah, who nodded, looking as if he was still in a state of disbelief. "I feel like I literally died and went to heaven," Jen said. "Living here, and with a chef sharing the place." She grinned at Isaiah, who didn't notice. She sighed in a way that made her flesh seem to melt into her bones.

I showed them all the ins and outs of everything from the ventilation system to the security alarm, as well as the care and feeding of Damien. As we made our way through the condo, the bird kept up his mantra — *Dangerous woman, Dangerous woman, Dangerous woman* — but without his former enthusiasm. I wondered if he knew I was leaving. Jen would probably keep him better company, but I believed he would miss the sound of my life as much as I'd miss his snarky comments, the echo of his laughter. Maybe the wild cockatoos in Australia would talk.

It couldn't have worked out better for me. Jen and Isaiah would be so numbed by their luxury they wouldn't spend time giving thought to all the things they didn't know about me, to considering anything that didn't add up.

When I was finished with the instructions, I mixed three martinis and we went out to the balcony. The sun was going down, leaving the sky watery blue near the horizon, darkening to inky blue above. It was still warm, the last of a pleasant San Francisco spring before the typical summer fog settled in to confuse all the tourists with the damp, chilling breath of winter.

Soon, I would be skipping ahead to the start of winter. The

idea was difficult to get my head around, but I was eager to slip out of San Francisco quietly, on those foggy little cat feet mentioned by Carl Sandberg, leaving behind the chimera of my connection to unsolved murders and seemingly accidental deaths.

A NOTE FROM CATHRYN

Thank you for reading The Woman In the Bar. I hope you enjoyed reading the story of this confident, secretive sociopath as much as I enjoy writing about her. Since the day the voice of Alexandra first appeared on the page, I've sometimes been as surprised as readers by some of the things she thinks, and says, and does. I'm constantly entertained and she honestly makes me a little nervous at times.

If you want to tell other readers what you thought about the book, please consider leaving a review.

I love hearing from readers. You can email me at Cathryn@SuburbanNoir.com or get in touch on social media.

CATHRYN'S BIO

Cathryn is the author of sixteen psychological suspense novels and the ALEXANDRA MALLORY series, featuring a sociopath you can't help but love. Readers have called the series "addictive".

The things that torment us in real life—obsession and revenge, guilt and envy and longing—are endlessly fascinating in fiction and she never grows tired of writing stories about characters struggling to overcome the worst.

Cathryn also writes ghost stories because who knows what lies beyond our senses—The Haunted Ship Trilogy and the Madison Keith series of novellas.

When she's not writing, she's usually reading, walking on the beach, or playing golf, going way out of her way to avoid hitting her ball in the sand or the water. She lives on the Central California Coast with her husband and her cat, Cleopatra.